DRAGONS REALM

BY TESSA DAWN

Published by Ghost Pines Publishing, LLC
http://www.ghostpinespublishing.com

First Edition Trade Paperback Published October 31, 2015
10 9 8 7 6 5 4 3 2 1

ISBN-13: 978-1-937223-17-5
Printed in the United States of America

Author may be contacted at: http://www.tessadawn.com

This is a work of fiction. All characters and events portrayed in this novel
are either fictitious or are used fictitiously. Any resemblance to actual
persons, living or dead, business establishments, events, or locales is
entirely coincidental.

gp Ghost Pines Publishing, LLC

CREDITS AND ACKNOWLEDGEMENTS

Ghost Pines Publishing, LLC., *Publishing*
Damonza.com, *Cover Art*
Reba Hilbert, *Editing*

Quotes
Proverbs
Friedrich Nietzsche
William Shakespeare, *King Lear*, 1608.

In memory of Elaine Latkin, my eighth-grade English teacher.

PROLOGUE

IN A LAND as ancient as time itself, there were those who were born to protect the Realm, to rule over commoners, shadow-walkers, and warlocks alike, and those who were born to serve the rulers with blind obedience. The former carried the primordial blood of the Dragon in their veins; the latter bore the burden of a dragon's desires—his hunger, *fire lust*, and passion—on their shoulders.

It was a sacred duty.

An elemental obligation.

They were chosen females, taken from their homes at the tender age of twelve, reared by strangers at the Keep, and trained to serve, obey, and *feed* their masters in order to keep the dragons strong.

A select few, the Sklavos Ahavi, were singled out for an even greater purpose: to bear the future sons of a dragon's line. To wed the ferocious beings who were so deceptively human in outer form, yet primal, dark, and wild at the core.

The Ahavi were servants who belonged to their dragon lords.

The shadow-walkers and warlocks were reluctant subjects

who resented their dominant masters. The commoners were humans who lived in fear of all that inhabited the Realm.

And the dragons…

Well, they were a species apart—*and above*—all others.

PART ONE:
DRAGONS REALM

"He who fights too long against dragons becomes a dragon himself; and if you gaze too long into the abyss, the abyss will gaze into you."

~ Friedrich Nietzsche

CHAPTER ONE

MINA LOUVET WAS only twelve years old the day she was taken by the Dragons Guard, the day she was ripped from her mother's arms in order to be schooled in the ways of the Ahavi, those who would serve the Dragon. She had been chosen for her aptitude in linguistics, her burgeoning ability to speak multiple languages, both those of ancient tongues and foreign lands, and for her rare, almond-shaped eyes.

She had been chosen because Wavani, the king's witch, had assured the king that Mina would one day be one of the few, the chosen, the Sklavos Ahavi, a female who could not only bear healthy children but would *only give birth to sons*. The witch had seen it in a Seeking Vision, and the revelation had been enough to change Mina's life forever.

Now, at the age of eighteen, Mina, along with two other *chosen* females, entered Castle Dragon for the first time. As she stepped into the grand receiving hall, she had to will herself to be strong, to hold her head up with pride, to keep her shoulders from slumping in defeat. She had to consciously keep her knees from knocking together in fright.

Her eyes darted around the enormous foyer in anxious, furtive glances, as she gawked at the numerous examples of opulent wealth: The architecture was cutting-edge and grandiose. The artwork was rare, refined, and priceless. And the floor beneath her feet was made of exquisite marbled stone, reflecting the purest blue veins and pearlescent arroyos Mina had ever seen.

The ceiling was beyond magnificent. It must have stood at least fifty feet high and, heavily coffered in ornate tiles, its large uncut beams framed the massive structure like a celestial curtain. And the sparse but ornate furnishings—the round table by the grand entry; the golden wing-back chairs, placed on either side of the enormous staircase; the pair of vintage, velvet sofas that sat up against the textured walls—they all looked too elegant to touch, too expensive to sit upon. This was the Dragons' home. The castle where King Demitri once lived with his infamous Queen Kalani, a Sklavos Ahavi who, prior to her death, had given the king four noble sons: one who had died by his own hand, and three, still living, who would remain in the gigantic fortress to serve the Realm along with their newly acquired Ahavi.

At least until the Autumn Mating.

For once the sons were wed, they would be sent out into the three rural provinces, along with Mina, Tatiana, and Cassidy, to set up their own royal courts and rule as dragons of old.

A soft echo accompanied a dainty set of footfalls as Pralina Darcy, the Ahavis' governess, descended the grand staircase, rounded the corner into the foyer, and strode regally before the girls, her head held high enough to intersect with low-lying clouds. "Welcome to Castle Dragon," she said in a cocky drawl. "This will be your new home for the next five months, and I will be your mistress."

Mina swallowed a lump in her throat and glanced longingly over her shoulder at the main castle doorway. She had half a mind to take off running, to dart beneath the high wooden arches, dash into the nearby woods, and escape the boundaries of the Realm forever.

She wanted another reality.

She wanted another life.

She pressed her palm against her lower belly and curtsied instead. "Governess."

Pralina began to walk in slow, demeaning circles around the cluster of girls, her face a mask of disinterest. She appraised the group much like a common farmer might appraise a herd of cows at market, studying their features, scrutinizing their figures, and assessing their postures with barely concealed disdain. And then she reached out to grab a lock of Mina's raven-black hair. "Do you shampoo with rose water?"

Mina nearly teetered in place. "I…I…yes…sometimes."

Pralina frowned, her severe gray eyes reflecting dubious shadows in their depths. "You stutter?"

Mina shrank back. "N…no, ma'am. I'm just nervous."

Pralina bent low to Mina's ear. "Do not stutter in the presence of the dragons."

Mina nodded, unable to reply, unwilling to risk another misstep.

Pralina let go of her hair and stepped to the side, evaluating Tatiana next. "Your name?"

The shy girl winced and averted her eyes. "Tatiana Ward." Her voice was barely audible.

Pralina fingered the high, lacy neckline of Tatiana's gown and scowled in reproach. "Are you a prude, uneasy, or just stupid? You cover your shoulders, your breasts, and your throat…on *this* day?"

When Tatiana started to tremble, Mina wanted to reach out and slap Pralina across the face, governess or not. Of course they were all nervous and uneasy—who wouldn't be? They were the future brides of dragons, glorified slaves, offered like lambs to the slaughter for the supposed good of the Realm. And even if that had not been the case, Tatiana would not have been well suited for this duty. She was unbearably shy, far too sensitive, and this heartless woman, this prickly governess, was nothing more than a bully—*as if they didn't have enough to fret over already.*

Mina bit her bottom lip in an effort to hold her tongue. She watched as Tatiana curled inward, her frail frame retreating like a tortoise's head inside of a shell, and thought about how hard the girl had struggled at the Keep, how deeply Tatiana had grieved her inescapable destiny.

Like Mina, Tatiana Ward had been born to a common family in the poorest province, only Tatiana's family had desperately needed her help on the farm. Unfortunately, that fact had not mattered at all to the Dragons Guard or the imperious king—not one iota. Once Wavani had discovered that Tatiana was a Sklavos Ahavi, her significance as anything more than a servant to the Realm, a future bearer of a dragon's sons, had been completely disregarded. It was as if her value as a person no longer mattered, as if she were nothing more than a commodity to be traded.

Mina sighed, understanding it all too well.

Even as a child, Mina had been a rare beauty: Her long, raven hair fell in thick, glossy waves down her gracefully sloped back, the silky tresses a flawless complement to her deep green eyes; and her uncanny ability with languages, her miraculous ability to memorize and understand foreign dialects, had ultimately sealed her fate. The fact that another rare beauty, Tatiana Ward, had also excelled in economics, that she understood the complex dynamics of running a royal treasury and seemed to just *get* the finer nuances of a ledger, had rendered any possible objection to her service futile. With ringlet, auburn curls and soft, amber eyes, Tatiana was stunning, plain and simple. She was a fiscal asset to the Realm, and her body was ripe to bear sons. The fact that she was painfully shy and far too delicate to withstand the lustful, temperamental demands of a dragon simply didn't matter to the powers around her. And that fact, that harsh reality, had been a devastating blow to Tatiana's family and, quite frankly, a cruel twist of fate Tatiana didn't deserve.

None of them did, really.

Well, except, *perhaps*, for Cassidy.

Even before Pralina could approach the obnoxious female, Cassidy took a bold step forward. She flipped her shoulder-length blond hair, batted her crystal-blue eyes, and angled her jaw in defiance. "I am Cassidy Bondeville."

Pralina drew back in surprise. "Did I ask you to speak?"

Cassidy manufactured a frown as severe as Pralina's. "No, ma'am. You did not." Her voice was clipped and brazenly unapologetic.

Pralina raised her open palm and held it just inches from Cassidy's jaw. For a moment, Mina could have sworn the governess was going to slap her, but then, as the tension slowly ebbed, she stroked the side of Cassidy's rosy cheek with her thumb, instead. "Ah yes, Cassidy Bondeville, born to a high-bred family in the common province. Eager to get on with it, I see."

Cassidy shrugged her shoulders with haughty indifference. "Eager *enough*...to serve the Realm."

Pralina snorted. "I see: *to serve the Realm*." She laughed out loud, and then she took several steps back and regarded all three girls circumspectly. "As Cassidy has so humbly reminded us all"—she spat the word *humbly* with heavy sarcasm—"you are here to serve the Realm." She snickered. "More importantly, you are here to serve the king. More *specifically*, you are here to learn what you must over the next five months in order to *serve* Damian, Dante, or Drake Dragona however they see fit." She cleared her throat and smiled, and it was a wicked parody of mirth. "When the leaves turn color in autumn, which they inevitably will, the witch will make her recommendations to the king. Those recommendations, along with whatever petitions His Majesty receives from his sons, will ultimately determine your fate, which one of you will be bound to each dragon son. You have no say in the matter, and if you were not already fit for this appointment, you wouldn't be here. It is my job to make you *worthy* before then, to ensure your absolute obedience. It is your job to comply."

Tatiana choked back a sob, and Mina reached out to take her hand, hoping to provide whatever comfort she could. "Ignore her," she whispered beneath her breath. "She's just trying to scare us." She left out the fact that it was working.

Tatiana squeezed Mina's hand in desperation, and Mina responded in kind.

It was the wrong thing to do.

Pralina instantly stiffened and glared crossly at Mina. "What did you just say to that girl…a moment ago?"

"Nothing, Governess. I just—"

Pralina seized Mina by the arm and dug her nails into her flesh. She squeezed so hard that her bony fingers drew blood, and then she slapped Tatiana's linked hand away. "You just told this girl to ignore me. Are you insane?"

"No," Mina said, realizing she should stop there but unable to hold her tongue a moment longer. "I didn't tell her to ignore *you*. I told her to ignore your flagrant attempt at intimidation, your obvious need to humiliate us." She clasped one hand over Pralina's, unpeeled the bony fingers from her bleeding arm, and met the governess's icy stare head-on. "I told her you were just trying to scare us." This time, she didn't stutter.

Pralina drew in a sharp, angry breath. "You willful, insolent…*whore*! Do you not know that I could have the flesh peeled back from your bones, have that tongue cut out of your insolent mouth? There are dozens of Ahavi at the Keep just waiting for the opportunity to take your place. Do you think you are irreplaceable, you stupid, rebellious wench?"

Mina clenched her fists and her arms began to tremble. She was *this close* to taking a swing at Pralina's jaw when the room suddenly grew cold, and the air grew inexplicably still. It was as if someone had thrown open a window in a dark, creepy attic and a glacial mist had swept into the room. As the eerie, otherworldly wind swirled about the foyer, a tall, imposing male stepped out of the fog.

Great ghosts of the original dragons, Mina thought. This was not someone to toy with.

The male had to be at least six-foot-two, and he was dressed in form-fitting breeches and a silk black shirt, one that bore the unmistakable emblem of the dragon in the upper left corner. The royal sigil was a deep blood red; the dragon itself was embroidered in gold; and in the center of the dragon's eye, just below his angry brow, there was a polished inset diamond. It was roughly cut and blazing with light. In fact, it almost appeared alive, as if it were waiting...and watching...guarding the dragon's heart.

The male was just as cryptic.

His angular features were drawn so taut they appeared to be chiseled in stone, and he practically glided when he walked, slinking forward in the most inhuman manner. His muscles contracted and released in waves, rising like the haunches of a predatory cat, descending like an ocean's foam, as his rich onyx hair shifted in the preternatural breeze, cascading around his proud, broad shoulders. Power radiated from his hidden aura; danger settled in his wake; and all the while, his midnight-blue eyes shone like dark sapphires, emerging from hidden flames.

His movement, *his very essence*, was chilling yet deceptively calm.

He was utterly terrifying in his animal grace.

Pralina stepped back and bowed her head, and for a moment, Mina thought about doing the same. Heck, she thought about climbing underneath the nearest piece of furniture, but she stood, transfixed, watching Pralina's obedient, submissive behavior.

It reminded her of a pack of wolves she had observed while living at the Keep.

It had been the dead of winter, and she had been gathering wood in the forest when she came across an alpha, a pack leader, snarling at a beta pup. The pup had tucked in his tail, bent back his ears, and exposed his underbelly in submission, much like Pralina was doing right now.

Mina shivered.

The governess's body language was more than acquiescent—it was positively withdrawn. "Milord." Pralina spoke the word with *reverence* and more than a little fear.

The male spared her a glance and waited.

For what?

Mina had no idea.

But the seconds seemed like hours as the bizarre scene dragged on. And then, all at once, realization dawned on her: This wasn't about Pralina or her piteous show of submission. It was about the royal prince reining in his beast. Somehow, Mina just knew he was telling his barely leashed, primordial instincts to heel, that he was commanding himself *not* to hurt the governess.

And then, just like that, his countenance softened.

He shrugged his shoulders and inclined his head, casually regarding all three girls without meeting their eyes. "Governess…" His voice was laced with unspoken command.

"My prince?"

He gestured toward the Sklavos Ahavi. "Name them."

Pralina nodded far too enthusiastically, and her tongue darted out to lick her quivering lips. "As you wish, milord." She pointed at Mina first. "My prince, Dante: This is Mina Louvet, from the southern province. She is renowned for her aptitude with foreign languages and her knowledge of distant cultures." She turned her attention to the shy beauty quaking in her boots. "Tatiana Ward is also from the *commonlands*. Although she hails from a poor family, she is now well-educated and shows great promise in mathematics and commerce. I believe she is the most obedient of the three." She cut her eyes at Mina as she spoke the previous phrase, and then she immediately turned her attention to Cassidy. "And Cassidy Bondeville is from a well-bred family, wealthy and respected. She is eager to serve the Realm."

Dante listened, but he kept his eyes averted, his head cocked slightly to the side.

He didn't look at any of them.

He simply nodded after each introduction, and then, without saying a word, he silently turned on his heels and strolled to the castle doors.

The dismissal—*the absolute disregard and ownership*—was as glaring as his silence and far more foreboding.

Both gave Mina the chills.

She watched as he walked away, both silent and proud, without bothering to look back or even dismiss the governess, and something inside of her recoiled.

Mina didn't know what she had expected, what she had hoped would happen the first time she laid eyes on a dragon, but this wasn't it: Perhaps she had expected an interrogation or a sharp, condescending diatribe, outlining exactly what was expected of each girl, what would and would not be tolerated. Perhaps she had expected the dragon to snarl when he spoke or to radiate cruelty with his eyes, to regard them with hostility or disdain, even vulgar innuendo—after all, they were *his* to do with as he pleased—but this, this casual disregard and quiet dismissal, it was truly beyond the pale. After six long years of servitude—living, working, and training in utter desolation at the Keep—after nearly a decade as nothing more than a ward of the kingdom, Mina had expected something more.

Anything.

More.

Somehow, Mina had at least expected to be acknowledged as alive.

Just then, Dante turned around in the doorway, and his severe eyes met *hers*. It was as if he had heard her thoughts—was that even possible?

"Mina…" His voice was hardly more than a whisper. "There are two horses saddled in the courtyard, a black stallion and a white gelding. The stallion is my personal steed; the gelding is now yours. Take your mount." His voice was as enchanting as the night sky and just as dark. He didn't await a reply. He simply sauntered out the doors.

Mina's stomach turned over in sudden waves of nausea, and she locked her gaze on Tatiana's—the girl's face was positively ashen—before turning her attention to Pralina. "Governess?"

Pralina scowled. "Go, girl."

Mina winced. She looked down at her attire—she was wearing a calf-length, flowing tunic of emerald green and opal white over a tight-fitting undergarment that hugged her hips, thighs, and legs. "Should I not change first?" *Dearest goddess of light*, what did Dante want with her? Had he truly overheard her private thoughts? And if so, what then? Or had he actually overheard her prior insolence with Pralina before he entered the room? Was he going to take her into the woods and dispose of her?

Or worse?

"I…I don't understand."

Pralina took a menacing step forward, her frigid body drawing so close to Mina's that their noses almost touched. "Which part of this is giving you pause? Your *lord* has given you a command. *Go.*"

Mina swallowed her apprehension and nodded. This was what she had wanted, right? To be acknowledged as alive? Suddenly, the idea seemed utterly preposterous: Dante Dragona, the first-born son of King Demitri and Queen Kalani, was a dragon, a supernatural being with untold power, no matter how human he seemed. The last thing Mina wanted was to be alone with him.

She clutched the leather pouch around her neck, an amulet given to her by her mother before she was taken to the Keep: It contained a lock of her mother's hair, a likeness of her sister, Raylea, drawn by her father on an aged piece of parchment, and the petals of a tulip, one Mina had grown as a child in the family's humble garden; and it usually gave her strength.

Usually.

Today was altogether different.

"Of course," she finally mumbled, feeling more than a little bit queasy. Gathering her courage, she headed for the door.

CHAPTER TWO

MINA FORCED HERSELF to place one foot in front of the other, to simply keep her eyes on the cobblestone path before her, as she stoically made her way toward the white horse. A deep, guttural sound brought her up short—*was that actually a growl?*—and her eyes shot to Dante. She took an unwitting step backward. "Milord?"

"You're bleeding." He licked his full lips before waving her forward with his hand. "Come to me."

Mina's heart began to race in her chest. She glanced down at her wounded arm and quickly covered it with the palm of her other hand. "It's...it's nothing."

His voice dropped to a sultry purr, devastating in its intensity. "I said, *come to me.*"

Mina gulped. She raised her chin, took a slow, deep breath, and tentatively stepped forward.

"Closer."

She took another step forward. And then, with a wave of impatience, Dante narrowed his eyes on her feet, his pupils flashed burnt orange or crimson—it was too fast to tell—and she was suddenly standing before him, their toes nearly touching. *Blessed Nuri, Lord of Fire, the dragon had moved her body with his mind.* She quickly dismissed the thought; it was more than she could grasp.

"What happened?" he asked, as he reached out to take her arm.

Mina fought not to pull it away and tuck it behind her back. "Nothing."

He smiled faintly, but there was no joy in the expression. "Six years at the Keep and you still do not understand authority?"

She assumed the question was rhetorical, but she answered anyway. "No…I mean *yes*…milord." She watched him as he studied the wounds on her arm.

"I'll ask again: *What happened?*"

"Pralina," Mina whispered. When he glared at her angrily, she added, "She snatched my arm and dug her nails into my flesh."

"Why?"

"I…because…in response to my insolence." She bit her bottom lip.

He nodded. "*Pralina…*" And then he began to caress the wound absently with his thumb. He rubbed slow circles over the jagged incisions as he studied them more closely, and then he pressed his own thumbnail into the deepest of the cuts.

"Ouch!" Mina flinched.

"Shh, be still," he whispered, and then he did something as strange as it was unexpected. He slowly bent his head, his midnight hair falling forward in a silken frame that shielded his eyes, and lapped up the blood in three slow strokes of his tongue.

Mina gasped. She drew back her arm and stared at him in morbid fascination. She looked down at her arm and shuddered—the wounds were all gone.

He gestured toward the horse. "Your mount, Mina."

Mina took a courageous step toward the beautiful white gelding and reached for the sloped leather horn, and then she froze.

She had thought she could do this.

Heck, she had been trained for six long years to do *just this*, but the reality of the Dragons—the reality of Dante—was far more foreboding than she had expected. Nothing she had been taught had prepared her for this first real-life encounter, the overwhelming presence of the preternatural male standing so close beside her, the way he watched her with *those eyes*, the way he appraised her with barely concealed ferocity in his gaze. And she wasn't at all sure she could go through with it, that she wouldn't end up being executed for disobedience before the encounter was over.

She reached once more for the saddle horn, willing her body to comply with the prince's command. After all, what was the big deal? How hard was it to go for a ride on horseback? She was as sure in the saddle as anyone—all the Sklavos Ahavi were—they were trained to be so. Just the same, her hand trembled, and she could barely remain steady on her feet. She released the saddle horn and wiped her sweaty hand along the front of her tunic. "Where are you taking me?" she asked, hoping to distract him while she regained her composure.

Dante measured her thoughtfully. He glanced at the horse, assessed her trembling hands, and then looked off into the distance, as if giving her a moment to collect her wits. "I am going to show you the castle grounds, the land around the settlement, and you are going to commit it to memory."

Mina nodded. That sounded innocent enough. "Why?" she whispered. "I mean, *why me?*" She waited with bated breath.

Dante grew motionless, far too still, and he stood like that, like a granite statue, for what seemed like an eternity before reaching out to take her by the arm and spin her around to face him. "Look at me, Ahavi."

Mina looked up into his bottomless dark eyes and almost faltered. His face was haunting in its perfection yet terrifying in its subtle brutality. There was something unidentifiable lurking just beneath the surface of those eyes, something ancient, wise, and *deadly*. They held fire and ice; war and blood; passion and pain in their depths.

Power beyond imagining.

Mina tore her gaze from Dante's and studied his features instead: His cheeks were chiseled, as if in stone, the harsh, unyielding angles just *shy* of cynical and cruel. His nose was straight and noble, sculpted at the tip as if by the hands of an artisan, and his brows were perfectly arched, not too straight, not too thin...not too full. His chin was strong; his mouth was sultry; and his skin was as smooth as the day he was born. *Do dragons age?* she wondered. *How long do they really live?* Legend had it that they were nearly immortal, and if that were the case, what would become of her, Tatiana, and Cassidy as they grew older?

Again, the thought was too unsettling to ponder, so she dismissed it.

Forcing herself to meet his steely gaze, she asked, "Are you going to answer me?" She wished her mouth would just stay *shut*.

Dante held her gaze, unblinking, until she finally turned away. And then, he raised his right hand to touch her nose with his index finger, a light tap on the tip of her flesh. "Don't ever question me like that again, Mina." His voice was cold and uncompromising. "You may ask questions if you're curious, but don't ever insist upon an answer."

Mina's eyes grew wide. Oh, *hell's fire*, she knew better. What was happening to her? Her knees grew weak in fear of retaliation. "Forgive me," she whispered, not so much because she regretted breaking the rules, but because she understood all too well just who *and what* he was. She closed her eyes. "Apologies, milord."

He clasped her by the chin and gently tilted her head upward. "Open your eyes."

She obeyed, half expecting him to strike her.

"Beautiful," he whispered, slowly releasing his hold. "Now then: I am taking you on a ride around the grounds so that you will know which areas are safe and which are forbidden. I will show you the best places to find fruit…and flowers…and the best places to hide should the fortress be attacked."

Mina's head was spinning, her thoughts swirling around like rain in a nor'easter wind. *He wanted to show her where to find fruit…and flowers…and where to hide?* What was he? A lover or a sadist? She stood, motionless, waiting for him to continue.

"As for *why you?*" He rubbed his chin thoughtfully. "Because you are the Sklavos Ahavi I have chosen for my mate."

Mina's mouth dropped open. She tried to gather her thoughts, but her fear got the best of her. *Was he kidding?* What did he mean *he had chosen her as his mate?* It was way too soon! He hadn't even looked at the other girls in the foyer. In fact, he knew nothing about her beyond Pralina's initial introduction. And besides, the witch, Wavani, had to make the final recommendations. "The choice is your father's," she blurted in a rush, "the king's." Oh great goddess of mercy, she could not be wed to this fearsome creature.

Dante smiled lazily, his countenance unperturbed. "Mm, perhaps that is true, but I am the king's firstborn. He will respect my wishes."

Mina gasped. "But you just met me! You haven't even spoken with Tatiana or Cassidy yet."

Dante reached out to twirl a lock of her hair through his rugged fingers, and he sighed. "Your hair is like mine, as dark as the midnight sky." He ran his thumb along the side of her jaw. "Your eyes are the color of emeralds, as rare as they are exquisite." He clasped his hands behind his back and studied her from head to toe, without apology. "You are beautiful," he whispered, "and our sons will be strong."

Mina gasped and took a step back, grasping at straws. "But… but…" The words wouldn't come.

He placed his open palm against her heart, his thumb settling far too close to her breast. "And you have fire in your soul, Mina Louvet. More than enough to feed a hungry dragon."

Mina tried to remember her place, to restrain from removing Dante's hand from her chest—*she really did*—but the terror was beginning to overwhelm her. Brushing his hand aside, she held both palms up to usher him back. "Please, my prince. Don't touch me like that." She felt her body begin to tremble, and she might have given vent to tears if she hadn't been so deeply opposed to giving him the satisfaction.

She waited quietly then…

To die.

Dante stared at her with a disapproving gaze, but there was no hint of retribution in his eyes. His brows didn't furrow, and his jaw didn't stiffen. He didn't grow scales or fangs. Only, his eyes, those glorious, dangerous eyes; they glowed with the reflection of flames in the centers, a dragon's fire barely restrained. "Take your mount, Mina," he growled, turning away to gather his stallion's reins.

Mina exhaled in relief, stunned that she was still standing.

Still breathing.

Loosely grabbing the reins, she reached for the horn on her saddle, set a foot in the stirrup, and started to hoist herself up. Yet, and again, her trembling grew unmanageable. Cursing herself for her weakness, she froze where she perched and simply tried to take in air, one breath in, one breath out. "*Inhale deeply, Mina, then release it*," she whispered beneath her breath.

Dante was instantly behind her, his massive frame towering above hers. He placed one hand on either side of her waist, pressed his chest blatantly against her back, and bent to her ear. "Relax, Ahavi. The beast can smell your fear."

Mina looked up at her horse. He was beginning to snort and prance in place, and she knew her emotions had transferred to the intuitive animal. She shook her head to clear the cobwebs. "*Of course.* I don't mean to frighten the horse. I'll try—"

Dante rested his chin on the crown of her head. He nuzzled her hair and sighed, his body growing noticeably tense. "I wasn't referring to the horse."

Mina dropped the reins. She quickly stepped to the side, eyed the pasture just beyond the courtyard, and then, without thinking or reasoning, she took off running, her legs moving faster than they had ever moved before. Her arms pumped furiously and her lungs burned like fire as she glanced repeatedly over her shoulder, awaiting the dragon's pursuit.

Dante stood by the horses and watched as she placed more and more distance between them. He didn't call out to her, and he didn't shift into whatever form a dragon took. He simply watched her run as if she were putting on a show for his amusement. Finally, he said something to the animals and began to walk in her direction.

Mina picked up the pace, frantic to get away.

She scanned the surrounding fields, searching for a place to hide, while Dante just kept walking.

When, at last, she reached the edge of the woods, he made his move.

He jumped.

Or flew.

Whatever it was, she couldn't be certain, but it propelled him forward at enormous speed.

Dante Dragona was no longer a man, yet he wasn't a dragon, either. He was simply a blur of motion, an impression of light, traveling faster than time or space should allow, hurtling toward her with lethal purpose. "Stop!" The force of his voice brought her up short as surely as if he had bound her hands and feet in a pair or iron shackles.

Mina tugged against the invisible binds, the mystical power that held her in place like an unseen hand. "Release me," she pleaded.

"Be still," he barked.

Mina struggled mightily against…*against*…against what? She was desperate to break free. "Please, Dante. I can't do this. I don't know how to do this."

"To do what?" He encircled her from behind, again. Only, this time, he clamped his powerful arms around her waist and pulled her back against him, the tops of both hands brushing indecently against the sides of her breasts. "Do what?" he repeated. "This?" He tightened his hold.

"Yes," Mina cried. "*Please.*"

"Please, what?" he repeated.

She ceased her struggles. "Please, let go."

He bit her on the neck, just between the juncture of her throat and her collarbone, and his teeth felt much sharper than they looked. He held her like that, like a lion restraining a cub, until at last she froze beneath him, and he let go. "You will not question me, Mina," he growled. "You will not tell me when I may touch you and when I may not."

Mina grimaced. She tugged at his hands to no avail. "It's *my* body, milord."

"No," he whispered coldly. "It is not. It is mine."

Mina could hardly believe her ears. "But you haven't even considered Tatiana or Cassidy. All I'm asking—"

"You will not ask this again," he warned her. "Just breathe, Mina. *Relax.*"

She sighed in exasperation and more than a little defeat, and then she continued to stand perfectly still. "Please, just move your fingers down…a little…*please.*"

He grasped her tighter and moved them higher. "No."

She trembled, but she didn't fight him.

"That's it, sweet Mina. Just breathe. And relax. And *listen.*"

Her chest rose and fell like a turbulent ocean tide, fluctuating with every breath.

"If Damian had chosen you, you would be dead right now."

His voice was an icy rebuke. "Do you understand what I am saying? He is not a patient dragon. He is not a moral prince."

Her ears perked up as she tried to process his words. "Is he crueler than you?"

Dante laughed, and it was a haunting, wicked sound. "Damian would just as soon behead you as wed you. What he would have already done to you in this field would take months to recover from, if, indeed, you ever did."

Mina cringed. "And Drake?"

"Drake is not Damian. He is as noble as our kind can be, but he has no heart for war, no mind for elaborate strategy, no imagination for the schemes of our enemies. He cannot protect you from the threats within this realm, and there are many."

Mina shivered. "And you wish to *protect* me?" she scoffed.

"I wish to possess you—it is one and the same for a dragon."

Mina shook her head, still struggling to remain calm, to understand what he was trying to tell her: How could he possibly make a distinction between himself and his brothers? "You are all dragons."

"Yes," Dante agreed. "And that is why you must proceed with caution." When she didn't respond, he continued: "When you run, sweet Mina, the *dragon* gives chase. When you tell him *no*, he imposes *yes*. When you tell him he cannot have you, he *needs* to dominate you. He is not human. He does not think or reason. He is master of this realm, and if you tell him he is not, he will show you otherwise. Do you understand what I am saying?"

Mina suppressed a reservoir of mounting fears and tried to simply concentrate on Dante's words. It wasn't as if she had not heard them before, dozens of times, while being reared in the Keep: Dragons were predatory animals, beasts of instinct. They ruled with absolute power; resorted to force whenever they were defied; and exacted justice, swiftly and without mercy. They were powerful beyond measure, ruthless without restraint, and cunning without equal. She knew all of this, better than most. Still, she had not made the connection when it came to a dragon lord and his Sklavos Ahavi. Somehow, she had believed they would possess a gentler nature when it came to their females, their breed mates, their futures.

At least she had hoped…until now.

"So, when I question you, the beast responds?"

"He rises to the surface *quickly*, dear Mina."

"And when I tell him not to touch me—"

"He wishes only to force your submission."

She swallowed a lump in her throat. "And when I run…"

"He will *always* pursue you."

"And if I fight him?"

"He could hurt you."

"And you?"

"I am a dragon."

"Never a man?"

"I am *trying* to be a man as well as a prince." He spoke in a guttural snarl. "Only now. Only here. Only *for you*."

Mina finally understood.

And once she did, she recognized Dante's ferocity for what it was, an internal war between the prince and his beast. The hands that trembled, yet still remained *beneath* her breasts; the voice that rose and fell with dominance, reflecting tenuous control; the alpha creature that insisted upon her obedience—all were beholden to the dragon. "Forgive me, milord," she whispered.

"For what?" he said as his body stiffened.

"For my insolence and defiance. For displeasing you."

"Do not toy with me, Mina." His voice was laced with glacial warning.

Mina heard him clearly, the words beneath the words. "Is he close?" she asked, referring to his beast, not knowing if she really wanted the answer.

"So…*very*…close," he said softly.

Mina forced her hands to her side, ignoring the proximity

of Dante's thumbs to her most intimate anatomy. She inhaled deeply and tried to concentrate on something—*anything*—that would bring her mind back to a peaceful state: the color of freshly bloomed tulips in the spring, the sound of the Draconem River as it swept through the *commonlands* valley; Raylea's laughter, and the joy her little sister had brought her, before she had been taken to the Keep.

Dante's muscles began to relax and his iron hold softened.

She leaned back into him, giving way to the submission he craved, and he breathed an audible sigh of relief.

When, at last, he let go, he spun her around to face him. "Kiss me, Mina." It was as much a need as a test. The dragon was still angry, still searching for control.

Mina stepped forward into his arms, rose up onto her toes, and pressed her lips lightly to his, following the swirl of his tongue as it gently swept the outline of her lips. He growled—that *had* been him earlier—and then he backed away. "You are mine, Mina." Despite his burgeoning self-control, he snarled.

"Yes," she whispered. "Your Sklavos Ahavi."

"And when the autumn leaves turn, and the king gives you to me, I *will* take you in every way."

She gulped. "Until then?" If her words had been any more hushed, they would have merely been thoughts.

"You will come at my command. You will do as I please. And you will accept my feeding as well as my touch."

Mina didn't reply, but she did hold his gaze.

At least that was something.

"And you will stay clear of Damian as much as possible," he added. "He also has the right to command you, so heed my warning, Mina. If you displease him, he will kill you before the Autumn Mating. And no one will punish him for the deed."

Mina nodded, understanding, as grave as the reality might be. "And Pralina? Is she also a threat?"

He tilted his head, considering her question. "She can be, but not like Damian."

Mina bit her bottom lip. "Anyone else?"

"Oh," Dante said, "*everyone* else: the warlocks in the east; the *shades* in the west; the ancient Malo Clan of my father's enemies; the castle servants, when they are jealous or being petty; the Lycanians across the sea; and Wavani, the witch. You were protected at the Keep, and now you are here at Castle Dragon. You are on your own for the next five months."

Mina dropped her head in despair, even as she nodded with growing awareness. "And that is why you wished to show me fruit and flowers...and places to *hide.*"

He looked off into the distance, and his silence said it all.

"Is there no one I can trust?"

"Oh, there are always servants you can trust, but their loyalty ebbs and flows; however, there is one who will always remain faithful: Thomas the Squire, a nine-year-old boy who has been with us since he was orphaned at age two. His allegiance is not *entirely* with my father."

Mina didn't dare ask what that meant. Surely, Dante Dragona was loyal to the king, without question or hesitation, but then why did he speak so cryptically about this squire? She curtsied as she had been taught in the Keep. "Thank you," she said, not knowing what else to say.

He took a measured step forward, but only halfway. "Come to me." He crooked his pointer and middle fingers in a microscopic gesture, much like he had done earlier.

Mina stepped slowly forward until her toes were touching his. She looked into his eyes and held his penetrating gaze.

He stared at her so intently, it was almost hypnotic. And then he ran his fingers through her hair, traced her jawline with his thumb, and trailed the back of his hand lightly along her throat, across her collarbone, and over her breasts, stopping to trace the outline of each areola.

She shivered and gasped, but she didn't protest. Her heart pounded in her chest, and she willed it to slow down.

"Don't ever forget what I am, Mina," he said in a chilling voice. And then, much like he had done with Pralina, he straightened, shrugged his regal shoulders, and inclined his head. He was all at once as calm, clear, and steady as a crystal pond.

He whistled for the horses, and the two magnificent beasts pranced eagerly to their lord's side. He gestured toward the white gelding and nodded, returning to his original intent. "Take your mount, Mina."

As before, his voice was a quiet command.

CHAPTER THREE

DANTE DRAGONA SAT back in the well-worn saddle, adjusting his weight to flow effortlessly with the powerful gait of his majestic horse. He was deep in thought, trying to prepare himself for what was soon to come: the execution of two Warlochian traders at Dante's hands. His royal brothers, Damian and Drake, fell into an easy pace beside him, both of their mounts prancing excitedly beneath their imperial riders, as if sensing the drama to come.

He stared ahead at the winding path, considering the state of the Realm and the role he was soon to play as the prince of a tumultuous providence, wondering at the wisdom of his father's inevitable decrees…

King Demitri had already chosen a ruling territory for each of his three sons: Damian was to be given the western mountain territory of Umbras, home of the treacherous shadow-walkers, beings who assumed solid form in the day yet sank into the shadows like ghosts at night; Drake was to take the southern region, or the *commonlands*, where the mortal humans made their home, including the devious Malo Clan; and, of course, Dante was to reign over the warlocks and witches, with their infernal gargoyle pets, establishing a Warlochian Court in the east.

As far as Dante was concerned, the king's choices made sense.

Damian was the most aggressive of the three, the angriest by far, and he would rule with an iron fist, subjugate his citizens by force...and with fear. He would rule as a tyrant, yet his power would be respected. After all, the shadow-walkers—or *shades*, as they were often referred to—were nearly soulless beings who lived predominantly to satisfy their carnal natures, to prey on the souls of others. They revered power and treachery above all else.

Drake, on the other hand, had a much more reasoned mind. He was a shrewd and deliberate thinker, and as the prince of the *commonlands*, he would rule with wisdom and deliberation. His talents were best suited to a human population, and it could only be hoped that he would manage the Malo Clan with wisdom and finesse.

And Dante?

Well, he was as perceptive as he was cunning, not to be taken lightly or trifled with. His keen awareness of energy, as well as his proficiency with magic, would give him the greatest advantage when working with a race of beings who were always up to witchcraft.

He shifted in his saddle once more and took special notice of the vivid green leaves as they rustled in the tall linden trees which lined the winding path of Forest Dragon, the trade route that snaked from the royal district to the three outlining provinces, ultimately comprising the Realm. The forest was especially beautiful in May, alive with brilliant colors, teeming with wildlife, and bursting with infinite promise—it seemed strangely at odds with the ever-increasing burdens that weighed upon Dante's shoulders like a cloak plaited in stones.

He glanced sideways at Damian and sighed: The male's mouth was set in a harsh, implacable line, *as always*, and his dark brown eyes, framed by a faint one-inch scar on his right temple, were practically brimming with anticipation, alight with eagerness for the upcoming kill.

Damian was a loose cannon to put it mildly, and keeping him in line, or, rather, balancing his impulsive, reckless behavior with the mounting needs of the Realm would be one of Dante's greatest challenges. As much as it saddened Dante to admit it, Damian could not be trusted, neither with his subjects nor his court. He was simply too dangerous, *too broken*, too hard to contain. He was the second-born child of King Demitri and Queen Kalani—well, that is, if one didn't count Desmond, Dante's twin, who had taken his own life nearly ten years ago—and he had been conceived in brutality, nursed in black magic.

The story was as tragic as it was important...

One hundred fifty summers ago, at age nineteen, Dante's twin Desmond had fallen deeply in love with a simple peasant girl from the *commonlands*. Her name had been Evangeline Stone, and with eyes the color of polished blue glass, hair the texture of fine-spun silk, Desmond had been prepared to give up everything he held dear in order to make Evangeline his bride. Needless to say, the late Queen Kalani was not pleased in the least. Not only was Evangeline *beneath* Desmond's station, as far as the haughty queen was concerned, but by choosing her as a bride, it would mean that Desmond could not—*would not*—choose a Sklavos Ahavi as his consort when the time came.

And that meant he would not be guaranteed royal male offspring.

Although Queen Kalani had been the first Sklavos Ahavi in the history of the Realm to be elevated from the servitude of *consort* to the status of *queen*—in fact, King Demitri had gifted her with immortality in order to make it possible—she had repaid the king's gift *and his affection* with bitter betrayal.

She had ordered Evangeline's execution, and she had kept the order a secret until it was, at last, viciously carried out.

The loss of his *beloved* had catapulted Desmond into an

inconsolable state of grief, and the realization that his mother had ordered Evangeline's murder had ultimately pushed him over the edge. Alas, on a warm summer's night, beneath the softly hanging branches of a sycamore tree, just beyond the castle's outer walls, Desmond Dragona, second-born twin of the first royal birth, had consumed a vial of witches' tonic in his desolation, and when that hadn't worked fast enough, he had hanged himself in the tree, thus taking his own royal life.

Dante bristled at the memory, and his horse grew uneasy beneath him, as if sharing the painful recollection with him. Dante did not care to think about that fateful day, about the fact that he had not been there to save his twin, or about the truth of his mother and father's so-called marriage, who they had truly been and what they all had become after Desmond's tragic death. To this day, King Demitri remained a heartless, vacant shell as a result of the suicide.

Dante turned his attention back to Damian and what the tragic story meant for the Realm…

When the king found out what had transpired, he had flown into a virulent rage, his beast emerging with unrestrained ferocity, his temper flaring into merciless wrath: As far as King Demitri was concerned, his queen, a Sklavos Ahavi—*nothing more than a glorified slave*—had been handed the keys to the kingdom only to commit unspeakable treason. She had gone behind his back and given a royal order, one she was not entitled to give, and in that perilous act of sedition, she had cost the king his son. To this day, Dante didn't know if Evangeline's death had ever meant anything to his father, or if his rage had only been fueled by his wounded pride…by a dragon's need for revenge.

Either way, the results were the same.

He had punished Kalani with a brutal beating, and he had forced her to conceive another son, the coupling being an act of violation, not love.

While it had been too late to retract her coronation or reverse her immortality, too late to remove her from the throne, the king had withdrawn his affection and his respect, and the wound had never healed for either one of them. In retaliation, Kalani had cursed the unborn child. She had practiced dark magic throughout the pregnancy, in hopes of giving birth to an ally who would one day avenge her; but instead, she had given birth to Damian, a child without a conscience.

A prince without a moral compass.

A dragon with a tainted soul.

Two years later, the king had forced Kalani to conceive once again, and Drake was the result of the pairing. Not long after Drake's birth, she had died in her sleep. According to the king, her immortality had not completely taken—her conversion had not been properly sealed—and the pregnancy had weakened her beyond recovery.

Dante winced at the pathetic story.

Immortal beings didn't pass away in their sleep.

In fact, it took a grave act of violence to kill them.

Either way, Drake had been the last child the embittered couple had ever produced.

"Dante...*Dante!*" Drake's voice pierced the silence, jolting Dante out of his trance. "Are you alert, brother?"

Dante shook his head, as if he could physically dislodge the memories, before turning his attention to Drake. Drake was another responsibility altogether—rather than being born too wicked, he may have been born too kind. While he could certainly hold his own as a prince and a dragon, he was hardly a tactician of war. His Court would require constant military support and intervention, even if it was only comprised of humans, and the Malo Clan might prove to be his undoing if he didn't remain on his toes. "Yes, I can hear you," he called in response. "What is it?"

Drake inclined his head in a nod, gesturing toward the upcoming village. "We are approaching Warlochia...and the prisoners."

"You need to stay alert, brother," Damian snarled, reining in his horse. "This should be done swiftly and with authority."

"Do not counsel me on how to rule my future province," Dante retorted, avoiding eye contact with the surly dragon. "I know what needs to be done."

"Yay, indeed you do," Damian replied, taking no offense at the banter. *Strength*, he understood.

Dante scanned the approaching piazza before them—the townspeople were gathered in fearful clusters; the prisoners were already manacled to a pair of wooden posts; and at the center of a wide semicircle, the local sheriff awaited the prince's approach.

Summoning his dragon's fire, Dante kicked his horse into a run and galloped into the center of the plaza with authority.

*

The Warlochians parted to make way for the charging horse and the dragon prince, who sat so proudly erect on the stallion's back. No doubt, Dante looked like a knight of old, summoned to a field of battle, only this battlefield was a village square, surrounded by tall, spindly trees; bounded by a smooth earthen floor; and dotted with dilapidated old structures: an outlying stable, various rickety benches, and an aged stone well.

Dante dismounted in one lithe leap, landing directly before the prisoners, his thick raven hair blowing softly in the wind. "Sheriff," he called, waiting for the appropriate subject to answer.

A short, stout mage, nearly fifty years old, shuffled over quickly, all the while reining in his pet gargoyle on a short leather leash.

Dante ignored the obnoxious little ornament, refusing to acknowledge a three-foot-tall monster as a subject. "See to my horse and bring me the decree."

The mage bowed low, his obeisant eyes reflecting the fear that always shone in the presence of a dragon. "As you command, my prince." He turned to a nearby errand boy—the child appeared no more than eight years old—and gestured toward the stallion's reins. "Feed and water your prince's horse," he commanded, and then he turned back to Dante; retrieved a rolled-up scroll from a purse strung over his tunic; and placed it gently in the palm of Dante's hand.

Dante examined the seal.

It was blood red, embossed in gold, and in the center of the stamp, there was the outline of a dragon with a diamond-shaped eye. It was the unmistakable signet of King Demitri Dragona, the tenth of his line, the imperious ruler of Dragons Realm. He broke it and read the decree out loud in the common tongue, his voice traveling across the Warlochian Square like rolling thunder. "For the highest crime of treason against the realm, I, King Demitri Dragona, regent of the royal court, hereby sentence the traitors, Wylan P. Jonas and Sir Henry Woodson, to death by execution at the hand of their future sovereign. The execution is to be meted out on the fourth day of May in the 175th year of the Dragonas' Reign, the season of the diamond king."

The crowd grew deathly quiet as Dante approached the first of the two condemned men. "Wylan P. Jonas?"

The warlock raised his head, leveled a hate-filled glare at Dante, and spoke with heavy contempt in his raspy voice. "Yes, lord?"

"You have been found guilty by a court of your peers for the crime of treason: What say you?"

The prisoner mustered his remaining courage and spat at Dante's feet, and the effort cost him greatly, as his cracked, swollen lips immediately began to bleed. "I say you can all go to hell." His eyes flashed amber, glowing with rising malevolence, and his words trailed off with a hiss.

Dante remained unfazed.

He neither reacted to the abuse nor acknowledged the slight.

Rather, he stepped gracefully to the side. "And Sir Henry Woodson, you have also been found guilty of plotting against your realm and your king. Do you wish to speak on your own behalf?" He narrowed his eyes with singular purpose in an unspoken warning: *Think before you speak.* "Do you wish to beg your prince for mercy before you die?"

The second prisoner looked up and trembled.

After a long, piteous moment had passed, he shrank back against the post. "It is not in the nature of a warlock to submit to the rule of another mystical being, milord. I make no apologies for defying the Dragonas or the king's rule." He gasped for air, and it was readily apparent that his lungs had already been damaged from a previous beating. "However, I am also not a fool. If his lordship would send me to my death with honor, without the pain or scourge of fire, then I would humbly request that he do so."

Dante took a measured step back, regarding the second prisoner from head to toe. Mercy was not the way of the dragon, and ruthlessness was all the Warlochians understood.

He stepped forward, approaching the obstinate prisoner first, the one who had spat at his feet; and the crowd gasped as he tore Wylan P. Jonas free from the post and crushed the heavy iron manacles *effortlessly* beneath his powerful hands.

The iron crumbled into dust.

Wisps of smoke rose from the prince's palms.

And Dante kicked the prisoner to the ground with a booted foot and snarled, "You are an insolent fool, warlock, but at least you are brave. The merciful death will be yours." He grasped the hilt of his sword in its scabbard, brandished the blade in an audible chime of steel, and swiftly brought it down along the prisoner's neck, removing his head in one clean blow. Bracing himself against the spattering gore, he licked his lips, felt his fangs begin to elongate, and slowly re-sheathed the blade. "As for you, Sir Henry Woodson, you shall return to the pit of hell as nothing more than a pile of ash, so that even those who inhabit the underworld will know: A dragon's fury is mightier than a warlock's pride."

He took two large strides back and began to call his beast.

Orange and red fire began to circulate around his body, radiating like a macabre halo, even as pulsating tendrils, like miniature bolts of lightning, shot forth from his fingers. His fangs extended even further, growing perilously sharp and long, and a primordial growl rose in the back of his throat, shaking the ground beneath them. As his face began to harden with the emergence of primordial scales, and a pair of leathery wings punched through his back, he drew back his shoulders, bent both arms at his sides, and strained to arch his spine.

And then he parted his lips and threw back his head, releasing a deafening roar, as an unbroken stream of mystical flames shot forth from his mouth and scorched the second prisoner, without mercy.

The male cried out in agony.

He yanked against his chains and thrashed against the post.

He jerked in pain, writhed in misery, and spat curses, tinged in bloody, blackened mucous.

And yet, the torture persisted.

Which was Dante's intention.

He continued to channel the dragon's fire, the infernal, never-ending blaze, until the screams of the warlock were finally silenced by melting flesh and calcifying bones. Until the crowd turned away in horror and hid their revolted faces from the ghoulish spectacle before them.

Until the gathered Warlochians cried out for mercy on behalf of the prisoner, again and again…

And again.

Until, finally, Dante relented.

The flame turned white and the fire began to cool, until at last, there was nothing left but a charred stump and steaming ash where the post and the traitor had just been. Calling his dragon to heel, Dante fought to regain his center, to reconnect with his civilized core, and to extinguish the flame once and for all.

Having followed Dante into the square, Damian stepped

forward, beside him, and waited, his savage expression daring anyone in the crowd to speak, to even presume to meet their eyes; while Drake took a stance on Dante's other side, projecting unconditional solidarity and conviction with his presence. He may have been a logical thinker, a calming influence—he may have stood in the eye of the storm—but he was still a Dragona at heart. And, together, they wielded enormous power and influence.

When, at last, Dante's wrath had cooled—his fangs and his wings had retracted—he searched the crowd for the sheriff. The male was hovering behind the aged stone well at the back of the square, his face a mask of terror, and the moment their gazes met, the sheriff quickly shuffled to the front of the crowd. He stood before Dante and waited, his head dropped low in a deep, subservient bow.

"We will take drinks and refreshments at the tavern while you tend to our horses," Dante said. "And then we will be on our way."

Before the sheriff could answer, a young girl, perhaps ten or eleven years old, shot through the horrified crowd. She ducked beneath the warlock's legs and ran toward Dante, almost as if she were fearless. "Milord!" she cried out. "Milord! Please—*please*—hear my petition."

Dante looked down at the eager child and drew back in surprise. *Great Winter Spirits, she was human!* He could tell by the contour of her eyes. What was she doing here among the Warlochians? "What is the meaning of this?" he asked the sheriff, choosing to ignore the child.

The sheriff looked perplexed.

He shook his head back and forth; his eyes darted this way and that; and he finally shrugged his shoulders. "My prince, I…I do not know. Please—"

"*Raylea!* Raylea, come back!" Another human, a beautiful, middle-aged woman, darted through the crowd, coming to an abrupt halt in front of the dragons. She grabbed the child by the arm, snatched her frantically away from Dante, and tried to tuck her behind her back. "Forgive me, milord. She is just a child. She doesn't know what she is doing." The woman gathered her skirts and tried to curtsy—it was poorly, at best—her wide eyes brimming with fear. She looked down at the child and frowned, her face growing ashen. "Raylea, what have you done? Apologize to the prince at once!"

The girl stepped out from her mother's side, crossed her arms in front of her chest, and boldly shook her head *no*, although she was clearly shaking in her stockings.

The woman gasped. "Raylea!" She turned her pleading eyes to Dante and waited, presumably for his wrath.

Dante considered the girl and then the woman, each one in turn, before firmly pursing his lips together in thought. Finally, he said, "I assume this is your daughter?"

The woman trembled. "Yes, milord."

"And you did not think to raise her better than this?" Damian cut in, his voice reverberating with ire.

The woman fell to her knees in the dirt. "I have tried, my prince." She practically groveled on the ground, even as she tucked the child tight against her bosom in a gesture of protection. "I beg your pardon. Forgive her...or hold me responsible in her stead."

Drake took a measured step forward. He held up his hand to silence his brothers. "Your love for the child is apparent, but it still does not explain why she would dare to approach a dragon prince. The *commonlands* will soon be my jurisdiction, which makes you my imminent subject. Explain yourself: Why are you here amongst the Warlochians? And why has the child approached the Dragon Prince?" When the woman hesitated, as if she were searching for just the right words, Drake narrowed his gaze with impatience. "Speak quickly, woman. No one has time for these antics."

Dante waited in silence, curious to hear her reply.

The woman cleared her throat. "If it please you, milord…" She stared straight at Drake, pleading with her eyes. "This is my daughter, Raylea. She ran away from home several days ago, after she heard that the future prince of Warlochia would be traveling to this province for—"

"No! No, Mommy!" the girl cried, tugging on her arm. "You have to ask him about Mina."

The woman gasped and shoved her hand over her daughter's mouth. "Be quiet, child! Before it's too late for me to save you."

Damian withdrew a sharp, curved stiletto from his belt and held it out in front of the girl. He turned it slowly back and forth, rotating the shiny blade in the fading sunlight so that the reflection flashed in her eyes, and then he placed the curved edge against the child's throat. "If your daughter speaks out of turn one more time, I will remove her tongue."

The woman turned a ghastly shade of white, as hideous as one of the nearby gargoyles, and she pressed her hand even harder against the child's mouth. "Please, milord." Her eyes said everything she couldn't say: *I'm begging you not to hurt my baby.*

Drake placed a steadying hand on Damian's arm, indicating that he wanted him to wait for his direction, yet he was also wise enough to play his cards *just so*. He cast a sidelong glance at the angry prince. "Perhaps the child should tell the tale, Prince Damian, since she is clearly so…*eager*…to speak. Perhaps we should hear her petition before we cut out her tongue."

Dante waited for Damian's reaction, appreciating Drake's tactic: It appealed to Damian's pride without challenging his authority, and it was certainly better than mutilating a little girl in front of a village of gawking spectators, *for the gods' sake*. "But first, she must apologize for her insolence," Drake added, using his eyes to issue a clear warning to the child's mother: *The situation could quickly get out of hand, and none of the princes would stop it.*

The mother whispered hastily in the child's ear, and the girl stood tall. "Forgive me, milords." She curtsied like a proper lady, and then she knelt beside her mother.

"Speak," Drake ushered, nodding his acceptance of her apology.

Raylea raised her head and smiled, her dark, luminous eyes brightening beneath a veil of thick, curly lashes, her brows rising in ardent anticipation. She was nothing more than an innocent child, a bit immature and unruly, yet harmless. "It's just…it's just…I heard that there was going to be an execution…*for treason*…in Warlochia, and I knew that the princes would be here." She inhaled sharply, trying to modulate her breath. "So I ran away from home."

Drake frowned. "Why would you do such a thing?" He gestured at the village square. "An execution is no place for a child, and Warlochia is no place for a human."

She nodded quickly. "Yes, yes, I know, but I just had to see you. All of you. One of you. I had to ask about my sister, Mina."

"Who?" Damian asked irritably.

Drake held up two fingers. "Go on."

"My sister; her name is Mina Louvet," the girl answered sweetly. "She was taken to the Keep six years ago to be trained as an Ahavi, and then we heard that she had been chosen as a Sklavos and taken to Castle Dragon." She reached into a tattered sack and withdrew a homely, patchwork doll. "I made this for her with my own two hands. I just wanted"—she eyed all three of them warily—"I wanted one of you to give it to her…*for me*."

Damian scoffed in disbelief, and Drake slowly shook his head, squatting down so he could address the child at eye level. "The Sklavos Ahavi belong to the Realm, little one, not to their families. They are not permitted to maintain contact with their kin, at least not until after the Autumn Mating; and even then, it is at their lord's discretion. Do you understand?"

The girl swallowed, and her eyes filled with pressing tears. "I know. *I do*. But…but it's just…*I made it*…with my own two hands." She held the doll out to Drake, rotating it ninety degrees so that it stood upright, and the little button eyes stared back at him.

Damian stalked away toward the tavern, lest he do something rash—*thank the Spirit Keepers*—and Dante held his tongue, trying not to chuckle, waiting to see what his wise, benevolent brother would do next: Would he address his youthful subject with kindness, or would he address the doll, instead?

He looked on as the prince took the toy from the child, patted the object brusquely on the back, and then turned it this way and that in mock appreciation. "And what a fine work of craftsmanship it is. It is very well made." He looked back at Dante for support, and when none was forthcoming, he sighed. "What is her name?"

Raylea shrugged. "I don't know. I thought…maybe…Mina could name her."

Drake smiled then. He handed the doll back to the child, patted her on the head, and rose to his full five foot eleven inches. "You hold onto this, Raylea, and perhaps after the Autumn Mating, you will have a chance to give it to your sister yourself."

"But I haven't seen her in six years," the girl said, a fresh tear rolling down her cheek.

Her mother rose to her feet then and clasped the child by both shoulders. She shoved her behind her back once more; only, this time, she gripped her arm so tight she could have cut off her circulation. "Thank you, milord. You are far too kind." She averted her eyes and bowed her head. "I apologize for my daughter's impetuousness, and I assure you, it will not happen again. We pray that Mina will bring honor to the Realm"—her voice caught on a sob before she quickly regained her composure—"and we hope to see her after the Autumn Mating, should her master allow a visit." The fear and anguish in her voice were unmistakable, despite her best attempt at courage and decorum.

Drake pretended not to notice. "Very well, Mistress Louvet."

He spoke quietly yet sternly. "Your daughter's impetuousness is forgiven. *However…*" He leaned in and grasped her chin, forcing her eyes to meet his. "Keep a closer watch on her. Warlochia is no place for a child or a human woman. You are no match for these magical beings." His warning could not have been any clearer: Humans were afforded basic protections in the *commonlands*, where human decrees and law enforcement were in play, but once they left that province, once they ventured into Umbras or Warlochia, all bets were off.

"Yes, milord." The woman spoke quietly. She curtsied once again, first to Drake and then to Dante. "And thank you for your compassion as well, my prince."

Dante nodded, but he said nothing.

As he watched her walk away, ushering the child hurriedly in front of her, he turned toward a nearby warlock, an old man with a long white beard and a cane, and gestured him forward.

The man shuffled as quickly as his aged feet would allow. "Yes, lord? How may I serve you?"

Dante bent to the old man's ear, and in a voice so low it was barely audible, he whispered, "Have a courier bring the doll to Castle Dragon in the morning."

The old warlock looked surprised, but he stared after the departing mother and child and nodded profusely. "Yes, yes, of course, milord."

Dante nodded, waved him away, and then turned in the direction of the tavern. He suddenly felt the need to have a stiff drink with his brothers, and he wanted to get on with his day. It wasn't like the execution had bothered him; actually, not at all. And he didn't feel as if he had truly gone against Drake's wishes, either—at least not in a way that really mattered. After all, he had no intentions of repeating his father's mistake or his twin's tragic recklessness: A Sklavos Ahavi was not meant to be made immortal, nor was she born to be a queen. And desiring a woman, any woman, so much that a prince would sacrifice his duty to the

Realm in order to keep her affections, that he would take his own life in her absence, was unfathomable to Dante on every level.

No, Dante Dragona would not make the same mistakes his father and his twin had made.

He would *feed* as a dragon must; he would produce the required heirs; and the Realm would always come first.

Still…

What harm could there be in giving an Ahavi her sister's doll?

CHAPTER FOUR

Castle Dragon

MINA LOUVET GINGERLY climbed out of the slippery bath in her private bedchamber, careful to maintain a sturdy grip around the edge of the tin basin. She reached for a woolen towel, planted both feet solidly on the wooden floor, and began to dry off as quickly as possible. Shivering from the cold, she angled her body toward the hearth for warmth and glanced toward the doorway.

There was someone in her room.

A figure in the shadows.

A murky impression, like a waif or a ghost, and it flickered in the reflection of firelight, dancing in her peripheral vision.

Gasping, she quickly wrapped herself in the towel, turned in the direction of the shadow, and strained to take a second look.

It wasn't a shadow at all.

It was Dante Dragona.

And he was standing in the doorway like a notch in the frame, utterly melded and silent, as if he simply belonged there, as if he were part and parcel of the woodwork itself.

Mina cursed beneath her breath even as she exhaled in relief. *Thank the Spirit Keepers it wasn't an actual specter,* yet what it was—*who it was*—was far more daunting. Her heart began to race from a different kind of fear, and she struggled to steady her nerves.

As far as Mina knew, Dante was supposed to be away from the castle.

Just yesterday morning, he had traveled to Warlochia on important court business, and she was surprised to see him back so soon. Just what his business had been, Mina had no idea—the Ahavi were not privy to such matters—but by the weary look on his face, it must have been something grave. His eyes were haunted with subtle shadows. His jaw was set in a hard, implacable line, and his usual discernable expression was inscrutable.

"Milord?" She spoke cautiously, still wondering how he had entered her bedchamber without making a sound. She hadn't heard the telltale creaking of the large iron doorknob, nor had she heard the panel settling back into the frame—and the realization unnerved her. Dante was far too predatory for her liking.

"Mina." Her name was a mere whisper of breath on his tongue.

She unwittingly clutched the towel, bunching it up in her fist as she pressed it closer to her racing heart. "How did you—"

"Shh." His eyes grew dark with subtle reflections of mystery, and then he took a graceful step forward, his movement as subtle as the flutter of a butterfly's wings. "Come to me, Ahavi." His iron chest rose and fell in deep, even breaths.

Mina bowed her head and forced an uncomfortable curtsy: *By all the Spirit Keepers, she was trying to be obedient.* "Of course." She took a bold step in his direction and then halted. "Just give me a second to get dressed." Her eyes darted across the room to the enormous four-poster bed and the pale linen nightgown laid out so neatly on top of it. "I'll only be a moment." She tried to shuffle forward without meeting his gaze, hoping he would allow her this small indulgence.

A harsh, guttural growl brought her up short. "I said, *come to me*," he repeated, his voice like an icy wind.

Mina froze in place.

She got it.

She did.

The prince expected nothing less than immediate submission and absolute obedience from his servants, and she was no exception. Although she had no desire to oppose him, it was just so hard to jump at the snap of his fingers. And right now, she would have given her right arm to be properly dressed, to not feel so incredibly vulnerable. She linked her hands behind her back in an act of submission and peeked at him through mollified lashes. "My prince, I only wish to—"

"Silence." He shot her a clear, unmistakable warning with his eyes. "Not another word."

Mina stood motionless, awaiting his next command. She couldn't help but notice that the flames in the nearby hearth were flickering wildly in response to the dragon's rising ire; the crescents were swaying to and fro as if tossed about in a turbulent wind; and the macabre reflection cast a haunting red shadow against the bedchamber wall, almost as if it were decreeing a warning: *Now is not the time to defy or incite the beast.*

Mina contracted her diaphragm as she breathed, still trying to calm her nerves.

Surely, Dante understood the rules…

He had to know that there were boundaries governing the five-month introductory period when the king's sons selected their preferred Ahavi, lines that could not be crossed, principles that must be honored. Surely, Dante understood that the princes were not to *bed* their potential consorts before the Final Choosing, not a day before the Autumn Mating. It was strictly forbidden for so many reasons: Not only was it seen as distasteful and assuming, but to do so was akin to playing a dangerous game of chance, taking a perilous and unnecessary risk, flirting with imminent disaster.

Dragons were territorial by nature.

One male could not have *carnal knowledge* of his brother's wife, nor could he risk impregnating the wrong consort—who's to say he would not be devious enough to slip her the fertility elixir? Should a Sklavos Ahavi end up carrying the wrong prince's child, her rightful master would be inclined, if not driven, to destroy the illegitimate offspring, to murder his nephew in an act of dominance and territorialism. *No*, carnal relations were forbidden during the preliminary months. Unfortunately, they were about *all* that was forbidden.

Trusting what she had been taught at the Keep, Mina forced herself to meet Dante's intimidating stare head-on. She gathered her courage and took another step forward, moving clearly in his direction.

It must have been too little, too late.

His eyes flashed amber in response to what he clearly perceived as an unhurried pace, and then they turned even darker still—heavy, shadowed, and disapproving—as he used the power of his mind to wrest her forward more quickly.

Drawn by the dragon's power, Mina took five quick, orchestrated steps toward Dante, shuffling mindlessly like a marionette on a puppeteer's strings, until she finally stood before him, her toes nearly touching his. It was the same thing he had done that first day in the courtyard, and she felt utterly frustrated by the all-too-familiar situation.

It wasn't as if she couldn't learn.

Quite the contrary, really. She got it. She was just having trouble with the *immediate* part of obedience.

Holding her breath, she practically cowered before him.

"Why do you insist upon trying my patience, Mina?"

She sighed, feeling like she just couldn't win, knowing there was no acceptable reply. After all, what could she say? Dante had no idea what this was like for her, what it was like for a mortal to stand in a dragon's presence. And why would he? *How could he?* To him, her lame attempts at compliance were measly at best. To her, they were Herculean feats of bravery. She held her tongue, hoping to appease him with silence.

He stared at her exposed shoulders, unconsciously licking his full bottom lip while revealing the slightest hint of fangs, his mouth turning down in a scowl. "Ah, I see...silence."

Mina trembled as he openly appraised her from head to toe, as if doing so was his gods-given right, and truth be told, it probably was.

"Turn around," he commanded, subtly inclining his head.

Mina froze. Her heart began to race in her chest, and she instinctively clutched the towel above her breasts. She wanted to obey so badly it hurt, but his request was just so terrifying. Surely, Dante would not force himself upon a Sklavos Ahavi like a drunken commoner with a tawdry barmaid. Surely, he would not take *a virgin* in such a barbaric manner.

Dearest Ancestors, be merciful!

"W...why... milord?" she asked sheepishly.

Dante's perfect brows creased in frustration, framing his harshly beautiful face like an angry crown as he waited for her compliance. "Have I not warned you, dear Mina, about questioning your lord?" He lowered his voice and whispered, "About challenging *the beast?*" His eyes fixed on the towel, the way she was holding it just above her breasts with white-knuckled fingers, and his voice practically vibrated with heat. "Do you really want to challenge the dragon's dominant instincts *now*—in your present state of undress?"

Mina shivered. She drew in a deep breath and slowly turned around, clutching the towel even tighter, if that was possible. She could hear his breathing—it was shallow behind her—and the feel of his warm breath pulsated against her ears.

"Better," he said. And then he spoke so quietly, she had to strain to hear him. "At the Keep, you were schooled in all the ways of the dragon, were you not? You were taught when and how to submit?"

"Y…y…yes, milord," she whispered.

"Good. Then you understand our various appetites?"

Mina no longer just shivered. She literally quaked where she stood, her slender knees knocking together. She opened her mouth to reply, but no sound came out. She was terrified, beyond humiliated, and utterly speechless.

Dante reached out to touch her, although whether or not he meant to comfort her or threaten her, she had no idea. He slowly ran his fingers through her hair in a chilling caress, stopping to twirl several damp tendrils between his thumb and forefinger before letting them drop to her shoulders. And then he swept the lot of her hair away from her neck, placing it gently over the left side so that her right shoulder stood completely bare.

Her skin tingled beneath his ministrations. Her neck felt overly sensitive and unnaturally exposed, yet there she stood, frozen like a statue, submitting as a good Ahavi should.

Lowering his head to whisper in her ear, he said, "I am weary, Mina. Tired and famished. My dragon wishes to reanimate his fire."

Mina blinked back tears and bit her bottom lip. She didn't dare utter a word. She couldn't if she tried. A dragon's *fire-lust* was all-consuming once it began to burn. She knew this. All the Ahavi knew this. And if she tried to extinguish it now, she would only make matters worse, perhaps succeed at inciting another need altogether, a much more primitive, carnal hunger. She tried to brace herself for what was coming next, but her legs felt weak beneath her, and she had to take a quick shuttle-step to the side to keep from losing her balance.

Dante stiffened and stood up straight. Whether or not he had taken her silence as an affront, she didn't know. Whether or not he was feeding on her fear, she didn't want to know. She purposefully let her shoulders drop, just as they had been taught to do at the Keep, and then, in order to relax, to ease her rigid posture, she began to count her breaths, one after the other, silently in her mind. She paid careful attention to her diaphragm. She focused on the way her chest rose and fell. She visualized the air moving in and out of her body as a golden ray of light, and she concentrated on circulating it in smooth, even waves. She did everything she had been taught over the last six years. *Relax. Let yourself go. Drift away in your mind.*

Just breathe.

"Good girl," Dante whispered, and he genuinely seemed to approve. He encircled her shoulders with his powerful arms and lightly fingered the top of the towel. "Let go," he commanded.

Mina swallowed hard and tried to comply, but her hands would not obey.

He gently pried her fingers loose from the fabric. "Do not fight me, Mina," he warned as the thin towel began to slide down her waist.

Mina gasped as the towel fell to the ground and her body was instantly bared in the firelight, exposed to the dragon's gaze. Dante drew in a harsh intake of breath, and she clenched her eyes shut, trying to recall her training, struggling to remember her duty, endeavoring to return to the rhythm of her breathing.

When he took a step back, moving several inches away, she nearly collapsed with relief, but then he placed both of his hands on her shoulders and began to slowly massage her muscles. It was almost as if he were a potter and she were a lump of clay as he kneaded her arms, slowly ran his palms down her biceps to her elbows, and then gently traced the outline of her forearms to the junction of her wrists. He lifted his hands and repositioned them at her waist, measuring her slender midriff with ten splayed fingers, cupping her belly with his outstretched hands. When his palms brushed over the curves of her hips and his thumbs slid absently over her buttocks, she panted in near desperation, trying to dispel her fear.

He knelt behind her, and Mina's eyes grew wide.

Dear goddess of mercy, she was naked!

What was he about to do?

Her eyes flitted across the room as she desperately searched for a focal point, an object to fix her attention upon. She quickly settled on a brass oil lamp, situated next to a tattered tome on the fireplace mantel, and she could practically hear the governess at the Keep whispering in her ear: *When you're standing before him, and he is touching you; when the pain is too intense, or the degradation is too severe; when the demands he makes of your body feel too extreme, like you cannot comply, find a focal point or an object across the room and place your full attention upon it. Study it. Memorize it. Name its various parts in meticulous order. Count down the seconds, the minutes, or the hour; and do it in measurable increments.*

Mina studied the lantern and began to recite the various components in her head: *Burner. Wick. Collar. Chimney. Shade—*

And then Dante reached out to grasp her ankles, and she almost jumped in place. *For the love of the Spirit Keepers*, what would have happened if she had kicked him?

She swallowed her anxiety and stood as still as she could as he repeated the earlier process, only this time, performing the ministrations on her legs. He slowly ran his hands up the backs of her calves, massaging her muscles as he moved along, and then he rotated his thumbs over the backs of her knees and slid his palms along the outside of her thighs.

Mina cringed when Dante's seeking fingers came to rest at the crease of her rounded bottom, their progress all at once impeded by the soft, circular globes. His proximity to her *most intimate region* was far too close for comfort. She had never felt more exposed—or humiliated—in her entire life. When at last she couldn't stand another moment, she slapped at his wrists. "Prince

Dante!" Catching herself, she immediately withdrew her hands and softened her voice. "I mean, *milord*...what are you doing?"

Ignoring her disobedience, Dante chuckled low in his throat, the tenor a raspy, masculine sound. "I am measuring your heat, sweet Mina. I am checking for any blockages that may have gone undetected at the Keep, trying to discern how much of your essence I can take without doing you irreparable harm."

How much of her essence he could take without doing her irreparable harm?

Oh gods...

She trembled.

"I must say," he added softly, "it is hard not to become... distracted." He purred low in his throat and then groaned. "By all that is sacred, my Ahavi, you are more beautiful than I imagined." He placed a soft kiss *on her derriere*, and then he rose to his feet in one smooth, agile motion. He lightly trailed the backs of his fingers up, along her spine and across her trapezius muscles, and then he placed each hand on one of her shoulders and whispered in her ear. "Lean back against my chest, Ahavi, so you don't grow faint."

"Milord, please...I...I'm not ready."

"You will do as you are bid, sweet Mina." Before she could reply *or refuse him*, he tugged her back against him, swirled his tongue lightly over the area where the bend of her neck met her shoulder, and then swiftly made a seal over the moist circle with his mouth.

Mina felt the slow drag of fangs where his cool tongue and warm breath had just been, and she tensed, sending a silent prayer up to the Spirit Keepers for strength.

Shh, Dante whispered *in her mind*. And then he released his fangs and sank them deep into her flesh, taking the barest sip of blood in his first primal pull.

Mina jolted from the pain, and then she whimpered from the helplessness, clutching at his hands for support. He held her more tightly against him, locking her body to his in an iron hold, even as he continued to feed from her *essence*, no longer taking her blood. Although the pain began to subside, she still didn't want this. She just wasn't ready to *serve* him this soon.

But what choice did she have?

She was an Ahavi, a female sworn to serve the dragon, to feed his fire at his behest; and moreover, she was Dante's Sklavos Ahavi, or she would be soon, the moment the king decreed it—and that meant Dante's every wish was to be her command. It was simply the way of the Realm.

It had *always* been the way of the Realm.

And Mina thought she had been prepared for the inevitability of her duty, for this defenseless, subservient moment, until she began to feel the warmth seeping out of her body, the very nucleus of her soul draining from her flesh. Until the dragon continued to feed his fire with her heat, and her life force began to dissipate.

Inexpressible chills traveled along Mina's spine as her body temperature dropped rapidly and her energy waned. Frosty sensations, like fingers gloved in shards of ice, played along her skin—grasping, probing, taking—even as her muscles grew weak and her skin turned blue. She shivered and moaned.

Yet and still, Dante fed.

When at last he withdrew his fangs, she felt as if she might collapse from exhaustion, as if any moment now, she would draw one last shallow breath and just let go, pass on to the netherworld, drained from the core. She felt as if her body no longer contained the essence it needed to maintain *life*, as if her soul was no longer separate from his.

As if Dante had taken it all.

The dragon had drained her completely.

Dante sealed the puncture wounds with a rasp of his tongue, and then he began to blow a steady stream of fire over the raw, inflamed skin. She knew it was *blue fire*—or at least she hoped it was—because that was the *healing* color they were taught to expect at the Keep, the only fire that came from a dragon which gave life instead of taking it. Well *that* and silver, which was used to bestow immortality.

As the mystical flames licked at her skin, causing a dull, radiating pain to throb in her neck, she felt her body temperature begin to rise almost as rapidly as it had fallen. The strength in her muscles returned, and she became instantly reanimated. She was suddenly infused with amazing strength, robust health, and renewed vitality; and somehow, she knew she was stronger than before. Dante had sealed the wound with a powerful, healing fire.

And then he knelt behind her *again*.

Only this time, he picked up the towel; ran it along her smooth, delicate skin; and stood back up, reaching around to tuck the front into a loosely folded knot, just above her breasts. He was careful not to touch her indecently, or perhaps he just wasn't inclined to do so. Either way, he tucked in the towel and released it. "You did well, Ahavi." His voice was a silken purr in her ear, and she shivered at the unfamiliar vibration of his approval.

As tears of relief rolled down her cheek, she bowed her head in response. She felt *open*, exposed, and incredibly vulnerable, but not altogether despondent. "Then you are pleased?" she asked, not at all sure why it mattered, other than the fact that she hoped to continue living, even if this *was* to be her lot in life.

"Your essence, your heat, is like sunshine on a cloudy day. It is so much easier when you submit, is it not?" He placed a sweltering kiss on her bare shoulder. "I cannot help but wonder what *all of you* will feel like when the time comes."

Mina couldn't restrain her reaction. She spun around to face him, unwittingly taking several steps back. "Please, milord." She held up both hands to keep him at bay and then immediately thought better of it—Mina did not want to anger the dragon, but *goddess have mercy*, there was only so much she could take in one day. And *this*, the idea of submitting her body to Dante *completely*, it was just too much to deal with, far too much to take in. Dante's certain ownership, his proud *possession*, his proprietary ways were more than enough for Mina to contend with. "I don't wish to defy you," she said respectfully, "but you are terrifying me, milord. And I can hardly bear it another moment." Her white-knuckled grip on the towel turned blue, and she glanced anxiously around the room, searching for a place to retreat.

Or hide.

Dante swept his hand along the curve of her chin, traced her protesting lips with his forefinger, and then gestured for her to be silent. "It will not always be so, Mina. You will come to understand your role...and mine. You will learn to accept them both."

She raised her eyebrows and frowned. "And if I don't?"

He shook his head in quiet dismissal. "But you must." In that moment, he looked so fiercely predatory, so intrinsically regal, so harshly masculine yet beautiful that Mina was caught off guard.

She tried not to think of his words...

What they meant for her future and her life.

Instead, she eyed her nightgown, still lying across the coverlet on the large, four-poster bed, and wished she could don it with her mind alone. She needed to retreat someplace safe, to cover her body and protect her heart. She needed to feel in control, if only for a moment.

As if he could hear her thoughts, Dante stretched out his hand toward the object of her desire, crooked the tips of his fingers, and effortlessly drew the nightgown into his open hand from across the room. He handed it to her with grace. "Yesterday," he said, crossing his arms over his chest and leaning back against the wall, as if they had been carrying on a casual conversation all along, "I traveled with my brothers to the village of Warlochia to execute two traitors who were plotting against the king."

Mina's eyes grew wide, and she watched him carefully, even as she slipped the nightgown over her head *and above the towel*, before removing the wool from underneath.

"While I was there"—he pressed on as if the executions were nothing more than background information—"I met a young girl who gave me this." He reached behind his back and retrieved a figurine.

Mina held up her hands in question. She stared at the object for a protracted moment, her features distorting with confusion. "A doll? You met a young girl who gave you a *doll?*"

The corners of Dante's mouth curved upward, and Mina thought it was the first time she had ever seen him smile.

Well, almost smile.

Dante lowered his voice and snickered. "The child's name was Raylea Louvet, and she made the *doll* for her sister."

Mina continued to stare at the figurine, trying to make sense of Dante's words, and then all at once it hit her, and her hands flew up to her cheeks. "Raylea! *Raylea* made this *for me?*" Tears of joy spilled from her eyes, and she reached out to snatch the toy from his hands. She studied it meticulously, committing every detail to memory, wondering at the exquisite craftsmanship of her *baby sister*. Okay, so the eyes were a bit crooked, it was pitifully under-stuffed, and the features were a bit lopsided; still, it was the most beautiful thing Mina had ever seen, and she fought not to break down and sob.

Rubbing the belly of the doll against her cheek, she looked up at Dante through tear-stained lashes and genuinely smiled in return. "Thank you. Oh, *thank you.*" She didn't know what else to say.

Dante seemed somewhat taken aback by her emotion: His brow furrowed; his expression grew unreadable; and he cocked his head to the side. "You're welcome." His voice was even and controlled.

Mina struggled to compose herself as well. "It's just…it's just…I lost my sister to the Realm six years ago, when I was taken to the Keep. She was only four years old, and she lost me, too. I haven't seen her in so many years."

Dante nodded then, looking curiously out of place, and she felt instantly embarrassed, not because she had thanked him and not because she had smiled, but because she had shared something so personal and *intimate* with a dragon.

He took a deep breath and slowly exhaled. "We have all made many sacrifices for the Realm, Mina. For you, it was your lovely sister and your parents. For me, it was the freedom of choice and my brother, *my twin,* who died by his own hand. Perhaps you can take comfort in knowing that you may at least see your loved one again."

Mina inhaled sharply, surprised by his words. She dropped her arm to her side, letting the doll hang loosely in her hand. She knew of Desmond's suicide—of course she knew—they had all learned the Dragonas' history at the Keep, but it had never occurred to her, at least not before this moment, that these weren't just facts and histories. They weren't just details to be memorized or lessons to be learned: They were real-life events.

Accompanied by real loss and pain.

"Oh gods, Dante. I'm sorry. How insensitive I must seem." She unwittingly took a step forward, reached up to touch his face, and cringed when he jerked away.

"Your compassion is not necessary."

She withdrew her hand as if she had been burned, feeling even worse than before. "Apologies. I…I…"

"I did not give you the doll to court you, Mina," he added coolly.

She nodded then. "I see."

"You are my Sklavos Ahavi. *Mine.*" He reached out, took her hand in his, and placed it against his cheek. "I gave it to you because a brave child asked me to, and I knew that it would bring you comfort. That is all."

She bristled, feeling terribly confused. "So why would you want to bring me comfort then, *milord?*"

He tilted his head to the other side as if deeply considering her words. "We are so often compelled to do what we must to fulfill our duties to the Realm. It is a small thing to make life easier for a loyal servant."

A loyal servant.

Dante's words struck her like the tip of an arrow piercing through her heart, although she had no idea why. "Of course," she whispered. Turning her gaze to her hand, which was still being pressed to his cheek, she murmured, "May I remove my hand, *milord?*"

"You may," he answered quietly, letting it go.

She did just that, and then she rubbed her palm against the skirt of her nightgown, as if she could somehow remove the feel of his skin from her palm. Softly, she whispered, "If it is not my heart you wish to *court*, then what is it you desire?"

He reached out to finger a lock of her hair, and a sardonic smile curved along his lips. "Your obedience, sweet Mina. Always—*and only*—your obedience."

Mina blinked back a tear. "And when we come together… to create children…to create *your sons*, what then?" She couldn't believe she had spoken the words aloud, but so be it: It wasn't like her *purpose* was a secret, and she wanted to know *now* what she could expect down the road.

His eyes heated with desire, and his sapphire pupils reflected unspoken promises of dark languid nights filled with satin kisses and fiery caresses. "Then I will command your obedience *and* your pleasure." He narrowed his gaze on her lips. "Of that, you may rest assured."

Mina swallowed a flippant retort.

She had no doubt that Dante could please her body, dominate her will, and even possess her soul if he chose. After all, he was only a whisper shy of being a god; but still, what would her life be like without compassion, without companionship, without even the *possibility* of love? What would her life be like as the consort to a dragon, a being born of fire, who was fueled by feral passions yet devoid of tenderness and affection?

Glancing once again at the doll, still hanging at her side, she quickly dismissed the thought. Dante Dragona was indeed capable of tenderness—*and kindness*—and he would never know how much his little gift had meant to her, regardless of his reasons for doing it. "Whatever your purpose," she whispered, "I thank you, milord."

He inclined his head in a polite gesture of acknowledgment. "And I thank you for feeding the dragon, sweet Mina." He stroked her cheek once more, then backed away. "I will come to you again, *soon*."

With that, he simply vanished from the room, leaving her shivering, breathless, and perhaps just a little bit…hopeful.

CHAPTER FIVE

RAFAEL BISHOP, THE high mage of Warlochia, ducked under a low-hanging branch of a prickly ash tree, careful to avoid the dense, barbed undergrowth. He stared at the silent circle of warlocks before him, each male seated comfortably around the fire, and gently cleared his throat. "The slave trade was especially profitable last month: We managed to sell three girls and four boys to the shadow-walkers in the west and ship several others across the restless sea. Losing Sir Henry will set us back a bit—he was instrumental in hiding some of our early captures until we could arrange for their transport—but I don't anticipate more than two or three weeks before we're back in business."

"The fool got caught planning to raid Castle Dragon," Micah Fiske said, spitting into the dirt in disgust. "He thought he could break into the treasury. How foolish can one warlock be?"

"Well," Rafael said with derision, "he is dead, so perhaps we need not tread on his grave."

Micah scowled. "A grisly death by fire. He was foolish to provoke the prince."

"Again," Rafael said, growing increasingly annoyed, "no need to spit on his grave."

Micah crossed his arms over his bent knees, held his hands out to the fire, and rubbed them together for warmth. "By the way, we have a new girl, just like you asked for. Top grade: young, virginal, and pretty, not a single scar on her body. Caught her on Monday."

Rafael cocked a curious eyebrow. "Do you? And how did the capture go?"

Micah shrugged. "Like any other, I suppose. We cornered the girl and her mother in the forest. They were traveling alone by horseback, so it took very little effort to drive them off the path. Zakor, my gargoyle, jumped out at the child's mare from behind a tree, and the horse reared up in a panic. The kid was thrown from the saddle, and Zakor was able to snatch her by the arm before she hit the ground. He dragged her into the thicket, kicking and screaming all the way, I might add, and handed her over to me." He sniffed with something akin to insolence or pride, as if capturing a ten-year-old girl was truly a great feat of prowess. "At that point, it was just a matter of binding her hands and feet, gagging her so she couldn't scream, and then throwing her on the back of my horse." He stared off into the distance as if reliving the memory in nostalgic detail. "Her mother fought like a crazed banshee, though. She screamed and cursed like a madwoman, trying to charge after her daughter." He sniffed. "Hell, she must have given chase for a full five minutes because I swear my horse was winded by the time we lost her, but, ultimately, her mare was too old, not up for the task. We left her in the dust somewhere around Devil's Bend."

Rafael frowned, unimpressed by the dispensable details of the sordid tale. How hard was it to *cleanly* steal a little girl from her middle-aged mother? "And it didn't occur to you that the mother might report the incident to the constable once she gets back to the *commonlands*? Did you not think to take care of the only surviving witness? That perhaps you should have seen to *her* disappearance as well?"

Micah glared at Rafael with unconcealed insolence, his thin lips turned down in a scowl. Apparently, he was growing weary of being challenged. "Two women riding alone through Forest Dragon on horseback? As far as I'm concerned, they had it coming: They could've encountered anything from bandits to a wild animal. By the time she gets back to the Commons District, it'll be too late for the constable to do anything about it. Oh sure; the guard will take down a report. They may even send a missive to the Warlochian sheriff, since it happened inside his territory, but they aren't going to marshal any troops or send out any search parties, not to retrieve one lone, insignificant girl. Raylea Louvet will be written off as a casualty of the Realm, just as so many other children are...every day."

Rafael took a seat across from Micah, added another log to the fire, and used a forked, gangly branch to stoke it into a robust flame. "I suppose. But in the future, you need to take care of loose ends." Unwilling to endure Micah Fiske a moment longer, he turned his attention to Robert Cross. The warlock was staring into the fire like his long-lost love was perched on an emblazoned log, the pupils of his witchy eyes dilated and dreamy. "And you, Sir Robert? Do you have a buyer for the child already?"

Robert blinked several times as if coming out of a trance, and then he coughed, scrubbed his filthy hands over his already dirty face, and hawked some phlegm from his throat. Spitting it into the fire, he smiled. "I do. A shadow by the name of Syrileus Cain." His tone was unusually affable. "He lives by himself in a secluded cabin, far back in the Shadow Woods. I believe he is looking for a housekeeper and a cook—eventually, a wife, of course. The girl will do well, and he's willing to pay a handsome price for an untouched virgin: fifteen coppers."

Rafael nodded in appreciation. "Good. *Good.* The sooner we can turn the girl over to the shadow the better. We will need all his coppers to procure a new henchman, someone to replace Sir Henry Woodson, someone with a good-sized cellar in his barn and a helluva lot of loyalty in his greedy heart. The heavier the purse, the greater our chances of buying both."

Micah tore a piece of chicken off the horizontal spit suspended above the fire, and began to chew the meat in earnest, smearing ash and grease all over his surly face. "It's a damn shame she's only ten and the shadow is willing to pay a premium for her virtue." He spit out a gnawed piece of bone and smacked his lips together, spreading more grease around the corners of his mouth. "I'd love to take a turn with that little spitfire. She's quite the wildcat, that girl."

Rafael frowned and leveled a heated glare at his idiotic companion. "And that is why you will never be more than a gopher, Micah. You still do not understand the difference between business and pleasure, what it means to conduct an arm's length transaction. You still find pleasure in the subjugation of little girls." He rolled his eyes in disgust. Not that he was some paragon of virtue—far from it, really—but just the same, he at least liked to consider himself a man, someone who measured his feats of bravery against worthy adversaries.

Not helpless little girls.

Micah snorted, looking moderately annoyed. And then, without any warning, he threw his remaining chicken bone into the fire, bounded to his feet, and stormed toward Rafael, his warlock's eyes flashing red with thinly banked madness. "You think you're so damn superior," he spat. He thumped his fists against his chest and visibly swelled up with pride. "Then do something about it, warlock! Because I've just about had it with all your sanctimonious bullshit."

Rafael rose slowly…

Gracefully.

A sinister smile embellishing his tightly pursed lips.

He drew in a deep, measured breath of air, filling his lungs with the night's dark pleasures, even as he reveled in the sudden aroma of sulfur, wafting to his nostrils. He held both hands, palms out to the fire, and began to gather its heat. As the flame turned blue and began to swirl around his thick, knotty fingers, he chuckled deep in his raspy throat. "Have you not seen enough death and destruction for one week, Micah? Do you really want to join the ranks of Sir Henry and Wylan Jonas? Because, trust me, it can be arranged." He spun around to face him then, his dark cloak flapping behind him, carried on a sudden gust of cultic wind, and his body rose nearly four feet off the ground. As he hovered there, dangling in the air like a specter, his voice took on a gravelly tone, and his corneas flashed white with fire.

Micah took a cautious step back.

That's right, Rafael thought, *run, little rabbit. Go back to your hole and hide. Your magic is paltry and insignificant compared to mine.*

Micah held both hands up in front of him in a gesture of supplication. "Hey, Rafael, forget about it. I was just spouting off." He genuflected with a guarded wave and practically bowed his head. "You know I was just foolin' around. I mean, who would wanna take on a high mage? Let's sit down, have some more chicken."

The high mage spat at Micah's feet, and electric sparks rose from the spittle, dancing about the ground like little minions seeking Micah's toes. "Are you sure, Mr. Fiske?"

Micah nodded copiously. "Yeah, yeah, I'm sure." He lowered his eyes and snorted, searching for a way to swiftly change the subject. "By the way, did I tell you? That girl we caught; she's damn near royalty."

Rafael raised his eyebrows, descended from the air, and planted his feet firmly on the ground. "What do you mean, *she's damn near royalty?*"

Micah met Rafael's eyes and forced himself to hold the mage's gaze. "She's the sister of one of those Ahavi wenches, one that actually got chosen for the mating. I think—"

Rafael held out his hand to silence him, suddenly consumed with rage. He closed his fingers into a tight fist, constricting the warlock's heart in the process, and then tightened his grip on the male's aorta from the other side of the fire. "Are you insane? Are you absolutely daft?"

Micah clutched at his chest and staggered backward. "What the hell did I do now?"

"What the hell did you do now?" He released Micah's heart before the male fell down, dead, and could no longer answer his questions. "*What the hell did you do now?* You took the sister of a Sklavos Ahavi to be sold as a slave—to a shadow-walker! Did it not occur to you that word of her plight might get back to her sister?"

"So!" Micah shouted, his eyes wild with fear. "*So what?* The girl's a peasant, *a slave*, and so is her royal sister, if you wanna tell the truth." He gasped for air and rubbed his chest in slow, desperate circles. "Sure, the kid will be a maid and a cook for a while, but we all know why the shadow really wants her, to strap her to his bed and plant little shadow-walkers inside her someday. And that's the same damn reason the prince has her sister." He finally caught his breath, and his voice rose with conviction. "Oh, it might be some royal settee—or a feather-stuffed mattress—that the dragon straps her sister to, but the end result is the same. They're chattel. What the heck is your problem, Rafael? Money is money, and the girl is pretty—she's going to fetch a large coin. I got you fifteen coppers. "

Rafael shook his head in disgust, trying desperately to control his temper. "I swear, one of these days..." His voice trailed off and he licked his lips. And then he turned to regard Robert, the male who had found a buyer, before addressing the worthless idiot again. "You're not waiting to unload her. I want you to go with Micah, and I want the two of you to head out now."

Micah looked off into the distant forest and frowned. "Are you crazy? It's the middle of the night."

"Get the girl, and take her to Umbras. *Now.* Sell her to this Syrileus Cain before the week is over. Do you hear me?"

Micah popped his neck on his shoulders as if trying to relieve some stress. "Shit." He leveled a crosswise glance at Robert and winced in apology. "Yeah, I hear you."

Rafael raised his hand and seized the warlock's heart a second time, just to belabor his point. As Micah doubled over in pain, Rafael hissed his next words with venom. "I am not playing around with you, Micah. Get rid of her. *Now!*"

Micah clenched his fists over his heart and nodded profusely, sweat pouring from his tortured brow. His face was contorted in pain, and his cheeks were drenched in rivulets of anguish and fear. "Okay. Okay. Let me go." He huffed between words, and then he staggered backward, fell to the ground, and writhed in the dirt until Rafael released him.

He would either obey, or he would die.

The time for talking was over.

As Micah Fiske struggled to his knees, retrieved his traveling sack from the hollow of a nearby tree, and headed toward the makeshift corral to untether his horse, Robert got up to join him. "I'll see you in a couple days, Rafael," the wiser warlock muttered.

Rafael inclined his head in response, and then he watched his cohorts scamper away.

He didn't really perceive any danger.

After all, the girl would disappear into the southwestern mountains of Umbras, never to be seen again, just so long as Micah did as he was told.

Still, it had been so stupid and careless.

What if Castle Dragon got wind of it?

What if his own wicked mistress, Wavani, the king's witch, somehow sensed it and began to question her personal involvement in the slave trade? As it stood, she was difficult to contain, already.

Why barter for trouble when you didn't have to?

The realm was full of young, virginal girls, just ready to be sacrificed, violated, or sold, if not to the shades or other warlocks, then to the Lycanian shifters across the sea. There was no point in tempting fate by taking the sister of a Sklavos Ahavi. One never knew when something unexpected might occur, when unintended paths might cross.

All Rafael knew was that he was far wiser than Sir Henry Woodson and far more careful than Micah Fiske. He had no intentions of drawing the attention of a dragon prince to their little profitable slave trade, nor did he intend to suffer any fools, not a moment longer than he had to.

When Micah Fiske returned from selling the girl, Rafael would kill him.

He would capture his soul, trap it in a bottle, and sell it to the shades as an edible delicacy on his next trip to Umbras.

As he watched the warlocks take their mounts and head off in the direction of the cage that temporarily housed the girl, he snarled.

Good riddance to bad rubbish.

CHAPTER SIX

Three days later

MINA SLIPPED OUT of her bedchamber and padded down the steep servants' staircase at the far end of the musty hall, clutching a hand-drawn, rudimentary map in one hand and a dimly lit torch in the other. According to the map, she needed to follow the staircase until she came to a forked landing and then turn left. At that point, she could follow the hall toward the rear of the castle and enter a final narrow tunnel that would take her all the way to the kitchens.

Good grief, this was quite the maze.

Just the same, she was determined to sneak into the galley; retrieve some wine, bread, and cheese; and make her way back to her room before any of the castle's occupants noticed her absence. She was edgy, she was restless, and she needed the exercise. So what the heck?

The day had been unbearably long, and now that it was night, she couldn't sleep.

She hadn't seen Dante in at least three days—a fact for which she was grateful—and the idea of sitting by the window and gazing at the stars, snacking by lantern light, seemed calming, if not entirely peaceful, a momentary distraction from the incessant thoughts that rattled about in her head.

As she raised her pitch-covered torch and slowly made her way down the winding stone steps, she thought she heard the faint mewling of an animal, perhaps a cat or a stray puppy that had wandered into the castle. Whatever it was, it was coming from the bottom of the staircase, and it made the hair stand up on her arms.

Mina moved forward with caution, careful not to step on the hem of her robe. The last thing she needed was to trip and fall down the remaining stairs. She was just about to place the ball of her foot on a particularly narrow step when she thought she heard the sound again, only this time, it almost sounded human. She peeked cautiously around the corner, trying to identify the source, and she hurried down the remaining steps.

And then she froze in suspended horror as her eyes struggled to focus and her mind fought to comprehend the horrific scene before her: Tatiana Ward was lying at the bottom of the staircase, her body curled up into a pitiful little ball, her legs tucked tightly to her chest, almost in a fetal position; and her face was stained with rivulets of blood that trickled along the corners of her mouth. All the while, she emitted a coarse, drawn-out moan like the mewling of an animal.

Mina gasped.

She anchored her torch in a nearby iron stand and hurried to her friend's side, desperate to help her, frantic to stop her moaning.

The Sklavos Ahavi flinched at her approach.

"Tati?" Mina called out, stooping to get closer. *"Oh dear goddess of mercy…"* She reached for the girl's shoulders and immediately drew back when Tatiana shrieked.

"Don't touch me!" Tatiana cried, recoiling from Mina's touch.

Mina's hand went instinctively to her own heart. "What's

wrong, Tatiana? Tell me what happened." She glanced toward the top of the staircase and cringed, imagining her friend taking a horrible fall down the steep, winding passage. "Did you fall, sweetie? How long have you been lying here?"

Tatiana whimpered, but she didn't answer.

In spite of the girl's protests, Mina gripped Tatiana by the waist as gingerly as she could and gently turned her over, removing her arms from her face.

Oh. Dear. Gods.

Tatiana's face was a virtual wasteland, battered and bloody. Her left eye was practically swollen shut. Dark, crimson blood seeped from the corners of her mouth, and there were harsh red welts in the shape of fingers striped about her narrow throat. "What happened to you?" Mina repeated, immediately ripping a strip of cloth from her own nightgown in order to dot at the blood. She ran her hands over Tatiana's arms, her stomach, and then her legs, trying to feel for obvious injuries or broken bones. "Please, Tati," she pleaded, "tell me what happened." She was about to panic.

Tatiana winced in pain as she grabbed Mina by the arm. "Please, don't touch me."

Mina drew back as requested. "*What happened to you?*" This time, her words were only a whisper.

"The prince," Tatiana whispered.

Mina's brow furrowed in confusion, even as her heart sank with dread. "*What?* What do you mean, *the prince?*"

"Damian."

As if someone had just tossed her into a frigid lake, Mina felt her body stiffen, and the air rushed out of her lungs. "Prince Damian did this to you? Why? When? *Whatever for?*" Her mind was spinning with incredulity.

Tatiana winced as Mina tried again to remove the blood at the corners of her mouth, and then she met Mina's eyes with a cool amber stare of her own. "It doesn't matter," she mumbled. "There was no specific reason."

Mina was utterly dumbstruck.

Her thoughts were swirling around in violent eddies of anger and fear, but she had to focus. She had to stay grounded in the moment. *She had to help Tatiana.* "I don't understand," she whispered.

Tatiana shivered. "The prince has been with me—or should I say, I have been with him—off and on for the last three days." She thrust two fingers inside her mouth and bit down against the tips to offset the pain.

Mina rocked back on her heels and took a helpless seat on a cold stone stair. She didn't want to ask anything else—she did *not* want to hear what was coming next—but she had to. How else could she help her friend? She rubbed her brow in anxiety. "What do you mean, *you have been with him for the last three days?*"

Tatiana began to chew on her nails. "That first day, when Dante called you into the courtyard, Damian called me to his chambers to feed his dragon, and then he called me again on Monday and Tuesday"—she shook her head really hard as if she could somehow dislodge the memories—"and then again on Wednesday and Thursday…only…to fulfill a very different need."

Mina's stomach clenched as a wave of nausea swept over her, and bile rose in her throat. She bit her bottom lip, forced back her tears, and tried to restrain any coming reaction. "That's not… that's not possible. Not even Damian can do that. It's forbidden before the Autumn Mating. Surely, you don't mean what I think."

When Tatiana's eyes welled up with thick crystal tears and a heart-wrenching sob escaped from her throat, Mina had her answer. She wanted to wrap her arms around her friend to comfort her, but she was terrified that she would just cause her more pain.

Terrified, disgusted, and *furious.*

Who the hell did Damian Dragona think he was to flaunt

thousands of years of tradition in this beautiful girl's face, as if the customs were mere suggestions, rather than edicts, as if he was above and beyond reproach, even from the king? She wanted to kill him with her bare hands. "When King Demitri finds out, he will punish him," she snarled.

Tatiana almost laughed, the sound coming out as a desperate, hollow bark. "Oh, Mina, don't be so naive." She waved her hand as if to dismiss her own protest. "I really don't believe the king will do anything." She sniffled and drew in a deep breath. "I told Damian that it wasn't proper, that it wasn't allowed, and he laughed in my face. He said the king would not refuse him anything—he would give him whatever Ahavi he desired, and he desired me. He said that he could make the rules, break the rules, or *screw the rules*, and there was nothing anyone could do about it. And when I told him that his brothers might not feel the same way if"—she stumbled over the next words, her tears falling in unbridled rivers—"if I became *with child*, only to be promised to one of his brothers, instead, do you know what he told me?"

Mina shook her head.

"He said that there was nothing to worry about because I hadn't taken the fertility elixir, and besides, Drake was far too honorable to force himself on an Ahavi—and Dante was too afraid of their father. So even if something freakish happened, there would be no question of paternity…so why the hell not."

Mina swallowed a groan of protest. She pressed her hand to her lower belly and tried to steady her nerves. "Oh, Tati." She brushed a gentle hand over her friend's cheek and gently cupped her face. "I'm so sorry."

Tatiana sneered. "But you know what really makes it worse?"

Mina could not imagine *anything* making this worse. "What, sweetie?"

"I didn't fight him. I didn't try to stop him. I fed…*all his appetites*…two nights in a row. And tonight? He became enraged because Drake asked me to meet him in the gardens tomorrow for a stroll, something I have no control over, whatsoever, and Damian beat me like…like I was *nothing*…like I was a shadow, or a warlock, or another man."

Mina stared at her friend closely. Her eye looked positive ghastly, and her face was hardly recognizable as the beautiful portrait it had been before. Yet and still, she had felt Dante's barely restrained power, coiled in his hands. She had seen it in his eyes and felt it in his fire: If Damian Dragona had beaten Tatiana like a man, Tatiana would not be curled up at the bottom of a staircase. She would be six feet underground, rotting in an unmarked grave.

Mina kept her observation to herself. "Where is he now?"

Tatiana swallowed convulsively. "He's in the throne room, just beyond the Great Hall. All of them are. It would seem the king called a late meeting with his sons to discuss court business, something about their future appointments and the treasury—he wants to raise taxes or something."

"And he needed to discuss this at midnight?" Mina said, suspiciously. The question wasn't meant for Tatiana—she was more or less thinking out loud—disgusted by the entire situation and surprised that Damian had chosen to share so much information with a Sklavos Ahavi…right before he beat her. She placed a gentle finger over Tatiana's lips to keep her silent. "Okay…*okay*. Save your strength now. Don't waste your energy on speaking. Just give me a second to *think*." She stood up and began to pace the long hallway, hating to leave Tatiana alone, but needing a moment to collect her wits, to shake and clench her fists if she needed to, without further upsetting her friend.

She had to choose her next move *very* carefully.

There were so many dangers all around them. And as much as she wanted to rush in and help, she had to be deliberate: Where would she take her? Who would help her? And how would she keep them both safe? *Spirit Keepers forbid*, if Damian found out…

And why did he want Tatiana anyway?

The concept was maddening, especially when Cassidy was such an obvious choice—Damian and Cassidy were two peas in a pod, two selfish, power-hungry beings, cut from the same cloth.

Ah, but then she remembered…

Of course.

It was one of the reasons Tatiana was here: She was a wizard with numbers and a guru of economics. She could be used for more than her beauty or her body—she could be used to elevate the prince and solidify his district. Mina swallowed a lump in her throat and pressed her hands to the sides of her head, thinking. *Where could she take her? Who would help them?*

When Tatiana began to choke and spit up blood, Mina spun around on her heels. By all that was sacred, this was serious. The girl might be dying. She ran to the top of the stairs, stared hastily at the ominous line of golden strings, the cords attached to the servants' bells, and chose the one for the squire, Thomas. Dante had said the boy was an ally, although Mina had no idea why. She darted back down the staircase and waited, hooking her hands gently beneath Tatiana's armpits to try to pull her upright. "Try to sit up," she urged her. "I'm going to take you to my bedchamber and call the squire. You need a healer. Do you think you can—"

"No!" Tatiana protested, her voice thick with alarm. "Please, don't call any of the royal staff; it'll just anger Damian further."

Mina frowned. "And would he have you die in your present state? How would that serve him in the end?" She mulled it over in her head. "Very well, at least allow the squire to help you back to my chambers, and then I will clean you up myself." *And then I will go find Dante*, she said to herself, seething.

She didn't give a royal damn what Damian Dragona wanted. Perhaps it was time he picked on someone his own size.

His own species.

Not that Dante would oblige Mina—or ever defend a slave—but still, she had to try to intervene.

She had to.

This was beyond repugnant and reprehensible. It was immoral and unthinkable. It was evil and obscene. And then, she remembered Dante's words: *"He is not a patient dragon. He is not a moral prince…Damian would just as soon behead you as wed you."*

Mina shivered, fully understanding the danger she was in.

Just the same, she couldn't let this go. If nothing else, Dante had the power to heal Tatiana with his blue fire, to soothe her with his mind; perhaps he could even erase her memories. Who knew what all a dragon could do?

Mina knew better than to wander through the castle at midnight, to go anywhere near the throne room or the king, to dare to approach Dante for help when he could barely tolerate Mina as it was. She knew they were hardly allies or friends—she was only a glorified servant, and he was most certainly her *master*. It would be as foolhardy as it would be dangerous to seek him out…

Still, she also knew right from wrong.

There were some things, *some people*, worth sticking one's neck out for. And Tatiana Ward was one of them. She hadn't deserved this, and it would not go unanswered.

Fortifying her resolve, Mina shifted her weight beneath Tatiana's shoulders and prepared to lift her, just as a tall, skinny youngster descended the steps.

The boy walked as quietly as a mouse toward the Sklavos Ahavi, his curly blond hair reflecting a myriad of natural highlights in the firelight, his downcast eyes brimming with curiosity and kindness. "Yes, mistress Ahavi. How may I serve you?" His voice was as gentle as his countenance.

Mina lowered Tatiana back to the floor and took a careful step toward the squire. "Are you Thomas?"

"I am," he answered respectfully, still averting his gaze.

Mina forced herself to swallow her fear. "And you and Prince Dante have a *special friendship*, do you not?"

The boy's face lit up, and he raised his head, exposing bright hazel eyes that seemed to shimmer with curiosity and intelligence.

"We do." The words were merely a whisper, but Mina heard them just the same.

She nodded. "Very well, then can you keep a secret?"

He bit his bottom lip and frowned as if thinking it over. "What kind of a secret?"

Mina looked over her shoulder at Tatiana and gestured toward her battered body. "This kind."

The boy cringed as he stared at Tatiana's terrified, broken form, slumped on the ground like so much garbage. He swallowed a lump in his throat and met Mina's seeking gaze. "If nobody asks me a question, I will not say a word. But, if I'm questioned, I must answer honestly." He averted his eyes in a gesture of apology. "Even then, I will try to say as little as possible."

Mina slowly nodded.

It would have to do.

"Very well. I need you to help me get Tatiana back to my chambers, and then I need you to take me to the prince. To Dante."

Thomas's eyes grew as wide as saucers. "Oh, no, mistress. I cannot. *You cannot.* He's in the throne room with his father."

She thought she heard a clipped tone at the end of that sentence, almost as if he had spat the word *father*. "I realize that I can't go in the throne room, but I need you to show me where it is. Perhaps there's an antechamber or a nearby hall, somewhere I can wait for Dante?"

The boy wrinkled up his nose and looked off into the distance, thinking. "There's a storage room, just beyond the back entrance, but again, I don't think you understand: King Demitri would..." His voice trailed off.

Mina raised her eyebrow and waited. "*Well?* He'd what?"

He squared his jaw. "He'd kill you if he found you."

Mina was waiting for the catch, the contingency, the explanation that she knew must be coming, but there wasn't one: The king would kill her if he caught her approaching the throne room? Without asking questions first? She cringed. Somehow, she knew the boy was telling the truth. It was as if he had some personal experience with this side of the king. "I understand," she whispered. "Just the same, my friend may be dying, and I need Dante's help. Will you take me to this storage room or not?"

Thomas stared at Tatiana, who was now shivering uncontrollably on the floor, and slowly nodded his head. "Okay."

Mina sighed with relief. "Thank you." She appraised him from head to toe then—he had to be at least five-foot-seven, and although he was thin, he had wiry, adolescent muscles. He was probably far stronger than she was. "Can you help me get Tatiana up the stairs?"

He nodded immediately then. "Of course."

He stepped forward, slid an arm around Tatiana's waist, and began to lift her off the floor, even as she cringed in pain. As blood seeped through her nightgown, and her head lolled forward, Thomas the squire took the brunt of her weight on his slender shoulders and began to half drag, half carry her up the stairs, and Mina slowly followed.

"Oh, by the way," Mina whispered, placing her hands on Tatiana's back to steady her. "I'm Mina Louvet."

Thomas glanced over his shoulder and angled his chin. "I know."

CHAPTER SEVEN

"I AM GOING TO levy an additional property tax in the *commonlands*, nothing oppressive to the farmers or the merchants, just enough to increase the number of guards at the entrance to the state. And I would like to build several small, armed garrisons in Forest Dragon, posts that double as tollways between one province and the next, in order to try to address the illegal slave trade, which still remains out of hand. The tolls will provide added protection for the women and children being sought by the shadows, and if we can monitor who comes and goes across the borders, perhaps we can ferret out who is behind this costly, illegal activity." King Demitri Dragona sat back on his red velvet throne and leaned to one side, bracing a muscular arm against a golden support. "Dante? Are you listening?"

Dante Dragona regarded his father—*and his king*—circumspectly from the bottom step of the platform, just beneath the royal dais. "Yes, Father," he murmured. He straightened his back to demonstrate his attention, even as his eyes swept over his father's purple-and-gold brocade robe and the golden crown, inlayed with enough jewels to build fifty garrisons in every province, resting snugly on the king's head. He eyed the two fearsome Malo Clan guards, now perched at his father's side, captain and lieutenant, and shivered. Each male stood at least seven feet tall and would die without hesitation for the same Dragona banner that had enslaved their ancestors nearly eight centuries past. They were a barbaric race of muscle-bound heathens who could fight like demons, endure immeasurable suffering like heroes, and die like love-stricken brides welcoming their long-lost husbands. All without crying out for mercy. And just why King Demitri insisted on having the barbaric sentries beside him, even for private family meetings, Dante couldn't say. It was as if the king actually feared his own sons, when he had no reason to do so.

None at all.

"Very well," King Demitri drawled lazily, "then look like it, son." He turned his attention to Drake and sat straighter in his chair. "Now then, Prince Drake, have you calculated the figures I asked for, determined what percent of farmland holdings should be taxed as opposed to storefront leases and mortgages?"

Drake cleared his throat and began to speak, but his voice drifted off into the ether as Dante continued to consider the dynamics of his family and the current state of the Realm: Although he and his brothers had not always respected the king as a man or a father, while they may have even resented his cruel, sadistic treatment of them growing up, to say little of his heavy-handed conduct with his subjects, Dante could not deny that he respected the male *deeply* as a king.

As the supreme dragon of the Realm.

Sure, as a child, Dante had hoped—as all children do—that one day his father would recognize him in some indulgent, paternal way, that the tyrannical lessons and harsh beatings would somehow come to an end, and Dante would be welcomed into Demitri's inner circle of trust as an equal. In truth, he had loved his father deeply, but time had a way of bringing things into much sharper focus—and boyhood fantasies had a way of evolving into adulthood realities. Childish hope gave way to mature acceptance; juvenile dreams gave way to reasoned objectivity; and over time, Dante had come to understand exactly who and what Demitri Dragona was…

And was not.

No, he was not a loving father.

And no, he was not a patient or kindly king.

But he was an ancient, primordial dragon, the eldest of their kind, and at 269 years old, he was the only dragon in the Realm who could fully shift into pure *dragonian* form, at will. As it stood, Dante would not reach the *age of maturation* for another thirty-one years; Damian still had fifty-one ahead of him; and Drake still had fifty-four. Consequently, King Demitri Dragona was the single force that held the Realm together and kept their enemies at bay. He was the only creature powerful enough to incinerate an entire village in one fell swoop, turn the ocean tides into a raging sea with the flutter of his wings, or bury a city block beneath a crumbling crater with the simple wag of his tail. In short, he was death on wings if he chose to be: fire, ash, and fury at will.

And he was all that stood between the four provinces and the hordes of conquering Lycanians, shifters who lived across the restless sea.

Dante shifted his weight from one foot to the other and drew in a deep breath as the truth of that statement sank in for the hundredth time: Demitri Dragona was the sovereign king of a land that could explode into chaos and violence at any moment, simply because it housed so many savage, brutal, and powerful inhabitants. If his laws were not obeyed, if the shadows or the warlocks were to rise to eventual power, if the sheer numbers of subjects were to unite and stage an organized uprising, then it was King Demitri Dragona who could reestablish order. And while each of his sons played a critical role in maintaining the Realm's delicate balance—while each would rule his own district, sustain life, ensure prosperity, and maintain law and order—Demitri was the paste that held it all together.

The mere threat of his fury inspired obedience and awe.

The king cleared his throat in an unusually coarse fashion, and Dante's eyes shot back to the throne. "Dante, did you hear a single word your brother just said?"

Dante cast a sideways glance at Drake, as if he could somehow intuit the crux of the conversation from his brother's expression, and frowned. "I'm sorry, Father. I was—"

Just then, there was a loud bang from behind the eastern wall of the throne room, a sudden crash of crates or boxes, and the shuffle of small feet stumbling to regain their purchase.

A dragon's hearing was highly acute.

"What the hell was that?" Damian snarled, even as the Malo Clan guards stood to instant attention.

"Indeed," the king said, instantly forgetting his nit-picking with Dante. He flicked his wrist in the direction of the sound, indicating the private back entrance to the throne room, and both guards immediately headed in the direction of the clamor.

Dante, however, did not need to wait on the guards' report.

He had fed from one of the Sklavos Ahavi.

He had tasted her blood and consumed her heat.

And now that he was aware of an intruder, *he could smell her from here.*

Mina Louvet.

*

Mina stared through the narrow peephole in the cramped, dusky storage room, eyeing the elaborate throne room with its extravagant, ornate furnishings and listening as Prince Drake explained in minute detail how he intended to apply the new tax in the *commonlands*, according to the king's behest. While she couldn't make out every word—she was far more concerned about how she was going to get Dante's attention and tell him about Tatiana—any fool with eyes could read the royal dynamics between family members as they played out in the hall.

King Demitri was an intimidating figure to put it mildly. He looked like he could maim or kill with nothing more than a crook of his eyebrow, yet his actions appeared almost rote, as if he were a duty-bound king simply going through the motions, perhaps bothered by insomnia and engaging his sons in the middle of the night for lack of anything better to do.

As if the extremely late hour was irrelevant.

Prince Drake looked far more alert and awake, like he lived to please his father, like he lived to serve the Realm, and he was exceedingly focused on providing the king with clear, detailed information. Damian, on the other hand, was visibly irritated—perhaps at being summoned in the middle of the night?—and Mina's stomach churned, even as bile rose in her throat, as she stared at the cocky son-of-a-goat, strutting like some sort of overblown peacock at the bottom of the dais. She shivered at the malice in Damian's dark brown eyes. His deceptively handsome face barely concealed his disdain or his inner rage. Just the same, he gave his father a fair modicum of attention and respect, or at least the appearance of the same. In fact, if Mina hadn't thought him incapable of the emotion, she would have speculated that Damian's base motivation was not respect at all, but fear: The dragon prince was terrified of the powerful male on that throne, and he probably resented the hell out of having to supplicate himself to a clearly superior dragon.

She turned her attention to Dante, unable to stomach another moment of staring at Damian's face, and her insides turned over again, this time, from an entirely different set of emotions: a mixture of fear and intimidation, curiosity and…intrigue?

She shook her head to dismiss the thought.

The king's eldest son was being appropriately respectful to his father but perhaps a little too reserved. Under further scrutiny, it appeared as if he was tuning the entire discussion out, pretending to listen and pay attention, while biding his time to…exit the chamber? Go back to bed? Mina had no idea. She only knew that Dante looked like someone who had become bored with the whole monotonous process, oh, maybe about five decades ago.

She was just about to lean in closer, try to figure out where, when, and *how* she could get Dante's attention the moment the meeting was over, without attracting the attention of the others, when a huge furry rat dove from the top of a dusty shelf right at the center of her chest. Despite her need for caution, she leapt backward, swatting at the vile creature to keep him from biting her on the chin, and the storage crate she was standing on turned over with a clang.

As it crashed into a smaller set of boxes, all lined up neatly beneath her on the floor, she scrambled to regain her footing, and the pile of containers rattled together, causing a ridiculous *and loud* ruckus. "*Holy Spirit Keepers!*" she yelped in a hushed whisper, shoving her hand over her mouth to keep from crying out. She had to get out of there, *now*! She would have to do something else for Tatiana, find a different way to help her friend. As it stood, she had just placed them both in increasing danger.

She spun on her heels, moving faster than she had ever moved before, reached frantically for the sooty brass handle on the storage closet door, and almost jumped out of her skin. Standing directly in front of her, like a mountain of muscle, bone, and grim determination, was one of the huge Malo Clan guards, a giant with a fearsome, angular goatee, and in her forward momentum, she slammed right into his chest.

Mina screamed.

She couldn't help it.

And as she backpedaled to get away from the sentry, she tripped over the overturned crate, causing an even greater racket.

Mother of Mercy, could this get any worse?

She tried to duck around the enormous male, to dart out of the room, but the guard caught her effortlessly by one arm and scooped her up like she was nothing more than a sack of fresh produce. He hoisted her so high that her feet left the floor, and then he simply lowered his arm and dragged her behind him, causing the tips of her toes to sweep against the floor like the quills of a broom, leaving an obvious path in their wake.

Mina twisted and screamed to no avail, trying to break free.

She wrenched at his fingers, trying to uncurl them from her arm.

She even considered kneeing him in the groin or punching him in the gut, but her common sense finally kicked in, and she thought better of it—this male could crack her skull like a walnut if he chose to. He could slam her up against the nearest wall and crush her back. Hell, he could give up on her arm and drag her by the hair, nearly scalping her in the process.

The gruesome possibilities were endless, yet they all yielded the same result…

Mina could not get away from a massive Malo Clan guard, not in the best of circumstances, and besides, her presence was already known by the king.

She thought about what Thomas the squire had told her, and she cringed. She could only hope that her status as a Sklavos Ahavi would buy her some reprieve, that maybe, *just maybe*, Dante would have mercy on her and enough influence over his father for that mercy to matter.

She could only pray that the gods would intervene.

Because as it stood, both she and Tatiana were as good as dead.

CHAPTER EIGHT

DANTE DRAGONA STIFFENED his spine and bit down on his tongue, leaving a deep indentation in the flesh. He was trying *hard* not to react to the sight of Mina Louvet, the Sklavos Ahavi he intended to claim at the Autumn Mating, being dragged into the royal hall by an angry Malo Clan guard.

Part of his reaction was territorial, a dragon's instinctive dislike of any other male touching his female, but another part of his reaction was sheer irritation—he had just about had it *up to here* with the slave's disobedience.

What the hell had she been thinking?

Didn't she know that the king would never suffer her insolence?

Not for a microscopic second.

He bristled inside, feeling his inner dragon awaken in the form of rising heat. It was itching to command his outer, living flesh to wrench the girl from the sentry's paws and thrash her himself.

"Well, well, well. What do we have here?" Damian cackled,

sauntering away from the dais toward the center of the floor, where the guard now stood with Mina. He strolled up to the Ahavi with blatant arrogance and gripped her harshly by the jaw. "Your suite of rooms is on the *second* floor of the castle," he spat. He peered over his shoulder to make eye contact with Drake and snickered. "And I believe the rest of the castle is off limits after dark." He locked eyes with his father, who was now leaning forward on the throne, watching the entire scene with increasing interest. "And the royal hall, *my father's throne room*, is always off limits to the likes of you." He removed his hand with an insolent flick of the wrist, causing her head to snap backward from the dismissive gesture.

Mina gulped, and Dante restrained a growl. He prayed that the impulsive girl would *just this once* hold her impetuous tongue, at least with Damian. He crossed the floor in five long strides to join them. "What is the meaning of this, Mina?" He held her gaze in an iron stare, commanding her absolute attention.

She gulped again, and her knees rattled together as if they might just buckle beneath her. "I...I couldn't sleep. The fire went out in my hearth, and it was so incredibly cold in my chambers, I thought I might catch my death." She fidgeted nervously with her hands, apparently hearing the double connotation in her words. "I couldn't get it restarted, so I decided to search for another blanket—and to see if I could find some fresh kindling." She averted her eyes, clearly recognizing the fragility of her story.

Damian glowered at her. "You're lying," he snarled. "There are plenty of blankets in the upper wardrobes, and if an Ahavi requires more of *anything*, she need only yank on a chain at the end of a hall and call for a servant." He narrowed his gaze in disapproval. "Apparently, the only chain you are yanking tonight is ours."

Dante nodded. It was the truth, and there was nothing he could say at this juncture to mitigate the situation or substantiate the lie. It was pitiful, and Mina knew it.

Mina blinked, trying to think fast on her feet. Apparently she agreed with her captors—her story was pure, unadulterated rubbish. "Yes, yes, I know. That's true, but as I said: I couldn't sleep. Insomnia, I think." She bit her lip, like she knew she was drowning, and then she took another breath and pushed on. "So I thought a stroll might do me good, perhaps even warm me up." The last word was spoken with an inflection, more like a question than a statement, and Dante shut his eyes and dropped his head, slowly shaking it from side to side.

"Enough," he said, resurrecting his gaze in order to glare at her. He was trying to say *shut up* in so many words—the silly girl had no idea just how close to death she was standing. Taking a deep breath, he raised his chin and asked, "So you sought out a storage closet on the main floor, just beyond the *throne room?*" The question was going to be asked, so he may as well be the one to ask it. Maybe then, he could direct her answers.

Mina shook her head with vigor. "No. *No.* Not on purpose, anyhow. I just got lost, turned around. I wandered many halls before I stumbled across the back staircase, and then, when I turned to the left, I guess I just—"

Dante narrowed his eyes at her in a harsh, unambiguous glare: *Stop talking…now!*

She immediately bit her lip again and waited, even as Damian began to laugh.

"Father?" Damian turned to regard the king, no doubt in an attempt to incite the monarch's anger, and Mina took immediate advantage of the moment.

She reached out with a crooked finger and quickly hooked it inside Dante's sleeve to get his attention, and then she just as rapidly pulled it back, stared right at him, and leaned slightly forward, raising her eyebrows in determination. She was speaking volumes with her expression and angling her head *just so* as if to say…*something*: desperation, fear, and urgency.

Dante took a step back.

What was she trying to tell him?

When Damian started to speak again, Dante held up his hand to silence him, still staring intently at Mina. "Tell me, Ahavi," he said, "this insomnia, the conditions in your room; were they really that *urgent?*"

Mina squared her shoulders and raised her chin. "Yes. I felt that they were."

At this, Damian lost his patience.

He spun around and sauntered toward the throne, wisely stopping before taking the first stair. He bowed his head. "Father," he repeated coolly, "it may have felt urgent to this woman, but I think we all know better. She's lying. And what's more, a small indiscretion today will only lead to treachery and betrayal tomorrow. Rules are rules for a reason."

Talk about going straight for the jugular.

The king was no stranger to the treacherous, manipulative ways of a Sklavos Ahavi who was allowed too much leeway with the rules, who had been given too much room to roam.

Dante said nothing.

The king would either seek more information or render a premature judgment.

Just like that.

And there was no bargaining with Demitri Dragona once he had chosen a course of action.

The king stood up, and the entire hall fell silent.

Drake leaned back against one of the six enormous pillars that lined the center of the hall and crossed his arms in front of him, even as Damian took a cautious step back, awaiting their father's word.

"Which one are you?" the king bit out, pointing at Mina, his hard expression otherwise unreadable.

Mina turned toward the king and curtsied. Apparently, she at least had that much sense. "Your Majesty, I am Mina Louvet, a Sklavos Ahavi from the southern district of Arns." She bowed even lower. "And I meant no disrespect." She froze in that posture, her eyes plastered to the floor.

The king turned toward Drake, perhaps because he was often the most reasonable of the three princes. "She was chosen among the Ahavi, why?"

Drake cleared his throat. "They say she can speak many languages, that she has an intuitive understanding of foreign cultures. In that way, she yields us some advantage. She can act as a translator with our neighbors and an unlikely spy with our enemies."

The king harrumphed. "Hmm."

"And she's supposed to be unusually bright," Drake added. His voice neither rose nor fell, absent of conviction, either way.

The king chuckled merrily. "Apparently, not too bright." He took a step forward, but he did not descend the stairway. "Our rules are not optional, Miss Louvet."

Mina didn't reply. She didn't dare.

"Do you even understand the rules?" the king asked.

Dante hoped she understood the question: His father was testing her intelligence, her memory. If she said no, he would scorch her where she stood.

"Yes, Your Majesty," Mina replied, continuing to hold her body and her head in a subservient posture.

"Yet, you broke them?"

Mina choked back a sob. "Yes, Your Majesty."

"If I let you live, will you break them again?"

Mina stumbled to the side, clearly caught off guard by the bluntness of his words or the severity of her offense. Perhaps, now, she finally understood just how fragile a precipice she was standing upon—*if I let you live...*

She caught her balance and groveled even lower. "No, Your Majesty." Her face was the color of a pale harvest moon, yellowish white and absent of lucidity.

The king eyed Damian. "Son?"

He shrugged one shoulder in a gesture of disdain. "I say dispense with her. She's only a woman. We can replace her, and I have no patience for insubordination."

The king turned once again to Drake. "Prince?"

"Your will is my own," Drake said, smart lad that he was.

It wasn't that Prince Drake was cold and unfeeling, quite the contrary: The dragon had more compassion in his heart than most, but he had also lived for 146 years. And like the rest of them, he knew his father well. Any show of mercy would be seen as weakness, and more importantly, it wouldn't further Mina's cause. Demitri would ultimately do whatever he felt like doing, and more often than not, his choices were based solely on his passing moods.

"Dante?" the king asked, offering a seeking gaze.

Dante felt the moment like a heavy weight bearing down on his shoulders. Not unlike Damian, he took every incident of insubordination, every potential threat to the Realm, quite seriously, and a subject who could not follow the most basic rules was a loose cannon, an unpredictable element, something to be removed simply on principle. However, unlike Damian, he was not a sadistic egomaniac, and he would derive no personal pleasure in seeing a young female executed for such a petty offense.

Beyond even that, *this was Mina.*

He had fed from her, felt the inaugural stirrings of carnal desire for her body, begun to adopt a familial responsibility for her well-being, based on their potential future roles. He still believed she would give him strong sons and prove to be an ally one day, and he did not believe she was a threat to the Realm.

She could be tamed…

Or, at least, she could be corralled within reason.

He sighed, knowing that Demitri was merely a heartbeat away from incinerating the girl as she bowed, even as she continued to genuflect before him.

She would never see it coming.

And even a lengthy pause in Dante's answer could set the volatile king off, illicit the sadistic reaction.

"She should not be allowed to display such impertinence before the throne," Dante said firmly. "I think she should be soundly punished, succinctly taught a lesson, and if, *after that*, she commits another infraction, then her death will be on her own head." He held his breath, waiting, trying to appear more nonchalant than he felt.

"I see," the king replied. For all intents and purposes, he was probably trying to *gauge* his mood: *Do I feel like killing? Do I feel like watching? Would I rather go to bed?* His eyes flashed with resolution, and Dante knew the decision had been made. "Give her fifteen lashes with a spiked whip. If she lives, she will get another chance. If she dies, we will replace her. Perhaps, in this way, the gods will decide her fate." He sat back down on his throne and gestured toward the elaborate, archaic cabinet on the eastern side of the room: The lavishly carved chest was twelve feet high and nearly eight feet wide. It sat flush against the interior wall like a statue of a feudal knight, and it contained various ornamental boxes and hidden compartments inside, all housing the king's sadistic treasures, his favorite instruments of torture and amusement. "Do it now," he said to no one in particular, sounding almost as bored as he did resolute.

Damian's face lit up with zealous anticipation.

He strolled across the room to the massive cabinet, flipped open the ornamental doors, and chose a particularly gruesome but effective lash: It was a multilayered, braided leather strap, about ten feet in length, the thong protruding from a smooth wooden handle with the dragon's crest carved into the stock. About every three to four inches along the leather, there were barbed spikes made of iron, each one embedded in the belly like a spiny thorn. He cracked the lash in the air, just for amusement, chuckling as it echoed throughout the grand royal hall, and then he grabbed a handful of leather ties to bind her wrists and ankles and headed straight toward Mina.

The Ahavi jolted.

She gasped, whimpered, and started to run.

Dante caught her around the waist and held her in place. "Do not," he whispered in her ear, knowing the king would slay her as she fled before she ever reached the door.

Her eyes were as wide as saucers, and there was a deep primal fear radiating out of her pupils. She was utterly terrified and aghast. "Dante," she whimpered piteously. "Oh gods, please." Her beautiful, deep green eyes were shadowed with tears and haunted with desperation. *"Please."* She gaped at him like she had never seen his face before, like he was more than a stranger, more than an enemy, like he was a mythological monster, something to be dreaded and feared. Her knees gave way to their trembling, and she crumpled to the floor, doubling over in anguish and grasping at his shirt, his trousers, his boots, as she fell. "Please," she cried even louder. "My prince?" She sobbed. "Dante, I'm begging you." She pleaded with her eyes, and in that solemn moment, Dante saw only a helpless little girl who would have rather died than face the torture awaiting her. "You can't let him do this, my prince." Her lips literally quivered. "I know I've displeased you, but...but *this*?" She gestured to the side, indicating Damian and the lash with her hand, unable to turn her head in such a terrifying direction. Her eyes grew even wider, and her thick lashes sloped beneath the weight of her tears. "Please. *Please.*" The last word was a pitiable question. "Dante?"

As Damian drew closer, the king cleared his throat. "Damian," he said brusquely. "The lashing was your brother's idea, and this slave seems to expect mercy from *him*. Give him the whip."

Mina shuddered, and her mouth gaped open in shock.

Dante showed no reaction whatsoever.

He had expected as much to happen.

Damian declined his head in deference and extended the lash

and leather ties to Dante, smiling as his older brother gripped the handle and slid the wrist-loop around his arm. "As you will, Father," Damian said. He winked at Dante and took a casual step back, copping a lean against a nearby post.

Dante held the ties in his left hand and tested the weight of the lash in his right.

His father was watching everything.

As always…

Such endless tests of obedience.

He cracked the whip soundly, sending it sailing overhead through the air. He measured its movement, felt for the subtle motion of the fall, and memorized the *pop* of the crack. Satisfied, he then looped it over his shoulder and bent toward Mina, flexing to lift her from the ground.

CHAPTER NINE

MINA TRIED DESPERATELY to scurry away from Dante.

She kicked her feet in a useless, backward motion, sliding helplessly against the floor. She twisted this way and that, hoping to break free of his iron grasp, to no avail. And she tugged frantically against his powerful arms before she finally ceased her struggling and went limp at his side.

She simply could not believe this was happening.

It was too horrific for words.

Yes, she understood that she had taken a risk when she chose to seek him out, especially near the throne room; and yes, she knew that the king might kill her if she got caught. But this archaic torture? It was impossible to comprehend. Being ripped apart—flesh, muscle, and bone—by a barbaric lash, like some sort of animal, some sort of seditious traitor; it was more than her mind could process.

And Dante?

The prince who would one day claim her—wed her, lie with

her, father her children—he was going to do the evil deed with his own hand.

Oh, Great Spirit Keepers, Mina wanted to die then and there.

She had always been strong. She had always had a high threshold for pain. She had always been able to endure the unendurable, or at least she thought she had, but no woman could withstand a punishment such as this: the feel of the lash biting into her skin, the insult of the barbs grasping her muscles, flaying them free from her bones.

And over and over...and over?

Fifteen times?

He would kill her.

There was no question in her mind.

She felt like she was drifting far away in a tunnel, like blackness was overwhelming both her and the room, as Dante's strong, firm hands, the ones she had almost trusted just days ago, *the ones who had given her Raylea's doll*, grasped her by the shoulders, tugged her onto her feet, and began to drag her toward one of the tall imperial columns in the middle of the hall.

No.

No!

Oh dear Spirit Keepers in the afterworld, no.

She didn't know if she was screaming. She didn't know if she was crying or fighting or clawing for her freedom. It all felt so surreal. She only knew that she could not bear this—she could not survive this—and she had to make it stop.

She had to make it stop.

"Dante...Dante...*Dante*..." She heard his name coming from her lips like a mantra or a prayer, as if from some great distance, floating through an ever-darkening channel of disbelief. "No, Dante; *please*." She was sobbing like a baby. She had never felt so helpless, or desperate, or terrified in her life.

"Mina." His resilient voice cut through the fog, even as he secured her arms around the post and began to bind her wrists with the thongs, tying them high above her head. His weight felt oppressive against her back, yet she prayed it would never leave, that he would never leave, for once he stepped away, the whipping would begin.

No!

"Mina!" His voice was harsh now, almost angry, unyielding.

Her head fell back and she managed to peek at him from beneath tear-drenched lashes, her lips quivering, her eyes leaking like a sieve, mucous dripping out of her nostrils.

He tightened the bindings on her wrists and secured them swiftly to a notch in the post so she couldn't pull away. She tugged against them and tried to kick backward in his direction, which was the worst thing she could do: He unhooked the ties, raised them another several inches until she was standing on her tippy-toes, almost hanging off the post, and then refastened her wrists against the higher notch to keep her from gaining leverage. "Oh gods, Dante..." She was panicking now, beginning to hyperventilate, ready to come apart.

Dante pressed his sturdy upper body against her back and anchored her head from behind with his powerful hands, as if to demand her full attention. He bent his head forward, and his thick black hair fell about her shoulders and chin, shrouding them in a dark silky curtain of madness.

She was going to go insane. "Please, please...please."

He slid his hand forward and covered her mouth, nearly brushing his lips against her left ear. As his warm breath wafted across her lobe, she shivered.

This was really happening.

This was going to happen, and there was nothing she could do to stop it.

"Mina," he whispered in her ear. "Why did you come to the throne room? What were the *urgent* conditions in your bedchamber?"

She blinked several times, trying to gather her wits. She

couldn't think. She couldn't reason. She was about to die, but then there was...there was...

Tatiana.

And the Sklavos Ahavi was still upstairs, lying on Mina's bed, suffering and probably dying as a result of Damian's cruel machinations. *Oh gods, that's why she had made this sacrifice to begin with.*

For Tatiana.

Somehow, a strange clarity enveloped her; it descended upon her from nowhere, and she was able to find her words in the midst of her terror. "Tatiana," she whispered.

"What?"

"Tatiana—the other Ahavi, the one with auburn hair." She winced from the stretch in her back. "Damian beat her. He raped her." She drew in a ragged breath. "She's in my room, and she's dying."

Dante froze against her. He almost seemed to quit breathing, and then he slowly stepped back, looked down toward her feet—she could only see his profile—and waved Drake over to the column. "Hold her feet while I remove her dress."

Mina screamed.

That was it.

This was utter insanity, and she was beyond despondency.

Within moments, Drake appeared at the post, and she could have sworn Dante bent over and whispered something in his ear, *something about Tatiana.* But then she heard the back of her dress tearing, ripping open. Her chemise was swiftly removed, and the cold, stale air of the Great Hall kissed her bare skin like a brutal lover, her flesh now bared to the room.

She began to scream in earnest, over and over, like a wounded beast.

Dante stepped forward one last time and wrapped his hands around her throat. He didn't tighten his fingers or try to choke her. He just bent once more to her ear. "Listen to me, Mina." His words were guttural and imposing, and the force of each syllable felt like stiff, unseeded cotton being stuffed into her ears. "You need to scream like you are in the worst agony of your life, like you wish you could crawl through this post and disappear. I want you to hang from this column like you are dying, and you'd better make it convincing—*like your life depends upon it*—because it does."

*

Dante took ten measured steps back from the column, exactly the amount needed to wield the whip with lethal efficiency, and then he waited for Drake to address their king.

"Father," the youngest dragon prince said in a lackadaisical tone of voice.

The king acknowledged him with a slight tilt of his head.

"If it does not offend, I have no interest in the outcome of this proceeding." He gestured casually toward the post where Mina stood on the tips of her toes, trembling and panting in fear, waiting for Dante to begin her beating. "I am not particularly interested in this specific Ahavi." Now this was a risk. He was giving away his preference for the Autumn Mating—*was it Tatiana or Cassidy?* Dante wondered—and while the statement might very well backfire in the future, he had to sound convincing now. "At any rate," Drake pressed on, "I would rather continue working on the figures, on the taxes, if you please." He bowed his head in silent obeisance. "May I take my leave?"

The king pursed his lips together in thought, and then he grunted, not seeming to care one way or the other. "Very well." He dismissed his last-born son with a flick of his wrist.

Dante waited until the dual heavy doors to the hall opened and closed behind Drake, knowing that he would head directly to Mina's chambers to see about the other Sklavos Ahavi, Tatiana Ward. Once Drake was gone and his footfalls could no longer be heard receding down the corridor, he resumed his aggressive posture. "At your command, Father."

The king sat back in his throne and nodded, and just like that, Dante drew back the whip, cracked it bluntly in the air, and pitched it forward toward Mina's back.

The strike was deafening.

The leather sliced at an angle, making initial contact with Mina's upper right shoulder and then angling down across her slender spine to pare her narrow waist. She jolted and screamed, her entire body shuddering from the violent contact, and Dante drew in a deep, steadying breath, braced his feet further apart, and struggled not to stagger.

Do not wince. Do not cry out. Do not show a reaction, he told himself, biting down so hard on his tongue that he drew his own blood.

Fifteen, fourteen, thirteen...

He counted the piteous lashes down as he wielded them, one after the other, throwing all the strength he had into their sting.

At ten, he almost faltered.

His vision grew blurry, and he wondered if he could continue. He clenched his eyes shut, but only for a moment, and then he forced them open, determined to press on.

Nine, eight, seven, six...

Mina dangled, limp against the post. She still continued to scream, but her cries had changed to guttural moans and whimpers, her body swaying more than trembling with each strike of the lash. She was doing well; whereas, Dante felt the magic slipping—he had to maintain just a little bit longer.

Focus, he told himself. *Hold the spell.*

Five, four, three, two...

He was going to vomit. The pain was unbearable.

Every lash, every spike, every bite of the whip had been transferred from Mina's flesh to his own. Every ounce of pain and agony, every moment of terror and disgrace, was mystically contained, not in her delicate flesh, not biting deep into her trembling muscles, not tearing away at her shoulders—but at his.

Dante Dragona had transferred the lashing from Mina's back to his own. The whip might have seemed to strike her skin, but it was his that was flayed to the bone. The illusion of crimson anguish, the sight of so many ghastly rivulets of blood, might have appeared on her back, but it was his flesh that was oozing, seeping, and broken. Thank the gods, he was the only Dragona born with the sacred magic, and the only one with occasional second sight.

His knees began to buckle beneath him, and he stiffened his spine once more, almost passing out from that single, vertical gesture.

One more.

He could endure one more.

Thwack!

The whip crackled through the air, and his fist began to tremble. Turning to face his father, he inclined his head in a gesture of deference—or at least he thought he did; *he hoped he did*—and then he began to make his way to the column.

He untied Mina's wrists as if in a dream, working the knots like someone in a fog. He caught her body as it slumped from the pole and fell into his arms, and then he groaned inwardly as her weight pressed mercilessly against his battered flesh. He forced his powerful hamstrings to contract, his calf muscles to flex, as he pushed himself upward with all his strength, in order to heft her into his arms. No longer knowing which way was up, he somehow managed to toss her over his shoulder and stroll forward out of the throne room.

Bless the Spirit Keepers, his father let them go.

Even Damian simply stood and watched his retreat.

The moment the doors closed behind him, he stumbled, groaned, and dropped Mina from his shoulder onto her own two feet. "Help me up the stairs to your room," he grit out between trembling lips. "And hurry."

Mina gasped, momentarily speechless. She seemed utterly stunned that her body wasn't damaged, that her skin wasn't raw, and she instinctively placed her hand on his back as he bent over in agony. When she drew back a palm covered in blood, the realization began to set in. "Oh Dear Ancestors, *Dante*...how... *why?*"

He snarled, unable to speak, not wanting to get caught before they made it down the main corridor, through the receiving hall, and up the grand staircase to the second floor. "Now, Mina," he growled.

She nodded brusquely and quickly slid her slender shoulder beneath his arm, pressing hard against his side in order to sustain as much of his weight as she could on her diminutive frame.

She opened her mouth to speak and then closed it.

What could she possibly say?

Even Dante understood that words were wholly inadequate.

Finally, as she struggled to help him up the staircase and down the upper hall, she murmured, "Lean on me, my prince. I've got you. *I promise.* Just hang on."

CHAPTER TEN

THE TRIP DOWN the upper hall seemed never-ending. It felt like an eternity before Mina and Dante rounded the corner, passed the first set of private suites, and then finally arrived at Mina's remote chambers. In reality, the entire journey had probably taken less than two minutes.

Halting before the large wooden door, Mina pressed her shoulder further into Dante's upper body to steady his weight—and hers—and then she yanked at the handle, gave it a quick, downward turn, and kicked the panel open with her foot. "Hold on, my prince, we're almost there."

Thank the Spirit Keepers, the door swung right open.

The moment they stumbled across the threshold, Dante pushed away from Mina and fell forward onto the floor—it was almost as if his pride could not withstand another moment under her compassionate support.

Mina dropped down to her knees to check him, and that's when she saw the terrifying sight on the bed: Tatiana was lying on her back, her head and neck extended in an awful, uncomfortable arc, and Drake Dragona was perched perilously above her, like a creature on all fours, his feral mouth gaping open. Blue fire shot forth from his throat, coursing in a preternatural stream of incandescent waves, and tunneled its way into Tatiana's mouth. And all the while, she was helpless to stop him.

Mina narrowed her gaze and fought back a reaction. Crying out wouldn't help. Interfering wouldn't be wise. And besides, for all intents and purposes, it looked like Tatiana was *healing*, knitting back together from the inside out. Her skin was regaining its natural color; her wounds were closing, even as Mina watched; and her bruises were slowly transforming from a deep purplish blue to a light pasty gray.

Mina gawked in surprise and wonder, and then she immediately turned back to Dante. "My prince?" she uttered remorsefully. "Tell me what to do. How can I help you? What do you need?"

In a flash, Drake was no longer on the bed, but standing perilously above Mina, hovering over the scene, and his feral eyes were ablaze with anger. "What have you done to my brother?"

Mina stiffened. "Nothing!" She shook her head back and forth rapidly, practically straining her neck in the process. "I swear, I've done nothing. He…he somehow…he took the lashes for me."

Drake drew back in surprise and then stared down at his brother. Dante was writhing on the floor, shivering and moaning from the pain. Drake knelt down and ripped the now-bloody shirt from his shoulders and gasped at the multiple protruding welts, at all the deep, gaping cuts, the raw, fresh abrasions, and the crisscrossed lesions that had torn Dante's royal flesh. The dragon prince looked like a piece of freshly ground meat. "Great Nuri, Lord of Fire," Drake snarled. He glared at Mina, but only for a second, and then he sidled up behind her like he was about to do something indecent.

Mina held her breath and tried to crawl forward out of his reach. "My lord?"

He wrapped his left arm around her waist and pulled her

back against him, even as she continued to stare at Dante. He bent his head to her shoulder and thrust her neck to the side with unnecessary strength; and then, without warning or preamble, he sank his fangs deep into her throat, drew what felt like far too much blood from her vein, and began to consume her essence like a dragon, starved.

Drake fed until he was satiated, and then he sealed the wound with blue fire and pushed her away. "Get back," he growled. Once again, he bent over Dante's battered body, this time turning him over, ever so gently, onto his back and straddling him on all fours. "Brother, let me heal you."

Dante groaned, and his head fell back in an unnatural arc, much like Tatiana's had been just moments ago. It was an indirect gesture of consent, and Drake responded immediately. He opened his mouth, lowered it to Dante's, and began to channel the same healing blue flames deep into Dante's throat.

Mina sat on her knees and watched as Dante's shoulders slowly relaxed, his writhing ceased, and his wounds began to heal. She stared in both wonder and fascination as his bleeding slowed, his breathing began to deepen, and his face, at last, grew tranquil. When he was finally healed, he met Drake's eyes with a cold, empty stare of his own. "I'm fine."

Drake inhaled brusquely, retracted the fire, and then measured each of Dante's features, one at a time, as if gauging the truth for himself, before he slowly crawled off him. He sat quietly beside him, braced his arms on his knees, and then hung his head forward in fatigue. The male was exhausted, depleted, utterly spent.

Dante sat up slowly and growled. He glanced around the room, taking his first true measure of the situation, his keen eyes missing nothing. He stared at Tatiana, still lying dazedly on the bed; shifted his gaze to Mina, glaring at her in reproach; and then turned his attention to Drake and sighed. "I'll go fetch Cassidy," he said.

Mina sat erect, her mind at full attention. "Does he need to feed again?" she asked, testing her voice for strength. She quickly sidled up beside him and angled her head, offering Prince Drake her throat. While she still didn't feel completely well—far from it, really—it was the least she could do. Dante had saved her life. Drake had saved Tatiana's, and she owed them both immeasurably. Not to mention, Cassidy Bondeville could not be trusted. Not in the least. The power-hungry wench would try to use the situation to her advantage in any way she could, and if that meant spilling the beans to Prince Damian in order to gain his favor, or telling him everything she knew, she wouldn't hesitate to do so. It was better to leave Cassidy out of the equation.

Dante waved his hand and shook his head. "He can't take from you again, Mina. Not this soon. Not that much. It would kill you."

Drake rolled his head on his shoulders and groaned. "I'm all right."

"No, you're not," Dante snarled, standing up slowly and pacing the room. He bent over to pick up his bloody tunic, crumpled it in his fist, and tossed it into the corner, behind a high-backed chair. Then he gestured with his chin toward the bed. "Is she okay now?"

Mina hurried to the bed to check on her friend. "Tati? Can you hear me?" She gently helped her sit up. "Is that better?"

Tatiana moaned and rubbed her eyes. "What happened?"

Mina smiled. Her friend's voice was faint but familiar, a soothing balm to Mina's soul. She was going to be all right. "Prince Drake healed you. You're going to be okay." She ran her hands up and down Tatiana's arms, testing for weakness or reactions. She turned her friend's head from side to side, ignoring the matted, bloodstained curls, and she ran the pad of her thumb beneath a soft, arched brow, marveling at the sudden perfection, the normal, healthy eyelid, and the utter lack of swelling. "You look a thousand times better," she murmured, pulling her into a tender hug. "Oh, Tatiana. I was so scared."

"Save it for later," Dante growled, his harsh voice bringing Mina up short.

She released Tatiana and spun around on the bed to face him. "My prince, thank you for all that you've done."

Tatiana cowered against the headboard, clearly terrified of all things *male.*

Dante approached the bed restlessly, his cruel mouth curved into a frown. "Don't you *ever* pull some shit like that again," he snarled.

Mina recoiled. "Dante, *my prince,* I—"

He held up his hand to silence her. "What the hell were you thinking?"

She gulped. "I...I was *thinking* that Tatiana might die."

The fair, auburn-haired Ahavi clutched at the bedcover, drew it up to her neck, and cowered beneath it. She peeked back and forth between Dante and Mina and shivered. "I'm sorry," she whispered in a barely audible voice.

Dante shook his head, warning her to stay out of it.

"I'm sorry, too," Mina offered. "But it couldn't be helped."

Dante bristled at her last words, the muscles in his shoulders growing visibly taut as he clutched one of the four bedposts in his fist. "You really just might be too stupid to live," he said, and then he immediately turned his attention to Tatiana. "Get off the bed, and go get Cassidy."

Tatiana blanched. Her hands shook uncontrollably as she forced herself to turn the coverlet loose. She nodded in obedience, even as she glanced at Mina with wide, frightened eyes. "Yes, my prince." She swung her legs over the side of the bed, shuffled for a moment, in order to test her strength, and then hurried toward the door.

"Wait!" Mina called after her. "Cassidy cannot be trusted." She regarded Dante with fervent eyes, trying to ignore his last comment—perhaps she deserved it, considering all that had happened. "She's an opportunist, Dante. She's power-hungry and corrupt. She wouldn't blink at betraying any one of us just to further her own ends."

Dante tightened his grip around the post and drew a deep, regulating breath.

Mina shuffled backward on the bed and hung her head in obeisance.

He let go of the post, rounded the bed, and loomed over her in a threatening pose. "We're on a first-name basis now?"

Mina felt faint. "Please," she whispered, "I'm just trying—"

He moved so quickly she never saw him stir. He yanked her up by the swell of her arm, dragged her from the bed, as if she weighed no more than the pillows, and then spun her around to face his brother, who was still sitting idly on the floor. "Look at him," he growled. And then he addressed his next question to Drake. "How much time do you have before you grow ill, brother? *Dangerously ill?*"

Drake lifted his chin with no little effort. "I'm fine right now, Dante. Maybe thirty minutes, an hour at the most."

Dante nodded. He released his hold on Mina and angled his body toward Tatiana—his bare chest looked like sculpted iron, reflected in the firelight. "At the end of the hall, beneath the servants' bells, there is a square panel. Open it and tug on the braided chain inside." He fixed his gaze on Mina and scowled. "It will call one of the female courtesans, *the Blood Ahavi*. One of them can feed my brother."

Tatiana's expression registered her disgust, and before she could think better of it, she uttered, "You mean the sex slaves are real?" Her shoulders literally curled forward, and she looked like she might cry.

Of course they're real, Mina thought, *there were a lot more than three Ahavi trained at the Keep.* The Sklavos Ahavi just happened to be the only Ahavi capable, and deemed worthy, of producing offspring. She sighed. *Poor Tatiana.* Not only had Damian used her so brutally, but he had done so while knowing that he had his choice of numerous females just a chain's tug away, waiting to fulfill his every need.

Dante shrugged. "My father keeps his favorites at the castle." He frowned, although his eyes reflected little sympathy. "Normally, the Blood Ahavi are kept separate and hidden from the chosen"—he swept his hand in a wide arc, indicating the room they were standing in—"but under the circumstances, I think we are all beyond keeping secrets."

Mina also felt like weeping, yet she had no idea why. Once again, Dante had succeeded at both shocking her senses and wounding her pride. Would she never learn to just shut down her feelings, to name herself as what she was—*a slave*—and apparently, one of many? She nodded at Tatiana, signifying her consent, and then she immediately cowered, throwing both arms in the air, in an effort to shield her head as Dante raised his angry fist.

For whatever reason, he did not strike her. He just stood there, hovering above her, glowering angrily with those venomous eyes. "You would give *my* slave *your* consent?" His voice was thick with contempt.

Mina fought to regain her composure, to try to make sense of the situation. By all the gods, what had she done now? "No. *No.* I just"—she pointed absently at Tatiana—"we're friends. It was just an instinct. I was just agreeing." She stared at his fist and tried not to cower.

Dante lowered his arm, stormed to the door, and scooped Tatiana up by the waist. The female shrieked in protest as he carried her across the room and tossed her on the bed.

Mina watched in horror. "Dante, *no*! Please!"

He rotated his neck on his shoulders, like someone who was *this close* to snapping, and then he released his fangs. When he next spoke, his eyes were like molten lava, and his voice was dark with malevolent intent. "Shall I undo what Drake has done?" He cocked his head to the side. "Name your poison, Mina." He licked his feral lips. "Fire?" He splayed his fingers, widely apart, slowly releasing ten jagged claws. "Shall I undress her with these?" And then he reached down and unfastened the threads on his trousers with the tip of a nail. "Or shall I keep her clothes on and just make you watch?" He growled deep in his throat, sounding more like a beast than a man. "Which shall it be, sweet Mina? Which method of correction do you prefer?"

Mina's heart pounded furiously in her chest, both desperate and disbelieving. She ran to the bed and, without even thinking, dove across the mattress and planted her body between the dragon prince and his victim. "I'm sorry!" she said, nearly shouting. "My prince, *please* don't take this out on Tatiana. I'm begging you."

He turned to face her and held out both hands, his fingers curled inward as if he wanted to wrap them around her throat. "Why should I stop? *Tell me!*" His voice was ragged and cruel. "What the hell is it going to take for you to understand your place?"

"I understand," she croaked. "I swear. I do." She shuffled onto her knees, rising higher in order to meet his gaze. She was shocked by her own desperate courage, but she had to get through to the man—somehow, she had to get past the angry dragon, which she knew she had provoked. "Milord," she whispered, hoping he would focus and hear her, "before all the gods in the heavens, the lord of fire, bringer of rain, and the goddess of mercy, spirit of light…I swear to you, I *am* sorry. I did not mean to provoke your wrath or to question your supremacy. Never. Truly. *Never.*" She licked her lips in a nervous gesture and tried to steady her breath. "I just…oh, my prince, please…show mercy." She swept her hand around the room, much like he had done earlier. "I don't understand any of this. I don't pretend to understand you." She stared at Drake. "You sent your brother to heal Tatiana, so I know you have a heart…you have a soul. You have compassion."

She gestured toward the bloody, crumpled shirt, now tossed away in the corner of the room. "You took fifteen lashes *for me*, to spare me from pain and degradation. *You saved my life*, and I don't even know why, but you did it just the same. *My prince*," she slowly shut her eyes, and this time, as she spoke, her tears fell freely, "not only am I sorry; I am grateful. I am *not* defying you. I simply do not know how to please you…yet. But by all the gods, I swear to you, I will learn." She opened her eyes and shook her head. "Not because I have to, and not because I fear you, but because I want to. Because I owe you." She sank back down, settling her weight onto her legs, lowering her posture before him. "If you must punish someone, punish me. If you must teach a lesson, teach it to me. I am your willing servant." She held his gaze, and he took a measured step back.

His eyes flashed several times, retreating from crimson to ruby, from ruby to dark blue, and then he retracted his claws and refastened his trousers.

He glanced at Tatiana, who was shivering on the bed, still lying in wait and heaving with sobs. "Sit up," he said evenly. "Stop crying. I am not going to hurt you." He ran his hand through his hair in frustration, and then turned back to Mina and frowned. "I don't know how to teach you, Ahavi!" He sighed. "I don't know why it is…you can't learn."

Just then, Prince Drake stirred on the floor. He struggled onto his hands and knees, slowly pushed up, and staggered toward the bed, where he clutched at a post for balance. "Perhaps this Ahavi is like me, brother. Perhaps she is guided by reason." He met Mina's surprised gaze and nodded politely. "Perhaps, *just this once*, we might speak to our servants as allies. Allow them to ask questions. Give them answers. Perhaps that is the lesson she awaits." He turned to face Dante then. "The question is: Is it worth it…*to you?* To take this one opportunity to teach her in a way she might learn."

Dante stared at his brother like he had drool on his face, like he was truly confounded by the suggestion. Perhaps his dragon was just too strong, or perhaps something inside of him was just too implacable to shift… Nonetheless, he considered Prince Drake's words carefully.

Very carefully.

After several minutes had passed, Drake cleared his throat. "What say you, brother?"

And all at once, Mina understood: Damian was a true primordial dragon, nothing but fire and instinct and force; whereas, Drake was a thinker, a peacemaker, much more aligned with his humanity. No wonder the king had chosen him for Castle Commons, to lead the human province. And Dante? Well, he was a curious mixture of both: a feral dragon, easily provoked, yet a tempered soul, capable of reason. The question was one of boundaries, where to draw each line.

She waited, along with Tatiana, studying Dante's face.

His expression remained inscrutable, yet the wheels were clearly turning.

Finally, he nodded his head. "Perhaps. Just this once." He turned a steely gaze on Mina and then Tatiana, each female in turn, and added, "But I swear on the soil of my twin brother's grave, if a word of this…*candid conversation*…ever leaves this room, if you so much as even think of acting or speaking as an equal, with impunity, again—"

"We will kill you both ourselves," Drake supplied.

CHAPTER ELEVEN

DANTE NODDED, AND Mina shivered.

There was no question in her mind that they meant what they said. If the girls betrayed them, they would kill them.

She took a seat on the bed beside Tatiana, instinctively wrapping her arm around the frail Ahavi's waist, and then she waited for one of the princes to speak, showing proper deference by averting her eyes.

Dante took a deep breath and leaned into the post, stretching his back by arching into his arms; whereas, Drake shuffled weakly to the end of the bed and sat down gingerly, facing his brother. Although his frame was hunched over, his eyes were alert and vivid.

"How are you holding up?" Dante asked Drake.

The prince shrugged, showing his fatigue. "I'm fine for a while longer."

Dante shook his head. "Not good enough." He turned toward Tatiana. "Ahavi, go call a blood slave, then return. I'm sure Mina will share anything you miss."

Tatiana nodded several times in exaggerated compliance. Even Mina knew better than to get involved. She waited silently with the monarchs until the door closed softly behind her friend.

"Now then," Dante said, getting straight to the point. "If it's a matter of questions and answers, then ask. Speak freely. This is a one-time opportunity."

Mina gulped, but she hid her fear. She started to speak, but stopped. She was still so rattled, still so afraid, she hardly knew where to begin…or if it was truly safe.

"Go ahead," Drake insisted in a receiving voice. He angled his body ever so slightly toward the Ahavi.

Mina met his gaze with one of gratitude, and then she took a quiet moment to collect her thoughts. Finally, when she had garnered the courage, she looked down at the coverlet and spoke evenly. "I know that what I did tonight was reckless. It was stupid and dangerous, and I could've been killed." She pushed past her hesitancy. "But I was really desperate to save Tatiana." She raised her chin so that each male could see the conviction, the depth of emotion, in her eyes. "I don't understand how…*why*…Damian gets away with it."

"*Prince* Damian," Dante corrected her.

Drake held up his hand. "Go on."

Mina swallowed a lump in her throat and looked questioningly at Dante.

He nodded.

She wet her lips. "It is forbidden by your father, by King Demitri's very laws, for a prince to take an Ahavi before the mating, yet Prince Damian did just that—and he almost killed an innocent woman. I just don't understand. Nothing is like what we were taught at the Keep. How are we to obey or make sense of our obligations?" She bit her lip in anxiety, fearing she had gone too far.

Drake sighed. "Are you asking whether or not we can reason

with our father on Tatiana's behalf? Whether or not we can oppose our brother, or how to avoid Damian's wrath?"

Mina blinked, surprised by his candor. "Um, all of it, I guess."

Drake turned to Dante and nodded, apparently urging him to answer.

"Mina," Dante said pensively. He brought his fist to his mouth for a moment as if deep in thought. "Do you know how many bones there are in a child's body?"

She shook her head, a bit surprised by the question. "No."

"Well over two hundred," Dante said. "And do you know how I know this?"

Once again, she shook her head.

"Because my father broke all of mine, but seven, and that was before the age of six." His eyes grew murky with recollection. "A dragon's anatomy is a bit different than a human's, but I think I was innocent enough."

Mina started to recoil, but she caught her reaction before she could offend the prince with pity. *Don't you dare*, she said inwardly, reminding herself to remain impassive. The last thing this brutal dragon was looking for was sympathy from a woman. She clenched her teeth and declined her head in a nod of under-standing, and then she waited for Dante to continue.

"Do you know what a fourth-degree burn feels like, when even your bones are melting?"

Mina closed—and then reopened—her eyes. "You do?" she whispered.

He nodded, quite matter-of-factly. "Pray that you never will, because dragons heal from fire; humans don't." He stood up straighter and looked off into the distance. "Earlier, in the throne room, my *father* would have scorched you where you stood if I had not stepped in." He leaned in closer. "And as for *King Demitri*, he doesn't give a sweet damn about your friend, Tatiana, or what Damian does in his free time as long as it doesn't affect the Realm."

Mina did cringe this time. It was everything she had feared. She opened her mouth to speak, and then closed it, terrified by her very thoughts.

"What were you going to say?" Drake asked.

Mina quickly shook her head. "Nothing."

"What?" Dante growled. He didn't sound so much angry as insistent, as if this was her one chance to speak freely, and to him, it was an act of great benevolence. He was somehow determined to play it out.

She trembled as she spoke, voicing her question in a whisper. "Has anyone ever opposed him?"

Dante shut his eyes and the faintest of growls rumbled in his throat. It was as if the word *treason* floated through the room, and nobody had to name it.

Mina waited quietly, either to hear an answer or to be burned.

"My brother or my father?" Dante asked.

She was shocked that it wasn't Drake posing the question. "Either. Both."

Dante took a deep breath, crooked his ear toward his shoulder, and popped his neck, as if to relieve some tension. "My mother opposed my father," he said coolly. "That's where Damian comes from."

Mina pressed her hand to her stomach and swallowed rising bile. "And Damian?"

"Soon, Damian will rule over Umbras, the shadowlands, a region teaming with wickedness and violence, and he will need an iron fist. My father appreciates his *guile*."

The door to the room opened, and Tatiana tiptoed back in. "The Ahavi is in the hall. Should I—"

"Leave her out there," Dante snarled impatiently. "In fact, tell her to wait at the end of the corridor until we call her." He turned to face Prince Drake. "Are you—"

"I'm fine," he assured his brother. "She's not that far away, and I would certainly feed before I pass out." He regarded Dante squarely. "And if I do, pass out, that is, I trust that you will bring her to me before I die."

Dante smirked. "Not funny." He nodded at Tatiana. "Tell her to move to the end of the hall."

Tatiana responded with a proper curtsey, and then she quickly opened the door, whispered something to the waiting blood slave, and then quietly reentered the room, where she took an unobtrusive place by the fire, retreating into the background with her head bowed low. It was clear to all concerned that she was listening, but she had no intentions of joining in.

Drake cleared his throat. "I think we answered your question, about Damian and Father, but perhaps a few things remain unclear." He bent forward, and his own voice became a whisper. "King Demitri is the oldest living dragon on this planet. He is more than a man, more than a king. He is nearly a god."

Dante narrowed his gaze at Mina. "Do you understand what that means?"

Mina furrowed her brows. "Not really. Don't..." Her voice trailed off as she mustered more courage. "Don't you have the same powers he does? I mean, now that you're grown?" She eyed him warily, hoping once again that she hadn't gone too far.

"I do not," he said simply. "My father is a full shifter."

"That means," Drake said, "that while we can grow scales, breathe fire, manipulate the elements, and access various powers, our father can become a *serpent*. He can shift into a fully formed dragon and fly. He can scorch the earth and everything in it. No one—*and nothing*—is his equal."

All at once, Dante stared pointedly at Mina, his smooth dark brows rising in an arc. His expression hardened, and his eyes flashed with defiance as he squared his already angled jaw. "Son of a bitch," he snarled. "Let's just cut through all the bullshit, shall we?"

To his credit, Drake didn't react.

Mina flinched a bit, but she didn't respond.

"For the sake of argument," Dante continued, "let us say that something *unfortunate* were to befall our brother or our father. Then what?" He gestured toward Tatiana, whose face was a mask of terror and disbelief. "Who would rule the Realm?" He leveled a heated gaze at Mina. "You, Tatiana, Prince Drake, and me? Would we take over Castle Dragon, Castle Commons, Castle Umbras, *and* Castle Warlochia all by ourselves, and still maintain law and order throughout the realm?"

Mina shrank backward on the bed. She shook her head briskly and gestured with her hands. "Milord, I never suggested… I *never* asked—"

"Quiet," Drake whispered. "You need to understand."

Dante pressed on, sounding curiously apathetic. "And when the Lycanians sail their wooden ships across the sea, then what? Who will stop them? Drake? Or me, by myself? And what would you say to me then, sweet Mina, when the Lycanian shifters attack the Realm, set the kingdom on fire from the east to the west, murder your parents and rape your sister, let all the people starve. What would you ask of us then?"

Mina recoiled. "My prince—"

"Do you know what keeps the Lycanian shifters from invading our land?" Drake cut in. "Do you know what holds them back, even as we speak?"

Mina shook her head.

"Fear of our father. Fear of the king's wrath. Fear of the *dragon* that he would become."

Mina grasped the coverlet in her hand and tightened her fist around the soft material, further shrinking back on the bed.

"And let's also say, for the sake of argument, that the Lycanians don't invade our lands," Dante chimed in, "that our realm remains unmolested and intact—what shall we do with the shadows once Damian is gone? How shall we keep them in line, stop them from taking human women to breed like cattle, prevent them from devouring human souls out of mere gluttony, keep them from defiling your race's sons and daughters for mere pleasure? What should we do with the warlocks when they turn their gargoyles loose on their neighbors, like vultures on carrion, in order to seek dominion, when they sit on the throne in all four realms and rule the land with witchcraft? What will you ask of me then, when the entire realm is controlled by black magick, when the people are starving because the corrupt mages turn bread into gold and wine into silver? Will you be happy then because *Tatiana* is safe?"

Mina brushed a tear from her eye. Why was Dante speaking to her like this, like she had asked him to murder his brother, or worse, to commit outright sedition and go after the king? Despite her distress, she knew the answer: He had seen the questions in her eyes. He had felt the desire in her soul. He knew—*he somehow knew*—that she believed the Realm would never be just or fair, or even tolerable, with Demitri and Damian on their respective thrones. She was a dreamer, and he was a realist. And that's why their very spirits clashed.

As if he knew he had finally gotten through to her, Dante relaxed his posture. "Yes, Mina. Our enemies fear all the Dragonas, but for a reason. It takes an entire kingdom to hold them at bay, to keep *all those* you love safe and warm. You would chop the head off the snake because it is evil, when the body would devour the Realm. You understand nothing of the politics, dangers, or dynamics that motivate the monarchy, the concerns that supersede the value of any *one* life, how precarious our hold is over this land you call home."

The entire room grew quiet. Other than the crackling of the fire dancing in the hearth, not a single sound could be heard, not even the natural ebb and flow of their collective breath. Finally, when the silence had swelled to a deafening crescendo, Dante spoke stoically. "While what happened to Tatiana is despicable and tragic, perhaps even reprehensible, it is an unavoidable evil as long as King Demitri sits on the throne."

"And unless and until another dragon comes of age, he *must* sit on that throne," Drake added. "As long as all of us are needed to maintain order in this realm, it is important—nay, it is *imperative*—that the balance of power remains as it is."

Mina blinked back her tears and frustration. "I understand," she whispered.

Dante furrowed his brows. "Do you?"

She frowned. "*Yes*, I do."

"Then just ask it, Mina. Ask it and be done."

Mina shrugged. "I don't know what you mean. I—"

She halted.

She stopped protesting, and she stopped lying.

She stopped pretending, and she stopped holding back. Instead, she squared her shoulders to Dante and sighed. "And is there no one else with whom you could form an alliance? No one who would rise to your cause? Help you maintain law and order…without your father and brother?"

Dante actually faltered. He released the post and took a measured step back, his expression falling into a hard line of chagrin, and Mina understood. His Sklavos Ahavi, the woman who would one day bear him children, had just committed sedition. She had openly and verbally expressed a desire to overthrow the king, and he had given her permission to go there.

Drake drew in a labored breath and shuddered.

"Who?" Dante's voice was deceptively calm. "The humans?" He laughed then, and it was a hollow, piteous sound. "Are you kidding me, Mina? Have you ever seen a human in the clutches of a warlock? I have. It wasn't a pretty sight. And the shadows? Do you know what they would do with human souls if they were allowed? They would devour them, absorb them, suck the life-force right out of the men and place the souls of the children on their tables as desserts, even as they chained the women to their beds and used them to repopulate the Realm."

Mina felt her heart harden. "If they are that evil, that unredeemable, then couldn't the Dragonas destroy them all?"

Drake whistled low beneath his breath, and Mina shot him

a furtive glance of apology. By all the gods, she sounded like a traitor, even to herself.

Curiously, Dante answered her final question. "*All* the warlocks? *All* the witches? *All* the gargoyles and shades?" He smiled, yet the mirth didn't reach his eyes. "And then, when the Lycanians come from across the sea, there will be no armies to stand in their way, no warriors to meet them on the sands. Are you seriously advocating the destruction of our world and everyone within it?"

Mina bowed her head. "I…oh gods, my prince." Her eyes sought his for the first *real* time, honest, unchallenging, and raw. "I understand."

And for the first *real* time, his authentic gaze found hers as well. "I should slay you, Mina. Right now. Right here."

She wanted to protest, to plead for absolution, but the dragon prince was right. All those years being raised in the Keep, being taught more about the Realm than her non-Ahavi, human counterparts, she had actually been *sheltered* from the truth. She had been pampered and privileged and raised for one purpose, and even that, she had failed. Dante *loved* the kingdom she resented, and he served it, while she only rebelled. He kept her mother and her father and her sister…alive. "I'm an idiot," she whispered. "A willful, ignorant, idealistic *idiot*, who only thinks of herself."

Dante shook his head. "If that were true, I would have let you die in the Great Hall when my father caught you, when Damian suggested it." He took two measured steps away from the bedpost, rounded the bed, and reached out with a self-assured hand to finger a lock of her hair, and then he stroked the underside of her chin and bent to her ear. "One day, I will be as powerful as my father," he whispered, so that only she could hear. Well, perhaps, her and Prince Drake. "You may not live to see it, but you may still live to raise our sons. That is not a small thing." He stepped back, stood up straight, and regarded her squarely. "If you want to help me, Mina, feed the dragon's fire until he is strong. Pray that I live to come of age. Give me sons…many, many sons…

so that one day we might have impartial princes to rule. But do not *ever* ask me to commit sedition or high treason, to take on a primordial dragon that cannot be destroyed, or to oppose my brother at the expense of the Realm—to save one beautiful slave who would die anyway, at the hands of our enemies, should her persecutor be destroyed. Do not question me as your prince."

Drake sighed and clasped his hands together. As always, he injected compassion into the dialogue. "You can't avoid Damian if he calls you." He turned to regard Tatiana. "Neither of you can." He tightened his interlocked fingers like a single fist. "And you wouldn't be the first to suffer at his hands. If we can heal you, we will try—send a missive through the squire—but never, ever, approach my father's *lair*. Never break our laws. Try to avoid Prince Damian if possible. If not, then try to appease him, to please him the best you can, and pray to the gods for mercy. That is all any of us can do."

Tatiana emerged from the shadows like a specter rising from a grave: silent, ominous, and hauntingly alone. She padded to the foot of the bed, where Prince Drake still sat, and slowly fell to her knees. Bowing her head, she whispered meekly. "My prince. I have a question of my own."

Prince Drake sat forward, still clearly fatigued and waning, but he gave her his full attention. "What is it?" he asked. "Speak your peace."

The Ahavi swallowed repeatedly, her narrow throat convulsing in waves. "Only you know what is best for Castle Commons, what the province needs the most, but if all things are equal…" She began to tremble uncontrollably, and her eyes spilled over with tears. Struggling to keep from crying, she wrapped her slender arms around her waist and pressed on. "But if all things are equal, would you ask your father for me when the time comes? To make me your consort, instead of Damian's?"

Mina felt her chest constrict; her heart was breaking in two. Tatiana sounded so wretched and ashamed. She waited with bated breath as Drake inhaled sharply and stared at her companion's face, seeming to study each one of Tatiana's features in turn.

"So much has happened...I..." His voice trailed off, and he cleared his throat. "Look at me."

Tatiana met the prince's hazel gaze, and her lips trembled as she waited.

Like all the Dragonas, Drake was both handsome and robust. He kept the front edges of his midnight hair plaited in masculine braids, and his striking features were both noble and refined. Although not quite as tall as Damian or Dante, he was just as imposing, but his eyes were different—they were unusually kind. Just the same, he was a dragon by birth, a territorial predator at heart, and Tatiana was no longer pure. She had been used, and thus *marked*, by Prince Drake's brother.

He stared at Tatiana until Mina thought her own heart would cease beating, and then he simply nodded his head. "I will ask," he said.

Tatiana buried her face in her hands and sobbed.

Touched by the moment, Mina turned toward Dante and offered him a smile, as paltry as it was. "And you," she said, "thank you for what you did tonight. All of it. There are no words." She folded her hands in her lap. "And I'm truly sorry."

He lowered his head in the barest inclination of a nod. "Then we start again?"

She rose from the bed and approached him cautiously, until their toes were nearly touching. "We start again."

Dante held her seeking gaze for a moment longer than was comfortable. Then, gesturing toward Tatiana, he lowered his voice. "I think your friend is a bit overwhelmed. If you please, go fetch the blood slave. My brother, *your prince*, has waited long enough."

Without hesitation, Mina fell into a curtsey, spun on her heel, and headed for the chamber door to do the dragon's bidding.

CHAPTER TWELVE

The next day

"I ASKED MATTHIAS GENTRY to travel to the royal province." Margareta Louvet rested her elbows on the old wooden table and dropped her head in her hands, waiting for her husband's reaction. When he stared at her blankly, not saying anything, she added, "I asked him to try to get a missive to Mina." And then she simply waited…for the brunt of his anger.

His voice rang out, irritated but calm. "You did *what?*"

She sighed and lifted her head. "I spoke with Matthias."

Soren Louvet kicked back his chair, stood up, and paced to a nearby window where he stared out at the fallow pasture, his face a mask of disbelief. "When?" he snarled. "Why?"

Margareta turned around in her chair to face him and rubbed her tired eyes. She had no tears left to shed. "Yesterday, outside of the market. *Why?*" She shook her head sadly. "Why do you think, Soren? *Why do you think?*"

Soren crossed his arms over his broad chest and continued to stare out the window. "Matthias and Mina were best friends growing up. Hell, they were promised to each other in marriage by age five, before the Dragons Guard came for Mina, and you know that he is still very fond of her…" His voice trailed off, and he sighed. "What could possibly come of involving Matthias now? Do you wish to get the boy killed? Do you wish to get Mina killed?"

Now this set Margareta off.

She slammed her open palm down on the table, wincing from the pain, and stood to face her husband, even if she was only staring at his back. "They were never old enough to fall in love," she protested, planting her hands on her hips. "But yes, they were true friends, and Matthias may be the only one left who cares about Raylea! If anyone can get word to Mina, Matthias can."

Soren spun around, regarding his wife cautiously, his own bloodshot eyes drooping beneath heavy-burdened lashes. "Margareta…"

"What?" she huffed. "What would you have me do? The constable has done nothing! The insensitive fool simply took a report and filed it away." She turned her nose up in disgust. "We are so sorry for your loss, Miss Louvet. We mourn what has happened to Raylea along with your family, but we have no extra resources to send on a fishing expedition. We will, however, look into the matter, as the slave-rings are a top priority for this province." She gestured angrily with her hands, her voice rising in angst. "What the hell does that mean, Soren? The slave-rings are a top priority? They basically told us to forget Raylea and go on with our lives. She's gone." Margareta slumped back into her chair and lay her head down on the table, as if it were too heavy to hold up. "Raylea is gone," she repeated in a forlorn voice. "She's just… gone. And so is Mina. What was I to do?"

Soren stepped away from the window, crossed the room in three long strides, and stood behind his wife, placing two firm hands on her shoulders. Despite his best attempt at valor, his hands trembled against her dress. "We will continue to search for her, ourselves. By all the gods and goddesses, I promise you, I will not stop looking. I'll never quit. *Never.* Not until we bring her home, or find out—"

"That she's dead," Margareta supplied.

Soren shut his eyes and shook his head. The mere possibility was unthinkable, and Margareta knew the stubborn man would *never* give voice to such a possibility. "She has to be alive," he said with conviction. "She *has* to be all right."

"All right?" Margareta echoed, her voice catching on a sob. "No, Soren. She is not all right. You and I both know how the raiders work, the purpose of the slave trades." She swallowed hard and searched for her own brand of courage, a bravery she could no longer find. "Why they would take her...what they would want of her...what they will do to her...eventually." She tugged on a lock of her hair, carelessly twisting the ends into knots. "And that is why we cannot wait, Soren! Every minute, every hour, every day we procrastinate, Raylea is in the hands of monsters. Even if we find her—"

"*When* we find her," he growled, his face a mask of iron determination.

"Even if...or when...we find her, she may not be the same. Her soul may not be the same. Her laughter, her joy, her spirit may be gone." Margareta's tears fell freely then, and she made no attempt to hold them back. "Oh, gods, Soren! She survived the loss of Mina—we all did—but how can anyone survive this? *How?*"

Soren pulled a chair in front of hers and sat down to face her, taking both of her hands in his own and squeezing them far too hard. His knuckles turned white as he grinded his teeth, trying to find the right words, and it was as if the entire humble cabin groaned in response. The old wooden floor-planks creaked; the dilapidated shutters settled with a grumble; and the rundown shingles, high above their heads, seemed to sigh with an audible moan. The cabin, like their lives, was falling apart. "Raylea is *our daughter,* and her spirit is strong. She will survive intact. She has to. And so will Mina. We haven't lost her yet; there is still the Autumn Mating and—"

"And *the Sklavos Ahavi* belong *to the Realm, not to their families*," Margareta mocked. "*They are not* permitted *to maintain contact with their kin, at least not until after the Autumn Mating; and even then, it is at their lord's discretion.* That's what he said, Prince Drake, and he was the kind one!" She felt her expression harden, even as her ire rose like a sudden gust of wind, swirling upward in passionate eddies, fanning out in frustration and rage. "The *kind* prince, the one who showed even the barest amount of compassion, looked our daughter right in the eyes and told her that Mina belonged to him. And the other one, Prince Dante, he was like a block of ice or a slab of stone. We are nothing to these dragons! Nothing, Soren—you didn't see his face." She clutched a potted urn that was sitting on the table, serving as a centerpiece, and ran her forefinger along the petals of a single pale rose, planted in the center. "And Damian Dragona, our future prince of Umbras? He was the Dark Lord himself, Keeper of the Forgotten Realm. He was evil incarnate, Soren. There was nothing in his eyes: no soul, no compassion, no mercy. He held a dagger to Raylea's throat—a ten-year-old child!" She stood in a sudden storm of fury, tossed the pot across the room, and watched as so many shards of clay scattered about the cabin, ricocheted off the walls, and dispersed across the floor in a dissonant pattern. "Who do they think they are? What gives them the right? To take our children, our little girls, and use them like common whores!" She fisted her hands at her sides and glared at her husband with scorn. "You are not a woman, Soren." She felt horrible saying it, but she just couldn't help it. "I know you love your daughters, of course you do, but you can't possibly imagine. I would rather slit my own throat than be forced to breed a son for the Realm with one of those princes. And now, Raylea, too? Oh great Spirit Keepers, why? *Why!*" She slumped to the floor in a ball of anguish and began to weep uncontrollably.

Soren knelt down before her and tried to wrap his arms

around her quaking shoulders, but his own anger, his barely concealed helplessness and rage, rose from his being like fog from the sea, and joined her fury in the room. He was coming apart, about to break down, utterly mired in feebleness and contempt. "I...I..." He bowed his head and shuddered. "I don't know what to say. I would kill them all if I could, but it wouldn't bring our daughters back." He tightened his grasp around Margareta's slender frame and buried his fingers in her long, auburn hair. "I swear to you, my love. I will find Raylea or die trying." His deep, masculine voice broke then, giving way to anguish and tears. "I'll bring our baby home...or I'll die trying. *I swear.*"

Margareta clung to her husband as if her life depended on it—and maybe it did—because in this fateful moment, she no longer possessed the will to go on. She had no idea how to get up in the morning, how to stumble through each day, or how to carry on with the business of life and farming when all she had lived for was gone.

Hell, she didn't even know how to draw her next breath.

By all that was holy—or unholy—the Realm had stolen the most precious gifts she had ever been given: her babies, her angels, her daughters...

First, Mina.

And now, Raylea.

It was just too much to bear.

And even though Margareta had escaped the attack in the forest with her life, just barely, she did not wish to continue, not like this. Not without her youngest daughter. It was hard enough to accept the fact that Mina was living on the other side of what felt like the world with those three demonic dragons, but to give Raylea up, too? It was simply impossible.

She was just about to pry Soren's hands from her hair when she heard a hard, crisp knock on the door, and she froze. Oh gods, what if it was the constable, or worse, a member of the Dragons Guard? The words she had just spoken were treason, and they wouldn't hesitate to take her away. She stared at Soren blankly and shrugged her shoulders, her lip beginning to quiver.

"Miss Louvet? Master Soren? Are you in there?" Matthias Gentry's deep, melodious voice reverberated from the other side of the panel.

"Matthias?" Margareta called out, quickly rising to her feet and ushering her husband to follow. She hurried to the door and unhitched the latch.

The boy, who was now a proud and formidable man of twenty summers, stood on the front stoop like a soldier: his angled chin held high, his proud shoulders pulled back, his deep blue eyes narrowed with steadfast purpose. His familiar crossbow was slung over one of his broad, muscular shoulders, and his long, wavy blond hair rustled in the wind as he fixed his gaze on Margareta's. "Ma'am. I'm here to retrieve that missive. I'll be heading out for Castle Dragon come morning."

Margareta took a cautious step back and gestured for the youth to come in.

He stepped past her like a cool, welcoming breeze on a scorching, unforgiving day, and immediately regarded Soren. "Mr. Louvet," he said by way of greeting.

Soren nodded. "Matthias." He shook the youngster's hand. "I think there's been a misunderstanding, son." He leveled a crosswise glance at his wife. "We can't ask you to get involved in our private affairs, to do something this dangerous. My wife was distraught, and she—"

Matthias held up a gracious but firm hand to silence him. "With all due respect, sir, I think I'm old enough to make my own decisions." He pitched his voice a bit softer out of esteem. "Mina was—*is*—my friend. And Raylea is like a little sister to me. So if you think I can just go on with my life as if nothing has happened or changed, well then, you don't know me as well as I thought you did."

Soren appraised Matthias carefully then, his mouth turning

down in a frown. "Son, this has nothing to do with your character or the place you have in our hearts. You desire to speak man-to-man, then I'll speak to you with candor: If you go to that castle, you're gonna get killed. You might even get Mina killed in the process. My friends and I, we will continue to search."

Matthias' bright blue eyes turned dark with disapproval. "I understand that, sir. I'm not a fool." He tapped his crossbow. "My aim is not to storm the castle like some lunatic or to try to get to Mina, but I've got a really strong arm, and I can thread an arrow through the eye of a needle at two hundred yards. All I need to do is get the missive to her, *somehow*. I'm thinking of attaching it to the end of an arrow—she'll recognize my fletching."

Margareta cast a hopeful glance at Soren, waiting to hear his reply.

He shook his head in consternation. "Aren't you engaged to be married next summer to the Walcott girl?"

Matthias nodded, and his handsome features seemed unusually stern, far too serious for a lad his age. "I am."

Soren frowned. "Then I just can't ask you to do this." He gestured toward his wife. "*We* just can't ask you to do this."

Matthias stood quietly, seeming to weigh his words very carefully. After a thoughtful, protracted moment, he finally replied, "I understand that you can't ask, Mr. Louvet, but I'm offering." He held up his hand to silence any protest. "And when I'm done, I'm offering to ride with you and some of the other farmers into Warlochia, through the dragon forest, all the way to Umbras and beyond if needed, to help you search for Raylea." He cast a brief, compassionate glance at Margareta before turning his attention back to Soren. "Look, I understand your reservations as well as your many concerns. *I do.* But this isn't just about my friendship with Raylea or my *past* with Mina. It's about my honor as a commoner and a citizen of this realm." He eyed Margareta warily, as if wanting to temper his words—*and their meaning*—in the presence of a woman. "The dragons take our women, our girls—hell, our futures—and they lock them up in that gods-forsaken Keep, training them to be servants, consorts, and worse; and we allow it because we have to. The warlocks do the same, only instead of just taking our young women, they also steal young boys—they make them all but indentured servants, and we never get them back. And the shades, they come for our souls, and there is little protection. Now, this? Raylea? For what? By whom?" He shook his head in disgust. "We have to fight back, Mr. Louvet. We have to form our own militias and guards. We have to start resisting. Surely, the scattered descendants of the Malo Clan, the giants, are not the only humans who secretly detest the king."

Soren shrank back in alarm. "You would oppose the Dragonas and their laws? Align yourself with the descendants of slaves, who are few and far between, not to mention carefully watched by the Dragons Guard? You would oppose traditions as old as time in a realm controlled by magic? Son, we could never win."

Matthias shook his head in opposition, displaying a more reasonable frame of mind. "No. I don't mean to change the way of the Realm. I understand why the Ahavi are needed, even if I don't agree with how they are acquired and kept from their families." He pursed his lips in frustration before pressing on. "The moment we weaken the dragons, the Umbrasians and the Warlochians will be the least of our worries: The northerners will come across the restless sea, and the Lycanians will make every sin committed in this realm seem like child's play by comparison. They'll scorch the farmlands, murder the children, rape the women, and leave our corpses like bare husks in their wake on their way to overcoming Castle Dragon, in an attempt to overthrow the king. No," he insisted, "we need the dragons—we need their protection—and they need to remain strong by having dragon sons. But this? Common thieves and raiders? Slave traders and mercenaries, capturing ten-year-old girls for their own deviant purposes? This is my province too—I grew up in Arns—and I have a personal investment in making it safe. I have the right—*we have the right*—to fight for our own."

Margareta took Soren's hand in hers and squeezed it, beseeching him with her eyes. "Please, Soren. Let him go. At least let him try." She practically held her breath, waiting for an answer.

Soren appraised Matthias more carefully then, taking his measure from head to toe, and Margareta couldn't help but appraise him, too: The adolescent had grown into a powerful young man with the broad bearing of a warrior, standing at least six feet tall. His lean, muscular frame was robust and vibrant, practically radiating with the infinite energy of youth. He was strong and sturdy, sound of mind. And he had always been a fiercely determined lad, as skilled with that crossbow as the most adept, professional soldier. If anyone could get the missive to Mina, it would be Matthias.

All at once, Margareta frowned, thinking about another issue that plagued them, another potential complication: From what she had seen of the princes—Damian, Dante, and Drake—it wasn't as if any one of them would bother to lift a finger on Mina's behalf. It wasn't like her daughter had any political power or pull. So what if Matthias *did* achieve the near impossible—he successfully got the missive to Mina, all the while remaining undetected? Would Mina then turn to her masters for help? What if she approached one of the princes on behalf of Raylea, begged them to intervene, and her request was met with hostility, seen as disobedient? Matthias could very well be placing Mina in grave danger, even if he succeeded in his mission.

But what else were they to do?

Margareta had clung to every hope that Soren and his companions would find Raylea somewhere…*somehow*…and bring her home safely. She had prayed for it every night since Raylea was captured, but she had also stood in the Warlochian square and watched Dante Dragona execute two prisoners, severing one's head as easily as one might halve an apple, scorching the other to ash. He was, indeed, a frozen block of ice: cold, calculating, and ruthless. And his brothers were his equal.

Still, there was an alternate possibility, one that renewed her hope: What if Matthias *did* get the missive to Mina; Mina somehow appealed to one of the princes—perhaps the most reasonable of the three, Prince Drake—and the prince actually took mercy on Raylea's plight and stepped in? With so many resources, such supernatural power, all at the tip of his fingers, the king's son could have Raylea home by the end of the week.

If anyone could save Raylea, a Dragona could, and Mina *was* very resourceful…

Margareta could only hope that her eldest daughter was still as strong and creative…and single-minded as she had always been growing up. She could only pray that the gods would show her favor. Or mercy. And bless Matthias and his powerful arm.

"Soren?" she entreated, her voice rising in a hopeful plea.

Soren reached out, placed a firm hand on Matthias's shoulder, and slowly nodded his head. "Thank you, son." He paused for a moment and murmured, "I wish…things had been different for Mina…and you."

Matthias's nose twitched, almost imperceptibly, and then he declined his head in a polite nod. "What is done is done," he said, in an unusually acquiescent voice. "It is not for us to try to alter the will of the gods. But the will of evil men, bent on their own carnal pleasures and destruction, well, that's a different matter."

Margareta stared at Matthias's expression and shivered.

There was just something *so unusual* in his eyes: something dormant, something dangerous, something powerful and ancient. She shook her head, dismissing the wayward thought.

Matthias was…*Matthias.*

His resolve was implacable.

His determination was rock-hard and fierce.

She took an unwitting step back and wrung her hands

together. By all the Spirit Keepers, the Dragonas were not the only formidable beings in the Realm.

Not anymore.

*

Raylea Louvet tugged against the heavy chains that bound her wrists to the damp stone wall. She blinked back tears of terror and gazed out the small iron-barred window above her, trying to figure out just where she was now.

A dungeon?

A cellar?

A rat-infested hovel?

But in what territory?

She thought about her mother and that calamitous day in the forest, the day they had traveled back from the execution in Warlochia, the day the old man has asked for her doll in order to send it by courier to Castle Dragon, and the day they had been attacked near Devil's Bend. Raylea trembled as she replayed the awful events in her mind, the way that nasty gargoyle had leaped out from behind a linden tree and frightened her horse half to death, how terrified she had been when he had reared up and she had fallen, and what it was like when she'd looked into her captor's eyes: those vacant, evil, witchy-gray eyes. He had looked at her like he hated her, and for the life of her, she hadn't understood why. What had she ever done to him? To any of them?

She winced, remembering how her mother had screamed, wheeled her horse around, and tried to charge at the slavers. Raylea had wanted to run to her mom so badly to get on the back of her mother's horse and go home to her father. She had been so excited about the prospect of her doll making its way to Mina.

But none of it had mattered.

It hadn't mattered at all.

The Realm was a wicked place full of evil people just waiting to prey on the weak, and she had been one of them. As angry tears welled in her eyes, she wished she could wipe them away, but those damnable chains clutched her little arms like a dragon's talons, and it was simply impossible. She was just about to scream in frustration when she heard a key rattle in the lock. The iron door swung open, and a shadow-walker entered. *Oh dear gods*, she was being held captive by a *shade*, an abominable creature that fed on human souls.

It must have been past twilight because the *shadow* no longer held his human form. He was wispy and somehow skeletal, like half of his flesh was gone. In fact, he slinked, more than walked, toward the back of the room, where Raylea watched him with rising terror.

"My name is Syrileus Cain"—he spoke with a hiss—"and I am your new master, your benefactor, and your god."

Raylea literally recoiled, pressing her little body as tight against the stone wall as she could, wishing she could blend in with the rocks.

"You will worship me, obey me, and see to my every need." He flashed a wicked, contemptuous grin, his front yellow teeth gleaming in the moonlight that shone through the iron bars, and Raylea felt instantly faint.

She tugged against the chains and screamed bloody murder, praying that someone could hear. That someone would please… *please*…help her. She was desperate to get away from the shadow, but there was nothing she could do. Nowhere she could go. Her lungs burned in her chest, and her voice became raw from her effort.

And all the while, Syrileus just licked his thin lips and laughed. *He laughed.*

As if her terror and her pain were nothing, mere performances to amuse him. And then he took several steps toward her, and she flinched. As she tucked her head forward, nearly pressing her chin to her chest, he reached out with a ghostly, shadowed hand and scratched the underside of her jaw. His fingernails were long, pointed, and disgustingly dirty, and he purposely nicked her flesh in order to draw a droplet of blood.

And then he tasted it.

Oh gods—he tasted it!

His thin, slimy tongue snaked out of his garish mouth, and he sucked the droplet off the end of his finger.

Raylea began to retch, even as she continued to twist this way and that in her chains, trying to put some distance between herself and the shadow-walker. And then he opened his distended jaw and bent toward her, not for a kiss, but to sample her soul... to draw out the first taste of her essence.

Raylea's eyes rolled back in her head as fear consumed her.

True or false, her young life passed before her eyes, and then the entire world went black as she *blessedly* passed out.

PART TWO:
DRAGONS WAR

"Come not between the dragon, and his wrath."

~ William Shakespeare, KING LEAR

CHAPTER THIRTEEN

Two weeks later

MINA LOUVET STARED out the open, stained-glass window in her private bedchamber, enjoying the view of the immaculate gardens below. Things had settled down nicely over the past two weeks. Okay, so *nicely* might be too strong a word, but they had settled down. Mina and Dante had fallen into an amiable, predictable rhythm, both in terms of Mina feeding his dragon and the two of them exchanging cordial banter. Tatiana had completely healed from Damian's brutal attack, at least physically, if not emotionally, and life at Castle Dragon had settled into an affable routine, at least something she could anticipate.

She glanced askance at the mantel, smiling as she eyed Raylea's doll, remembering the day Dante had presented it to her, and feeling grateful for the priceless gift even now. The prince *did* have a heart, albeit deeply buried beneath all that battle-hardened Dragona armor, and she was finally learning how to navigate around the rough, thorny edges.

A high-pitched whistle hummed beneath the open window,

piercing the tender silence of contemplation like a blade, and she instinctively leaned over the sill in an effort to identify its origins. And that's when she saw the wooden arrow with its bright, twisted quills sticking out of the bushes.

Mina sucked in an anxious breath and leaned out further, staring at the familiar fletching.

She would know that arrow anywhere.

The telltale bright-colored plumes; the narrow wedge-shaped design; the superior craftsmanship of the wood—that arrow belonged to Matthias Gentry, one of her oldest and dearest friends.

A boy she had once been promised to in marriage.

She ducked away from the window and grasped the outer layer of her tunic, absently glancing to the left, then the right, as if someone might be watching. *Great Spirit Keepers*, she needed to calm down…

Of course no one was watching.

Mina knew she was alone.

She peered out the window once more, this time scanning the distant surroundings for the archer, and that's when she heard the swallow's nervous call from within a weeping willow, the rapid, high-pitched chirping that alerted her to a stranger's presence.

Ancestors be merciful, what was Matthias doing?

Why had he come to the Castle Dragon?

Was he trying to get himself killed?

Wasting no time at all, she dashed across the room, snatched her parka, and sprinted toward the back castle staircase, where she flew down the steps like a falcon intent on surprising its prey, eager to get to the archer.

Dante had given her a wide berth when it came to exploring the castle grounds, just so long as she took reasonable precautions. She didn't think her sudden exploit would be noticed.

Throwing open a heavy door, she emerged on the eastern end of the grounds, quickly traversed the small sunlit plaza, circled the bubbling fountain, and then headed in the direction of her bedroom window toward the shady end of the gardens. The moment Mina approached the huge willow tree, she bit her lip, kept her eyes focused downward, and swiftly made her way toward the low-arcing branches. And sure enough, her childhood friend stood up, his broad, muscular shoulders held in a proud, easy stance, his long legs crossed at the ankle as he copped a lean against the trunk of the tree and turned in her direction.

"Matthias!" she exclaimed. "What in the name of the gods are you doing here?" She planted her hands on her hips and tapped her foot in nervous anticipation.

Matthias rose to his full six-foot height and ran a long, slender hand through his thick blond hair. "I've been traveling for the last ten days. I have news concerning Raylea." He nodded in the direction of his spent arrow, indicating the vertical quills, still standing upright, beneath her bedchamber window. "I can't believe my luck, that I saw you standing in a window, but you'd better retrieve that arrow—there's a missive attached to the tip."

Mina glanced over her shoulder and nodded. She drew back her shoulders and strolled leisurely toward the arrow, stopping to admire a cluster of bright pink-and-violet peony bushes along the way, just in case someone was watching. She bent over slowly, as if to check the hem of her skirt, pulled the arrow out of the ground, and tucked the shaft beneath her arm, concealing the object in the various folds of fabric. Then she checked the gardens one more time to make sure they were alone as she slowly strolled back toward Matthias.

Ducking beneath the cover of the willow, she handed the arrow to Matthias, waited as he placed it back in his quiver, missive and all, and then squatted low to the ground. "Get down." Her voice was unintentionally harsh. "You're not safe here, Matt."

He immediately followed suit. "I know, but it was really important. Your parents are having a very hard time."

Mina felt something inside of her constrict, perhaps her

stomach growing queasy or her heart beginning to ache. She knew Matthias would not have traveled all the way from the *commonlands*—he would not have taken such a risk—if the matter had not been of the utmost importance. *And it was about Raylea.* She almost wished she had read the missive the moment she had pulled the arrow from the ground, but that would have been stupid, not to mention unnecessary. It would be better to hear it from Matthias. *Oh gods.* Her palms began to sweat from anticipation. "Well," she finally whispered. "What is it?"

Matthias captured her gaze in an unwavering stare. "Your mother and Raylea were attacked in Forest Dragon, nearly three weeks ago, by a band of warlocks and their gargoyles. We believe they were slave traders, those who sell to the *shades* in the west." He shook his head, and his eyes grew cloudy. "Your mother got away. Raylea did not."

Mina gasped, and then she immediately shoved her hand over her mouth to stifle her outcry as the emotion slipped out. "Oh, gods...*no*." She practically whimpered her next words. "What happened? Do you know where she is? What is being done?"

Matthias sat down on the ground, and Mina mimicked the action. She could hardly contain her panic, but to her credit, she waited for Matthias to collect his thoughts and answer when he was ready.

He drew a crude diagram in the dirt. "Her horse was here, not far from Devil's Bend." He pointed at a rock about two inches from the slash which indicated the horse. "The raiders came from behind a thick grouping of trees." He drew another slash in the primitive illustration, presumably to designate the trees. "We believe it was a band of Warlochian slavers led by the high mage Rafael Bishop, but we don't know who actually took her—Rafael runs with a very dangerous crew: Sir Robert Cross, Micah Fiske, and Sir Henry Woodson, at least before he was executed, just to name a few." He waited for his words to sink in, fully expecting her to recognize the notorious names. "And we believe Raylea was taken to be sold—not sacrificed or consumed—but the constable refuses to follow up. He isn't doing a thing. They're just too busy to organize a search." His jaw stiffened in a visible attempt to subdue his anger. "Or perhaps they're just too indifferent." Before Mina could pepper him with questions, Matthias pressed on. "Your father and several nearby farmers organized a search party of their own, but they haven't had any luck. We feel like…your mother feels like…unless you intervene, unless you can get one of the princes to intervene—*right away*—Raylea may be lost to us forever."

Matthias's words swept over Mina like a cold, bitter wind, chilling her skin and causing her body to shiver. She grasped her head in her hands as she rocked forward in anguish. Oh, heavens above, not Raylea, not sweet, innocent, beautiful Raylea. What were those monsters doing to her little sister? Trying to contain her grief—it wouldn't help, and Raylea could not afford the wasted time—she tried to think of something she could do. Would Dante actually help her? Would he send a faction of the Dragons Guard to search for Mina's little sister? Would he actually go himself?

She honestly didn't know.

It was a lot to ask.

A lot to consider.

Before she could formulate her next words, seek advice, or ask Matthias for suggestions, a distinctive, familiar sound caused the hairs on Mina's arms to stand up: the crackling of crisp, brittle leaves beneath footfalls, alerting the two of them to an approaching visitor.

Someone was coming toward them.

Mina slid onto her belly and rolled toward the trunk of the tree, even as Matthias scurried behind it.

"Too late, you little witch. I knew you could not be trusted." Pralina Darcy's shrill, heartless voice penetrated the tense atmosphere. "Get off the ground, you stupid little whore, and tell your lover to come from behind that tree." The castle's spiteful governess glared angrily at Mina as she stood before her like a looming bastion of evil, her skeletal hands planted firmly on her bony hips, her thin blood-red lips pulled back into a scowl. She looked positively murderous.

"Mistress!" Mina bounded to her feet, unconsciously placing her body between the witch and Matthias as he crept from behind the tree, his knees bent low to the ground, his considerable weight shifted forward, as if he were prepared to spring. "What are you doing in the gardens?" Mina persisted, trying to sound indignant. "Were you *following* me?"

Pralina threw back her head and howled like some sort of demented animal, utterly insane.

"Pralina!" Mina curled her hand into a fist and thought seriously about striking the governess across the jaw. "Be quiet!"

Pralina's severe gray eyes narrowed in rage as she howled again, this time calling for assistance. "Guards! *Guards!* Come quickly!"

Mina's heart constricted in her chest.

She spun around to face Matthias. "Go!" she ordered, hoping her sudden, imperious command would startle Pralina into silence, at least long enough for Matthias to slip away. "Get out of here. Quickly! Before she wakes the dead."

Matthias rose nimbly to his feet, his nervous eyes scanning the nearby commons, even as he took a cautious step backward, preparing to run. "What about you?" he whispered softly, his overwhelming concern etched into his forehead.

Before Mina could answer, Pralina stepped forward and glared at Matthias, challenging him to even flinch. "You dare to step foot on these royal grounds, commoner!" she snarled. "To approach one of the castle's Sklavos Ahavi without escort or invitation? I will see your head on a spike."

Mina sucked in wind, her clenched fist convulsing with spasms. She was going to kill this witch—

Right here.

Right now.

This was not a game.

She fixed her attention on Matthias and placed all the volume she could muster into her voice. "Go!"

Matthias hefted his quiver onto his back, clenched his bow in his right hand, and spun around in quick retreat, heading toward a thicker grouping of trees on the outskirts of the gardens, just as a tall, looming figure entered the private setting from the east. *Oh dear ancestors, have mercy!* It was Damian Dragona.

He was dressed in black from head to toe; he had a wicked-looking sword dangling in a scabbard at his hip; and he was striding forward like a tornado bent on destruction. Mina saw her life flash before her eyes—*to hell with it!* She cupped her mouth in her hands and shouted from the top of her lungs. "Dante!" She arched her back, turned toward the castle, and shouted again, this time abrading her throat. *"Dante!"* What were the odds that the prince could hear her? What were the odds that he was anywhere near? *Oh gods above,* she prayed for their divine intervention.

Damian stepped promptly in front of her, drew back his arm, and slapped her soundly across the cheek, sending her spiraling to the ground on her knees. And that's when Matthias halted, drew an arrow out of his quiver, and turned back around. Mina stared in stunned stupefaction as Matthias Gentry nocked the arrow in his crossbow, pointed it directly at Damian, and sidled forward toward the willow tree.

Blessed Nuri, protect them all.

He was going to confront the prince.

The ground shifted beneath her knees; the sky spun in dizzying circles of pastel blue above her head; and her stomach churned like a vat of curdled milk heated in a kettle as Mina reached up with a quivering hand and tried to distract Damian. "My prince," she garbled the words around bloody spittle, *"please*...this is all a big misunderstanding."

Matthias took a bold step forward. "Don't touch her again."

Damian came to a sudden halt. He cocked his arrogant head to the side, measured Matthias from head to toe, and laughed: a loathsome, scornful sound. "What are you going to do with that bow, boy?" he snarled.

Matthias's eyes betrayed his fear. He blinked several times in quick succession and then planted his feet a shoulder's width apart below trembling knees. "I don't want to do anything, my lord, just...but...we all need to calm down." His voice was wobbly, despite his deliberate attempt at bravery. "Mina is right. This is all a misunderstanding. I came in peace."

Damian snickered. His bicep twitched, and his sword hand covered his scabbard. "Mina is right. *Mina?*" He glanced down at her trembling form. "You mean my insolent slave?"

Pralina leveled a hate-filled glare at Mina, stepped forward, and grasped her by a handful of hair. "Get up, bitch!" she ordered.

Mina clutched her scalp, fury overwhelming her, and stumbled to her feet, trying to keep the roots of her hair from ripping out with every jarring movement. "Let go of me," she cried.

Pralina tightened her fist and tugged against Mina's scalp, drawing pleasure from her pain. She dug several sharp, jagged nails deep into Mina's flesh and cackled, staring at her nose-to-nose.

That was it.

Shoving the heel of her shoulder into the hag's stomach to throw her off balance, Mina went for blood: She raked her nails across the woman's cheek, barely missing her eye; kicked her in the shin; stomped on her foot; and then elbowed her in the neck. The moment Pralina let go of Mina's hair and began to choke, Mina followed up with a quick uppercut to the jaw, causing Pralina to bite her own tongue. The governess yelped and jumped back in surprise, trying to regain control.

"Son of a bitch," Damian swore, crossing his arms over his chest and relaxing in spite of Matthias's bow. His laughter grew raucous and loud. "You're a regular hellcat, aren't you, woman?"

He shrugged a cocky shoulder. "Perhaps I should ask my father for you, after all." And then he grew callous in the blink of an eye.

Without warning or preamble, the dragon prince flicked his wrists, pointed one forefinger at Mina, the other at Matthias, and shot them both in the chest with a supernatural bolt of lightning, stunning them where they stood. The air whooshed out of Mina's lungs, and she froze in place like a statue, even as Matthias went flying into the air, tumbled in a violent circle, and cried out in agony as his crossbow singed his hands. Damian rotated his forefinger in two small circles, and Matthias's bow and quiver soared away from his body as if caught in an unseen wind, spiraled high above the tree, and then plummeted to the ground, splintering into a dozen pieces.

Mina gasped, but she couldn't move. She couldn't even speak. All she could do was watch in abject horror as Matthias stopped spinning and began to drift upward—further and further—heading toward the high, winding branches of the willow tree. And then the twisted limbs began to moan and stretch, wrapping their rigid arms around the human's waist, his throat, and his hands.

Oh gods, Damian was using the tree as a restraint, binding Matthias in wooden chains, suspending him above the ground, in order to…in order to…*what?*

Mina's eyes grew wide, and she fought against the evil prince's magic, desperate to turn away, as Damian took several paces backward, opened his feral jaw in the most grotesque contortion she had ever seen, and released his pointed canines. Smoke bellowed from the corners of his mouth; his lips turned fiery orange, and deep red flames began to dance like twirling vapors, emerging from his throat.

Mina recoiled inwardly, even as she forced an outer moan.

No…

Please…

Oh, gods…no.

She did not want to watch Matthias burn.

Please, Damian, she begged in her mind. Her tongue was still thick and laden like it was coated in goo. *Oh, ancestors, where was Dante? Where was Drake? Where were the gods when they were needed?* Bitter tears stung her eyes as Damian's lip drew back in a primitive snarl, and he hissed a final pronouncement. "You dared to place your feet on the king's land. You dared to speak to a Sklavos Ahavi, to a wench that belongs to me and mine, and you dared to raise a weapon to your lord. For these crimes, and just for the hell of it, I sentence you to death." A primal roar escaped his throat, and he opened his mouth even wider to release the fatal flames.

"Prince Damian! *Prince Damian!*" An agitated band of castle sentinels rushed into the garden, led by the two Malo Clan guards who had been present at Mina's scourging. "My prince," the seven-foot guard with a pointed, scruffy goatee grunted impatiently. "The king demands your presence in the throne room at once."

Damian didn't turn in their direction. He didn't turn away from his fury. He didn't even acknowledge their presence.

The second guard stared at the piteous human dangling from the tree and grimaced as understanding registered in his dark, seedy eyes, but he pressed on with his own entreaty. *"My prince!"* His voice was gruff and insistent with appeal. "The watchtower sentry spotted at least two dozen Lycanian ships sailing this way across the restless sea."

"They're headed toward Dracos Cove," the first guard cut in.

"An attack is imminent. You are needed in the throne room *at once.*"

For the first time, both Malo Clan guards glanced absently at Mina, still frozen like a piteous effigy where she stood, and then at Pralina, her face bitter with anger, ashen with humiliation, and speckled with welts, each streaked with blood. The first guard snorted. "There is no time for"—he swept his hand in a dismissive arc, indicating whatever had gone on with the women—"for *this.*" And then he straightened his spine, squared his shoulders to the prince, and bowed his head in deference. "We were told to bring the Sklavos Ahavi, all three of them, to the throne room as well."

"The king said *now*," the second guard added with just a bit of vehemence and more than a little distaste.

Damian shook his head briskly as if trying to snap out of a daze. Undoubtedly, he was accustomed to the Malo Clan guards and their brusque, heavy-handed ways. More than likely, he was trying to bridle his dragon, retract the beast's fire, and regain some semblance of control. Moments felt like hours as Damian blinked several times; his eyes flashed back and forth between red and dark brown; and he finally drew in a measured, easy breath.

The fire abated.

He tilted his head to the side and glared at Mina, and for a moment, she didn't know if he planned to release her or murder her, right then and there. "Compose yourself," he ordered, flicking his wrist in her direction, and just like that, her invisible bonds were removed. She was no longer paralyzed.

She shivered and groaned from the strange sensation, watching in trepidation as he turned his attention to Matthias, who was still terrified and hanging, suspended from the tree. *"Oh please, oh please, oh please, sweet goddess of mercy,"* she breathed.

Damian frowned, but his ire had already cooled.

His attention was clearly elsewhere.

He raised his open palm toward the top of the tree, curled his fingers inward, and the branches simply let go, dropping Matthias to the ground, where he landed at Damian's feet. The sadistic prince kicked him in the ribs, and then spun around to face the leader of the guards, the barbaric giant with the menacing goatee. "Take this human excrement to the dungeon—we can execute him later." As several guards rushed forward to seize Matthias, Damian turned toward Mina once more. "And clean her up—*quickly*—then bring her to the throne room."

"As you wish, my prince," a normal-sized guard said, leveling his gaze at Mina.

As if she were utterly clueless to the gravity of the situation, Pralina Darcy huffed in exasperation, rushed toward Damian, and grasped him by the arm, her jagged nails unintentionally biting into his skin. "My prince," she panted, "forgive me, but I must insist on this Ahavi's immediate punishment. Did you not see what she did to me?"

Damian's eyes narrowed into two tiny slits, the pupils drawing as thin as a cat's.

"I am your father's most faithful domestic. I have served him honorably for the past ten years, and that bitch had the audacity to strike me." She kicked a mound of dirt in Mina's direction, her voice growing hoarse with disgust.

Damian licked his bottom lip. Slowly. "You insist?" His words were barely audible.

Pralina cleared her throat. "It's...well...it's very important that the slaves know their place. So in that respect, yes; I insist."

Damian nodded slowly. He glanced back and forth between Pralina and Mina, his face an iron mask of disdain, and then he fingered his scabbard, drew his sword, and gutted the governess from stem to stern in one graceful thrust of his blade. As Pralina's eyes bulged in their sockets, swollen with shock and horror, she grasped at his lapels and groaned.

"I couldn't agree with you more. Slaves should know their place." With that, he withdrew his sword, shoved her away with a booted foot, and watched as her body slumped to the ground. Turning to Mina, he extended the blood-soaked blade. "You," he snarled, placing the tip of steel to her throat. "Ten words or less: Why were you meeting with that human? Why did you call out for my *brother*? And what made you think you could get away with attacking Pralina?"

Mina swallowed convulsively, feeling the hard, cold edge of the sword taut against her throat.

Ten words or less?

How did he expect her to answer?

He increased the pressure, nicking her skin in the process and drawing a trickle of blood. She steadied her nerves and spoke slowly. Deliberately. "He brought a message from home. I was scared. *Apologies.*"

Damian withdrew the sword and sheathed it in its scabbard. "What was the message?"

"My sister was kidnapped by slavers."

He nodded slowly. "I see. And you thought Dante would... *what?* Help you find your sister? Protect you...*from me?*"

"My prince." The second Malo Clan guard vied for Damian's attention, presumably to remind him of the urgent situation, the need to get to the throne room post haste, but his captain swiftly seized him by the arm and shook his head in caution.

Shh, he mouthed the warning.

The lieutenant looked away.

"No, my prince," Mina answered quietly. "I...I just panicked. There was no thought. I...I'm just better *acquainted* with Prince Dante, thus far."

"*Acquainted,*" Damian echoed nastily as he nodded again. "Hmm. And Pralina?"

Mina bit her bottom lip. "She...she..." There was no polite way to put it, no clever way to restate it, so she chose to shut her mouth.

Damian leaned forward until he met her at eye level, and his harshly sculpted nose twitched. "She was a royal bitch," he whispered. This time, Mina nodded, and the corner of his mouth turned up in a sadistic smile. "Well, I don't think she'll bother either of us again, do you?" He narrowed his gaze with *such* contempt...

Mina closed her eyes and waited, expecting anything to happen.

She had no idea what the prince would do next.

To her surprise, Prince Damian stood up straight, brushed the dust off his tunic, turned on his heel, and pompously strolled away.

CHAPTER FOURTEEN

MINA CROSSED HER arms over her chest, gripped both triceps with her palms, and rubbed her exposed flesh briskly in order to stave off the chill as she entered the throne room of Castle Dragon.

Again.

How well she remembered the last time she had stood in this massive hall with its cryptic walls, enormous columns, and elaborate trappings. She still recalled the king's heartless words—*give her fifteen lashes with a spiked whip*—and the brutal flogging that had followed thereafter. She still remembered Dante's courageous sacrifice as he had endured her pain, accepted it as his own, and she understood, more intimately than most, how quickly one's fate could turn from bad to worse at the whimsical nod of this king.

Making her way toward the back of the room, she scurried to the left side of the hall and took an inconspicuous place beside Tatiana Ward. The two exchanged wary glances before Mina took her best friend's hand. "Hi, Tati," she murmured, still staring straight ahead.

Tatiana was practically cowering in the corner, and she welcomed Mina's touch with a firm squeeze of their interlocked fingers. "What is this about?" the frail, auburn-haired female whispered in an anxious tone. "And where were you earlier?"

Mina shook her head. She wasn't about to go there. She pressed her shoulder to Tatiana's, leaned in her direction, and whispered in her ear: "The Realm is under attack, or at least it will be soon: Lycanians from the north, sailing across the sea."

Tatiana shot her a furtive glance. "How do you know this?"

Once again, Mina shook her head. "It's not important." She shrugged. "And as for where I was earlier—I'll tell you later." As the crowd grew around them, courtiers filling up space, Mina tugged Tatiana by the arm and shuffled several paces back until they were both leaning against the far western wall. She took the opportunity to survey the hall, to observe its occupants, and to gather information. She was preoccupied with thoughts of Raylea and Matthias, terrified of Damian and his sadistic behavior, and she was anxious to get this mandatory meeting over with so she could concentrate on her much more pressing concerns.

As always, the king was perched like a god on his throne, but he wasn't leaning back in that grand, relaxed manner that told the whole world he was in control. On the contrary, he looked more than just a little uneasy—he looked equal parts angry and determined, as he sat suspended on the edge of his seat, rested his elbow on his thigh, anchored his chin on his fist, and leaned forward to speak with his sons. Dante, Damian, and Drake surrounded the king in a loose semicircle, and Mina couldn't help but notice that, for the first time ever, King Demitri's crown looked too heavy for his head.

As for the princes, they cast a powerful, uneasy visage of their own: Unlike the first time Mina had viewed the throne room, they were not standing in a lesser, symbolic position, staring dutifully at their father from the bottom of the dais, displaying a quiet, perhaps even resentful, reverence. They were each standing tall. They were offering the king counsel. And they were function-ing as a cohesive unit. The thought gave Mina chills. It was hard to see Damian as anything more than a vicious brute, a rabid dog that should be put down by its owner.

She shivered, watching as the two familiar Malo Clan guards paced back and forth behind the throne, throwing off a lethal energy of their own, and then she turned her attention to the greater hall.

Standing toward the front of the room, about twenty-five feet away from the bottom of the dais between two mighty columns, was a virtual entourage of important dignitaries: the high priest in all of his ceremonial garb, the king's chief regent, and the royal scribe, who was carrying the official seal of Castle Dragon, a quill, some ink, and two trundled scrolls, along with three small vials of mysterious liquid, all placed on a velvet-lined tray. Serving the dignitaries were several servants of lesser importance, including Thomas the squire.

"Are you looking at that?" Tatiana whispered, tugging on Mina's hand. "What's on the tray?"

"I have no idea," Mina said somberly, yet her stomach began to churn as she stared harder at the small mysterious vials. Their shape and color were vaguely familiar, reminding her of some-thing she had seen at the Keep: a hand-drawn picture, stuffed inside an ancient tome, about the fertility rites performed at the Autumn Mating. The Sklavos Ahavi were born with a rare gift of fertility, the ability to produce dragon sons for the Realm, but this gift did not blossom unassisted—the females were given a sacred, magical elixir that awakened their reproductive potential for thirty-six hours at the time of their formal mating. And that mysterious potion was stored in bottles that looked an awful lot like the ones sitting on the royal scribe's tray.

Mina shook her head. *Nah, that couldn't be right.* It made no sense. The Realm would soon be under siege; the king was worried about an imminent attack; and his sons were involved in the kingdom's defense—not exactly the right time or place for fertility rites. Mina sighed and dismissed the thought.

"Are those generals?" Tatiana asked, pulling Mina away from her curious, unsettling thoughts.

Mina blinked several times and followed Tatiana's gaze to the center of the hall, where she tried to make sense of the various males in their military regalia. There were humans, warlocks, Malo Clan loyalists, and *shades*, all congregating together, with one important distinction; they were loosely separated into four distinct clusters, each group gathered by a huge jutting column, each column festooned by a familiar district flag: the banner of Castle Umbras; the standard of Warlochia; the pennant of Castle Commons, and of course, the over-arching emblem of Castle Dragon, raised higher than all the others.

"Sweet goddess of mercy," Mina whispered. "They must account for half the warlords in the kingdom." In addition, a host of the king's private guards were milling around the throne room, releasing mysterious latches and tugging on thickly corded ropes. *The king was clearly preparing for battle, and his guards were clearly preparing to open the mighty dome.*

Tatiana fidgeted with her tunic, shifting her weight nervously from one foot to the other. "Are we in real danger, Mina?" She glanced toward the top of the dais. "I mean, beyond the usual, the obvious?"

Before Mina could formulate a reply, Cassidy Bondeville sauntered in their direction, elbowed her way through the crowd, and sidled up to Tatiana's free side. "Afternoon, ladies," she said in her usual haughty tone.

Mina regarded Cassidy sideways, peeking around Tatiana, grateful that she wasn't standing right next to the witch. Trying hard not to roll her eyes at the utterly ridiculous formal gown Cassidy had donned for the somber occasion, she forced an insincere smile. "Hello, Cassidy."

Tatiana nodded her head in kind. "Hi, Cass."

Cassidy curtsied, more likely than not to show off her gown, and gracefully inclined her head. "Any idea what's going on?"

"No," Mina and Tatiana lied in unison.

"Well, whatever it is," Cassidy persisted, utterly unaware, "it must be bigger than life." She shifted her crystal-blue gaze to the top of the dais, quirked her rosy lips into a smile, and feigned like she was going to swoon. "By the gods, those dragons are gorgeous, are they not? Especially Damian, don't you think?"

Mina struggled not to cough, even as Tatiana visibly flinched.

Lord of Agony, Mina thought, *Cassidy is such a clueless dolt.* "Well," Mina whispered, trying to conceal her disdain, "perhaps the gods will smile upon you, and you can have him in the autumn."

Cassidy cocked her shoulder in a dismissive gesture. "Perhaps," she mused. "Although I have to say; I guess it doesn't really matter. I've already fed them all, and while Damian is certainly the most dark and deadly of the three, Drake is far from a pushover. And Dante? Could the Bringer of Rain have created a more fearsome, sexual creature? He makes my knees weak."

Despite her heavy heart and her overburdened mind, something in Mina's stomach tightened as Cassidy's words set her teeth on edge.

Cassidy had already fed them all?

Which meant she had fed Dante, too?

Really?

When?

Why?

She shook her head in disgust.

Who cared…

It wasn't like it really mattered, or that the process didn't still scare Mina senseless. As far as the princes were concerned, all the Ahavi were interchangeable in that regard. They were slaves with a practical purpose, and even if Dante chose Mina at the Autumn Mating—even if the king agreed—that didn't mean he would never feed from another Ahavi. If anything, Mina should be thanking Cassidy for serving Drake and Damian.

The shrill sound of a tubular horn, the bugler calling the gathering to order, brought Mina's attention back to the royal dais. Like everyone else in the hall, she grew instantly quiet as she strained to see the king above the throng. She was prepared to hang on his every word, content to be safely ensconced in a corner, at the back of the room, watching with the rest of the room.

The king wasted no time getting down to business. He stood and cleared his throat. "As all of you have surely heard by now, the kingdom is facing a very grave threat. Not long ago, while manning the watchman's tower, Titus Beckham sighted a distant fleet of Lycanian ships sailing southeasterly toward the port of Dracos Cove. He believes the ships will begin to arrive this night, that all shall arrive by dawn on the morrow, and based on the size of the fleet, the formation of the vessels, and the display of several dark-colored flags, we can safely assume the Lycanians are not coming here to parley or to trade. They are here to invade our realm." He paused to let his words sink in, and then he gestured toward the center of the hall, indicating the myriad of high-ranking soldiers clustered beneath the four district flags. "I have already discussed strategy and defense with my sons and my generals, and we will be dispatching an army from Castle Dragon forthwith"—he held up a finger to emphasize his next point—"but that is not all. By sundown this eve, several militias from the remaining three provinces will make their way to the beach. It is our hope—*it is our conviction*—to contain the shifters when they dock before they have a chance to spread out from the port of entry." His aquamarine eyes flashed red with anger and maybe a bit of angst. "I don't have to tell any of you what would happen to this kingdom should the likes of these immortal shifters spread out like locusts across our land—the devastation would be immeasurable, the loss of life, immense." He pointed toward his chief regent. "I have asked my proxy to join us for one purpose, to reside over matters of court in my absence for the next several days."

The crowd grew enigmatically quiet, waiting for King Demitri to explain. A barely audible growl rose from the dragon's throat, and the rafters above them began to shake as the king stood even taller. "Because of the serious nature of this threat," Demitri continued, "I will not wait until my kingdom is under the sword and ablaze to summon the wrath of the dragon." He spoke over a collective gasp. "This night, as the full moon rises and the ocean tides ebb and flow, I will feed and call forth the primordial beast that guarantees each man, woman, and child in this realm their ultimate protection. And come the break of morn, I will meet our armies and our enemies on the sands of Dracos Cove, and the easterners—should any survive—will write legends about the slaughter."

A chorus of shouts and fearful bellows rose in the hall, even as two armored sentries threw open the massive throne-room doors, and another pair of castle guards began to lead a bedraggled group of prisoners—men, women, and children, all shackled by the wrists, feet, and throat—into the hall. Some were enemies of the state; others had simply failed to pay their taxes; yet others… Mina just couldn't tell.

All were of lowly status, whether commoners, witches, warlocks, or *shades*.

Tatiana squeezed Mina's hand so hard it felt like she might crush her bones. "What's happening?" she asked, her voice growing frantic. "What are they going to do with those people?"

"Mm," Cassidy murmured, before Mina could answer, leaning over to whisper in Tatiana's ear. "Looks like the dragon king's dinner has arrived."

Mina grinded her teeth and whirled around to face the insensitive wench. "Would you shut up, Cassidy!" she snarled. She watched as three familiar Blood Ahavi, women who were not born as Sklavos, nor slated to bear sons for the Realm, raised their chins in misplaced pride and led the haggard bunch toward the throne. The women were all wearing sacrificial garb. "Dearest goddess of sorrow," Mina exhaled.

She was at a complete loss for words.

"What is the king going to do?" Tatiana asked, pressing the subject. She turned toward Cassidy for an answer, evidently uncaring who supplied the information. She just wanted an answer.

"He is going to *feed* his beast, my sister," Cassidy said in a dispassionate voice. "He is going to take their blood, their heat, and their essence until nothing sentient remains. He is going to bleed them dry, the entire lot of them." She shrugged. "How else could he summon a fully formed dragon?"

Mina gulped. She felt sick to her stomach.

"And the Blood Ahavi?" Tatiana said. "They're going willingly? *Why?*"

"What choice do they have?" Mina said.

Cassidy frowned. "Makes that womb of yours—*of ours*—a bit more precious, does it not?"

Mina pressed her hand to her stomach and fought not to puke, and that's when she saw the human male at the end of the line, dressed in prisoner's rags. His legs were hobbled and bleeding. His wrists and his ankles were chained, and his eyes were hauntingly familiar:

Matthias Gentry.

Her childhood friend.

The boy she was supposed to marry before the entire world had flipped on its axis.

"Oh gods," Mina blurted as her vision swam. She stared up at the dais, trying to lock eyes with Dante. He had to do something. About all of it. The feeding, the soon-to-be slaughter, the inevitable war. She knew her thoughts were jumbled, that none of it made sense; after all, what could Dante possibly do to stop it, any of it?

Yet and still, everything inside of her was crying out against the injustice...

And that's when the bugler sounded his horn once more, and the king commanded the court's attention. "Silence!" he bellowed into the clamoring hall. "We are not done with our most important business." And just like that, he had dismissed the presence of the slaves, the meaning of their sacrifice, and the visual reminder of what was to come.

The king ushered his scribe forward, and the young man hurried up the dais with the tray containing the vials, the quill, and the scrolls. Demitri reached for the first of the two cylinders and unfurled the parchment. Without preamble, he began to read. "On this, the twenty-fifth day of May, in the 175th year of the Dragonas' Reign, the season of the diamond king, I Demitri Dragona, one and the same, hereby set forth into law for all perpetuity the following decrees: First, to my eldest son, Dante Dragona, I bequeath the province of Warlochia, the castle, the court, and all the lands therein, and I place him at the head of the Warlochian army to lead his subjects in battle as he sees fit. Effective today, this decree shall supersede the autumn coronation. Second, to my next-eldest son, Damian Dragona, I bequeath the province of Umbras, the castle, the court, and all the lands therein, and I place him at the head of the Umbrasian army to lead his subjects in battle as he sees fit. Effective today, this decree supersedes the autumn coronation."

The king continued to read the proclamation, bequeathing the *commonlands* to Drake, his youngest son, and also placing him at the head of the corresponding army. It was clear to Mina that he wanted each of his sons to have absolute sovereignty for the upcoming battle, and he was willing to circumvent the autumn ceremony in order to make that happen. So what did that mean for them, the Sklavos Ahavi?

As if the king had read her mind, Demitri Dragona stepped forward to the very edge of the dais, his long brocade robe flowing down the top two steps as he scanned the crowd and briefly locked gazes...*with Mina*. Turning back to the general audience, and ignoring the doomed slaves before him, he raised his imperial chin and gestured lavishly with his right hand. "I will not send my sons to war, where they may die at the hands of perilous shifters, without first bestowing upon them their birthright *and* their selected mates, the chosen Sklavos Ahavi. Both their castles and their females are now theirs to claim, and they may take them to the port of Dracos Cove as they see fit. Should the Bringer of Rain choose to claim one—or any—of my children, may He first bless them with a dragon son." He nodded at the scribe, who glanced down at the vials on the velvet-lined tray, and Mina knew—*oh gods, she knew*—they were indeed the fertility sacrament.

The scribe opened the second scroll, which was apparently unmarked, raised a quill, and dipped it in ink, waiting for the king's final proclamation. King Demitri then turned to face his sons and nodded at Drake. "From this day forth, until death shall part them, I bestow upon my youngest son, Drake Dragona, the Sklavos Ahavi known as Tatiana Ward. May she faithfully serve her lord, Castle Commons, and the Realm, and may the gods bless them with many sons."

Tatiana swayed on her feet with relief, and Mina had to reach out to steady her—her own heart was beating like a clay tambour in her chest. *Gods of the underworld*, the princes had not had a chance to petition their father for their chosen mates...

Or had they?

Wavani, the king's witch, had yet to make a recommendation.

Or had she?

Maybe that was good.

Mina held her breath and waited as the scribe finished penning the first matrimonial proclamation, and the king turned his attention to Dante. "From this day forth, until death shall part them, I bestow upon my eldest son, Dante Dragona, the Sklavos Ahavi known as Cassidy Bondeville. May she faithfully serve her lord, Castle Warlochia, and the Realm, and may the gods bless them with many sons."

Mina's face flushed with heat, even as her arms and her legs began to tremble.

Wait…

What had she just heard?

Dante and Cassidy?

No, that couldn't be right.

That wasn't right.

Time seemed to stand still, and everything around her spun in befuddled circles as the king continued to speak: "From this day forth, until death shall part them, I bestow upon my second son, Damian Dragona, the Sklavos Ahavi he has requested, known as Mina Louvet. May she faithfully serve her lord, Castle Umbras, and the Realm, and may the gods bless them with many sons."

Mina's jaw dropped open, but she couldn't form an articulate sound. She stared up at the dais, her gaze desperately seeking Dante's. Was he trying to say something to his father? Was he asking for a private word?

Yes—*yes*—of course he was, and surely the king would hear him out.

There was a short exchange between the two Dragonas, and then King Demitri held up his hand, cutting Dante off, abruptly. The monarch flicked his wrist in sharp dismissal, and that was… that was…what?

The end of it?

No! It couldn't be the end of it.

"Noooooo!" Mina's soul was screaming. "Dante, please… help me."

Nothing was real.

"Be quiet!" A sharp slap. *Cassidy's hand? On the side of Mina's cheek?*

"Mina. *Mina!* Can you hear me?" Tatiana bracing Mina by the shoulders?

"We're wanted on the dais!"

Cassidy, again?

For the life of her, Mina could not make sense of all the random words and sensations, the pain in her face, the pressure on her arms, the words...*the words*...the faraway words.

And Dante?

What just happened?

At someone's insistence Mina took a tentative step forward toward the dais, and then, the next thing she knew, she was lying on the floor, cocooned in darkness.

CHAPTER FIFTEEN

DANTE DRAGONA WAS seething inside, still stunned by the recent proclamations, but he couldn't process it now. He couldn't feel any of it. There just wasn't time. The Warlochian army—*his army*—was marching from the east toward the northern shore, toward the port of Dracos, and he wanted to catch up with them before they got to the sea. While the warlocks and their gargoyle pets might be formidable foes, far more dangerous than their human counterparts, they were still no match for preternatural shifters, for the Lycanians hordes. They would need a dragon by their side, even if Dante couldn't fully shift.

He stormed down the upper hall of Castle Dragon, gathering the last of his important belongings: his heavy lance, his great sword, and a series of strategic maps. As he rounded the hall to descend the grand staircase, he glanced over his shoulder toward Mina's bedchamber and stiffened. Gods, he could still see her beautiful face, the glazed-over tears in her emerald eyes, the shock that widened her pupils, and the trembling in her bottom lip as fear took a firm and inexorable hold on her heart. He could still hear that piteous scream: *"Noooooo! Dante please…help me."* He cringed at the memory. She had cried out in such despair—*in front of the entire castle court.* She had recoiled at the mere thought of being mated to Damian, and her strong, tenacious mind had literally shut down rather than embrace the reality of her fate.

Damian would beat her bloody for the public insult.

A deep, primal snarl rose in Dante's throat, and he clenched his fists at his sides. His father had gone too far—perhaps for all the right reasons, perhaps not—but it just didn't make any sense. Why had King Demitri done it? Why had he chosen Mina for Damian, and Cassidy for Dante; and why had he been so closed off to opinions? Yes, there were much more important matters to attend to, things that couldn't wait, but the king had made the call. He had chosen to conduct a lesser rite of the Autumn Mating, *now.* The least he could've done is hear his sons' opinions.

All his sons' opinions.

"Dante. *Dante!*" Cassidy Bondeville came prancing down the hall, hurrying in his direction, her thick blond hair brushing the tops of her shoulders and swaying like a pendulum in response to her eager motion. "Ah, I'm so glad I caught you, my love."

He planted his feet and squared his shoulders. "My prince," he snarled.

"Excuse me?" she drawled in that infuriating, sugar-sweet voice.

"*My prince,*" he said coolly. "Don't ever call me your love. That is not what we are."

The Ahavi blanched, clearly taken aback by his blunt words. She opened her mouth to protest, but apparently thought better of it. "Oh, yes, of course. Forgive me." She curtsied…perfectly.

"I don't have time for this, Ahavi. What do you want?"

"Cassidy," she said softly, smiling. "You may call me Cassidy."

Dante bristled from head to toe. He took a menacing step in her direction, allowing his dragon to heat the pupils of his eyes, and then he leaned forward. "Think carefully before you *tell me* what to do. What. Do. You. Want?"

Cassidy took one wary look at his glowing eyes and stole a cautious step back. "I...I simply wanted to see you off, and I had hoped"—she bit her bottom lip like a petulant child and tried to bat her bright blue eyes—"I was still hoping you might take me with you to the cove."

Dante was finished with the conversation.

He had not lived 169 years as an immortal dragon to explain himself to a foolish human who wore a ball gown to a war conference, Sklavos Ahavi or not. Ever since that insignificant, regretful night when he had passed her in the hall—the one and only time he had fed from her because he was on his way to spar with Drake and didn't care to bother Mina—Cassidy had acted like she had some clandestine claim on him, like he had some carnal interest in her. She had acted brazenly and wantonly every time she saw him, as if *she* were the monarch and *he* was hers to command...

As if every female in Castle Dragon—*nay, all of the Realm*—was not his to take at will.

He knew he couldn't stand her then, and he couldn't stand her now. As for the fact that she was his mated female, well, he would sort that out later.

Much later.

Perhaps when it was time to procreate.

He turned on his heel and began to descend the staircase, dismissing her with a sidelong glance.

She ran after him.

"Dante. *My prince.*" She caught up to his side and reached out to take his arm.

He spun around and snatched her by the throat, moving so quickly she never saw it coming. He was hardly aware of what he was doing—his dragon was teetering on the edge. "Is this what you want, *Cassidy?*" he snarled, digging his claws into her delicate skin until the tips scored her flesh and her neck trickled with blood. He released his fangs and hissed. "If I bite you, you *won't* enjoy it."

She was no longer his Ahavi.

She was his prey.

"My prince," she whimpered plaintively, her eyes wide with fright. "Forgive me if I've displeased you."

He snorted and fought to release his angry grip. "The sands of port Draco are no place for a woman." He softened his savage tone on purpose, calling back the beast. The scent of her fear was heady; her heart was pounding in her chest; and her blood was swirling like a siren's song in her veins, just calling...calling...calling...

Take me.

Drain me.

End me.

In an effort not to harm her—*not here, not now*—he retracted his claws, grasped her by both arms, and tossed her to the top of the landing, away from his beast and his rage.

She froze, uncertain, as if she had no idea what to do next: Should she run, try once more to appease him, or beg for his mercy? And Dante knew—*oh, great dragons of old, he knew*—if she moved even an inch, he'd strike.

"My prince?" she whispered cautiously.

He cocked his head to the side, pressed his finger to his lips, and growled deep in his throat. "Shh. Don't speak." She scooted backward on her rear, and he held up his hand to stop her. "Don't move."

She froze.

"Good girl," he finally whispered, and then he took a deep, steadying breath. He would unleash his dragon soon enough—on his formidable enemies, the Lycanians. There was no need to attack one piteous, misguided, self-important woman. "Cassidy," he said evenly, finding his voice as a man.

She sniffed. "Yes?" At last, she was completely submissive and without guile.

"Your place is not at Dracos Cove, and it is not by my side. Never by my side. Don't ever test me like that again. You may be mine, but I am not yours. Do you understand the difference?"

As she slowly nodded her head, he wondered at the cruelty of his words: Setting boundaries was one thing—and this female needed it, *badly*—but there was something else inciting him, something just beneath the surface, something larger than one woman's careless behavior. Something—*no, someone*—with hair the color of a raven's wing and eyes the shade of piercing emeralds. Someone whose defiance once infuriated him; whose stubborn, implacable will needed to be broken; someone who hovered on the verge of insanity and the edge of *walking tragedy* because she didn't know how to constrain her heart, to live in the eye of the storm with her gaze fixed on her duty, or to see herself—and her role—as simply one or many threads in a much larger tapestry… someone he could neither love nor let go.

His dragon wanted to roar with defiance: to hunt, maim, and destroy.

Damian might claim her. He might take her, use her, and destroy her. But he would never have her.

He would never own *Mina's* soul.

She had already given it to Dante.

That first day in the courtyard…the night he had given her Raylea's doll…

And yet again today, not less than an hour earlier, when she had cried out *Dante's* name in the throne room before all of Castle Dragon, before Damian and the king.

Yes…

Whether she knew it or not, Mina had ceded her soul to Dante Dragona, despite all of her stubborn will…

Despite all of his perilous warnings to do the opposite.

She had led with her heart, yielded to her emotions, and now she was paying the ultimate price.

Indeed, she had always been a walking tragedy.

*

"Get up!"

A cold splash of water to the face, followed by a boot to the ribs, sent Mina jack-knifing off the floor and scrambling into a seated position.

What?

Where?

Oh gods…

"Get the hell up!" Damian shouted. He sounded insane.

Mina arched her back to appear even taller. "I'm up," she panted, shielding her waist with her hands. *"I'm up."* She glanced anxiously around the room, trying to regain her bearings. *Where was she? What had happened?*

"Well, it's about time," Prince Damian snarled.

What the heck?

Why was she here…in her room…and with Damian of all—

Oh gods…

They were mated.

The king had made the decree in the Great Hall.

"Prince Damian," she whispered, desperate to subdue his anger, hoping to make reparations. "I…I…forgive me. I don't know what to say. How may I serve you? What can I do?"

"I should kill you," he drawled nastily, and then just like that, his voice grew chillingly calm: "Right here. Right now. I should take your life. But I don't have the time."

She looked up into his dark, ominous eyes as he lorded over her with that massive six-foot-four frame and shivered. There was nothing behind those pupils, no soul in their depths, no spark of empathy, just two empty orbs: deep brown, hollow, and demonic.

He meant what he said.

"Shouldn't you be on your way to Port Draco?" she asked, almost wishing he would just get on with it—his fury—and her death.

He grinned like a proverbial cat, toying with its prey. "I should. Yes, I should." He looked around the room and turned his nose up in disgust. "My brother, Prince Drake, is on his way to Castle Commons to meet up with his cavalry and head to the cove with Tatiana. I believe Dante is leaving Cassidy here, but he's probably already on the road." He gestured regally, and then held up his hands. "But me? I'm standing in the bedchamber of a *slave*, trying to awaken the poor swooning wench so we can get on with the business at hand—*the imminent invasion of our lands.*"

Mina sucked in air and tried to avoid direct eye contact.

"A slave," he continued, still speaking in that falsely tranquil, utterly petrifying voice, "one who howled my brother's name in front of all Castle Dragon's courtiers. A *slave* who fainted at the mere thought of being mated to me. A *slave* who begged *Prince Dante* to save her."

Mina shut her eyes. *Goddess of mercy; just get it over with.* "I'm sorry," she whispered. What else could she say?

"You're sorry?" he repeated, the echo coming out as a hiss.

"Yes," she whispered. "I'm so very sorry."

When he didn't respond, she peeked at him through barely raised lids. He was terrifying in his placid fury: On one hand, he was obviously riding a razor's edge, demonstrably unstable, yet his voice remained *so calm*—so entirely controlled—when every pore of his being radiated madness. "If I thought you could still ride a horse, I would break every bone in your body," he purred.

Mina winced, but she didn't reply. When he took a sudden step toward her, she flinched like he had struck her and curled into a ball.

He laughed, a humorless sound, and then he reached into the pocket of his breeches and withdrew a small vial—the fertility elixir from the velvet-lined tray—and snorted. "The high priest administered this to Tatiana and Cassidy, but I guess we'll just have to do it our own way."

This couldn't be happening.

This just wasn't happening.

In a series of long, supple strides, he stepped over to the mantel and smashed the tip of the bottle against the heavy, broad stone, sending tiny shards of glass scattering in all directions, and then he strode back toward Mina, squatted down in front of her, and grasped her harshly by the hair, yanking her head backward. Forcing her mouth open with his fingers, he barked, "Drink this!" And then he poured it into her mouth.

The concoction was bitter, and she had to force her throat to swallow.

When the contents were all gone, he tossed the flask into the fire and strode to the door. "The house servants will pack our trunks and other necessities. As for you: one minute; three items; pack, so we can be on our way."

Mina jumped to her feet, rounded the corner of the bed, and grabbed her woolen satchel from atop a nearby chest. She snatched a heavy cloak for warmth, tucked Raylea's doll into the bottom of the bag, and, for reasons she couldn't comprehend, grabbed an ivory-and-bone hair comb off the dressing table and stuffed it in her pocket. She tried to slink by him as she rushed through the door, but she wasn't that lucky. His heavy, muscular arm came around her, encircling her from behind, and without warning or initiation he tugged her firmly against his chest, bit her in the throat, and began to siphon her essence, taking her warmth and her blood in a furious, continuous gulp. When he had finally had enough—and frost began to form on her skin—he withdrew his painful fangs and blew a thin stream of blue fire over the bite to seal the wound. "Do you speak Lycanian?" he asked, completely out of the blue, spinning her around to face him.

She frowned, needing a moment to collect her wits.

Her mind was hazy, and she felt weak enough to topple over

sideways in the doorway; yet she held herself together, steadied her resolve, and concentrated keenly on his question. "Northern or eastern?" she asked, wanting to answer correctly.

"Either." He shrugged his shoulders with impatience. "Both."

She nodded faintly. "I understand the basic northern dialect, at least well enough to get by, to translate what I'm hearing; but yes, I can speak the eastern tongue fluently."

He seemed to go somewhere else in his mind, mulling over her words. When, at last, he met her gaze again, he was no longer a sadistic animal, but a calculating prince considering the needs of his realm. "Can you decipher and transcribe the syllabary as well?"

Once again, Mina nodded. "Yes."

"Good. Then you may come in handy should we capture any prisoners since I can't be in all places at once." He snorted, apparently satisfied with her answer. "I will let my generals know."

Mina bowed her head and averted her eyes, still trying to maintain her composure and her balance, and that's when he leaned back in the doorway and crossed his arms over his powerful chest. "Look at me," he growled. His voice was no longer placid.

Mina met his heated gaze.

"I am not a merciful dragon, Mina Louvet. I hurt Tatiana because I could, because she was weak and pathetic and easy to hurt, and because it simply felt pleasurable. I killed Pralina because she challenged me—and scratched me—and frankly, I was tired of hearing her voice. And I will make the rest of your life a bitter pill to swallow, one long, monotonous day at a time, because *that* is your lot in life. You will pay dearly for calling my brother's name; you will not go unpunished for embarrassing me in public; and I *will* eventually break you—your stubborn will, your pliant body, and your independent mind. But—*and this is the part you really need to hear*—I will also keep you alive as long as you are useful, as long as you serve the Realm and give me dragon sons. And you will at least be safe from my *corrections* when you're pregnant, so the sooner, the better…for you." He stroked her cheek like a wistful lover, and then he grabbed a fist-ful of her hair. "But know this, *my* Sklavos Ahavi: If you ever defy me again, disobey one of my commands, or even hesitate to do what I say, the moment I say it, I will tear out your throat with my teeth and laugh as you expire, with your spine still dangling in my mouth. Are we clear?"

As an icy breeze of hatred and resentment swirled in Mina's heart, wrapped around her arteries, and calcified to stone, she released every emotion other than determination—and she curtsied.

Yeah, they were clear.

Damian would spend his every waking moment making Mina's life a living hell, and Mina, a commoner, a female, and a lowly slave, would spend every waking hour trying to solve an age-old riddle, one that had baffled the greatest of minds throughout time:

How to slay a dragon.

"We're clear, my prince," she whispered, waiting patiently for the evil fiend to release her hair.

CHAPTER SIXTEEN

KING DEMITRI DRAGONA groaned from the pain in his gut, the fire that was searing his belly like lava, the poison that was scorching his veins. He stared at the rampant carnage before him, surveyed the bloodstained floor of the throne room, and gazed absently into the vacant eyes of the last corpse, the final prisoner he had consumed as a sacrifice.

The boy had been young.

He had been favored by the gods with a thick pelt of wavy blond hair that fell into deep blue eyes, and he had argued for his life like a seasoned counselor, rather than a powerless captive. Yet and still, he had also made a critical mistake, earlier that day: The courageous lad had dared to anger the king's middle son, to trespass onto the grounds of Castle Dragon, uninvited, and to approach a Sklavos Ahavi.

King Demitri frowned, almost feeling sorry for the misguided lad.

Almost.

He stared closer and scowled. The boy's forehead was still drenched with sweat, his divinely appointed crown of hair was now matted and plastered to his temples, and he didn't look peaceful in death.

The king shoved the carcass away.

What did it matter if the youth had died a gruesome death?

So had the three sacrificial Blood Ahavi, who had presented themselves with pride, and they had been beautiful as well. He grimaced, remembering the fiasco. Each girl had ultimately writhed in agony, groaned in delirium, and cursed the very king they served as the dragon had drained every last ounce of their essence and blood.

Still…

So be it.

They were all pawns, each and every one of them, just like the king and his sons, born to serve the greater good of the kingdom. And this day—this fateful May afternoon—would go down in antiquity, along with Demitri's voracious sacrifice, as one of the most pivotal moments in the Realm's glorious history. The defense of the Realm was no small matter. It required a great ransom and a terrible sacrifice. And the courage to see it through required a great and indomitable king, a ruthless servant of the people.

Hell's fire, it was a very simple equation: It required a *dragon* that could shift.

As King Demitri ran his thinning, elongating tongue along the tips of his still-protruding fangs, he struggled to relax his body and welcome the beast that was buried within him, to let the change come naturally. It wasn't as if breaking every bone, transforming every cell, and growing scales, wings, and a massive jagged spine was going to be a walk in the park for him, either.

He groaned with pleasure as the serpent inside him stirred, luxuriating in all the fresh essence, heat, and blood, snarling in anticipation of the upcoming transformation.

Soon.

The change would start soon, any moment now…

And as it transpired, the king would do his best to simply let it happen, to sleep the night away if he could, and arise at dawn as a fearsome, primordial beast. He would take to the skies as a dragon of old, nearly 270 years old, and then he would lay waste to the Lycanian fleet in grand, Dragona fashion. He could only hope that his formidable sons could hold back the shifters until then, fight like the monsters he had made them.

As his eyes rolled back in his head and his skin began to boil, he shrieked to release the pain and welcome the vitality. And then, in the whisper of a moment, just a fleeting breath of time, he thought he saw something move out of the corner of his eye, something—*no, someone*—stirring before him.

But no; that was impossible.

The king had drained them *all*.

He had fed very, *very* well.

Falling to the floor and sprawling on his back, he extended both arms outward, like the wings of an eagle, arched into the pain, and bent his neck until his chin pointed skyward so the vertebrae could stretch. The first spasm hit him, and he began to writhe in pain.

"Come, my beloved dragon...*come*."

*

Matthias Gentry came awake with a shout.

He punched wildly with his arms, kicked violently with his feet, and roared like a lion, an angry, cornered beast, protesting his agony from the very depths of his soul. *Oh, dark lords of the underworld,* he thought. *Make it stop!*

The king had trapped him like an animal, locked his upper torso in what had to be iron-clad arms, and tossed Matthias to the floor as if he were nothing, weightless and unsubstantial, climbing atop him like a scoundrel seeking to deflower a maiden before gnashing his teeth in warning and baring his lethal fangs.

Matthias had taken one hard look into those dark, primordial eyes and panicked. He had bucked like a wild horse; twisted this way and that; and struggled pointlessly to get to his knees—*to somehow crawl away*—before he had slid on the soppy floor and collapsed into a pile of fresh blood and gore, succumbing to the king's superior strength. He had screamed like a child. He had begged for his life. He had argued the merits of his existence, espousing his value to the Realm, and, finally, when all of that had failed, he had prayed to the Giver of Life for a quick and painless death.

The Giver had not answered.

The king had torn into Matthias's throat like it was a succulent piece of meat, slurping on the blood, gnawing on the flesh, worrying the bone—drinking, swallowing, gulping—devouring its very essence…inhaling Matthias's soul.

And the pain—*was there no mercy left in the universe?*—the pain had been unrelenting…unimaginable…impossible to bear. And then, just like that, the throne room had disappeared. The world had gone dark. And Matthias had welcomed peace.

Until now…

Until he came awake with a shout and started punching furiously.

Matthias raked a wild hand, festooned with coiled claws, at the visage of those two demonic orbs, the king's dragon eyes. He slammed his head forward, hoping to strike the king's skull with his own bony brow, and jolted in surprise when he only struck air.

What the hell!?

He tried to land a solid punch.

He tried to knee the monarch in the groin.

He tried to bite him back, as if such a thing were possible, and once again, he came up short. Nothing landed. And nothing connected. Because there was nothing—*and no one*—there.

The room was spinning.

"Are you…still alive?" The youngster's voice came from behind a heavy column, sounding distant, hesitant, and utterly wrought with terror as the nine-year-old scribe seemed to rise from the

ashes of the carnage and tiptoe toward Matthias, still holding his quill in his trembling right hand.

What had the king called the boy earlier?

Oh, yes, Thomas…Thomas something or other.

And he had forced the child to remain in the hall so he could record the names of the dying for posterity's sake. He had forced the young scribe to enumerate the wretched sacrificed souls as they *fed* the dragon, believing their names would one day become folklore, epic legends, intimately associated with a great historic battle, immortalized in the annals of war.

Matthias reeled from the immorality of it all and the desecration before him.

Was he dreaming?

Reliving his death?

He couldn't make sense of anything.

And the pain!

Dear Giver of Life, he just wanted to make it stop!

It had stopped.

The king was no longer before him. The pain was no longer material. And other than the trembling utterances of the young lad with the quill, the throne room was eerily quiet.

Matthias rose to his knees and patted his chest, stunned to find his bare sternum completely unblemished beneath the dried, crusted blood. He reached for his throat to feel for the gashes, and then he stared at the inside of his palms. Everything was normal—beyond normal, really—Matthias felt invincible.

Was he truly…*still*…alive?

The young squire blinked rapidly, swallowed convulsively, and started to pant. "That's, that's, that's just not possible. I saw it. I saw him, the king, he…he ate you."

Matthias rocked back on his heels, and for the first time since he'd—*awakened?*—he scanned the entirety of the macabre hall and began to retch. There were tortured, mangled bodies everywhere, blood as far as the eye could see, and at the bottom of the dais, lying on the floor and writhing in brutal agony, was the king of Castle Dragon undergoing some morbid state of transformation.

Matthias sprang to his feet. "We've gotta get out of here!"

The scribe shook his head furiously and scampered away, ducking behind another column. "You're supposed to be dead," he called from behind the pillar. His voice was hoarse with fear.

Matthias dropped down into a crouch and stared at the youngster. He snorted, snarled, and then swayed to the left. The boy dropped his quill and took off running like a bat out of hell, trying to reach the throne-room doors. At this, Matthias chuckled, deep in his unfamiliar throat. *What in all the worlds was happening?* Was this some kind of supernatural game? Was he caught between dimensions, neither dead, nor alive? Or was he at the gates of the Eternal Realm of Peace—*or the Eternal Realm of Suffering*—no longer a sentient being?

Matthias had no idea who he was or where he was, if anything around him was real. He only knew that he felt all at once glorious, formidable, powerful beyond reason, and as something foreign inside of him stirred—something deep, primordial, and clawing to get out—he began to see the child as prey.

The boy moved so slowly, like a mouse trying to elude a cat.

Matthias could track his every movement, predict the fluctuation of each and every muscle before it flexed or relaxed. Hell, he could hear the boy's frantic heartbeat, measure his every breath. A sudden surge of energy pulsed through Matthias's veins, and he snarled again, much louder this time, preparing to give chase.

In an instant, he was at the throne-room doors and on top of the mouse, pinning him to the floor by the throat...*with his fangs*.

The boy squealed in horror, and Matthias let go.

What was happening!

"Sweet Nuri, you're a dragon," the scribe gasped. "How can that be?"

Matthias shook his head. *What?* He lumbered backward into

a squat, trying to create distance between himself and the scribe, trying to calm his inner...beast?

And then the boy sat upright, an awestruck look in his eyes, and regarded Matthias with reverence. His quivering mouth dropped open, and he stared beyond Matthias's shoulders, toward the dais, and watched the writhing king. "How old are you?" he whispered, barely able to form the words.

Matthias frowned.

"How old?" the boy repeated.

"Twenty summers," Matthias growled.

The boy's face turned ashen and he nodded. "What is your mother's name?"

Matthias had no idea where this was headed, but he didn't have time to play *two dozen questions*. He had to get out of that throne room, away from that crazy king, and hopefully back to the *commonlands*, before the dragon arose.

"Her name!" The boy's voice cracked with insistence.

Matthias turned back to stare at the scribe. "Why are you asking me this?"

The child licked his lips and tried to stop his teeth from chattering. "The king taught me to transpose all the Realm's dialects into the common tongue, using the formal script, and I've been transcribing the historical rolls for two years now. This one time, I came across something I was never meant to see—like a missing page from a scroll or something—it was hidden in the wall of the archives, stuffed between two loose stones."

Matthias frowned, more confused than ever.

The boy shook his head and pressed on. "You don't understand. It was a missing leaf from the record of the Ahavi, the girls taken to the Keep, those who were accepted and those who were rejected. In the original scroll, there was a short entry about a dismissal, not that unusual, except...the witch rarely gets it wrong. Never, really."

Matthias was losing his patience as the child rambled on. What the heck did any of this have to do with him—and his urgent need to get *away* from the king? "What witch? What are you talking about? And what does she never get wrong?" He peered over his shoulder and shuddered. The king was growing scales.

Thomas labored to catch his breath. "I'm sorry. I'm not making any sense, am I?"

"No," Matthias answered bluntly.

"Please…just don't eat me."

Matthias shrank back. *What the hell?* For lack of anything more appropriate to say, he murmured, "I won't."

The boy leaned forward then, taking Matthias's measure from head to toe, staring deep into his troubled eyes. He held his gaze for an extended period of time before coming to a decision, apparently, to trust him. "Let me try again. There was a very beautiful girl from the *commonlands*, from the lower district of Arns, who was taken to the Keep because the king's witch, Wavani, believed she was Ahavi, one who would serve the Realm. At first, Wavani swore she was Sklavos as well, capable of bearing sons with the help of the fertility elixir, but the gate keeper disagreed. So she was brought before the high priest, and ultimately, she was culled from the ranks of the sacred. The priest said she was nothing special." He sighed. "*But*…she spent three days and nights in the castle under the analysis of the king before she was allowed to go home, and the rumors and conflicting accounts abound: Some say the king fed from her just to be sure, to see if he could taste something special in her essence. Others say he took her to his bed to use her because she was so incredibly beautiful. But the missing page from the scroll says the king put the fertility elixir in her tea to see if her scent would change, that he waited three days and nights to be sure, and then he let her go. The truth is: No one really knows for sure if she was truly his mistress or not, but I do know this: There was a special Ahavi—*she was real*—and she would've been here, at Castle Dragon, twenty-one years ago." He stared at Matthias with a shrewd, insinuating gaze. "Like I said before, Wavani the witch has never...*ever*...been wrong. What if the girl was Sklavos, after all? And the king *did* use her as his mistress before he let her go?"

Matthias crossed his arms over his chest, trying to make sense of the whole sordid tale. Despite the boy's obvious conviction, none of it rang true. "And what does that have to do with me?"

The scribe huffed in exasperation, and then he steadied his resolve. "What was your mother's name before she married your father?"

Matthias frowned. "Penelope."

"Penelope *Fairfax*," the child supplied.

Matthias jerked in surprise, growing intensely uneasy. "How did you know that?"

The boy ignored the question. "Is she still alive?"

Matthias shook his head. "No, she died in childbirth."

The boy sighed. "Of course. They can't birth a dragon without the help of a priest."

Matthias snorted, his anger rising in a virulent, ascending wave. "That's impossible!" he insisted, wholly unconcerned that the child was shuffling away. "I am *not* a dragon. As you have already pointed out, I am twenty summers old. I think I would know if I grew scales and breathed fire." He instinctively glanced over his shoulder to check on the king and the looming beast he was becoming. The dragon's scales were now fully formed, and the king's spine had morphed into a tail—but for all intents and purposes, King Demitri seemed to be lost in a trance, cocooned in slumber, suspended in an unconscious state, although he still writhed in unspeakable pain.

As if emboldened by the visage of King Demetri, firmly ensconced in a preternatural shell, the squire found his courage. He raised his chin and puffed out his chest, commanding Matthias's attention. "Ancient Lords of the Sky, Volume Five, Scroll Three: *And the dragons could only beget sons from the wombs of the sacred, and those sons could only become fully animated beasts over time, as the fire cured and ripened through the ages. But the sacred powers that made them immortal; these were gifted from father to son at birth, passed down through the dragon's saliva through the taking of blood and heat. The kiss of a dragon father awakens an immortal son."*

Matthias shifted uneasily, bracing his palms against the ground. *The powers were passed down through saliva, from father to son, through the taking of blood and heat.* He twisted back around in order to survey the horrendous, bloody throne room—*yet again*—and nearly recoiled at what he saw beneath the obvious, outer carnage: King Demitri has shared his saliva with each and every victim. He had taken their essence, their blood, and their heat. Yet Matthias was the only one who had survived…who had somehow arisen from the dead.

He shook his head like a rabid dog, enraged by the very implication.

No!

It simply wasn't true.

Penelope Fairfax was not a Sklavos Ahavi whom his father had mistaken for a common maiden. She had not been the mistress—or the victim—of the king.

His father would have known.

Penelope would have told him.

Matthias's mother—*bless her eternal soul*—was a mere mortal, a commoner, a fragile, unfortunate woman who had died in the prime of her life, unable to bring Matthias into the world because…*because…*

Because why?

As an inexplicable panic swelled inside him, Matthias spun around to face the squire with barely concealed rage. "Don't you ever speak those words again, *not to anyone*, and especially not to me! Rumors belong in taverns, sung by minstrels, or in the company of five-year-old girls as they play with their little dolls, not in the serious discussions that take place among men." His voice grew in proportion to his angst. "I am Matthias Gentry, son of Callum Gentry, a blacksmith and a farmer, and Penelope Fairfax was my father's first and only love. My *human* mother." He stood up abruptly, sidestepped around the squire to reach for the door, and snatched the handle with a trembling fist. "I do not know why *or how* I survived this bloody massacre, but for whatever reason, *I did*. And now? I am free." He wrenched at the large ornate handle, and the whole of the iron broke loose from the door before crumbling inside his palm. "Bloody hell!" he cursed, slamming his fist into the panel. As the thick, sturdy oak exploded upon impact, splintering into a dozen fractured pieces, a conical orange flame shot from Matthias's mouth and singed the remaining layers of fortification, leaving a charred hole in the center of the door.

Thomas stood slowly, cowering beside Matthias. He stared up into the male's angry eyes and pointed at the scorched, missing circle. Taking a cautious step forward, he gently shoved at what remained of the door and pushed it open. "I agree: You need to get out of here. But first, I think you need to see the hidden page for yourself, and then maybe, just maybe, you should read a little bit more about dragons...and find a Blood Ahavi. There are a couple we can trust."

Matthias frowned, still reeling from what had just happened. "Wh...*why*...a Blood Ahavi?"

Thomas squared his shoulders and planted his feet, regarding Matthias gravely. "Because you need to *feed* before you hurt someone."

CHAPTER SEVENTEEN

Dracos Cove

MINA LEANED AGAINST a thick sectional tent-post at the rear of the large provisional shelter and burrowed her bare feet deep into the sands of the beach, offering a heartfelt prayer of thanks to the goddess of mercy: The tent of Umbras was about one mile east of Dracos Cove, and Mina was more grateful than words could express that Damian had chosen to meet with his soldiers immediately upon arriving at the barracks. In fact, she could have fallen to her knees and wept with gratitude at the mere fact that she was finally— well, mostly—alone.

She stared beyond the heavy regal canopy out at the bustling encampment—with all its scurrying soldiers, nervous horses, and crudely erected tents—and endeavored to fix her gaze on the dark blue waters of the northern sea. Indeed, it was as restless as the camp. She dug her toes into the sand, reveling in the feel of the soft, warm granules as they tickled the heel of her foot, and she sighed.

She couldn't believe she was here.

Standing at the back of an enormous, magisterial tent, beneath the flag of Castle Umbras.

As a child, her dreams had been so simple, her desires so easy to define: She had loved to plant tulips in the fall and await their colorful blooms in early spring; she had envisioned getting married one day, perhaps to Matthias Gentry, and filling the chapel with the same lovely flowers that grew in the garden. She had imagined a family and a simple life, and she had cherished her life in Arns with her family. It all seemed like a lifetime ago—just a fanciful childhood story in the pages of an ephemeral book—a fleeting castle built in the sand, washed away by a tide of indifference, by all the cold, lonely years lived at the Keep.

She absently smoothed her skirts as she brought her attention back to the present, swallowed the bitter pill of her new reality, and surveyed the upheaval before her.

Here she was…

Surrounded by shadow-walkers and Umbrasian soldiers, supernatural servants of the Realm, who averted their eyes when she passed by, genuflected when they spoke, and pretended as if her role was something sacred. If she didn't know better, she would almost feel like royalty, someone of great importance and stature.

Oh, but she knew better.

Damian had made her true position crystal clear.

In truth, each and every fighter on the beach was loyal to Prince Damian—and Prince Damian, alone. Their only job was to serve their master, and if their master included his new Sklavos Ahavi in that obligation, then so be it. But make no mistake; they would slay her where she stood if the prince commanded it.

Dismissing the morbid thought, Mina spun around to nod at a maidservant who had been hovering behind her for the last ten minutes, gawking at Mina like she held the secrets of the universe in her eyes, Mina forced a congenial smile. "Daughter, would you mind giving me a little space?" The familial term meant *daughter of the Realm.*

The servant girl curtsied, causing her light brown ringlets to bounce, and took two insignificant steps back, bowing her head in supplication.

Mina bit her tongue—that wasn't exactly what she meant. Shaking her head in frustration, she tried to ignore the servant girl's presence as she bustled around the room, unpacked several items from her trunk, and placed them in a heavy armoire. It was mindless work and a *stupid* necessity—the fact that so many accessories had been brought to the beach and stored in the tent, just a mile away from a bloody battle.

Just the same, she could use the distraction.

She needed a moment to think.

Mina was trying desperately to hold it all together. She wanted to take each and every horrific event, all the madness from the last twelve hours, and lock it away somewhere safe in her mind. She could always retrieve the details later, when she was better equipped to look at it...to think about it...to *feel it.*

Her stomach clenched as her mind failed to obey her directive, as thoughts of Matthias and his hideous death stole into her consciousness like a thief in the night: the fact that he had been sacrificed to such an evil, barbaric king, the fact that he had expired in such a brutal, gruesome way, the fact that he had been captured while trying to bring news of Raylea...to Mina.

Bitter tears stung Mina's eyes as she folded several useless sections of linen, slips to adorn Damian's pillows, into neat little squares and struggled not to imagine what the king had done to Matthias. It was too gruesome to contemplate, too terrible to envision. Yet and still, the pain of it gnawed at her gut, and she knew she could not live with the outcome. Somehow—*some-way*—she had to rescue Raylea. Matthias could not die in vain.

Mina shivered and quickly donned a cloak to stave off the chill. She had no idea how to find Raylea, let alone how to stage a rescue and bring her back home, especially with Damian Dragona standing watch as her new gatekeeper.

Heck, she didn't even know if she would live to see the sunrise.

Flashing back to ten o'clock that morning, she tried to recall every single detail of Matthias's news, to put all the jumbled pieces together in her mind. She envisioned the diagram he had sketched in the dirt and rehashed the various particulars: So Margareta and Raylea had been attacked in Forest Dragon, near Devil's Bend, more than likely by a band of roving slave-traders. The slavers were led by Rafael Bishop, the Warlochian high mage, and they would have taken Raylea to some sort of holding station, perhaps for a couple of days, before traveling west to the shadow lands—*to Umbras*—to sell her to a *shade*. That meant Raylea was being held in Damian's division of the Realm. She was being held in Mina's new territory.

The Sklavos Ahavi clenched and unclenched her fists as her determination grew. A snow-white owl, perched on a nearby post, hooted three times and turned its head in her direction—a significant omen to be sure—but what did it mean? Were the hoots indicative of three major events: Raylea's capture, Matthias's imprisonment, and Mina's ensuing misfortune, being given to Damian as his slave? Or did it refer to the future: three days, three months…three years?

She sighed, having no way of discerning the meaning.

She did not possess the gift of sight.

"Mistress Ahavi." The voice of the maidservant, meek and uncertain, drew Mina away from her contemplation. The girl cleared her throat, wrung her hands together nervously, and clutched at her skirts until her knuckles turned white.

"Dear lords," Mina observed. "What is it?"

The maid licked her lips. "Um, I…forgive me for interrupting your *space*, but I was wondering…well, I was hoping…" Her voice trailed off.

Mina relaxed her shoulders, trying to appear less intimidating. "Yes?"

The girl tugged at her skirts again.

"You're going to worry the thread right out of that fabric if you're not careful," Mina said, trying to relax her. "Please, just take a breath and say what you have to say. I don't bite." Considering the current situation, the fact that they were both standing in the bedchamber of an immortal dragon prince, it was probably the wrong thing to say.

Nonetheless, the maid curtsied with appreciation.

Great Nuri, Mina thought, *she's so nervous.*

"Mistress Mina?"

Mina smiled. At least she was using her name this time. "Yes," she repeated—once again—with inordinate patience.

"May I"—the servant looked away, her nervousness getting the best of her—"May I ask you for a favor?"

Mina frowned. She was hardly in a position to grant well-wishes, let alone favors, to anyone, and she didn't even know this girl. "What kind of favor, child?" She crooked her finger, bidding the girl to come closer, out of the shadows.

The maid reclaimed the two meager steps she had surrendered when Mina had asked her for some space. "Just something... um...I know it isn't proper, but I was just hoping—"

"Out with it," Mina said, hoping her voice did not reflect her growing suspicion.

The girl nodded briskly. "My older sister, Anna; she traveled with the caravan from the *commonlands* to the encampment, and she's staying with other members of our clan. Would you...could you possibly...would you be kind enough to hold her hand? Just for a moment or two." She rushed the last words.

Mina frowned in confusion: *Would she be kind enough to hold the woman's hand?* She shook her head, dismissing the thought—first things first: "The caravan? What do you mean? *What caravan?* Why would commoners travel to this volatile, hazardous cove and place themselves in such grave danger? For what purpose?"

The girl seemed to relax as if she were finally faced with a series of questions she could clearly answer, a subject that didn't make her squirm. "The caravan of merchants and laborers, those who have traveled to the beach to support the soldiers, to feed them, attend to their wounds, build weapons and repair apparatus, those who are here to support the armies and serve the king."

Mina nodded. *Of course.* War was more than a clash of two opposing forces on a particular battlefield. It was a multi-spiked wheel, a burgeoning enterprise, and it required the efforts of many to keep the wheel turning, not just the heroes and warriors who fought on the front lines. "Are there caravans from all the provinces?"

"Yes, mistress," she answered quickly. "All have something to contribute."

Mina bit her bottom lip, deep in thought. "I see. And so your sister—*Anna*—she is part of the convoy from the *commonlands*? What does that have to do with me? And why would she wish to hold my hand?"

The girl shifted her weight nervously from foot to foot before twirling a lock of her light brown hair into what was surely to turn into a knot.

"Please," Mina encouraged, "speak freely. You don't have to be afraid. I would never harm you in any way."

The girl let out an anxious sigh, and then she raised her chin. "My sister Anna has been wed for seven years now to a wonderful man, a shoemaker named Jarett, and he treats her so very well. But…" Her eyes clouded with tears. "She has suffered five horrible miscarriages, and the last one almost took her life. According to the midwives, there is no help for it, nothing they can do. The only cure for her malady is to hold the hand of a sacred, of a Sklavos Ahavi." She genuflected with her hands. "I know it's improper—and I really shouldn't ask—but we just can't bear to see Anna suffer again, and we certainly can't bear to lose her. You see; she's pregnant again."

Mina's heart went out to the poor girl and her family. She knew all too well what it felt like to nearly lose a sister—wasn't that why she was willing to risk her own life and well-being in order to search for Raylea? Although she had no personal belief in the ancient superstition, she understood the power of *belief.* She smiled softly. "What is your name?"

"Jacine."

"Even if I was willing, Jacine, you do understand that it is forbidden for me to interact with any of my lord's subjects, unless he is present, don't you? Outside of our private guards and my personal servants—" She cleared her throat and crossed her hands neatly over her skirts to disguise her fear. "—the prince would be displeased." She didn't say what she really thought: *And when Prince Damian is displeased, bones get crushed, virtue gets taken, and lives no longer have any value. He's a monster.*

The look of instant disappointment and heartfelt desperation that swept over the girl's face made Mina want to cringe. Jacine nodded slowly and swiped at a tear. "I understand," she murmured sadly. "It was a lot for me to ask."

No, Mina thought, *it was brave and kind...and compassionate.*

She was just about to follow up, perhaps offer some words of encouragement, offer to say a prayer on Anna's behalf, when three Umbrasian guards sauntered by, about five yards from the rear of the tent.

"Sir Robert Cross is here at the encampment." One of them spoke to the others in guttural, informal Umbrasian. "He brought the latest...catch."

"One of Rafael Bishop's girls? A slave or a prostitute?"

The crude, stocky guard, the one who had spoken first, cupped his groin and cackled, casting a sidelong glance at Mina and her maidservant. "A fifteen-year-old slave, not as fancy as that one, but fresh from the market."

They all laughed in unison, feeling utterly confident that their words were unintelligible, that neither Mina nor her lowly maidservant could understand a single word they were saying. They couldn't have been more wrong. Mina spoke perfect Umbrasian in all of its bastard forms.

"How much for a virgin?" the third sentry, who was missing half his front teeth, asked.

Mina's ears perked up: So Rafael hired his mercenaries to catch them, various Warlochians probably hid them, and Sir Robert Cross sold them—that was important information. *And Rafael was here, close to the Dracos Cove camp.*

"Depends on whether you want to use or to buy," the first guard answered.

"I heard he sold a ten-year-old virgin from a *commonlands'* farm to Syrileus Cain, just a few weeks back, for a full fifteen coppers. If the untouched babes garner fifteen, she'll probably go for ten." The thickset guard raised his eyebrows in appreciation, and Mina bit back a reflexive gag, keeping her eyes fixed ahead: She pretended to stare at the ocean. She pretended to be utterly oblivious to the vile conversation.

The third soldier snickered and cocked his head in Mina's direction, as if she couldn't read his roguish body language. "Screw the ten-year-old: What would you pay for a turn with that one?"

They all turned in unison toward Mina and looked her up and down, careful to avoid meeting her eyes, and then the first guard shivered as if he had suddenly caught a chill. "Watch your tongue, shadow," he said to the third guard, "before the prince cuts it out. *That one* is off limits."

The toothless idiot picked at his nose and then quickly changed the subject. "So where can we find Sir Robert and *Rafael's*...girls?"

"They're camped on the far western end of the cove, about a mile and a half inland from the beach, on the other side of a dry ravine. All the traveling merchants and laborers are there."

Mina stepped back into the shadows.

So...

Sir Robert Cross had sold a ten-year-old virgin about three weeks ago for fifteen coppers? Could it possibly be her Raylea? She wanted to confront the abhorrent, despicable guards, to demand that all three males drop to their knees, grovel in the dirt, and choke on their apologies; and as Prince Damian's Sklavos Ahavi, she actually had the right to demand just that—though the prince would surely frown upon her slanted abuse of power. Just the same, she needed to be wise. These males, as revolting as they were, were speaking of the illegal slave trade, of *Rafael Bishop's chattel*, and they had clearly named his dealer. If this Sir Robert Cross was the man to trade with, the one paid in exchange for selling *Rafael's* illegal slaves, then one way or another, the bastard would know what became of Raylea, whose possession she ended up in.

Waiting for the soldiers to pass, she spun on her heel and regarded her maidservant squarely. "Jacine, how badly do you want to help your sister?" It was a shameless and selfish tactic, especially in light of the fact that Mina didn't even believe in the midwives' superstition; however, it was clear that the servant girl and her sister, Anna, did. And if Mina was going to risk Damian's wrath by disobeying a fundamental regulation, stepping farther and farther outside the lines of demarcation, chancing the forbidden, then there had better be a worthwhile exchange in the end: a valuable reward to offset the invaluable cost.

A price she may very well pay in blood.

"Excuse me, mistress?" Jacine answered, appearing all at once confused. "I don't understand—"

"You may bring your sister to my chambers, and I *will* take her hand in mine—but there's a price."

The girl visibly wilted as if Mina had just asked her to slay an imperishable monster. She pressed the back of her thumb against her lower lip and bit down on her nail, appearing to absorb the statement. "But of course," she finally mumbled, and then she forced her spine to straighten. "I swear by all the gods of the eternal realms; if we can pay it, we will."

"Not *we*," Mina whispered. *"You."* She gestured toward the maid's shift and her skirt, and then nodded at her shoes. "I want you to switch clothes with me; give me your traveling papers; and then bring me your sister. I will hold her hand as you've asked, and then afterward, the two of you will remain in my bedchamber, sealed off from the rest of the tent. From that moment on, *you* will pretend to be me, whilst your sister will pretend to be your maid. *My maid.* Do you think you can do that?"

Jacine's face turned a ghastly shade of green, even as her slate-gray eyes grew cloudy. "My lord would have my head."

"Yes, he would," Mina said truthfully. "That is, *if* he caught you. If he caught me. But I will only be gone for five or six hours, and he will be fighting long into the night, likely until the early hours of dawn." She steadied her resolve and amplified her persistence. "I know it's risky, and I'm asking a lot—but that is the price. *That*, your secrecy, and the secrecy of your sister. The three of us must take this deception, this temporary ruse, to our graves."

In this callous and shameful moment, Mina hated what she had become. Her palms were beginning to sweat, and her insides were turning to jelly. This was not her way; this was not her character. And yet, what choice did she have? What power did she wield? She was as much a servant and a pawn as Jacine or Anna, and her life was in just as much jeopardy, if not more.

There were all kinds of dangers lurking in the dark between the tent of Umbras and Sir Robert's camp, not the least of which were her master's loyalists, Umbrasian rapists, and Warlochian thieves, the whole depraved lot of them. Suddenly, Prince Dante's words made a whole lot of sense: *We have all made many sacrifices for the Realm, Mina.*

Truer words had never been spoken...

Yet she knew, deep down in her heart, that the sacrifice she was making—the one she was asking—was more for herself than the Realm.

It was for Raylea.

It was for Mina's conscience.

It was far more selfish than she cared to admit.

She crossed her arms over her chest and stared impassively at the trembling girl, all the while feeling increasingly horrid with every second that passed. Just the same, she would not give in. The maid had asked Mina to disobey the prince on behalf of the child's beloved sister, to take a calculated risk on Anna's behalf…

This wasn't that different.

The stakes were just much higher.

When it seemed as if the maid would never answer, Mina cleared her throat and tapped her foot on the floor—*gods help her, she felt like she had turned into Pralina.* "Well, Jacine? I'm waiting. What will it be?"

CHAPTER EIGHTEEN

"WHERE IS DRAKE?" Dante barked, coming face-to-face with Damian for the first time since the fiasco in the throne room. He adjusted his preternatural vision to see his brother's features more clearly in the moonlight.

"So nice of you to show up," Damian grunted. He met Dante's seeking stare with a scowl of his own before whirling around to stand back-to-back with the prince, all the while raising his sword and shield.

"Drake?" Dante repeated, falling easily into step with his brother.

"He hasn't made it to the beach yet," Damian clipped. Since Drake had to travel *to and from* the southernmost district in Dragons Realm, he had a lot further to go.

"So it's just you, me, and our soldiers?" Dante asked.

Damian angled his chin toward the various soldiers who were amassing nearby, adjusting their armor, drawing their swords, and nocking deadly arrows into tautly drawn bows. "Indeed. Two dragons and their faithful minions." Damian turned his attention to the ocean.

The first of five encroaching Lycanian ships had anchored about fifty yards from shore, and the wild, supernatural eastern-ers were not waiting for their companion vessels or the bulk of the remaining fleet, which was still at sea, to attack. At least ten Lycanians leaped from the deck, vaulted into the air, and shape-shifted as they dove, transforming into every manner of predatory fowl: giant hawks, enormous eagles, and huge prehistoric raptors with razor-fine talons and sharply edged beaks. At the same time, another twelve warriors dove into the sea, shifted into sharks, stingrays, and sea snakes, and darted toward the beach. Yet another eight or so males, with caches full of weapons strapped to their backs, remained in human form and jumped into the water before hitching a ride on a fin or a tail, shouting mortal war cries as they rapidly advanced.

Dante squared his shoulders, dropped down into a crouch, and rocked gracefully onto his toes, ready to pounce. Only the gods knew what the pagans would shift into once their bel-lies, feet, or talons made contact with the sands. If there were thirty males on the first vessel, which could easily carry ten to twenty more, then they needed to be ready to ward off up to 230 enemies in this first brazen attack. As it was, Dante could only pray to Nuri, the lord of fire, that the bulk of the fleet would not reach harbor before dawn, and the other four encroaching vessels would take their time anchoring in the bay. While Dante and his brother could see clearly in the dark, the same could not be said for their brave and loyal soldiers.

He could hear the heartbeats of the humans, shadows, and warlocks thundering all around him: swelling, pounding, and beating furiously in their chests. He could smell the acrid tang of the commoners' fear and the Umbrasians' hunger, as well as the sulfuric taint of the Warlochians' magic. All were as smoke, rising from a sodden fire, billowing into the air.

"Air, water, or both?" Dante shouted to Damian, knowing that the soldiers would wisely wait to see what appeared on the beach: The archers would step forward with a frontal assault on the invaders, while the others would form semicircular clusters in defense of their princes, aligning their shields as a wall. The warlocks would cast spells and wield magic, targeting their enemies, one by one, even as the shadows would follow on the warlocks' heels, waiting to devour the weak and absorb their dying souls.

"Both!" Damian snarled, releasing an ear-shattering roar.

It was all Dante needed to hear.

In the breadth of a second, he sprang to his feet and hurled twin bolts of lightning from his fingertips at two massive birds of prey, charring them in the air. He then focused his attention on a gigantic raptor and an enormous eagle, which were coming in low and fast, and seized their wings with telekinesis, crushing the hollow bones. As the wounded creatures plummeted toward the sea, he called his inner dragon and heaved a sweltering breath of fire, incinerating them both as they plunged.

Damian arched his back and stiffened, sending a blazing arc of flames into a narrow channel of the sea in an attempt to boil the water. Dante joined his cause, and together, they burned another seven shifters before the males could reach the shore.

"I hope you fed well, dear brother," Damian snarled, using the full power of his mind to sling a charging shifter backward, spiraling through the air, before impaling him on the mast of the anchored ship. "Father is still eight and a half hours away."

Dante formed an imaginary circle around the skull of a distant invader, and then he began to rotate the palms of his hands in slow, deliberate circles. He continued to twist, turn, and tighten his fist until, at last, the enemy's head imploded, and the Lycanian's corpse slumped to the ground. "Worry about yourself, Prince," he scolded.

And then all hell broke loose.

Predators dipped down from the sky and attacked the soldiers en masse: They gouged out eyes with their talons and severed arteries with their beaks, even as the archers released wild, panicked arrows in a frenzied attempt to drive them back.

The bulk of the arrows missed their targets.

Sharks leaped out of the water, shifting into giant wolves and marauding cats, even as snakes rose up on their tails and began to stalk forward as beasts. Dante and Damian donned their armor, but it wasn't a manmade shield. Rather, they withdrew into their inner dragons and coated their flesh with scales.

"Behind you!" Dante shouted, as a serpent the size of a small windmill coiled behind Damian and drew back to strike.

Dante didn't have time to watch: A raptor swooped down from the sky, slashed him across the cheek with a talon, and then instantly shifted into a primitive beast, some sort of hybrid between a lion and a bear.

Dante released his solid form and lunged at his opponent, passing right through the shifter's torso as if stepping through a wall. He spun around behind him, solidified his hand, and plunged a clawed fist through the creature's back, deftly extracting its heart. He tossed the bloody organ to the side and turned to check on the others' progress.

The prince was still wrestling with the giant serpent, one hand anchored about its upper fangs, another clasped to its lower jaw, and he was about to tear the mouth in two. A pair of warlocks had turned a werewolf into a dog, and they were ripping the snarling creature to shreds. The archers had littered several Lycanians with arrows—three, who had remained in human form—and the shadow-walkers were devouring their souls as they cried out in horror from the pain. Still another soldier had impaled a man-sized cat with his sword; the injury had only managed to anger the beast, and the feline was *this close* to shredding the soldier's throat with its wicked canines.

Dante covered the distance between himself and the soldier in a flash.

He pounced on the werecat's back and sank his own lethal

fangs into its haunches. The cat spun around with a snarl, swiped at the unwanted weight, and thrashed wildly, trying to toss the two-legged rider from its nape. The two clashed like a pair of otherworldly demons, each one vying for supremacy, each one trying to serrate the other's throat. Sand shot into the air; spittle dotted the sands; and blood soaked both fur and flesh, until at last, Dante released his feral bite and scorched the beast with fire, melting away its enormous teeth just moments before they sank home.

Dante tossed the creature to the side and scrambled back to his feet just in the nick of time. The Lycanians had regrouped. Sensing the futility of the battle, they had withdrawn from their individual attacks against the soldiers and were pursuing Prince Damian as one cohesive unit, all ten of the remaining shifters joining forces, ascending from land and descending from air.

The humans, warlocks, and *shades* rushed to Prince Damian's defense. They surrounded the prince and the Lycanians with lances, swords, and clubs, striking and spearing the enemy as best they could, but the battle was moving so swiftly—the supernatural shifters were changing shape and position so rapidly—that it was hard to track the fury of their movement with a naked, mortal eye, let alone in the dark of night.

Damian fell onto his back, and Dante knew it was up to him to intervene.

And quickly.

Not that Damian couldn't hold his own in any position; but hell, no one could ward off ten Lycanians at once—save, perhaps, their father Demitri, in his full primordial form.

Just as Dante began to rush forward, to dive into the fray, the strangest thing began to happen: For reasons he could scarcely explain, he began to see everything in double images. Distant memories flashed before his eyes, exposing painful glimpses of the past, just as current events continued to unfold, revealing the perilous battle before him.

As a husky Lycanian shifted into a wolf and pounced on Damian's chest, Dante saw a flashback of Thomas the squire being bludgeoned with a club—he saw Damian toss the bloody stump into the river, along with the innocent boy, leaving a six-year-old Thomas to drown…

Forcing Dante to dive in and save him.

One of the *commonlands'* soldiers speared the wolf with his lance, even as another two Lycanians, still in human form, retrieved sharp, jagged daggers from wet leather sheaths and lunged in the prince's direction, but Dante couldn't follow the trajectory of the blades. He could only see *Tatiana Ward*—broken, beaten, and terrified—lying on Mina's bed, following Damian's rape.

Right before Drake had healed her.

Prince Damian flung the daggers away using basic telekinesis, and then he flattened his back to the ground and tucked his knees to his chest in an effort to keep the invaders from advancing. A cruel smile distorted the features of one of the two Lycanians, and then it quickly morphed into another insidious grin, far more familiar, yet no less toxic—only, Dante saw Damian Dragona standing in the throne room, choosing Mina's lash. He saw the delight in Damian's eyes at the prospect of Mina's whipping, and he saw the immense pleasure the prince had taken in choosing the most lethal implement he could find.

Damian cried out in surprise.

Someone had just landed a blow, and Dante blinked several times, trying to bring the present scene into focus. Yet all he could see was another place and time, an image of Damian seared into Dante's memory: The merciless prince was standing on Desmond's grave, spitting into the dirt and proclaiming for all the world to hear that Desmond had been "too weak to survive." If Dante hadn't known better, he would have sworn Damian had *celebrated* Desmond's suicide.

Why hadn't he noticed all of this before?
Or had he?

Perhaps he had just buried it, tucked it away like the myriad of shells beneath his feet, hidden in the moonlit sands.

The sands.

Dracos Cove!

The beach!

The battle…

Dante sprang into action, determined to make his way to Damian's side. What difference did it make if his brother was cruel, weak of spirit, or dead of heart?

He was still a dragon prince.

He was still King Demitri's son.

A child conceived in violence, carried in madness, and born of rape—a soulless creature, to be sure, but one whose knowledge, skill, and lineage were very much needed in defense of the Realm.

The grinning Lycanian managed to land another blow, and Damian grunted.

Only Dante heard *Mina* scream…

He heard her plaintive wail in the throne room, just moments after the king had pronounced her fate: "From this day forth, until death shall part them, I bestow upon my second son, Damian Dragona, the Sklavos Ahavi he has requested, known as Mina Louvet."

Why the hell had Damian requested Mina?

As the Lycanians continued to land blow after blow, overwhelming the beleaguered prince, Dante shook it off.

Why didn't matter!

What was done was done.

He was just about to come to his brother's aid when Damian regained his advantage. He drew back both fists, plunged them forward with preternatural speed, and broke through the breastplates of the two attacking Lycanians, seizing their still-beating hearts from their chests and tossing them onto the sands.

Dante didn't wait for the rest to advance.

There were still seven Lycanians left.

He lunged forward, dove into the fray, and in a wild clash of fangs, fire, and claws, he fought like a demon possessed on behalf of his wicked, unredeemable brother. He fought on behalf of the Realm and all its innocent, helpless inhabitants, and he refused to come up for air until Damian was no longer in danger, until *together* they had dispatched the remaining seven barbarians.

Silence settled over the scene like dew on the morning grass as Dante and Damian finally rose—*as one*—to survey the ensuing carnage and enumerate the dead. A trumpet blasted, interrupting their count, and Dante turned to see the third point of the dragons' triangle, his brother, Drake Dragona, riding toward them with his army behind them and his flag before him.

He was just about to step forward and greet him, make some sort of snide remark about being late to the party and riding in like a girl, but there wasn't any time: The remaining four ships had just anchored in the harbor, beating the bulk of the fleet by at least eight hours, and just like before, the Lycanians rushed to attack.

CHAPTER NINETEEN

Five hours later

MINA LOUVET SLIPPED into the shadows beneath
the cover of a thick maple tree, careful to remain
concealed from the radiant moonlight above her. It
had to be at least two or two thirty in the morning; she was weak
and exhausted, in desperate need of sleep; and every muscle in
her body ached to give up and go home.

But she had come too far to turn back now.

Having switched clothes with her maidservant, Jacine; having
waited patiently to meet Jacine's sister, Anna, *and to hold her desperate hand*; having watched the vulgar guards consume enough
spirits to become sufficiently inebriated, Mina had finally donned
a hooded cloak, presented the maid's traveling papers to the main
sentry, and strolled right out of the tent under the guise of fetch-
ing water for her mistress.

None had been the wiser.

Now, after walking westward for an hour beneath the
benevolent cover of darkness; turning inland for another hour,
traversing much rockier and slower terrain; and finally coming

to the narrow, dry ravine that marked the entrance to the traders' camp, she was utterly and completely exhausted as she surveyed the site from the shadows and tried not to collapse.

She pressed her hand to her lower belly and took a deep, fortifying breath—she couldn't give up that easily. Raylea's life might depend upon her perseverance. Fortunately, she had managed to avoid all manner of hazards, pitfalls, and dangerous encounters thus far—*perhaps the gods were with her*—and by the distant, echoing sounds of the battle taking place on the beach, feral roars and snarls, clashing steel and iron, the cries of predators—*birds of prey?*—screeching overhead, and the unmistakable glow of bright orange fire flickering like distant candles in an ominous night sky, she knew the Realm's soldiers would remain busy for some time. No one would be looking for a wayward, wandering maid.

She also knew that the princes were leading the fateful battle: Damian, whom she hated and feared with all her heart; Drake, whom she prayed would keep the commoners safe; and Dante, whom she simply refused to think about, at all.

Until now…

Reaching beneath her cloak to fetch a small piece of dried venison, she chewed it slowly and forced herself to swallow in spite of her queasy stomach. She needed the sustenance. She needed to maintain her strength. Chasing it with a hearty drink of water from a deerskin canteen, she leaned back against the trunk of the tree and finally allowed the forbidden thoughts to creep into her mind:

Dante Dragona, the king's eldest son…

The one who had claimed her the first day she had arrived at Castle Dragon.

The one who had let her go without so much as a serious protest.

As she shuffled to the side to avoid a knobby outgrowth in the bark, she absently placed her foot in an uneven divot and nearly twisted her ankle. "Damnit," she grumbled beneath her breath, looking down at the ground to secure her footing. She was angrier with Dante than she had let on.

Not that it was Dante's fault.

Not that it was anyone's fault, the way things had turned out. But still…

Mina's future was doomed.

Damian would surely break her—body, mind, and soul—if he didn't outright kill her before the month was through; and if knowing that wasn't enough to unsettle her stomach, there was something else disturbing her, too.

Something that tore at her heart.

Something that made her feel uneasy.

She could still see Dante standing in her bedchamber, presenting her with a lopsided doll. She could still envision those haunting eyes, the firm set of his jaw, and the way his broad shoulders enhanced his dominant, implacable frame. She could still hear his deep, throaty drawl echoing in her ears, that first day in the courtyard when she had asked him *why*—why had he requested her company. "Because you are the Sklavos Ahavi I have chosen for my mate…your hair is like mine, as dark as the midnight sky." He had swept his thumb along the side of her jaw. "Your eyes are the color of emeralds, as rare as they are exquisite." He had clasped his hands behind his back and studied her from head to toe, without apology. "You are beautiful," he had whispered, "and our sons will be strong."

Mina shivered at the memory.

She had been so very afraid; yet now, looking back, there was a deep, aching chasm in the center of her chest. *Blessed Nuri, lord of fire, what had she been so afraid of?* Dante was the epitome of justice and benevolence when compared to his brother Damian, who had brutalized and tortured Tatiana without a moment's hesitation. The male didn't have a conscience—he didn't have a soul.

She sighed.

Damian.

Hadn't he already threatened to do the same thing to Mina in so many words?

A bitter tear escaped her eye as she tried to wrap her mind around this vicious twist of fate, as she struggled to make sense of her inexplicable grief, her deep *sense* of loss, when it came to the reality of Damian and the *absence of Dante.* For truth be told: Her sorrow went much deeper than her fear of Damian; it went much deeper than the substitution of one tyrannical master for another. If Mina was being honest—and at this point, *why not?*—then she had to admit that, despite her best attempts to avoid it, despite railing against it, she had somehow become *attached* to Dante Dragona.

On some subtle, hidden level that she couldn't explain, she had come to look forward to those midnight-blue eyes, to watching the dark, haunted soul within gaze back at her with so much passion—*so much hunger*—and she knew that, despite all his warnings, his endless admonitions about service, duty, and obligation, wanting nothing more from her than her obedience, she had still hoped, if not believed, that he would one day grow to love her.

Mina Louvet had fallen for the eldest dragon son without even knowing it.

And while it may not have been love—and it certainly wasn't mutual—the seeds of possibility had been sown.

Trust had not fully blossomed…*yet.*

Honesty was still emerging…*slowly.*

And their tenuous foundation was still so deeply mired in the thorns of fear, inequity, and obligation that it rarely rose to the surface. Yet and still, Dante had somehow stolen her heart.

And now, all of that—whatever had been possible between them—was as dead as the soldiers and Lycanians who were falling on the beach. Like the fleet of unsuspecting vessels still sailing this way, those who would meet the wrath of a dragon with the dawn, Mina's hidden hopes and dreams were as good as dead, soon to be burned to ash.

Two deep, husky voices jolted Mina out of her musings, instantly bringing her ears to attention, her thoughts to the current situation—there were two males crossing the ravine, and they were headed her way, sauntering in the general direction of the maple tree.

Acutely aware of the imminent danger, she quickly scurried behind the trunk, ducked down into a squat, and peeked around the base to watch the men approach. *Blessed Spirit Keepers*, they must have come within seven paces of the tree before stopping, checking their surroundings to make sure they were alone, and then resuming their conversation.

"Ten coppers for the slave," a tall, skinny shadow said, his chapped, reedy lips drawn back in a smile, his nearly translucent skin gleaming pale, due to the hour.

"Exactly ten," the other male replied. This one was clearly a warlock—his dim, witchy eyes gave him away, not to mention the long brown cloak fastened at his neck.

The shadow clapped the Warlochian on the back. "You're a fair man, Sir Robert."

Mina's breath hitched in her throat.

Sir Robert Cross?

Then this was him?

She leaned forward to take a better look, careful not to rustle any leaves on the ground or jostle her canteen, praying that the moonlight wouldn't cast a shadow beyond the tree.

Sir Robert held out his filthy hand and waited patiently as the shadow retrieved a leather purse, counted out ten coppers, and dropped them in his palm.

"When do I get the girl?" the shadow asked.

Mina's ears perked up.

"You will have her soon enough," the warlock answered. "We do have to be a little bit…discreet."

The shadow snarled, clearly disliking the answer. "You wouldn't cheat me, would you?" The warlock's eyes glowed red, and the shadow took a cautious step back, raising one hand in supplication. "No offense intended."

Sir Robert smiled then, his sorcerer's eyes dilating with artificial mirth. "Do think before you speak, Rohan. I would hate to see a pleasant transaction turned into something less civilized." He smirked, and it distorted his already unpleasant features. "Besides, you are this close to having a fresh young bedmate to do with as you please. Why spoil that now?"

Mina's stomach clenched in nauseating awareness: *Great Nuri, these men were foul.*

The shadow gulped and extended his hand, instantly appeased. "Of course, of course," he muttered, nodding his head like a dolt.

The two shook hands and turned to depart, heading back toward the narrow ravine, and Mina's heart nearly jumped out of her chest.

No!

No, no, no, no!

Sir Robert Cross was right there!

Standing directly in front of her.

She couldn't let him vanish.

She had to know what he knew; it might be Raylea's only chance.

Turning the various outcomes over in her head, Mina quickly assessed her options: If she confronted the warlock directly, it would be to her peril. For all intents and purposes, she was a traveling maidservant, a commoner, alone in the forest—she would become Sir Robert's next available slave. If she stayed to the trees and bushes, tried to follow him and listen, she would only make it so far before they approached the hub of the camp, and she would never remain undetected in the midst of so many travelers. If she tried to attack him and restrain him—*well, yeah, that wasn't going to happen*—she would die in some horrific manner, right there beneath the maple tree. And if she somehow got detained, was not able to make it back to the beach before dawn, Damian would discover her hoax, and he would probably have her head.

She didn't know what she had expected when she had set out for the camp. Perhaps she had hoped to stumble across a group of captives; to run into Raylea, herself; or to meet up with a lesser foe or an ally, perhaps a sympathetic human who would discreetly share information or intervene with the slavers on Mina's behalf—pretend to purchase a slave in order to gain information.

None of that mattered now.

This was the fate she'd been handed, and she had to make a choice *right now.*

Recognizing that the only true weapon she really possessed was her identity—she was the Sklavos Ahavi to one of three princes of the Realm, and Sir Robert Cross, as well as the shadow, certainly feared Damian Dragona—she removed the hood from her head, stepped out from behind the tree, and took a confident step forward, ignoring how she really felt. "Greetings from the province of Umbras," she said in perfect Warlochian.

Robert Cross spun swiftly around, and it was immediately evident that he was a sorcerer of tremendous power: His eyes flashed red, his cloak began to float behind his back, and his feet rose several inches off the ground. He was prepared to strike at the intruder.

Mina held up a graceful hand, careful to keep her voice both steady and calm. "You would be wise to think before you act, Warlochian. You don't yet know who I am."

The warlock narrowed his malevolent gaze on Mina, even as the shadow began to slink back into the shade, blending in with his surroundings. *How incredibly creepy*, Mina thought.

"You look like my next twenty coppers," Sir Robert snarled boldly.

Mina's expression darkened with anger. "Well, then you'd better look again." The Warlochian tongue flowed so smoothly from her lips that the mage tilted his head in surprise, leaned forward to angle his ear, and then furrowed his brows, as if he were trying to make out her accent.

"A commoner does not speak with such a fluent tongue." Sir Robert floated back to the ground. "Who are you?"

Mina took three confident strides forward. "I am the mistress of Umbras, the Sklavos Ahavi of your royal prince, Damian Dragona, and I understand that you have my sister."

This caught the warlock off guard. His cocky demeanor lessened and he smoothed his brow as if erasing all hints of emotion. "Yet you speak Warlochian?"

"I speak all your vile tongues," Mina replied, without hesitation. This time, she answered in Umbrasian before repeating the phrase in Warlochian.

Rohan hissed from the shadows in acknowledgment, and Sir Robert nodded his head. "I see." He crossed his arms over his chest and narrowed his already scrutinizing gaze. "And my lord, *the prince of Umbras*, has sent a *woman* to the traders' camp to confront a powerful mage of his *brother's* kingdom…alone? Hmm." He pursed his lips and sneered. "What's wrong with this picture?"

Although she was a bit surprised to hear how fast news from the castle had spread, reaching the major players in the Realm, Mina held her ground. So Sir Robert knew about the provincial assignments already? *Good.* That meant he also knew about the Sklavos Ahavi, who each female had been given to. He knew Mina was telling the truth. "Doesn't matter," she snapped. "Anything and everything could be wrong. I could be acting on my own. I could be a rebel or a recalcitrant mate—'tis really none of your business. But what is truth, and what does matter, are these three simple facts: As the Sklavos Ahavi to the prince of Umbras, you are forbidden to touch me. In fact, you are not even supposed to look into my eyes." She stiffened her spine and raised her voice. "And don't fool yourself into thinking no one's watching; you and I both know it would be a simple task for Wavani the witch to cast a seeing spell in order to find out what happened to Prince Damian's *consort*. Now then, the second fact that should concern you is this: The slave trade is illegal, and your king does not support it, which you already know. So I'm sure he would be quite eager to hear that Sir Robert Cross, a citizen of Warlochia, and Rohan, a disloyal *shade*, exchanged coppers in the forest for the purchase of a fifteen-year-old girl, and at the battle of Dragos Cove, no less, when they were supposed to be serving the Realm. Hmm. I don't believe that is something you would like me to repeat, which brings me to my third and most salient point: You took my sister, and I want her back. We can either make a trade—my sister for my silence—or we can split hairs over the details and both get caught, in which case we all die at the hands of our beloved prince. The choice is yours, and I don't have a lot of time." She tapped her foot on the ground to demonstrate her point.

Sir Robert Cross stirred uneasily, his upper lip twitching with disdain. He opened his mouth to comment, but a horrible snarl brought him up short: a terrible rumbling from within a nearby cluster of bushes, a roar so ferocious that it clapped like thunder, striking terror into the wicked mage's heart…and Mina's, too.

In the blink of an eye, two enormous feline beasts sprang forth from the bushes, their almond-shaped eyes ablaze with fury, their sharp, lethal fangs protruding from their gums like twin polished blades, their saliva-soaked lips twisted back in matching, maniacal snarls.

Lycanians!

Shifters had escaped from the beach.

"*Oh dear goddess of mercy,*" Mina breathed. They had broken through the soldiers' barricades—they had breached the princes' final line of defense.

She spun on her heels to run, her heart thundering in her chest, and everything happened at once: The first beast sprang toward the elusive figure in the shadows, toward Rohan the *shade*, and the second deadly creature sprang at Mina's back.

CHAPTER TWENTY

THE BATTLE AT the beach had waged on for five harrowing hours, leaving a bloody trail of carnage in its wake: humans missing their limbs and heads; shadows deflated into mere husks of their former selves; and warlocks withered from the inside out as their magic consumed their organs at the moment of their deaths.

Dante, Damian, and Drake had fought like wild things alongside their faithful subjects, struggling to keep the Lycanians at bay, desperate to contain them in the cove, needing to buy *just a little more time* until the king's feral dragon could awaken at dawn to destroy the last of the initial invaders as well as the remaining fleet.

The sun typically rose at 6 AM, and by 2:30 AM, the battle had become precarious at best—the ferocious Lycanian beasts had attacked, pursued, and hunted their prey as if they possessed no fear of death. And in a fleeting, chaotic moment, when Dante, Damian, and Drake had been surrounded by the enemy, two feline shifters on the outskirts of the scuffle had bounded away from the beach, scurried into the night, and headed swiftly inland toward the provisional encampments, bent on wholesale slaughter.

And still, there were countless ships sailing their way.

Noticing the breach in the defensive battle line, Damian had called frantically to his brother for help: "Dante! Go after them! Don't let them get away! If they reach the settlements, they'll murder everyone in sight, and other shifters will follow. I'm fine. *We'll be fine!*"

Prince Drake, who had been facing off with a ten-foot serpent, its powerful tail coiled around his legs, had nodded with fury. "Go, Dante. You're faster than me." He hadn't needed to say the rest: *and Damian is better equipped to control our* shades *and* warlocks.

Although Dante hadn't liked the idea of leaving his brothers alone, he'd had no other choice. Damian had been right. If the shifters made it to the temporary encampment—or worse, if they made it to the actual settlements—there would be a night of mourning like nothing the Realm had ever seen. The dead would be too numerous to count.

Hesitating just long enough to see Drake dispatch the serpent, Dante had slowly nodded his head. "Father will be here at dawn," he'd reminded his brothers, as well as the courageous soldiers, and then he'd slipped into the night.

Now, as he broke through a thick patch of brush and entered a small circular clearing, just yards away from the traders' ravine, a shocking and terrifying sight drew his attention away from his quarry.

Mina Louvet!

Damian's Sklavos Ahavi.

Standing beneath the low-hanging branches of a maple tree, wearing a simple, dark brown doublet cross-laced with black threads, over a plain white underskirt, the attire of a houseservant, and she was facing off with a warlock and a *shade.*

What the hell was going on?

"You took my sister, and I want her back. We can either make a trade—my sister for my silence—or we can split hairs over the details and both get caught, in which case, we all die at the hands of our beloved prince. The choice is yours, and I don't have a lot of time." She was nearly trembling with barely leashed rage, yet she held her chin at an authoritative angle and tapped her foot on the ground with impatience. She was clearly desperate and channeling her fear.

Before Dante could make sense of the strange meeting—*how the hell had Mina made it to the traders' camp, and what the heck did she hope to accomplish, other than losing her life?*—the two escaped shifters sprang from behind a nearby bush, one of them lunging toward the shadow, the other charging at Mina.

Dante sprang into action as if he had been born for this moment, careening into the werecat's side and knocking him off target, pitching him away from the Sklavos Ahavi. The cat shifted position in midair, rotated its flexible spine so it could lunge at Dante's throat, and forced them both downward toward the ground. The moment they hit dirt, the shifter sank its lethal fangs deep into Dante's neck and began to tear at his flesh.

Dante stiffened and let out a roar, his inner dragon consumed with rage.

Shocked by the ferocity of his own feral nature, Dante jolted and bucked as a spiked tail shot forth from the base of his spine, crackled through the air like a brandished whip, and wrapped around the shifter's neck with lethal dexterity and ease. Dante tightened his grip on the Lycanian's throat, choked off the beast's air, and yanked the werecat backward with his tail as he dislodged the wicked fangs. Wielding his tail once more, this time as a lever, he coiled it around the werecat's waist, spun him onto his back, and pounced on top of him, glaring into his eyes with a matching bestial stare. He sucked in a deep breath of air and sent it back as a blistering column of fire, scorching the werecat's features from the surface of his face.

Dante's own wounds healed instantly, even as the werecat's skull began to melt.

Yet it wasn't enough.

Not nearly enough…

The beast had to die!

He had threatened the dragon's female.

"*Mine*," Dante snarled in a red delusional haze, and then he dipped his head down to the shifter's chest, released his own lethal fangs, and tore out the Lycanian's heart with his teeth. In the space of a moment, he shot into the air, coiled like a serpent about to strike, and hurled his body at the second Lycanian, who was now devouring the *shade*. With one angry swipe of his claws, Dante punctured the beast from the side, wrapped his fist around the knobby spine, and yanked, removing the vertebrae from the shifter's body.

The Lycanian sank to the ground, eyes still open wide in death, and the dragon whipped his head around in a daze, unconsciously retracting his tail.

Humans were rushing from the encampment, heading toward the fray, gawking in fear and surprise, even as the warlock sidled up behind the female, trying to conceal something in his right hand.

A knife?

Was he going to stab her?

"Go back!" Dante roared at the crowd, his voice bellowing like thunder. "The next human who so much as glances this way goes up in flames!" As the ferocity of his wrath shook the ground, and the crowd took off running in the opposite direction, Dante took three long strides toward the Warlochian, crushed the hand that was holding the blade, and sank his fangs deep into the thick, ridged collarbone, just beneath the warlock's throat.

The dragon's female screamed as he drank, inhaling blood, heat, and essence.

"My prince, please, stop! *Don't kill him.*"

The dragon dismissed her pleas, intent on destroying this *thing* that had dared to threaten what was his.

"Dante!" Her voice was growing louder—*frantic*—more

insistent. "Oh gods, Dante, please. He took Raylea! He has my sister! Or at least he might know where she is. The girl who gave you the doll—*he made her a slave.* If you kill him, I'll never find her. Please, Dante; stop!"

The dragon snarled with displeasure and sucked even harder.

The female groped at his arm. "Oh, my prince, please… *please…please stop.*"

The dragon allowed the prince to listen, but only for a moment, and then he drank even faster.

Raylea.

The little girl with the doll.

The warlock's skin was turning blue, his body beginning to tremble. His flesh was the temperature of ice, and his heartbeat was slowing…diminishing…rapidly shutting down.

He has my sister.

He made her a slave.

If you kill him, I'll never find her.

"Dante, please! *I'm begging you.*" The female was on her knees, yanking on his trousers. She was sobbing in desperation, but the warlock's essence, his terror, and his power—*Great Master of Vengeance and Fire*, it tasted *so good.*

As the body went limp in his arms, and the heart began to stutter, Dante lapped his tongue over the gaping wound and sank his fangs in deeper. He wanted it all. He needed it all. The moment of death would be utter bliss.

And then he felt the female's hand pressed against his chest, quivering over his heart. "If you ever felt anything for me…if *any* part of you ever cared…then I beg of you, my prince, please help me save my sister." She sounded so piteous and forlorn.

As the dragon took one final drugging pull from the warlock's vein, Dante seared his consciousness into the warlock's mind and sucked out his memories, transferring each vile transgression to his own lucid awareness.

The warlock's body froze into a block of ice.

The dragon withdrew its fangs.

And Dante Dragona shoved the corpse forward, watching as it struck the ground with a thud and then splintered into a thousand brittle, irretrievable pieces.

*

Mina gazed at the frozen shards in shock.

Sir Robert Cross was dead, and Dante had killed him.

She would never find Raylea.

She took an unwitting step back, dropped her head in defeat, and let her arms fall to her side, simply trying to come to grips with the gravity of the moment.

Simply trying to reconcile the fact that Raylea was gone... forever.

A deep, angry growl rose in the dragon prince's throat. "*Mina. Louvet. What the hell are you doing here?*"

Her head shot up and she gulped. Dante was staring at her like he had half a mind to drain her dry as well. His mouth was coated in blood; his throat was convulsing with need; and his claws were still extended, adorning hands that were covered in hard leather scales. Yet and still, he looked deathly calm—his eyes were two vacant caverns—tranquil in a way she had never seen him before.

And Dearest Bringer of Rain, the prince had grown a tail!

It was gone now, but still...

She took a second, cautious step backward and screamed as Dante opened his mouth, hurled a sweltering ring of fire in her direction, and caged her within the dancing, circular blaze. Turning to the left and then the right to appraise the fiery fortress, she wrapped her arms around her midriff and trembled. "My prince?" Her voice was a mere whisper of a sound.

He cocked his head to the side like some kind of animal, rather than a man, like he was straining to make sense of her words, like the *human* language was a foreign tongue. "I have no time for your games," he spat in a gruff, guttural clip. "What are you doing here?"

Mina was about to curtsey, but the flames were much too close. Eyeing them through her peripheral vision, she nodded. "No games, milord. Life and death. The warlock that you killed was named Sir Robert Cross. He works for the high mage of Warlochia, Rafael Bishop, and several weeks ago, the day you rode to the district to execute the traitors, their band of slavers attacked my mother and my sister. They took Raylea prisoner and—"

Dante waved his hand through the air to silence her, and she instantly shut up. "I know this," he grunted. "I absorbed his memories."

Mina's mouth dropped open in surprise, and she nearly shuddered with relief...*and hope.* "Just now? Before you killed him?"

Dante nodded coolly.

Her eyes filled with tears and she bit down on her lip. An emotional whimper still escaped, and she clasped her hand over her mouth to contain it. "Thank you," she whispered into her own trembling palm, which was now quivering against her face.

He sighed, seeming to regain his composure. "You came here in the middle of the night, without Prince Damian's permission, to do what? Confront a warlock? Provoke a *shade,* a *soul eater?* For what purpose? To try to somehow rescue your sister?"

Mina gulped, trying to hide her fear. "I know it sounds crazy, but I was desperate. I thought maybe, just maybe, Raylea might be here...in the traders' encampment."

"And you would somehow...what? Just stumble upon her?"

Mina shook her head. "I know it was a long shot, crazy, maybe even suicidal, but so what? What do I have left to live for, anyway? A life with Prince Damian? A life of torture, rape, and humiliation? Yes, Prince Dante, I risked *everything* to come here, including your brother's wrath, which has already been promised to me, for a snowball's chance in a dragon's fire of saving my ten-year-old sister."

She took a cautious step forward, careful to avoid the dancing flames, and raised both hands in supplication. "How far would you have gone to save your twin?" The moment she said it she regretted it. "Oh gods, I'm sorry. I didn't mean that. I—"

Dante waved his hand through the air, extinguishing the fire with a slight and simple gesture, and then he stepped forward into the space where the flames had just been and glided closer to Mina. He moved with the grace of a predatory animal, and he didn't stop coming until his broad, powerful frame towered over hers.

Despite her resolve, Mina took a cautious step back—he was just too intimidating, his supernatural presence completely overwhelming.

"Sweet…rebellious…Mina," he crooned, reaching out to stroke her jaw.

She flinched before settling her nerves and allowing his touch—as if she had a choice.

Tracing her cheek with the pad of his thumb, he whispered, "Raylea is in a cabin in the mountains of Umbras with a shadow named Syrileus Cain. The warlock who made the sale is dead." Before she could speak, he pressed his forefinger over her mouth. "Shh. I will find her, and I will bring her home, return her to your parents. I promise you this." He narrowed his gaze with conviction. "But you; you have to promise me that you won't grow weary of serving the Realm." His eyes scanned her visage as if he were *drinking her in*: first, her dark green eyes, and then, her raven-black hair. And his own sapphire-blue reflection deepened with some emotion that Mina couldn't quite name. "Gods, you are so beautiful," he said. "You always were." The corner of his lips quirked up in the barest hint of a smile. "And smart. And crazy. And stubborn." His smile turned into a frown. "And I do regret, *deeply*, what my father has done, but you cannot take such foolish chances, Mina. Whether he knows it or not, my brother needs your influence. He needs your gifts and your tenacious will. The Realm needs your strength."

Mina's jaw dropped open in surprise, and she quickly pursed her lips to close it: On one hand, she was intimately touched by Prince Dante's words—he had *never* spoken so affectionately, so personally, to her before, as if she were more than a slave—but on the other hand, she was sickened by his conviction, wondering if he even understood…

Damian did not want or need her. In fact, the only thing he desired was the callous use of her womb. And for what noble purpose? To create soulless dragon offspring in his own abhorrent image? To spawn monsters just like him? Children she would neither be allowed to raise nor love? And *gods forgive her*, she didn't think she could if she tried: love them, that is.

As if he had read her mind—and truth be told, he probably had—Dante's expression turned as hard as stone, and he cupped her jaw in his hand. "Mina…" He spoke softly in spite of his stony resolve. "You will love your children. No matter what occurs, no matter how much they resemble Damian, you *will* love them."

She chuckled then, although the sound was absent of mirth. "Will I, my prince?" She shook her head before he could reply. "Regardless, it doesn't matter. I won't have any influence over their upbringing. In fact, I'll be lucky to even survive…to live long enough to have more than one child."

"Then fight for yourself and their future!" he insisted, his vehemence taking her aback. "Just be smart about how you do it. You're resourceful, Mina. You're determined, and you're imaginative. So make yourself indispensable. Fight to stay alive."

Dante's powerful words brushed over her like an unexpected breeze, yet they didn't cool her despondency. She just couldn't see it, imagine it, even conceive of it—finding or making a way, *any way*, in a universe governed by Prince Damian. "You know your brother," she whispered respectfully. "To oppose him, even in the slightest, is to die." She averted her eyes because she really wasn't trying to argue—the truth was simply the truth.

He snorted in defiance. "Really?"

She met his gaze once more and gawked at him, at a complete loss for words.

"Did you not fight for Tatiana?" he asked her, raising his dark, sculpted brows. "Have you not done everything in your power—no matter how limited—to oppose me since the day we first met?"

"That was different," she mumbled.

"Different? *How!*" he exclaimed. His large shoulder muscles contracted, then grew rigid, as he leaned forward, grasped her by both arms, and raised his voice. "Was Tatiana more worthy—am *I* more worthy—than yourself?"

She laughed then, another hollow sound. "I *love* Tatiana!" she argued, feeling her anger start to rise. "It was an instinctive reaction, not well thought out. And I thought I could love"—she caught her words, recoiled in surprise, and immediately changed direction, steadying her voice—"I never opposed you out of disobedience or malice, Prince Dante. *Never.* I was simply trying to understand you, to understand the Realm…and my duty to it. I was simply trying to get along." Her voice softened as her heart joined her words, and both began to flow as one in a pure, unadulterated stream. "I wanted to find my place with you, some place with you—*any place with you*—that was real. I wanted to somehow know you, if only from afar." She rolled her eyes at her own audacity, realizing she was about to purge her soul. "I knew that I was only a slave, your servant, just one of many, but despite that knowledge, despite that certainty, I was still just crazy enough…*stubborn enough*…to believe…*to hope*…that this whole thing"—she swept her arm in a wide arc around them, ignoring his iron touch, indicating the nearby encampment, the broader territory beyond the north, the entire Realm—"that this whole thing would be easier, at least for me, if I could find a way to serve you with my body and my heart, if I could find some way to care for you, even if you couldn't care for me."

She averted her eyes in shame and rushed to spit out her next words before the prince could silence or condemn her. "I know. *I know.* I heard you, each and every time, and you were right all along: Duty, obligation, obedience—that's all there is. You told me and told me, but I refused to listen. I didn't want to hear it—I couldn't accept it—not with the *duty* I was facing; and I'm sorry that it took me so long..." Her voice trailed off as she swiped several angry tears from her eyes and forced herself to meet his penetrating gaze. "But I get it now. I hear it now. I even accept it, but don't ask me to fight for such a meaningless existence anymore. Don't ask me to oppose Damian for the sake of our unborn children. Not now. Not when everything has changed. Not now that you're gone." The last sentence was nothing but a whisper. "Not when I don't have any love or rebellion left."

Dante grew deathly quiet, and time seemed to stand still as he processed her words and studied her features, as he searched for a way to respond. Finally, after several long, tense moments had passed, he cleared his throat. "Earlier, in the throne room, you collapsed before the high priest could administer the sacred rites. Did Damian—"

"Administer the tonic?" she interrupted, knowing exactly what he was referring to. "Did he give me the fertility drug?" She scoffed. "Yeah; he broke the vial over the mantel and shoved the contents down my throat, broken glass be damned. Yes, he *administered* the rites."

Something dangerous and foreboding flashed through Dante's eyes, and then his forehead creased in a deep, brooding frown. "Then he also..." For whatever reason, he couldn't finish the sentence—he couldn't quite muster the words—but Mina caught their implication.

"No," she whispered. "Not yet."

Damian had not raped and impregnated her...yet.

There were still twenty-one hours left inside the thirty-six-hour window when pregnancy was guaranteed by the serum.

Dante nodded, stoically. He ran a taut hand through his

hair and sighed. "You are a woman who is led by her passion, Mina Louvet, a woman who must fight for a cause. And you are the poorest excuse for a slave I have ever seen." He withdrew his hands from her arms and strolled away, pacing around her in what could only be described as predatory circles. "You have given me the courtesy of the truth. Now, I will do the same: In thirty-one years, I will be capable of fully shifting. You already saw what happened with the Lycanian—the change has already begun. And when that day comes, I will be strong enough to challenge my father. My sons will be strong enough to lead this realm at my side."

Mina visibly recoiled at the seditious words. She couldn't help it—it went against years and years of stringent indoctrination—yet she watched him astutely, curiously, as he turned on his heel, stalked directly toward her, and cupped her face in his hands. "Until that day, you *will* love at least one child, and you *will* fight to stay alive."

Mina trembled like a baby bird in the hands of an inquisitive child.

She was emotionally exhausted, physically worn out, and she couldn't track where the prince was going with this line of thought. Did he intend to take control of her mind? To force her to feel something for Damian—*surely not!*—or at least for a future child? "I'm sorry, my prince, I don't understand."

Dante took her hands in his and tightened his grasp, almost painfully, sinking the tips of his fingers, now those of a normal man, deep into her palms. His eyes grew distant, and he bit down hard on his lower lip, drawing a trickle of blood. If Mina hadn't known better, she would have sworn he was wrestling with his own indoctrination, battling some ancient demon, inside. He glanced at the moon, peered at the earth, and then gazed beyond her shoulders, as if seeking guidance from the northern shores. Then just like before, a white owl swooped down, perched atop a low-hanging branch of a tree, and hooted three times, revealing a mystical sign.

Dante must have understood it because his eyes grew all at once clear, and he met her seeking gaze with a look of absolute certainty. "You *will* fight for me. You *will* fight for the Realm. And you *will* fight for your unborn son because the child will not be Damian's—he will be mine."

CHAPTER TWENTY-ONE

MINA GASPED IN alarm, even as Dante swept her up by the waist, carried her into the thick of the trees, and dropped to his knees with Mina still in his arms, effortlessly laying her down along a soft patch of grass. "My prince!" she protested, trembling from head to toe as he crouched above her with fierce glowing eyes.

There wasn't a question in Mina's mind that Dante had made a decision, that the *prince* was asserting his privilege, or that the *dragon* was now in control. It was evident in Dante's regal but ruthless posture, his gentle yet possessive grasp, his determined and hungry gaze. There would be no dissuading him from his chosen path.

Yet and still, she had to try.

What he was suggesting was beyond dangerous or improper. It was betrayal at its worst, adultery at the least, illegal, no matter how one turned it over. "My prince, we can't," she repeated the objection.

He snarled, flashing the barest hint of fangs. His eyes swept lower, beneath the neckline of her cross-laced doublet, and his hand instinctively followed, his finger trailing a provocative line between her breasts.

She snatched at his wrist. "Stop," she panted, truly beginning to panic.

"Shh," he uttered, dipping down to brush her lips with his. The contact was fire and ice, sweltering heat and arctic cold, creating a shocking sensation of alarming intrigue, and despite her fervent protests, Mina's head began to spin.

"My prince!"

"Look at me," he commanded in a deep, raspy voice, arching forward to rest the bulk of his weight on his powerful arms while he gazed into her eyes beneath sultry, hooded lids. "Tell me what you see."

Mina blinked rapidly, trying to bring things into focus, trying to clear her befuddled mind...trying to still her racing heart. His onyx hair was disheveled and unruly, falling forward into his stunning, mystical eyes; his sculpted lips were full and parted, just barely, adding interest to his regal mouth, and *blessed goddess of mercy*, his chiseled, commanding frame—that rock-hard chest and those strapping shoulders—were practically trembling beneath his effort to restrain his passion. He was darkness and light; stealth and grace; beauty and anguish, all intertwined.

He was the most magnificent being Mina had ever seen, and his countenance—his otherworldly dragon's aura—swirled around them like an elemental coronet of light, bathing her body, her mind, and her soul in his primordial heat. "I see...I see..." *The only male she would ever love.* "I don't see anything."

"It's in your eyes, sweet Mina," he rasped. "You are already mine." He bent to brush his lips against hers a second time, and her stomach clenched in response. It was as if he truly did own her—and not as a slave or a citizen of the Realm—but as an intimate extension of his own primal body: like she was made by him, *of him*...for him.

No...no....no.

This wasn't right.

It couldn't be.

He pressed a firm, languorous hand over the expanse of her chest and splayed his fingers over the region of her heart before he deftly began to unlace her bodice. And his touch was pure, unadulterated magic.

Mina gulped.

Oh dear lords, he probably *was* using magic—*literal magic.*

She shivered beneath his tantalizing caress, and tried to grasp his wrists. "My prince!"

"My Ahavi," he mimicked with a satirical smile, pushing her hands aside. "Don't you see?" His voice lost all traces of satire, becoming all at once deep, resonant, and serious. "The Realm is bleeding." He dipped down to taste her throat, swirling his tongue over the tiny punctures he had just made with his fangs. "Our enemies are attacking." He lapped up the slight trickle of blood and groaned into her throat. "And my brothers are fighting alone." He made a seal over the wound, healed it with cooling fire, and lavished her neck with a passion so intense it made her shudder. "Yet I am here with you. *With you.* Submit to me, Mina. We don't have much time."

She mumbled something incoherent, shivering beneath his expert ministrations, before trying again. "Your father would—"

"*What?*" he drawled lazily. "Scold me? Kill me? My father will never know." He cupped her face in his hands and wedged his hips to hers, making it abundantly clear that he was more than ready to consummate their union.

"But Prince Damian, he would—"

"Damian must never know." He tapped her lightly on the tip of the nose, making sure he had her attention, while roguishly stressing his point.

"But, won't he be able to tell? I mean—"

"Not this early. Not if I mask my scent." He drew a slow, tantalizing outline along her upper lip with his tongue before nipping her gently on the bottom lip and then following the love-bite with a beguiling kiss.

She sighed in pleasure, losing herself to his undeniable appeal, unable to restrain her involuntary reactions to his magnetic charm. And then the reality of what was about to happen if he continued—*what she would be helpless to resist if he continued*—finally got the best of her, and she shoved at his chest. *"My prince..."* Helpless tears escaped her eyes, and she struggled to hold them at bay. "Dante...*please.*"

In a moment of unexpected tenderness, Dante pulled away, and to Mina's complete surprise, he shifted his weight to the side, sat up abruptly, and leaned back against a nearby tree. Before she could react, he pulled her into his arms, tugged her back against his chest, and sheltered her between his powerful thighs, nuzzling his chin in her hair. "Mina, my darling; you are trembling. You want this with every fiber of your being, yet you are utterly terrified." He pressed a soft, almost chaste kiss against the crown of her head and sighed. "That is not what I want."

Mina could not have been more stunned if he had slapped her. Who was this gentle dragon? This fearsome, all-powerful being who tempered passion with empathy and desire with... *respect*?

Despite the fact that the Sklavos Ahavi were considered special—*sacred*—they were still slaves, property of the Realm, and Prince Dante was free to take what he wanted, despite the dire repercussions. Realizing that her actions were also a blatant act of disobedience, she murmured an apology, and then she began to sob as all the pressure and angst of the past few days rose like a tide, surged to the surface, and spilled out in waves.

"Don't be," he whispered. "Just let me hold you."

Mina swam in a sea of disbelief as her tears continued to fall, as this utterly unimaginable, wholly incomprehensible moment continued to play out. It was as if the world as she knew it was no longer on fire; the Realm was no longer under attack; and her terrifying obligation to the kingdom—and to Damian—was no longer looming larger than life. For one blessed, indescribable moment, Mina Louvet felt safe. She *almost* felt free. Dante Dragona, one of the most powerful creatures she had ever known, was *holding her*, protecting her, cherishing her as if she were actually precious in some intangible way—as if the two of them had all the time in the world to linger together, when she knew it wasn't true.

Finally, when her tears were all spent, Mina cleared her throat and whispered, "My prince, I can't...I don't..." Her voice trailed off, and she tried again: "Why are you doing this...*for me?*"

Dante drew in a long, labored breath, and she felt the weight of the world shift upon his shoulders like golden coins upon a scale, being lifted, recounted, and then scrutinized again. "You and I are not so unalike," he said softly, his sincerity taking her aback. "We are both beholden to our duty, creatures molded by our pasts, and equally determined to find some meaning, some honor, no matter how insignificant or small, in this perilous world we live in. Would it be so wrong if, just this once, we lived in the moment...for ourselves?"

Mina's breath caught in her throat as she struggled to make sense of his words: How could Dante bedding Mina—and giving her a child to pass off as Damian's—equate to a moment for themselves? True, she would have a son to cherish, but she would also have a volatile and explosive secret to carry to her grave. "And you possessing me...taking me...forcing me to submit...that would be a moment of our own?"

"No," Dante said harshly, "*that* would be an abomination. But Mina..." He ran his fingers through her hair, weaving the pads in and out of the thick raven strands. "Has it not been your desire since the day we first met for me to simply treasure you, just once, to show you true affection?"

Her heart tightened in her chest, and she felt her tears return. "But you don't love me, my prince, and that's just it."

Dante sighed in frustration. "Oh, sweet Mina." He breathed softly, pausing for several interminable heartbeats. "I cannot afford to love. I hardly know what love is. As a child, I loved my father, and he beat it out of me. As a youth, I loved my mother, and she turned her back on me out of favor for Damian. As a brother, I loved my twin, and he hung that love in a tree because his heart belonged to a mortal woman. And through it all, I learned that love makes one weak. I learned to be strong, and I vowed not to love *anyone*...ever again." He rested his hands on her shoulders and pulled her more tightly against him before wrapping his arms firmly around her chest. "You, with all your fire and passion and noble ideas, are only beginning to learn the lessons that I've learned. Your heart bleeds for Tatiana, for your sister, and now for the injustice of your fate, and yet, you still love." He nuzzled the nape of her neck, deeply inhaling her scent. "Oh, sweet Mina, if I could've loved any, I would've chosen you: your fire, your beauty, your strength. And had my father given you to me—*as I desired*—I would've held you in high regard as much as any dragon can. I would've shown you pleasure and rewarded your obedience. I would've given you the Realm on a silver platter to make your obeisance easier. And yet, it would not have been enough, not for your sensitive soul. And now...now you have Damian, a terrible cross to bear, and what little I can offer you, I still wish to give: a child of your own, another soul to love that is worthy of your passion, and maybe, just maybe, you can give the babe what I no longer possess, a heart that isn't dead."

Mina closed her eyes, letting all she had heard sink in. "My prince," she finally said, "to me, that is so very sad."

He smiled, and she knew this because she felt his lips curl against her hair. "Perhaps. Perhaps not. Do you know what I think is sad?"

She shook her head and waited.

"That you can't see this rare, invaluable moment for what it truly is, for what it can be."

"And what is that?" she asked.

"A frozen moment in time. A chance—*just one chance*—for two souls who owe everything, yet control nothing, to have something to call their own: a memory they will never forget. A chance for two servants, who have never had a choice, to finally choose for themselves."

Mina glanced over her shoulder to gaze into the prince's eyes—she was desperate to read his expression—and when their eyes met, his were soft with compassion, uncharacteristically *alive*. They were filled with conviction, and he seemed to be searching her very soul with his gaze. Through quivering lips, she mouthed the words: *What would we be choosing?*

He smiled at her, and his features became resplendent. "Eyes the color of emeralds," he said. "A heart that can still love. I would be choosing *you*, Mina Louvet, over my father, over my brother, over my duty...if only for a night, an hour, a frozen moment in time. I would be choosing you."

Mina closed her eyes and basked in the warmth of Dante's soothing words. She took them in and buried them deep in her heart, someplace sacred, private, and untouched, where she could find them—and retrieve them later—to be used as a balm for her troubled soul. His undivided attention was rejuvenating, like water flowing through a barren desert after years of an aching drought, and she couldn't absorb enough. His strength surrounded her. His voice appeased her. And his certainty cast away all doubts...

Yet she knew she wanted more, needed so much more.

If only for a frozen moment in time.

So what if it didn't last forever?

So what if it wasn't true love?

What could be truer than this exquisite, candid moment? Then the fact that Dante had promised to save Raylea; that he had spoken honestly to Mina, from his heart; that he had offered to give her a child to love...

The ultimate defiance of Damian.

Rocking forward to break free from his embrace, Mina turned around and knelt between his legs. Biting her bottom lip in a cautious, nervous gesture, she, once again, sought his penetrating gaze. "I have to pretend I love you," she whispered, her own eyes brimming with tears. *"I have to."*

"Shh," he whispered, placing two firm fingers against her quivering lips. "Then don't pretend, sweet Mina. *Don't pretend.*"

Her mouth fell open in surprise, and he claimed the offering with an ardent kiss. As his arms snaked around her waist, he pulled her to him, shimmied away from the tree, and reclined on the soft green grass, settling Mina on top of him.

"Dante." She breathed the startled word into his mouth as he fisted his hand in her hair. Although she froze for a moment, she didn't object, and he immediately deepened the kiss, caging her between his powerful, possessive arms.

She moaned in contentment, and he began to explore her body with his confident hands: first, her back, then her shoulders, then her arms; next, her waist, then her hips, and her thighs; finally, her buttocks, then her stomach…and her breasts. His exploration was both gentle and strong; his mouth was both hungry and sweet; his body was equal parts dominant and acquiescent—taking, giving, exchanging—until she found herself virtually groping at his masculine form, stunned by the strength of her need.

Sensing her growing desire, he growled in her ear, rolled them both over, and pinned her beneath him.

Mine. He mouthed the word, and Mina shuddered.

Tugging at the laces of her bodice, he at last freed her breasts and drew a taut pink areola deep into the cavern of his mouth, where he began to suckle, taste, and tease, tantalizing each and every nerve she possessed with the skill of a philanderer and the mastery of a god.

The heel of his hand found her heat, and he rotated it in

maddening circles, causing her to cry out in astonishment, shock, and awe. She writhed beneath him and arched her back in offering: *Sweet goddess of mercy*, the dragon had set her on fire, and he'd yet to breathe a single flame.

"*Oh, gods, Dante...*" She let the cry of passion slip, and the entreaty called his beast. His eyes flamed red; his head fell back; and his manhood jerked against her stomach, growing massive and engorged. Before she could react to the strange sensation, he was bunching up her skirts, tugging at the ties of his breeches, and sliding out of his trousers.

She blinked three times, and her undergarments were being tossed to the ground, even as he rose above her and locked his gaze with hers. "Mine," he growled again, sending her entire body up in flames. "I want to hear you say it."

Mina gasped in fear and anticipation as he rocked forward, positioned his hips between her thighs, and nestled the head of his desire against her core. She panted, trying to keep from groaning, and her eyes latched onto his, like a moth to a flame.

"Say it." He froze: waiting…watching…trembling with need.

"Yours," she whispered softly, and from the very depths of her heart, she meant what she said.

A wisp of smoke wafted from his nostrils, and he looked positively magnificent in his raw, primal need, cloaked in pure, primordial hunger. And then to her stark surprise and wonder, a pair of pitch-black leathery wings punched through his back, enfolded her in a midnight embrace, a satin cocoon, and he thrust his powerful hips forward, making them one.

With patience and adept perception, Dante led her beyond the pain, taking her to new heights and sensations, until at last, they rose together to the Land of Enchantment, climbing greater and greater peaks until they hurtled over the edge—*together*—and slowly drifted back to the Dragons Realm.

PART THREE:
DRAGONS LAIR

"Unless a serpent devour a serpent it will not become a dragon.
Unless one power absorb another, it will not become great."

~ PROVERBS QUOTES

CHAPTER TWENTY-TWO

IT WAS AROUND five AM when Mina thanked the trader-camp guards for their escort, ducked into the tent of Umbras, and quickly hurried to her bedchamber. It had been a simple and effortless feat for Dante to enter the traders' minds, convince them that the Sklavos Ahavi from Umbras had been sleep-walking in the night, and compel them to return her safely—*and quickly*—to the tent of Umbras, where she would remain securely tucked away until the end of the battle. They had even traveled by horseback in order to make up for lost time.

A sly smile tugged at the corners of Mina's mouth, and she pursed her lips to keep it from showing: While the story may have been implausible—in fact, it was a bit ludicrous to believe a sleeping woman could've traveled such a distance—mind control was an amazing thing. The three traders had bought Dante's lie hook, line, and sinker; and in their conviction, they had convinced Damian's guards of the same, using a very persuasive argument. It didn't hurt matters *at all* that the Umbrasian guards were terrified of Damian. In fact, they had been so horrified upon learning that their mistress had slipped away into the night, so fearful of

Prince Damian's reprisal, that they were more than eager to settle the entire affair, swiftly, and in secrecy, without ever alerting their prince. Now, as Mina dismissed her maidservant and her pregnant sister, Anna, she truly only wanted one thing…

Sleep.

She was mentally exhausted and physically spent, completely overwhelmed by an inner cauldron of conflicting emotions, and totally drained by the gravity of what had transpired between her and Dante. She absently pressed her hand to her lower belly and shivered, heading toward her bed…toward *Damian's bed.*

She shook her head to dismiss the morose thought.

She would think about that later.

Dimming the wick on the lantern atop the bedside table, she crawled beneath the covers, snuggled against the soft feather-stuffed pillow, and was just about to close her eyes when she saw something move in the shadows, a figure, crouched low, behind a heavy wooden trunk.

She gasped and sat up straight.

The guards knew better than to enter her chamber without first announcing their presence.

"Who's there?" she called into the darkness, and just like before, the faint hooting of an owl echoed three times outside the apron of the tent, and the hairs stood up on the back of her neck.

Three owls.

Three appearances.

Three omens?

First, when she realized that Raylea was in Umbras; then, when Dante decided to give her a child; and now…*what?*

The lean, preadolescent figure of a young boy hastened forward, scurrying from behind the trunk like a startled mouse. "It's just me, mistress. Thomas. Thomas the squire."

Mina rubbed her eyes, reached for the lantern to turn up the wick, and strained to get a closer look. "Thomas?" She pulled the covers up to her chin. "Whatever are you doing here?"

The youngster sighed. "Apologies, mistress Ahavi. I...I have...news."

Mina slid from beneath the sheets, tucked her toes into a pair of waiting slippers, and donned a nearby robe. She stood anxiously at the side of the bed. "What kind of news?"

Thomas averted his eyes. "It might be easier to just show you." With that, he waved his hand toward the deepest pocket of shadows, a triangular cavity behind a heavy armoire, and a tall, familiar form stepped out.

Mina jolted. "Matthias!" At first, she could hardly believe her eyes, but after scrutinizing the male a half-dozen times—his wavy blond hair fastened in a leather thong; his lean but muscular frame, carried with informal confidence; his deep blue eyes sparkling in the lantern light—she knew without a doubt it was her dear friend and childhood playmate, Matthias Gentry.

But how?

"Dearest goddess of mercy," she mumbled absently, "is it really you?" She brought her hand up to her mouth. "I thought you were dead. I thought the king...executed you."

Matthias stepped further into the heart of the light and nodded his head. "He did," he said in a calm, steady voice. "But...I didn't stay dead."

Mina shivered. She padded to the edge of the bed, wrapped her trembling arms around his shoulders, and hugged him with all of her might. And then, as a sudden wave of dizziness came over her, she sat down on the edge of the mattress and just stared blankly ahead, her mouth gaping open in shock.

Matthias smiled. "I assume, because you are a Sklavos Ahavi, you were taught everything of import at the Keep?" Mina nodded warily, and Matthias continued. "So you must know that when a dragon is born, his father *awakens* his powers through the exchange of saliva and blood—it is called the dragons' kiss—and it is in that moment that he becomes an immortal being."

Mina cocked her head to the side in confusion, much like a

bewildered canine, and stared blankly at Matthias, waiting for his words to make sense.

"King Demitri *fed* from all the prisoners. He drained us as he executed us, consuming the core of our essence, and it destroyed everyone…but me." He let out a slow, deliberate breath, waiting for her to fully comprehend his words.

Comprehension didn't come.

Mina looked quizzically at Thomas, and then she cocked her eyebrows, feeling more than just a little sense of dread. "I don't understand," she whispered, still trying to process the cryptic words. "Why didn't it destroy you?"

Thomas the squire cleared his throat and dove into the conversation with blunt objectivity. "Because Matthias is the king's own son."

Mina swayed backward, catching herself on the bed with both arms anchored like tent spikes behind her. She pushed forward again and cocked her head to the other side. "Come again?"

This time, Matthias spoke plainly. "King Demitri is my father."

She wet her lips with her tongue and furrowed her brow. "You're…Demitri's son?" she echoed, nodding her head dumbly as if she were willing to play along for a time. "But…how can that be? I mean, I've known you all my life. You're the child of Penelope Fairfax and Callum Gentry—I know your father, and the two of you walk…and talk…alike."

Matthias sighed, understanding. "That may be true. After all, he raised me, but my mother was already pregnant when my father married her." He began to share the story about the lost Sklavos Ahavi, explaining how the beautiful young maiden became a subject of controversy between the high priest, the witch, and the king. He went on to describe Penelope's time at Castle Dragon, the scrutiny she was under for three days and nights, and why they suspected King Demitri of taking her as a lover, how she had ultimately escaped…or the king had let her go.

And then he waited quietly for Mina's reply.

Mina let out a nervous chortle, feeling like a fool. She was still having trouble making sense of the truth. "I'm sorry," she explained, "but it's just...I've known you all my life. You are a gifted hunter and a skilled fighter, to be sure, but a dragon? Matthias, I've never seen you say or do anything that might imply—"

Just then, the boy she had known all of her life stepped back from the edge of the bed, held out his hands, turned them palms up, and began to extend his claws, ten perfectly serrated talons. He sniffed in defiance, and a faint hint of smoke filled the room, even as his deep blue eyes began to glow a dark, fiery red. And then he retracted his claws, released a cavernous breath, and watched as a small orange flame trailed in the wake of his exhalation.

Mina gasped. She opened her mouth to speak, and then closed it, completely at a loss for words.

And that's when Thomas the squire stepped in. "Mistress Ahavi, we need your help." He glanced at Matthias and inclined his head. "We need your protection. If the king finds out...if he notices Matthias's body missing, he might put two and two together. At the least, he'll hunt him down and kill him."

Mina practically recoiled—at both the danger and the request. "My protection?" she scoffed, not meaning any disrespect. "You want some kind of protection *from me*?" Her heart sank as she reached out to take Matthias by the hand. "I have no power in Dragons Realm. None, whatsoever. In fact, I am hardly safe myself." She turned to regard the squire directly. "And you of all people should know this. I belong to Damian now—do you remember what happened to Tatiana?"

The boy nodded. "I do. Of course, I do. But I also have eyes, and I know that someone healed her." He began to fidget with his hands, for the first time showing his youth. "I know that the eldest prince favors you, Prince Dante. And I also know that Mistress Cassidy cannot be trusted, but perhaps if you appealed directly—"

Mina held out her hand to silence him.

This was a dangerous game they were playing.

All of them.

And the stakes had just grown higher.

How would she get to Dante...*again*? When? Where? And what would she tell him?

What could she tell him?

And why would he be inclined to help a half-brother—a bastard son of the king—whom his father would likely detest?

Dante also had a precarious role to play in the Realm, more so now than ever, and all of them were balancing on a razor's edge.

She unwittingly placed her hand on her stomach and sighed. "I don't understand what you think I can do...or say," she argued, feeling her heart constrict at the untrue words, "but even if I did, why would Dante get involved?"

The squire lowered his lashes and averted his eyes, glancing at the floor. "Because...because he is my friend."

Mina leaned forward with expectation, even as Matthias regarded Thomas sideways.

"Explain," Mina prompted. She didn't mean to sound so abrupt, but the three of them were literally playing with fire, and if there were any unknown or pertinent details, then she needed to know them all.

The squire raised his chin and drew back his shoulders, as if donning a cloak made of manufactured pride; he swallowed something akin to fear—*or maybe shame?*—and then he began to speak in a soft, rote manner, almost as if he were reciting from a scroll. "Many years ago, when I was only six summers old, the king asked me to accompany him and his sons on a pheasant-hunting trip—they were to practice their archery, and I was to carry their bows, their arrows, and his ale." He shrugged. "I can't explain it: the king enjoys his petty tortures, mocking those he thinks are weak."

Mina started to squirm, and she had to force herself to sit still.

At six years old?

Thomas clenched and relaxed his fists in a barely noticeable effort to control his emotions and pressed on. "Anyhow, we walked many miles into the woods, and needless to say, I grew tired, too tired. The weight of all that gear was just…too much." He gulped several times, and Mina wanted to say something to comfort him, but she restrained the impulse, held her tongue, and remained deathly quiet, instead. "We came to a fairly deep stream, and the king commanded me to get the princes a drink of water and him some ale, but he wouldn't let me set the hunting gear down." He bit his lower lip, and his eyes clouded with moisture, but other than that, he showed little emotion. "I dropped Prince Damian's bow, and it broke—so the king told Damian to teach me a lesson." The squire could no longer look Mina or Matthias in the eyes, and he slowly turned away. "I thought he would beat me with the bow, but he found a piece of wood, like a club, and he just…he wouldn't stop until I was nearly unconscious." He smiled then, and it was the most incongruent, paradoxical grin Mina had ever seen. "But he didn't stop there. He tossed me in the river, and I was too badly injured to swim. I would've drowned, but Prince Dante dove in and saved me." A single tear escaped his eye, and he brushed it away with an angry swipe, clearly upset that he had let it fall. "I don't remember anything else that happened that day; except, I learned later on that the king was so enraged that he broke both of Dante's arms, and then he made him carry me—and all the equipment—back to the castle. And apparently, Dante did it without a single whimper."

Mina brought both hands to her face and cupped them over her mouth, trying to choke back a sob—that was the last thing this brave little squire wanted or deserved—and she wasn't about to diminish his courage with pity. Still, she knew there was something else churning in her gut, something she could no longer deny: She was both grateful *for* and proud *of* the new life she was carrying inside her. And she would cherish this child with all of her heart, almost as much as she would delight in defying the king and Damian. Thomas had been an innocent, helpless little boy, and Dante, well, he had been a lion. A brave and defiant dragon.

He still was…

He still was.

"So, you see…" Thomas's words snapped her out of her musings. "Prince Dante has always been more than my lord. To me, he is a friend, and he knows that he has my undying loyalty… even unto death."

Mina sat taller. She stiffened her spine and nodded her head, even as her heart still wept from the story. "I see," she mumbled softly. She was just about to add that she would do whatever she could to help both Thomas and Matthias, even if it meant trying to talk to Dante, when a gale-force wind swept through the barracks, battered the posts beneath the high arches, and sent the heavy armoire sliding three feet back. A sound, so furious and ferocious that it pierced the ears, rocked the ground beneath them, and she jumped up from the bed. "What was that!" she cried as a chorus of voices began to rise outside on the beach: *The king! The king! The dragon is coming!*

Thomas instinctively ducked. "The battle!" He turned to Matthias. "Quickly! Put on your hood and cloak." And then he turned toward Mina, his eyes wide with fright and more than just a little bit of wonder. "It's the beating of the dragon's wings!" he exclaimed. "The king is finally here!"

*

Mina, Matthias, and Thomas bounded outside the tent and began to run along the beach in the direction of the cove, in the direction of the crowd, toward the apex of the battle. The Umbrasian soldiers either didn't notice or they didn't care—such was the commotion and the obsession with glimpsing the primordial creature in the sky. Every soul on or near the beach, every subject present from the Realm—man, woman, or child; slave, servant, or free—had only one objective in that moment: to catch a glimpse, no matter how distant, of the mighty primordial dragon as he slayed the Lycanian fleet.

The air bristled with power and crackled with fear as Mina and her companions finally rounded the corner and caught their first real glimpse of the primary cove. There were Lycanian ships filling the harbor as far as the eye could see, dozens upon dozens of massive vessels unloading their deadly cargo, and even as the hand-to-hand combat continued on the sands, the air began to crackle with thunder.

And then the entire cove grew as dark as midnight.

It was as if the sky, the emerging sun, and the stars from the previous night had suddenly been snuffed out. The pitch-black shadow descended like a vulture, a living nightmare, gathering, intensifying, and spreading out with a sudden, ominous flair, the dragon's enormous wings appearing as the absence of light.

And then, out of the cryptic darkness came an utter explosion of fire. Blistering columns of flame abruptly illuminated the beach, hurtling in all four directions at once, ascending and dipping, above and below. The massive beast struck with such amazing precision—he flung dazzling spirals of heat with such remarkable accuracy—that it appeared as if the Master of Vengeance, the lord of fire himself, had unleashed ten thousand flaming arrows upon the sands.

Shifters of all shapes and sizes dropped to the ground, melting into steaming piles of ash, even as their opponents remained untouched, standing upright beside them; and ships the size of grand, multilevel houses erupted into flames, their terrified, panicked cargo leaping into the boiling, turbulent waters, screaming in agonizing pain.

The dragon didn't stop there.

He circled like a buzzard, soaring, sweeping, dipping one leathery wing down in order to bat the other, the force of the ensuing wind sending each adjacent ship crashing into nearby rocks. Those who tried to escape were seized in the creature's talons, all four legs working in perfect accord to annihilate, crush, and tear the dragon's prey to shreds.

Mina shrieked as the pale green dragon spun his head to the side in a wild, serpentine motion, opened his mighty jaws, and tossed half a dozen Lycanians into his mouth with his hind claws, catching them in his venomous, serrated teeth.

The monster snarled as he ripped them into slivers, his jagged, uneven fangs gleaming in the preternatural light; his terrible arced horn pointing downward toward a waterlogged ship; his flared ears, like the armored horns of a devil, creating a triangular compass pointing *true north* toward his next Lycanian meal.

When the dragon struck the target, the carnage was too horrible to behold, and Mina finally turned away, but not before the image of severed limbs, detached heads, and flaming torsos was seared into her memory forever.

Blessed Nuri, Creator of Fire and Life; was this what she carried in her belly?

Was this what Dante would one day become?

And *if and when* he challenged his father, what would such a battle look like?

Dearest goddess of mercy, King Demitri was truly a deity on Earth, and this was indeed the *Dragons Realm*. It had been this way since time immemorial, and so it would always be…

Always.

Suddenly, Mina felt so insignificant, as if seeing herself for the first time as a single, fragile thread in a much, *much* larger web. Dante had been right all along: She understood "nothing of the politics, dangers, or dynamics" that motivated the monarchy, the concerns that superseded the value of *any* one life.

She scanned the sands all around her, hoping to check on her friends, and her heart nearly seized in her chest: Matthias was bent over in agony, rocking on all fours, his spine twisting this way and that as if it had a mind of its own. He was panting loudly, and his features were contorted with both menace and pain.

He hardly looked human.

"Matthias," she whispered, falling to the ground and reaching for his shoulders.

He snarled like a wild beast. "Too close," he rasped. "Too close to my father."

Mina slowly backed away. Turning to Thomas, she held up both hands in confusion and concern. "What do we do?"

The squire frowned. He pointed westward and raised his brows. "He's too new to his beast, too unfamiliar with the energy. We need to get him out of here, quickly. We need to head inland before the battle is over, before anyone sees him, before they know he's still alive."

Mina swallowed her initial protest. Of course Matthias would need to flee, but where would he go? How would he live—especially now that he knew he was truly a Dragona? She nodded, acknowledging his words. "By *we*, you mean—"

"Matthias and I," Thomas replied. "I need to get him home to the lower district where he can calm down, settle in, and begin to learn more about who and what he is. Where he can start to make the adjustment, whatever that ends up being." He glanced around the beach nervously, eyeing the devastation. "The cleanup may take weeks, and the organization will be chaotic. In a few days' time, when things have settled down, I'll return to Warlochia and try to speak with Prince Dante. No one will miss me before then." He sighed. "If you get a chance to speak to him before me, try… Otherwise, unless you hear from one of us, you need to return to your tent, and *we* need to get away."

The dragon king roared an ear-piercing bellow, shaking the land below as he shot into the sky like a comet spiraling backward, twisted his nimble body in midair, flipping his spiked tail like a whip, and dove toward another cluster of vessels in order to make another lethal pass.

Mina shivered. "Go." She stared at Matthias, and her heart nearly broke for him. "Matt, will you be all right?"

Her childhood friend shook from head to toe, trying to control the unfamiliar convulsions that were wracking his body with relentless frequency. He opened his mouth to speak, and a dollop of sweltering drool ran down from the corner of his lips. He had no idea how to control his inner beast. She could only pray that Dante's friendship with Thomas was as solid, deep, and binding as the squire had said—that the dragon prince would listen to the story, take mercy on his afflicted half-brother, and somehow agree to help.

Either way, she would not be party to the outcome.

She would be in Umbras with Damian.

As Thomas helped Matthias to his feet, Mina offered a silent prayer to the gods, begging them for her friend's protection: *Blessed deity of light, bringer of rain, lord of rebirth, I beseech you for protection and mercy. Go with the squire and Matthias. May their travels be swift; may their hearts be strong; may their path be illuminated by your wisdom. Keep and protect their innocent souls even as you grant me the courage to endure the path I must travel. Protect me from Damian...*

She paused and bit her lip.

At least long enough for Dante's child to be born.

She glanced up at the sky and took one last look at the fearsome, murderous dragon.

Somehow, some way, restore justice to this realm.

With that, Mina turned on her heel, headed in the direction of the Umbrasian tent, and refused to look back.

It was all in the hands of the gods now: what happened to Matthias, what happened to the squire, what became of Mina and her unborn child. The web was truly too intricate to unravel; the stakes for each and every soul too high to calculate or conceive; the depth of intervention needed on the Realm's behalf beyond the power of mere mortals.

CHAPTER TWENTY-THREE

DANTE DRAGONA DID not join his brothers and his soldiers on the beach in order to watch his father annihilate their enemy. He knew all too well what was taking place—*exactly what was transpiring*—the death and destruction; the fire and the fury; the enormous loss of life.

And somehow, he simply had no desire to see it firsthand.

Now, as he stood alone in the tent of Warlochia, his heart was heavy with awareness, thick with the gravity of the situation, burdened with the knowledge of what he had just done with Mina Louvet...

What he had just done to his brother...

What he had just done to the Realm.

Betrayal was betrayal after all, even if he had no regrets.

He splashed a handful of cool water from a tin basin over his face and stared into the looking glass, a flat piece of polished bronze, hung circuitous at an angle above a rough wooden pedestal, and then he jolted, overturning the basin, as he hastily jumped back.

Great lords of fire!

For the briefest moment, the reflection cast back at him from the mirror did not contain the midnight-blue irises he had come to expect, nor the strong, polished features that branded him as his father's son, but a huge leathery dragon with pointed horns, jagged teeth, and *three* fiery glowing eyes: *Dante's eyes*. The beast was positively enormous, surrounded by a radiant purple light, and behind the dragon's crest, just above and beyond the top of its head, was a shimmering image, a profile in silhouette, the likeness of Dante's brother *Desmond*. And it hovered within the bronze, staring out at Dante like a ghost from the past, seeking his attention; searing daggers into his soul; commanding his immediate consideration.

Dante turned away from the mirror and shook his head abruptly.

He was desperate to expunge the vision, yet it wouldn't go away.

When, at last, he glanced at his reflection a second time, the likeness of his brother sharpened, came more fully into focus, and Desmond locked his gaze with Dante's in a severe, unblinking stare. *"Behold, the greatest king to ever rule the Realm."* He spoke with the dragon's voice, and Dante practically quaked in his boots.

An enormous crown, inlayed with precious jewels and rare exquisite etchings, began to rotate in soft, luminescent circles above the dragon's head. It was strangely akin to a halo or a mystical aura, and it drew attention to the dragon's *third eye* in a way that could only be described as a focused beacon of light, a supernatural allegory for the dragon's second sight…

For Dante's second sight.

Desmond spoke again. *"Just as the apex of a triangle sits like a king on a throne, supported by two sides and one base, so shall the greatest ruler of this realm be made wise and strong by the three legs that will support his foundation."*

Like a sudden gust of tumultuous wind, clouds gathering before a storm, three distinct masculine figures swept across the screen—two of them flanked the mighty dragon with the crown, one on his left and one on his right, and the third knelt at the serpent's feet.

Dante's mouth fell open as he stared at the masculine personas—three strong, healthy lads—and while their age was impossible to determine, each one possessed an unmistakable regal bearing, the countenance of a prince; and each one, *to a lad*, had deep green eyes, the color of...*Mina Louvet's*.

The storm passed as quickly as it had mounted; the children were simply gone; and Desmond spoke again: *"Three children. Three decades. Three acts of deception—three betrayals. The prophecy has already begun. Do what you must to strengthen the Realm; seek justice, morality, and peace; obey our father in the light of day, but rise to your calling in the dark of night."* Before Dante could speak or react, Desmond whispered, *"Brother, you are never alone."*

Then, in the blink of an eye, the apparition was gone.

Dante took three generous steps back from the mirror.

He brushed his hands over his face and shivered, recalling each and every word from the vision, committing both the verses and the visage to memory, memorializing the dragon's eyes.

And he knew—*he just did*—exactly what it meant.

The dragon in the glass was his future self, and he would one day be king of the Realm. He would, indeed, usurp his father: not Damian, not Drake, but him. He would rise to power in a sudden surge, like the swell of a rapid storm, and the winds that would carry him to greatness would not be his determination, backed by the fealty of his two brothers, but the loyalty and strength of his sons, of children he had yet to sire, children born of *Mina's* womb.

Suddenly, the tryst near the traders' encampment took on a whole new meaning, and his choice to deceive his brother seemed less like a betrayal and more like a ploy, like his destiny unfolding...for a reason. Yet he also intrinsically knew that the shift in power would be subtle and unassuming, until the day of reckoning came. He would have to keep this omen and his intentions hidden, carefully concealed; he would have to make sure that the storm lay dormant for the next thirty-one years, until such time as he was able to fully shift.

He would have to be impeccable in his actions and his words.

Dante stiffened, understanding for perhaps the first time in his life what he was truly meant to do, both what and *who* he was fated to become: a dragon that ruled the Realm with smoke and fire; subtlety and strength; deception and morality.

He would have to be oh so very careful.

He would have to be cunning and deliberate.

And he would have to be as ruthless as he was patient.

For the good of the Realm, Dante Dragona would have to appease his father, continue his preassigned role, and bide his time; and somehow—*someway*—he would have to gain favor with *Mina Louvet*, for her involvement, secrecy, and complicity were integral to his success.

As hard as it was to believe, *Dante needed Mina.*

CHAPTER TWENTY-FOUR

DAMIAN DRAGONA EMERGED on the eastern side of the narrow ravine, about a mile inland from Dracos Cove, just before twilight. He was careful to remain on the distant outskirts of the traders' encampment, lest there be too many inquisitive ears and watchful eyes nearby, eager to witness his presence. He immediately scanned the dimly lit area for any hint of danger, an unknown enemy, or a member of the king's court who had managed to follow him into the interior. He had prearranged the meeting weeks ago with Thaon Percy, a heretofore enemy who was now an unlikely ally and cohort, a barbaric shifter, and the *rightful king of the Lycanians*.

He ran a splayed hand through his thick golden hair, readjusted the leather thong, and sighed as he kicked a dead squirrel out of his path and took a seat on a nearby hollowed-out log, waiting for Thaon to arrive. He and the crafty Lycanian had planned the entire conflict beautifully. They had done what needed to be done. And while many innocent players had lost their lives, and many more would carry permanent scars and injuries for the rest of their days, the cost and the collateral damage were miniscule when one considered the enormous payoff to the Realm, the gigantic leap forward that would be made on behalf of *all* its citizens.

For as long as Damian could remember, the Lycanians had bested the Umbrasians, Warlochians, and commoners in all manner of commerce and trade. Their fabrics were more refined; their engineering was more advanced; and their art was more valuable and exquisite. It made no sense to continue trading for goods and commodities the Realm could potentially produce for itself. Why limit the internal revenue and economic potential to restricted, local commerce and ever-increasing taxes when there was an entire world of export just waiting to be had? Why constrain one's labor force to narrow, antiquated districts; archaic, secluded villages; and proscribed but specialized merchants when the kingdom could bring in labor from other lands, enslave foreigners from other states, and revolutionize a whole new brand of industry, simply by taking a courageous step forward, by forging a lasting and mutually beneficial alliance with their oldest and most formidable enemy, the Lycanians?

Thaon had seen the vast potential when he had reached out to Damian over two years ago, asking the prince for an audience, and Damian had seen it too, the moment the wily shifter had described his ultimate vision: The Dragons Realm was rich in natural resources and ripe with raw, untapped power. It was teeming with magical inhabitants and imbued with preternatural strength, but the world beyond the Realm was so much larger, so much more expansive, than King Demitri understood. And that was the Realm's critical weakness. An alliance between the two most powerful species on the face of the earth—the dragons and the shifters—would not only be unstoppable, it would herald the beginning of a golden age, a time of absolute prosperity, influence, and dominion…at least for the powerful.

For the mighty.

For Damian Dragona and Thaon Percy, a shifter who was

as eager to usurp his brother, Bayard, as the rightful monarch of Lycania as Damian was to one day rule Castle Dragon in the place of King Demitri.

And so the two had plotted, schemed, and prearranged: Thaon had promised Prince Damian 1,000 years of peace, 100 seaworthy vessels that could be used to conquer and trade, and to openly share the lucrative, time-tested methods of Lycanian weaving, engineering, and artistry—with all the inhabitants of the Realm—in exchange for the indefinite military might and backing of a primordial dragon. True, it would be another fifty-one years before the two could fully seal their deal or cement their pact, before Damian could fully shift into a wholly formed dragon, but time was of little consequence to such long-lived beings. If Damian would promise to help place Thaon on the Lycanian throne—*right now*—to one day accompany the Lycanian fleet on slave raids and invasions, and to back Thaon's rule with his own indestructible might, that would be enough.

And so, together, the two had hatched a plot to overthrow King Bayard in one swift and definitive blow. They had agreed to stage an epic battle on the sands of Dracos Cove, a battle that would result in catastrophic losses for the Lycanian troops and invaders. They had convinced King Bayard that the Lycanians had an inside ally, a traitor, residing in Castle Dragon, who was intimately close to the king and only too willing to betray him, a rebel confederate who would insure the Lycanians' success. Furthermore, they had convinced King Bayard that the rebel had sworn to drug, shackle, and confine the powerful monarch from May 24th to May 29th, thus preventing the king from shifting for the duration of the invasion, for the entirety of the battle; and Prince Damian had demonstrated this traitor's ability to bypass the king and access the castle's resources by shipping one crate full of silver and gold coins, as well as a dozen illegal slaves, to Lycania, every other week for six months.

Convinced that King Demitri would be drugged, indisposed,

and shackled at the time of the incursion, King Bayard had commanded the invasion, sent his best ships and troops to the sands of the cove; and arrogantly awaited word of the destruction and booty.

Needless to say, things had not gone as the Lycanian king had planned. He had unwittingly led his armies to a wholesale slaughter, and the miscalculation would soon cost him his throne...if not his very life.

Now, as Damian waited to confer with his cohort, he couldn't help but smile at the stunning success of the plot. The shifters had taken the bait, and King Demitri had massacred the entire Lycanian fleet with the ease and alacrity of a giant dispatching a newborn kitten. Thaon would undoubtedly be named king in the weeks that followed, and Damian would one day be known as the greatest ruler—*the most powerful dragon*—to ever oversee the Realm. In a curious shift of fate, he would come to be known as the dragon who brought ultimate prosperity and progress to an antiquated land. All that remained to be done was to see Thaon safely home before Damian's father or his brothers discovered his nefarious role in the bloody, pre-orchestrated battle.

"Beautiful day for a devastating defeat." A gruff, menacing voice pierced the silence as Thaon Percy appeared, all at once, as if out of a mist, and sauntered up to the log.

Damian stiffened and stood up. "Indeed, my clever friend. *Indeed*."

"I'm glad to see you made it out of the scuffle alive."

Damian sneered. "Scuffle...*whatever*. It was a bit of a challenge for a few hours, followed by a blanket slaughter." He smiled. "And you, of course, hid out quietly—*and safely*—in our own traders' encampment, masquerading as a common human citizen of Dragons Realm." He waved his hand in silent dismissal of the menial topic and immediately turned to more important matters: *the victory*. "So how many Lycanian lives were lost, my good friend? Two thousand? Three? Great Master of Vengeance, it was a brutal massacre, was it not?"

Thaon grew uncharacteristically quiet, undoubtedly reflecting on the terrible carnage and the piteous loss of life. "Too many, my ally." He sighed. "But all necessary for the future we seek." He drew back his shoulders and raised his chin in proud defiance. "And what about on your side? How many loyal subjects of Castle Dragon were ushered into the Eternal Realm of Peace—or the Eternal Realm of Suffering—as the case may have been?"

Damian frowned, refusing to answer the question, refusing to give Thaon the slightest satisfaction in knowing his side had taken lives—it was of no matter, *whatsoever*, the unfortunate loss of life. In fact, all things considered, it had been a meager price to pay for an immeasurable gain. It was simply something that needed to be done. As it stood, King Bayard had made a grievous error; his reign as the monarch of Lycania was over; and now it was time to embrace the future. He winked at Thaon in a slightly derisive gesture. "You needn't worry about the Realm, my friend. Trust me; I have matters well in hand." A sly smile curved along his outer lips, and he raised his brows. "In fact, we were able to contain a potential *mishap* when two of your comrades broke through our lines and headed inland. My brother dispatched them as easily as my father dispatched our foes." He gesticulated impishly. "Well, Castle Dragon's foes—you and I understand that we are *all* mutual friends."

Thaon bristled at Prince Damian's cavalier words as well as the sparsely veiled superiority. "Your *brother* dispatched them?"

Damian nodded, unbothered. "Indeed."

"Prince Drake or Prince Dante?"

This time, Damian sneered. "What difference does it make?"

The Lycanian shrugged. "None, I suppose. Just curious." He crossed his arms over his chest, looked off into the distance, and squinted. "Hmm."

Damian didn't appreciate Thaon's tone. He didn't like the

curious look on his face or his subtle, self-satisfied demeanor. If they were to be allies—*and without question, they were*—then a bit of rival banter was fine, harmless and expected between powerful males—after all, they had been enemies for years—but *serious* disrespect of *any* kind? Well, that would not be tolerated, not in Dragons Realm. "Yes, my friend: *Prince Dante* dispatched the shifters. Does that satisfy your curiosity?"

Thaon turned his attention back to Damian, this time, biting his bottom lip and shifting his weight from one foot to the other, as if he was avoiding...something. "Then you've spoken to your brother, recently?" he asked.

Damian crooked his head to the side and unwittingly cracked his neck, waiting to see where this was going.

"I mean, about the battle and my...*comrades*...the ones who almost got away?"

Prince Damian slowly inclined his head in an amiable, affirmative gesture, yet his lips drew taut as he replied. "I was briefed on the situation by a watchman from my Umbrasian guard." He absently rubbed his jaw, relieving some unwanted tension—his teeth were clenched way too tight. He sighed. "Thaon, *my friend:* We have orchestrated a spectacular feat *together*—have we not?" He didn't wait for a reply. "And while I am more pleased than you could ever know with the outcome, I'd also like to keep the lines of communication open." He smacked his lips together in emphasis. "How shall I say this?" He toggled his hands up and down in the air as if searching for just the right words. "It's important that we...maintain some perspective...with regard to our relative roles. After all, I am a dragon, and you are a shifter. And while both of our kingdoms will benefit from this day, long into the future, one should not forget what that future will look like." He narrowed his eyes in contempt, foregoing all pretense of civility. "When that future arrives, I will be as my father was today: capable of absolute annihilation, capable of destroying an entire fleet—*of any enemy*—at my will and my discretion."

He immediately held up a placating hand, lest Thaon become offended. "You, of course, are not an enemy, nor will you be one at such time. However, it is important that you understand this notable *difference* between us, so that our light-hearted, masculine rivalries—our inevitable competitive banter—does not get out of hand." He softened his gaze. "Above all, I expect your undying loyalty, and always…your honesty. Like you, I am not much for playing feminine games."

Thaon snarled like the animal he was, but Damian didn't take any offense. It was a pure territorial reaction from a predatory beast, from his inner Lycanian monster, and to do any less would have been a great sign of weakness, unbefitting of a future king. "Of course," the Lycan hissed, even as his jaw tightened. "Just so long as you also…*understand*…that in less than one month's time, I will be the sovereign and solitary king of the most financially powerful, commercially lucrative, and densely populated country in our lands."

Damian smiled broadly. He bent infinitesimally at the waist and gestured grandly with his hand, drawing a wide arc through the air. "Of course, *Your Majesty.*"

Thaon drew in a deep breath of air and let it out slowly, nodding his head with deference. "*Very well, then…*" He took a moment to appease his beast. "And you're right: We should both be careful…being *two* alpha males and all." There was no need to elaborate.

Damian relaxed his posture and smiled again, understanding his ally's need to save face.

"And on that note," Thaon continued, "and, of course, in the spirit of friendship, there is something you should probably know." He paused unexpectedly, as if carefully considering his next words, and this piqued Damian's curiosity. "Unfortunately, it is somewhat of a sensitive nature, the type of thing one might consider personal, perhaps even…unwelcome."

Damian crooked his eyebrows and waited, though his gut was beginning to clench.

"As we both know, I have extremely sensitive ears and preternatural vision at night, so it wasn't that I was spying...or wandering...I just happened to—"

"Out with it!" Damian snarled, his temper getting the best of him. He tried to force a weak smile in the wake of his outburst and failed. "Just say what you have to say."

"Very well," Thaon replied. "Your brother bed your wife, or your slave—whatever you call the poor girls now, *your Ahavi*—and he did it no more than fifty yards from where we're standing." He averted his eyes out of respect...or maybe pity? "I heard the whole thing, and I'm sorry to say, but she seemed all too willing."

Damian's heart stuttered in his chest. "What did you just say to me?" There was nothing amiable or arrogant in his tone.

Thaon froze. "I...I just—"

"*What—the—devil—did—you—just—say?*"

"Prince Dante confronted two of my *comrades* near that large maple tree"—he gestured in the general direction—"and then he took the Ahavi, Mina, who was already here, laid her on the ground, and coupled with her." He pointed at a small rectangular clearing, in the midst of several adjacent trees, and indicated the leveled dirt and the ruffled grass. "I didn't hear the entire conversation—I was quite some distance away—but the prince said something about an elixir and bearing his offspring. I just thought you should know."

Damian's vision blurred, and his blood began to boil. He lunged at the shifter, grasped him by the throat, and lifted him several feet off the ground, calling his own primordial fire.

"Do not kill the messenger!" Thaon roared like the cornered beast he was, already beginning to shift into his aboriginal form in response to the unexpected threat. His jaw elongated into the muzzle of a bear; his eyes took on the cast of a jackal's; and his muscle-bound torso literally trembled from the effort it took to restrain the transformation—he obviously wanted to avoid a lethal confrontation. "Not after all we have done! Not after all we have achieved! We are so close, Prince Damian. *Think!* For the gods' sakes, consider the future!"

Damian shook from his rage, but he let the shifter go and took a measured step back, trying desperately to clear his head. He struggled to regulate his breathing—

Thaon was right.

The true fault was not with the messenger—it was with the scandalous Ahavi.

Yes, Dante had betrayed him as well, but that element he almost understood.

Almost.

Mina Louvet was a beautiful woman—stunning, really—and hadn't Damian already sampled Tatiana Ward for the very same reason? Truth be told, he was mildly impressed with Dante's audacity as well as his reckless virility.

Still, the duplicity could not go unchallenged.

It could not remain unanswered.

"You are right, Thaon." He nearly spat the words. "The sin is not yours." He quirked his lips in a half smile, half snarl, and growled in spite of his reason. "I will rip that unborn child from her womb; I will break every bone in her traitorous body; and then I will repair the damage, just so I can plant a true heir in her belly to replace Dante's bastard." He drew back his shoulders and raised his jaw in defiance, daring Thaon to utter a single, solitary word.

The Lycanian returned to his human form, and he didn't move a muscle.

"If we are finished…" Damian snarled.

Thaon inclined his head. "We are."

Damian nodded, and his voice grew eerily steady. "Then you know what to do. Travel southwest to Umbras and take lodging in the Gilded Chalice Inn. They will ask no questions of a stranger, but just to be safe, remain out of sight. In seven days' time, you will be escorted by my loyalists back across the sea to Lycania, and once there, it will be up to you to overthrow your brother, to usurp King Bayard."

Thaon flashed a wicked, bestial smile. "Alas, the task should be easy."

Damian snorted, but he didn't reply.

There were just no words.

There was only his Sklavos Ahavi…and his utter disgust… and his vengeance.

Oh yes, there would be plenty of vengeance…

He turned on his heel and strode away, headed for the tent of Umbras.

*

Beneath the moonlight, Thomas the squire wriggled against the cold, dry ground, shifting anxiously against a jagged rock that was poking him in the back. He shoved a pile of arid bramble off his chest, swept away the brittle leaves, and sat up in the ditch, turning to regard Matthias with alarm. "Did you hear that? What Thaon told Prince Damian?"

"All of it," Matthias grunted, his anger leaching through his words. "Enough to know that Damian is going to kill her."

Thomas nodded, his eyes wide with fright.

"I have to go, Thomas. Prepared or not, I know what I must do."

Thomas spit out a mouthful of sandy grit and grimaced at the bitter taste. "You're not strong enough, Matthias. Not yet. Not by a long shot."

"Am I not a dragon?"

Thomas sighed. "Not like Damian. Not like that. The prince will tear you in two. He will leave your body for the buzzards, Matthias. You cannot take him on. *You can't win.*"

Matthias narrowed his deep blue eyes and stared at the ground, as if in all his desperation, even he knew the squire's words were true. "Then you had better get to the tent of Warlochia *quickly*, in time enough to relieve me. Find Prince Dante. Tell him what we overheard. Even if the prince is not willing to protect a slave—the brother is unable to defy his own blood—surely, the *dragon* will fight to save his unborn son."

CHAPTER TWENTY-FIVE

I T WAS CLOSE to 9:30 PM; the beach outside the tent of Umbras was disconcertingly quiet—the sands of Dracos Cove were still filled with the dead and the dying—and Mina Louvet was sitting on the edge of her bed, *of Damian's bed*, wearing a cross-laced silk nightgown and combing out her hair.

Why she even bothered to remove the tangles, she couldn't say.

She certainly did not want to look beautiful for Prince Damian, *the evil hound*, and the gown had not been her choice—it had been packed by her maids. Yet and still, there was something detached and soothing about the mindless, repetitive motion, something calming about the feel of the ivory teeth and the stiff boars' hair bristles sweeping through her hair, something that kept her from leaping off the bed, running from the tent, and throwing herself into the restless sea to drown.

At the moment, drowning seemed like a much better option than trying to make a life with Damian.

She sighed, placing the comb on the bedside table, and glanced for the hundredth time at the entrance to the room: The evil prince should have been back by now. After all, the king had laid waste to the enemy, and the fertility elixir Damian had poured down Mina's throat only lasted for thirty-six hours. She was already on hour number thirty-three.

A wave of nausea undulated through her stomach, undoubtedly brought on by her nerves, and she almost retched from the stress. *Dearest Goddess of Mercy*, as if being there in the tent of Umbras—as if being Damian's whore—was not enough to contend with, she now had to worry about consummating their union within the next three hours. There was just no way around it. She had to "*get pregnant*" tonight, and she had to convince Prince Damian that the child she conceived was *his*. The thought made her want to curl into a ball…and die.

As if summoned by her mounting anxiety, the heavy canvas at the back of the tent flung open, and Damian Dragona stormed into the compartment like a crazed, wild animal, charging into a territorial fray. His nostrils were flared, as if he were struggling to breathe; his dark brown eyes were ablaze with fury; and his mouth was literally contorted in a savage, unnatural scowl. The dragon wasn't just angry—*he was murderous*. "Get up!" Damian shouted, spittle flying from his lips. "Get up! Come here! *And kneel!*"

Mina leaped from the bed and tried to run for the door. She had no idea what was going on, and she really didn't care. She only knew that she would rather be scorched from behind, burned to a crisp, than have her throat slit while she cowered before Damian on her knees. *And for what offense, this time? Surely, he couldn't know what she had done.*

The dragon moved with impossible speed.

He covered the distance between them in an instant, a mere blink of an eye, meeting her retreat with a swift and brutal backhand. She launched into the air like a giant stone shot from a catapult before landing squarely on her back, on the bed; and before she could scramble to her feet, try to flee once again,

Damian was on top of her, seizing her by the throat, and squeezing the life right out of her.

"My prince!" She choked as she spoke, her voice ripe with fear.

He slowly licked his lips and angled his head to the side. "My dutiful, *faithful* wife."

Mina froze at his words, too terrified to breathe, as the word he had used sank in.

Faithful.

Oh gods…

She didn't want to hear his explanation. She didn't care to see death coming. She could only hope it would be quick.

Damian sensed her surrender and relaxed his hands, removing them from her throat. He crawled off the bed, grabbed her by the ankles, and yanked her to the left, to face him. And then he simply stood there, hovering above her, towering at his full, imposing height, while glaring into her eyes, scanning her body from head to toe, and sneering at her middle. "Did you think I wouldn't know?" he whispered icily.

Mina gulped and bit down on her tongue, terrified of making a single sound. Dante had assured her that he had masked his scent, as well as the scent of the unborn child. He had sworn to her that he'd used some sort of magic…

She had no idea what Damian knew.

Perhaps he just suspected some sort of betrayal.

Perhaps it was something else…

So she watched him like a hawk.

And *gods be merciful*, whatever it was, he was going to beat the sense out of her—it was written all over his pitiless face. She drew a deep breath for courage, and he smiled. "My prince?" She finally found her voice.

He crossed his arms over his chest and leaned back as if the entire world was his to command. "I have yet to consummate our pairing; and yet, here you are, already with child. Tell me, *my Ahavi: How does that work?*"

Mina closed her eyes and tried to expunge her mind of all sentient awareness, but it didn't work.

Oh dear ancestors…

She was as good as dead.

But how did he know?

How could he possibly…know?

Was he simply baiting her for a confession?

What in the name of the gods was going on?

There was no point in speculating. There was no point in arguing or explaining. And there was no point in fighting back.

She opened her eyes once more and glanced at the back entrance to the tent, calculating the distance between the edge of the bed and the partially open flap. There were only two options that might yield *some* mercy, however slight: She could either escape, which was highly unlikely, or she could bait Damian into killing her swiftly.

She would try the former first.

She rolled to the other side of the bed, dove from the coverlet, and hit the ground running, pumping her arms at her sides to gain speed. Her bare feet kicked up sand as she scurried like a frightened rabbit toward the waiting door. Her heart pumped in a furious, unstable rhythm, but just like before, Damian moved like the wind.

One moment, he was standing on the other side of the bed, threatening her with *those eyes*; the next, he was simply standing in front of her, blocking her chosen path. His strong, muscular arms flexed—once, then twice—before he caught her by the shoulders, lifted her as if she were virtually weightless, and tossed her across the room, back onto the bed. He measured a hate-filled glower in her direction, and just like that, she was pinned to the mattress, shackled by invisible bonds. He was doing it all with his eyes—*with his intent.*

Mina whimpered like a pitiable child, wriggling beneath the invisible restraints, praying to an absent savior for pardon, for absolution...for death.

Damian paid her no heed.

He sauntered across the room to the fire-pit, removed a golden-handled dagger from his waistband, and placed the blade in the flames. While the bronze heated, he turned to regard her with contempt. "I will not kill you this night, my love." He savored every word. "Oh, no; that would be too easy, and we simply don't have time." He shrugged his massive shoulders. "Besides, I do not blame my eldest brother for mounting you. I'm actually rather proud of him for having the balls." He glanced over his shoulder to inspect the dagger, and Mina followed his gaze: The seven-inch blade was serrated on one side, and it had turned a deep coral red from the heat. Whether fueled entirely by the fire, or by his wicked intentions, Mina didn't know. Damian licked his lips. "No, I rather intend to make love to you, myself." He chuckled at the sardonic turn of phrase, and then he pressed his ear to his shoulder, lazily stretching his neck. "But you do understand that I must first remove that fetus." His face contorted into a mask of hatred. "That abomination that lives in your womb."

He reached into the fire with his right hand, as if he were simply dipping it into a bowl of water, and moaned at the exquisite sensation of pain as he withdrew the now-molten dagger from the flames. He held it up in the lantern light and grinned.

Mina screamed.

She bucked against the invisible chains, harder and harder, with every step Damian took toward the bed, and the moment he released her from the supernatural bonds, she kicked out at him with a fury.

He caught her ankles in his left palm—first her right, and then her left—demonstrating an uncanny level of dexterity, a complete mastery of speed and agility, that truly boggled the mind.

Mina never even saw him move.

It was all just a blur.

He pinned her ankles to the bed with his knees and crawled above her, lifting her nightgown with a calloused left hand, bunching it up at her waist as he creeped.

She gasped in horror. "No!" she shouted, unable to contain her panic. *"No, no, no, no!"* She bucked so hard she strained her back, and then she struck out at him with both clenched fists, swinging wildly at his jaw, his nose, his eyes—*anything*—just to divert him from his path.

Damian laughed like a hyena.

He was enjoying her fear almost as much as his own machinations. He *loved* seeing her squirm. He ripped the nightgown, straight down the front, and tossed the scraps to the side, watching as they floated to the ground like so much garbage. "Punch me again, and I'll break your wrists," he snarled. "I will crush them into dust beneath my hands, and your pain will be even greater." He stared at her bare, exposed breasts and groaned. "Think of it this way, my Ahavi: This is going to be a gruesome, bloody, and entirely unnatural process, butchering this thing from your womb"—he shrugged—"but once it's over, it's over. I can put you back together, and we can get on with our own exquisite coupling. So why don't you just concentrate on that." He bent low, drew a circle around her right areola with his tongue, and then drew back, flicking away the remaining vestiges of the gown with the knife, careful to avoid searing her skin with the heated blade.

For now.

It was all so sadistic.

When he transferred the dagger to his left hand, reheated the blade with his own dragon's fire, and then reached for the lace on her undergarment, she practically came undone: Mina fought like a hellhound released from the depths of the abyss. She twisted and bucked; kicked out and screamed; pummeled the dragon with blow after wild, desperate blow, utterly uncaring that she would further provoke his wrath.

She wanted his ire.

She needed his rage.

She *had* to incite him to kill—to take her life, swiftly and finally, right here and now: Mina Louvet wanted to die, and it was up to her to make it happen.

In a series of movements too rapid and exact to be countered, Damian snatched her by the throat, thrust her thighs apart with his knees, and braced her legs to the bed with his own, all the while, lowering the sweltering blade to her pelvis.

Mina shrieked in terror, and that's when Matthias Gentry lunged toward the bed. He snatched Prince Damian from behind, wrapped his powerful arms around the dragon's chest, and wrenched him backward. At the same time, he released a deadly pair of fangs and sank them deep into Damian's neck.

Mina gasped at the sight of Matthias Gentry snarling like a rabid dog. She could hardly believe her eyes as he wrenched his head to the right, and then the left, literally frothing at the bit, tearing into the prince's throat, bound and determined to eviscerate his esophagus.

Damian dropped the dagger and scrabbled for his throat, tearing Matthias's teeth from his flesh with careless abandon. He spun about in midair, an act of amazing legerity, and landed lightly on his soles, like a cat ready to spring into battle. His skin began to harden with the sudden appearance of scales, supernatural armor, even as his chest expanded in girth, his claws shot forth from his hands, and smoke wafted between his scornful lips. "Who. The. Hell. Are. You?" he bellowed, glaring at Matthias as the rebel crouched low before him, matching each of Damian's preternatural feats with one of his own.

"I am your father's son," Matthias snarled. And with that, he lunged forward and thrust a fearsome, serrated hand toward Damian's chest in an effort to seize the prince's heart.

Damian moved much too fast.

He sucked in his stomach, bowed his chest, and leaped backward, narrowly evading the swipe, even as he grasped Matthias's wrist and snapped the radius like a twig.

Matthias winced in pain, stunned but determined. As if drawing on some ancient, unconscious instinct, he sucked in a deep breath of air and released it with a hiss, conjuring a narrow redhot flame in the process and heaving it at Damian's golden hair.

The dragon prince disappeared.

He simply vanished in thin air, and Matthias spun around like a wild beast, trying feverishly to locate his prey. A huge, wicked gash opened up on Matthias's side, the ugly wound taking the shape of a barbed, triangular claw, as Damian reappeared to Matthias's left.

"My brother?" the evil prince mocked, and then he laughed like a certified lunatic. "Well, I'll be damned." His expression turned all at once serious; his glowing red eyes narrowed into two venomous slits; and he growled, deep in his bestial throat. He threw a right hook at Matthias's jaw and jolted in surprise when Matthias caught it in the palm of his hand and shoved the fist forward, sending Damian flying through the air, spinning into a summersault, and crashing into Mina's traveling chest.

The trunk split open, splintered into a dozen pieces, and littered the room with shards.

Damian catapulted to his feet and brushed the dust away. "Well done," he drawled lasciviously, seeming almost aroused by the game. "I'm impressed with your lineage, *dragon*; at least you have a heart. However, you are insane to think you are my equal, when you are yet a pitiful neophyte. Alas, it is time to end this silly duel."

Just like that, Damian Dragona unleashed the full fury of his wrath—the full powers of hell—calling on his feral beast for supremacy, drawing on his blackened soul: A pair of enormous webbed wings punched out of his back, and he flew at Matthias like a demon possessed, engulfed in a ring of fire. He latched onto Matthias with both sets of claws, making full use of his talons, his teeth, and his speed. He ripped at the fledgling's skin and tore at his muscles like a bird making sport of a worm. He undulated, coiled, and struck in precise serpentine motions, drawing upon *decades and decades* of training as he sliced, punctured, and withdrew. In a matter of seconds, Matthias was lying at Damian's feet—bloodied, battered, and broken—nearly lifeless on the floor.

His left arm was fractured in three visible places. His right leg was propped against a chair—on the other side of the room. And his intestines were spilling out of his stomach, the fluids, guts, and tissue oozing onto the bloody floor in a gory pile of mush.

Mina cried out in anguish; bitter tears of sorrow streamed from her eyes; and her heart broke with regret. Matthias was moaning in agony, and the torture was not over yet...

Damian bent over his torn, ruined torso, thumped Matthias on the chest, and carved a deep, circular gash into his flesh, over his heart. "Not yet, baby dragon." He spat the words with derision. "You don't get to leave us...quite yet." He turned to Mina and brandished his bloodstained claws in a clear and implicit threat. "This is the *same* male who approached you in the gardens, the *same* male who I had thrown into the dungeons, the *same* male that my father should have eaten! So I will ask you more specifically this time: What is his name? And what do you know of his lineage?"

Mina shivered, unable to find her voice, and Damian swelled up with rage.

"Answer me, witch! Or so help me gods..." He booted a heavy clay pot across the room, hurling it into the armoire, and the collision shattered the huge wooden bureau, breaking it into a thousand useless pieces. "I am no longer playing games with you, Mina! *This bastard is a dragon.*" He paused to catch his breath and lower his voice. "Taking Dante's unborn child from your womb is one matter, but *you*, continuing to defy me, will not be tolerated an instant longer." He ground his teeth together in fury. "I swear to you on my mother's grave, if you do not answer me now—*truthfully*—you will pray for death, but it will not come. You will curse the day your mother gave you life, and I will make your entire clan pay dearly. Yes, Mina, I will wipe your family from the face of this earth. Now answer me!"

Mina dug her nails into the sides of her arms, trying to gain control of her fear. She struggled to think, so she could answer, *to simply think*, clearly enough to speak. "His name is Matthias Gentry. He was...is...he's the son of Callum Gentry and...and... and—"

She couldn't think of the woman's name!

Who was she?

His birth mother?

The one...the girl...at the castle!

What was the name of the slave?

"The son of Callum and whom!" Damian roared.

Mina bit her lip until she drew her own blood and tried even harder to concentrate. *"Callum and Penelope Fairfax,"* she finally exhaled, breathing the words in a rush. Her palms grew sweaty, and her stomach roiled from panic. Dear gods, she was going to vomit. *No!* she told herself, vehemently. *Not right now. It will only push him over the edge.*

She pressed her hands, flat and hard, against her belly and cast her eyes to the ground. She had no doubt, whatsoever, that Damian Dragona could invent a lifetime of torture beyond anything she could imagine, beyond anything she could bear. Her tongue snaked out to wet her bottom lip, and she trembled. "Your father...my king...he had an Ahavi...um, a mistress... he...he...he kept her in the castle...at the castle. The priest didn't think she was Sklavos, but Wavani did...and she had to have been because...the serum...well, the king—"

"Shut up, Mina."

Mina gulped.

"I get the picture." He ran a tense hand through his hair and began to pace around the room, and then he stopped abruptly and flicked his wrist toward Matthias. "Who was this boy to you, and how long have you known him?"

Mina clutched her hair in her fists and tugged at the roots, as if she could somehow pull the information from her head or make her thoughts flow more freely with the gesture. "We grew up together in the southern district of Arns. He was my friend." She choked on the last two words, trying desperately to avoid the meaning behind them—she couldn't bear to think of Matthias Gentry as a child, of the two of them growing up as neighbors on nearby farms. She couldn't bear to listen, not for another tortured second, to his wretched, tormented moans: He was choking on his own blood, writhing in unspeakable pain, dying on the floor less than ten feet away from her, but his dragon's-blood would not allow him to perish. And she was helpless to come to his aid. "Please," she finally whispered, knowing she took her life in her hands. "Just kill him." She blinked several times, trying to steady her resolve, drawing courage from her childhood companion's unbearable suffering. "Please, Prince Damian...I'm begging you, milord...have mercy, and put him out of his misery."

A spark of satisfaction glittered in Damian's eyes, and his feral-red irises receded to dark brown. He relaxed his jaw, just a tad, as if he might consider her request. "How long have you known that he was a dragon, that he was my half-brother?"

Mina cleared her throat. The fact that Damian had used the word *was* rather than *is* was not lost on her. Matthias was as good as dead. The only question, now, was whether or not Damian would prolong his unspeakable suffering. "I've known since early this morning, perhaps fifteen or sixteen hours, my prince," she said softly.

"Does Dante know?"

Mina was surprised by the question. "No. Not that I know of."

Damian nodded. "Does my father know?"

Mina shook her head. "Not that I know of, my prince."

Damian furrowed his brow. "I see. Who else knows?"

Mina began to weep openly. *Oh gods, this was impossible.* "No one," she lied.

Damian grunted, knowingly. He walked over to Matthias, raised a bare foot, and stomped down on his pelvis, crushing the sacrum beneath his heel. As Matthias howled in pain, Damian turned back to Mina. "Who else knows?"

Mina would have gladly gone to her grave keeping Thomas the squire's secret, but the truth of the matter was this: It wasn't a secret that could be kept. Damian Dragona could extract the information from her mind at any time he chose. He was only asking her to force her obedience. He was only going through the motions because he wanted to watch her squirm. And maybe, just maybe—*lord of the Eternal Realm, be merciful*—he was actually considering putting Matthias out of his despair. "The squire knows."

Damian smirked. "Which one?"

"Thomas."

He let out a hollow chuckle. "Why doesn't that surprise me?" And then he frowned. "Lie back on the bed, Mina."

Mina recoiled. "Excuse me?"

He held up his right hand, displayed all five deadly claws, and hardened his tone. "We don't need the dagger. Lie back on the bed. Be as still as you can while I remove that child, and I will heal you straightaway when I am through." He glanced at Matthias, still writhing on the floor. "And I will even send my *brother* to the afterlife as your reward." He stepped forward and frowned. "But resist me, and you will both be eager to sell your souls to the Keeper of the Forgotten Realm in exchange for a mere hint of the *temporary* suffering I offer you now—*such* will be the depth of your suffering."

Mina felt her *soul* recede in her temporal body.

It was as if time suddenly stood still; sights and sounds intensified; and she could *feel* her own heart rising, falling, and beating in her chest. The entire moment was surreal, the haze of dreams and the sludge of nightmares, and she knew she had no choice: She belonged to a devil, perhaps the Keeper of the Forgotten Realm himself, and one way or another, he would have his revenge. He would take his due.

Fixing her eyes on a distant point across the room, Mina lay back on the bed. Before Damian could insist or instruct her, she moved her left ankle to one side of the mattress, her right ankle to the other, and grasped the coverlet in two clenched fists. Ignoring the helpless tears that leaked from the corners of her eyes, she drew a deep, ragged breath and waited, refusing to think of the child.

Damian approached the bed languidly. He sauntered to the edge of the mattress, his gaze fixed on hers, and crawled like the animal he was; until, at last, he knelt between her legs and lowered his wicked hand.

She held her breath, shivering, but she refused to whimper or beg. She could only pray that he would get it over with quickly— perhaps he would use his preternatural speed. Either way, she would simply hold her breath and stare into the corner.

"Look at me," he commanded, and her heart sank in her chest. *The bastard.*

By all that was holy, she would kill him one day if it was the last thing she ever did.

She never got the chance.

The evil prince's head jerked on his neck, toppled onto his shoulders, and then tumbled onto the bed, no longer attached to his body.

CHAPTER TWENTY-SIX

DANTE DRAGONA SHIMMERED into view, lowered his sword, and placed it back in its scabbard. He didn't even bother to wash off the blood.

His brother's blood.

He had just committed the worst betrayal—and treason— imaginable.

As anguish, guilt, and relief washed over him in turns, each one taking a stranglehold on his breaking dragon's heart, he fought to keep them at bay.

To do what he must.

"Aguilon," he said in an ice-cold tone. "Is your spell ready?"

One of only seven members of the Warlock's Council on Supreme Magic and Mystical Practices, a sorcerer whose skill was surpassed only by that of the high mage of Warlochia, stepped forward at his prince's behest and bowed his head in deference. "Yes, milord." His face was a mask of stunned disbelief, but he stripped all emotion from his voice.

Dante nodded. He waved his hand in an imperial gesture and turned his attention back to the bed. "Mina, get up and get dressed." He didn't express any feelings as the Sklavos Ahavi, the female who was carrying his offspring, scrambled from the bed, wrapped her naked torso in a sheet, and dug through the broken pieces of the armoire, trying to find a dress. "Thomas..." He spoke now to the squire, who had been waiting in the wings, hovering in the shadows, throughout the entire brutal scene.

The squire stepped forward warily. "My prince?"

"Is the soul-eater here?"

"Yes."

"Bring him in."

Thomas scurried to the rear of the tent, pulled back the flap, and stepped to the side as a tall, intimidating male ducked beneath the folds and entered the room. He was clearly a *shade*, and by the deeply etched lines in his brow and the pale silver cast of his hair, there was no question that he was an elder, an ancient, capable of stunning and powerful feats. "Your name?" Dante inquired, noticing how washed out the male looked at night.

"My prince," the shadow replied, "I am called Elzeron Griswold. I am a resident of the lower province of Umbras, your ever-faithful steward, and it is my honor to serve you this night."

Dante knew that the latter half of the statement was bullshit—shadows were arrogant, independent, and defiant down to their vile, carnivorous souls—but they weren't stupid, and they preferred to live as long as they could. The *shade* would do as he was bid. "We don't have much time," Dante said dispassionately, pointing at Matthias's body, still stunned by the revelation. "He is a dragon, so his soul will not leave his body or return to his ancestors until his flesh has been burned, but it will only remain viable for a time." He turned toward the bed and with calloused indifference sauntered over to Damian's body, hefted his torso in one hand, his head in the other, and carried both, like two sacks of grain, to the floor.

He dropped his brother's remains beside Matthias, and then he positioned Damian's head on his shoulders and sealed the two sections of the corpse back together using a powerful stream of blue fire, all the while, fighting mightily not to stagger…or vomit.

Not in front of his subjects.

Not in front of Mina Louvet.

What was done was done, and what was yet to come was absolutely necessary: a form of eternal retribution, an act of unforgivable sedition, but a required deed just the same. It was a solemn and inevitable duty.

This was for the Realm.

Damian had plotted with the dragons' mortal enemies—*the Lycanians*—behind their father's back. He had sent faithful and loyal subjects to their needless, gruesome deaths in an orchestrated battle with the shifters, and he hadn't even considered what would have happened to the Realm had his nefarious plan somehow failed—had the Lycans breached the beach and made their way to the villages.

And for what?

All to win favor with Thaon Percy, a jealous narcissist who wanted his brother's throne?

All to elevate his own station so he might one day overthrow the king?

Damian had maimed and raped and murdered one too many innocent souls. And the life that grew in Mina's womb was the final straw, the ultimate catalyst that had tipped the scales of justice.

Still, Dante Dragona had not acted out of vengeance or spite—or even unbridled emotion—he had acted out of wisdom, strategy, and duty.

He had acted out of necessity.

He turned to regard the suffering male, still groaning in misery on the floor, and knelt down beside him, wanting to *see* who he truly was, needing to *sense* his life force—this stranger who shared his blood. "Dear gods," he mumbled beneath his breath.

The human—*no, the dragon*—was beyond disfigured and torn. He was virtually eviscerated, nearly beyond repair.

And it didn't matter anyway—that was not why Dante had come.

The prince bent to his ear. "Brother, be strong. Know that your suffering will soon be over, and then all will be as it should." In a rare and tender act of empathy—or contrition—he pressed a soft, familial kiss against the young man's forehead, and then he steadied his resolve. Turning to regard the shadow-walker, he spoke in a clear and imperious tone: "Soul-eater: As I extinguish this young one's life, once and for all, you must devour his soul. Inhale it. Ingest it. But do *not* absorb it. It is not yours to keep." He rotated at the waist and gestured toward Damian's corpse. "Rather, you will place it into the prince's body immediately, expelling each and every vital particle into this carcass, until the skeleton is reanimated and the heart is alive and beating." He glared at the warlock next, making it abundantly clear that his words were an irrefutable command. "And you will use your considerable magic to conjure a resurrection spell—you *will* bring the prince of Umbras back to life." He didn't bother to tell them that he would either have to scrub their memories so completely that they went through the rest of their lives as simpletons, barely able to function, or he would have to kill them.

They could not be allowed to carry this secret.

It would be far, far too dangerous.

Before the warlock or the *shade* could reply, Mina Louvet rushed to Dante's side, wresting his attention from his morbid thoughts. She placed a trembling but gentle hand on his shoulder, and her fingers quivered in alarm. "My prince," she whispered, her voice tinged with unadulterated awe. "You mean to resurrect Damian?"

Dante shook his head. "No, Ahavi. Not Damian. I mean to resurrect Matthias…in Damian's body."

The scale of the deception was simply inconceivable.

Mina blanched. She let go of his shoulder, dropped down beside him, and extended her hand, as if to stroke his jaw, stopping just short of actually touching him. She earnestly beseeched his gaze. "Forgive me," she whispered, her voice thick with humility and respect, "but why not heal Matthias, exactly as he is? Can you not save his immortal body? He is a dragon, after all."

Dante's lips turned down in a frown. "Oh, Mina—we are still beholden to the Realm. *Always* beholden to the Realm. We are still my father's subjects. We cannot destroy his middle son and expect to walk away unscathed." He narrowed his eyes in an all-pervading glance, and met her desperate passion with his own. "And you must know that I do not do this for you. I would not betray my lineage and my obligations to the Realm for my own selfish gain." He reached out to brush the backs of his fingers against her quaking belly. "Not even for the life of my child." He closed his eyes, if only for a moment, and it felt as if the weight of the entire world was resting on his shoulders. When he reopened them, he was even more certain than before. "I do this because Damian's heart is irretrievably black, because his soul is tainted and he can no longer lead our people with the wisdom of a prince. I do this because his many decades of training and his superior acumen—as both a dragon and a prince—are far too valuable, far too honed, far too irreplaceable to simply abandon… to surrender in death. The Realm needs Damian's courage and his dragon's strength. It needs his keen intelligence and his innumerable skills, as much as it ever has; but it can no longer sustain his insolence, his selfishness, or his corruption. I do this because we need Damian's supremacy, tempered by Matthias's soul. We need my brother's power, his sovereign ability to rule, and my half-brother's integrity, his transcendent ability to reason. And we need it *all* in a body that my father will recognize as his own beloved pedigree: the child he has raised for nearly one hundred fifty years."

As if she understood that any argument would be futile, Mina looked away. She gathered her courage and placed her hands in her lap. "Whose memories will he have?"

Dante smiled then, albeit faintly, encouraged by the brilliance of his plan. "He will have both. His consciousness will belong to Matthias, for that is the origin of his soul. He will see through Matthias's eyes and think as Matthias thinks—for all intents and purposes, he will *be* Matthias Gentry, but he will wear Damian's skin, he will bear Damian's name, and he will know *all* that Damian knows in terms of memories and skill. He will speak Warlochian, Umbrasian, and the common tongue, and he will wield both sword and dragon like a maestro. True, it will be an enormous adjustment for a human from the *commonlands*—a *dragon* from the *commonlands*—yet there will be no learning curve in terms of Damian's knowledge and military prowess. Matthias will know what Damian knows. He will know how to please and appease our father."

Mina shuddered before she nodded, as if she were enumerating all of Damian's hideous crimes, his cowardly acts of brutality. Matthias would awaken, intimately bound to both light and darkness, in a body made strong through cruelty.

He would live with Damian's memories forever.

Still, to her credit, Mina nodded her head and shuffled back, moving out of Dante's way, and in this fateful, life-altering moment, the prince appreciated her obedience more than she would ever know.

With a crook of his finger and a nod of his head, Dante ushered the shadow and the warlock forward, and then he bent to Matthias's throat and swiftly drained him of blood…

Of heat…

And of essence.

Slowly withdrawing his fangs, he turned to his loyal subjects and gave them a single command: "*Begin.*"

CHAPTER TWENTY-SEVEN

WHILE THE ARDUOUS task of cleanup began on the beach—enumerating the dead, treating the injured, and assigning all available citizens and soldiers their various dreary tasks—Dante Dragona had much more important matters to attend to. Unsure of whether he should burden Drake with the truth, he had left his youngest brother in charge of Dracos Cove and set out with Thomas the squire and Matthias Gentry, who, in every practical sense, was now Damian Dragona, for the Gilded Chalice Inn to confront Thaon Percy face-to-face.

Matthias had only been the bait.

It was far too soon for the dazed and overwhelmed dragon to take an active role in matters of the Realm: He still needed to come to terms with his new fate and identity: to process, internalize, and categorize his numerous conflicting memories; to learn the ropes around Castle Dragon and Castle Umbras—well, to recall them anyway—and to slowly ease into the part he would be expected to play for the rest of his immortal life.

Due to the neophyte's frequent bouts of vertigo and extreme

fatigue, the journey to Umbras had taken five long days by horse-back, and the confrontation with Thaon Percy had been dicey at best. Prior to their arrival, Dante had planned to murder the traitorous Lycanian where he stood, the moment they entered the inn, but critical news, via messenger pigeon, had reached a previous village along the way, before they arrived, and intercepting the early missive on day four of their journey had changed Dante's plans: *"Our dragon king has executed a swift and decisive victory over the Lycanians"*—this was nothing Dante didn't already know—*"and the king of Lycania, Bayard Percy, has been murdered in his palace, the apparent victim of poisoning. His brother will succeed him as king."*

This, on the other hand, was critical information.

Like it or not, Thaon Percy was the new king of Lycania, and a kingdom without a ruler was far too politically unstable to manage or predict. Not to mention, the last thing Dante needed to contend with were questions and suspicions about the mysterious disappearance of the second royal brother. Why buy extra trouble? In the end, Dante had been forced to reevaluate his strategy, and he had struck a new alliance with the terrified, yet visibly irate foreigner, who couldn't comprehend why Damian had turned on him after all they had achieved, why the seedy prince of Umbras had revealed their duplicitous plot, as well as their future alliance, to his law-enforcing brother.

It was of no matter.

Thaon had been between a rock and a hard place, and he had swiftly made allowances to save his own skin and ensure that he made it back to Lycania…alive. In the end, he had agreed to a thousand years of peace between the kingdoms, fifty seaworthy vessels for the Realm's commercial use, and the same, original offer he had made to Damian: to provide the citizens of Dragons Realm with knowledge and training in Lycanian weaving, engineering, and artistry, all in exchange for *personal* military protection for the duration of his rule, liberal use of the Realm's warlocks and witches in matters of healing and medicine, and *two hundred pounds* in copper coins as payment for the ships, none of which would begin until King Demitri's rule was over. They would not whisper, conspire, and bleed the castle's treasury behind King Demitri's back. It was far too risky…and far too stupid.

Peace for peace.

Knowledge for knowledge.

And fair payment for the seaworthy vessels.

There would be no dragon-support in raiding innocent villages, and there would be no expanded, legal slave trade in Dragons Realm, not ever: The Realm had its own sordid history with the practice of slavery as a primary resource for labor—the embittered and treacherous Malo Clan was a result of that experiment—and Dante understood only too well that the vile practice created lifelong adversaries for the monarchy, inevitable wars in the form of uprisings, and a lasting hostility, based on racial and clan identity, which was hard to overcome. In short, it placed the most embittered enemies of all, those with virtually nothing to lose, in the very midst of the Realm. The Malo Clan's hostility had lasted for *eight centuries*, even though there were very few descendants of the original slaves left: Why capture, breed, and cultivate a new local opponent?

In the end, Thaon had taken the deal because he'd had no other choice. Whether or not he would stick to it remained to be seen.

Now, as Dante dismounted from his black stallion, tethered him to a tree in the thick of the Umbrasian Mountains, and approached the modest cabin tucked deep into the forest, he was glad he had sent Matthias and Thomas back to the Castle of Umbras, about eight hours ahead. He would meet back up with them shortly.

This was something he needed to do alone.

*

Raylea Louvet tossed the dirty water from the mop bucket out the back door, secured the raggedy mop against the top inner corner of the doorframe, and slowly made her way back into the front room of the cabin to kneel before her captor.

Syrileus Cain.

Despite telling herself, over and over, that she would not tremble, she would not beg, she would not give the monster the satisfaction, her skinny, knobby knees knocked against one another beneath her filthy, tattered dress. Her stockings were torn to shreds, yet he insisted that she wear them, and her shoes no longer fit her feet, causing blisters on her toes. Yet and still, she kneeled like a "proper lady," just as Syrileus instructed.

The tall, wispy shadow-walker rose from his lazy repose in his favorite chair, crossed the room with unnerving silence, and loomed over Raylea with menace, his vacant gray eyes perusing her from head to toe, even as his thin, reedy lips drew back in a parody of a smile.

"I have finished my morning chores, master," Raylea whispered. She knew the routine. He was waiting for her to make the same tedious announcement—three times each day—and then he would make a calculated decision that always struck fear into her heart: He would either take her back into his bedroom, where he would try to ravish her and fail, or he would drag her back to the cellar and chain her to the wall.

Raylea wasn't sure which option was worse.

In truth, the old man had never managed to truly violate her, at least not in *that* way—his old, decrepit body would not allow him to do what he wanted to do—and so he would slap her mercilessly instead, venting his frustration. Whereas, if he chose to take her to the cellar, the only repercussions would be raw flesh where her wrists met the manacles and the cool, damp air that left her shivering from cold.

She almost preferred the thrashings.

At least when he was finished, he would often leave her alone.

She could exit the cabin for a time, feel the sunlight on her face, feel the wild grass beneath her feet, escape her confinement in her imagination and travel back to Arns, pretend she was still living with her parents…and Mina.

Syrileus reached out a long, bony finger and tipped her chin upward to force her gaze, his dirty nails nicking her skin. "I shall have you in my bed," he crooned.

Raylea closed her eyes, but only for a second. The threat was always chilling, even though she knew he could never follow through. She drew a deep breath for courage and slowly inclined her head in capitulation. "As you wish." Then she rose as gently as a lamb and padded across the wide-planked floors to the back bedroom, where she stoically began to remove her outer gown in order to lie on the bed—there was no need to remove her undergarments.

"Do not." A dark, deadly voice rang out from the shadows, and Raylea immediately searched the corner of the room to identify the source. She could see nothing. There was no one there. "Keep your clothes on and crawl to the far side of the bed."

Raylea gasped, stifling a scream. She didn't know whether to run, call out to Syrileus for help, or follow the disembodied voice's commands. Every beat of her heart pattered with rising hope—had the Spirit Keepers finally come to rescue her? Was the Bringer of Rain, at last, on her side? Or was this some cruel trick perpetrated by her master—had he finally sold her to someone else, perhaps to a warlock or another *shade* who *was* capable of defiling her? She shivered and instinctively followed the specter's command.

Syrileus sauntered into the room, his masculine anatomy visibly aroused as it always was in the beginning. He glanced toward the bed and frowned. "Why are you still dressed?" His voice dripped with the venom of his displeasure.

Raylea bit her bottom lip and trembled.

"Because…" the disembodied voice purred, drawing the serpentine word out. "She will never suffer your advances again."

In a flash of light that sparked like fire emerging from flint, the dark, handsome male flickered into view. His thick onyx hair cascaded in virulent waves about his shoulders, framing his angry jaw, even as his sapphire-blue eyes deepened to crimson red.

Raylea clutched at the covers, her jaw dropping open. She would know that face anywhere, that proud, regal bearing, that terrifying, indomitable frame. It was the prince she had met in Warlochia, the one who had ultimately asked the old man to retrieve her doll.

It was Dante Dragona himself, and he was standing in *her* cabin.

Threatening Syrileus.

Her eyes welled up with tears, and she quickly blinked them back, struggling to catch her breath.

Syrileus spun around to face the corner as if he were a much younger man, his movements both rapid and true. He narrowed his gaze at the intruder, and then he jerked back, faltering for a moment in fright.

So he recognized the dragon, too.

Dante stepped forward and smiled. "Do you know who it is that you have enslaved?"

Syrileus took a cautious step in retreat, his evil eyes narrowing into fine, wary slits. He gulped in place of an answer.

"Do you know that the slave trade is illegal in this realm?"

Syrileus turned a garish shade of white. "My p-p-prince,"— he stuttered over the word—"the high mage of Warlochia both allows and supports our meager industry." He genuflected like a clown, flashing a broad, congenial smile. "I would never defy my liege if…if…if only I had known." He waved his arm around the room as if to dismiss its true barbaric nature. "Truly, it is a harmless pastime, all in fun." He fixed his gaze on Raylea and gestured with an open palm. "In fact, you may have her if you wish. She is young and eager and beautiful." He frowned. "Well, when she's cleaned up, but I can have her washed and ready in no time if you'd like."

"You have yet to answer my question: Do—you—know—who—she—is?" Dante bit out each word separately, as if the shadow was too dense to understand.

Syrileus's thin, slimy tongue snaked out to wet his lips. "I—I—"

"She is the sister of a Sklavos Ahavi, one who now carries my child. She is under my protection."

Syrileus turned from white to green and moaned. "I didn't know, my prince. I swear to you on the souls of my ancestors, I...I really didn't know."

Dante nodded affably. "You didn't care, shadow-walker. You thought only of yourself and your perverse desires." His brow knitted in disgust, and his voice rang out like thunder, rattling the rafters above the room. "She is a child!"

Syrileus opened his mouth to protest, then shut it, clasping both hands in front of him in a gesture of supplication, instead. *"My prince..."*

"Kneel."

Syrileus eyed the floor dubiously, and Raylea held her breath.

In the blink of an eye, the prince drew his sword from his scabbard, lowered it, and slashed it crossways through the air, cleanly slicing the lower half of the shadow-walker's legs from his body, just below the knees. Syrileus fell to the ground with a shout, even as Dante singed the bloody stumps with a steady stream of bluish fire, instantly cauterizing the wounds. "I said *kneel.*"

The stunned shadow-walker scrabbled to his knees, such as they were, and shrieked in agony as he tried to tuck the steaming stumps beneath him. The next slash of Dante's sword was far more harrowing and disastrous: With a quick circular twist of his wrist, the prince made sure that Syrileus was no longer a man.

As the shriveled appendage fell to the floor, the shadow-walker screamed like an animal being slaughtered, and once again, Dante scorched the wound with fire, instantly staunching the flow of blood. "Raylea, it is two to three days' travel where we are headed. Gather what you need for the road."

Raylea jolted, unsure of what to do. She understood the prince's words—he had spoken in the common tongue—yet she was stunned by his simple directive. *Did he really intend to remove her from this hell? Blessed Spirit Keepers, it was too good to be true.*

Finally, the dragon prince's words sank in, and she scurried from the bed, darted out the door, and numbly gathered a satchel, filling it with a blanket, a loaf of bread, and a large canteen of water. When she returned to the threshold of the bedroom, mindlessly moving by rote, her eyes flew open in horror, and she gaped at the macabre sight before her: Syrileus Cain was hanging upside down from the ceiling, trussed by his thighs and his waist with linens from the bed, and an iron spike from the headboard skewered him through the ribs, like a pig being roasted on a spit. His scalp had been torn from his skull, and it lay atop a conical fire-pit beneath him, while mystical flames of red, orange, and yellow danced beneath his head. Sweat poured from his brow as he swayed back and forth above the fire, writhing and jerking in pain.

"The fire will grow no larger," Prince Dante said, obviously sensing her presence, since his back was still to the door. "Nor will it grow any hotter." He straightened his lapel. "His death will be slow and painful. His eyes will melt; his hearing will falter; and his skin will peel away from his bones." He turned around slowly then, and met her gaze with one of compassion, the color of his fearsome, deep red eyes receding back to blue. "It is not enough…for what you've endured…but at least it is something."

Raylea recoiled at his words, unsure of what to say or do. On one hand, she had never been so relieved or grateful in all her life. On the other, she had never been more terrified or disturbed.

Falling into the familiar obedience she had practiced over the past three and a half weeks, she bowed her head and averted her gaze. "Thank you, my prince." Despite herself, large salty tears streamed from the corners of her eyes, and that's when the prince approached her.

He strolled to the open door, squatted down in front of her, and slowly—oh so gently—drew Raylea into his arms. They were the strongest arms she had ever felt. "You are safe now, little one," he murmured. "The nightmare is over."

As if all her anguish, fear, and hopelessness had been bottled behind a dam—a thick, invisible barrier erected to insure her survival—the dam broke loose, the floodgates opened, and Raylea wept like the child she was, clinging to Dante's shoulders for dear life in an effort to keep her soul from being swept away in the current.

Time stood still as she sobbed; until finally, there were no tears left to cry. Dante pressed a soft but firm kiss against her temple, and the kiss felt *funny*. Her mind felt *hazy*. And then, all at once, it was like a burden the size of a boulder had been lifted from her chest: She still held the memories, the knowledge of her captivity in the shadow-walker's cabin, but the deeper understanding was no longer there. She couldn't remember the pain. She couldn't feel all the anguish and fear. She couldn't connect to the horror that had been her very existence for what felt like as long as she could remember.

It was as if it had simply been erased.

Raylea was staring at a scar that had healed over a hideous wound. She knew what had happened, what existed underneath, but it was no longer open or festering.

And there was something else missing.

Something else that seemed like only a blur: Dante's words…

Earlier.

In the cabin.

Something he had said about Mina—or a woman he knew

in the Realm—someone was carrying someone's child…or had recently given birth?

She reached for it, but she couldn't find it.

And truly, it didn't matter.

The eldest prince of Dragons Realm had saved her from a monster.

There was nothing else—*nothing else*—she could possibly need to know.

CHAPTER TWENTY-EIGHT

Two days later

MINA SAT ACROSS from Matthias—*from Damian*—in the front parlor of Castle Umbras, trying not to stare. She had been with him for a total of eight hours now, and still, the bizarre combination of Damian's all-powerful presence imbued with Matthias's gentle soul was jarring. Every now and then, Damian's dark brown, almond-shaped eyes would soften, transition from harsh, brutal orbs to stunning, thoughtful globes, and she would glimpse a hint of her childhood friend's soul. But then they would harden again, and she would have to catch her breath.

Matthias's mannerisms were prevalent, dominating the six-foot-four strapping torso: the way the *prince* gesticulated with his hands when he spoke, the way he tilted his head ever so slightly to the side when he contemplated a question, and the way he softly furrowed his brow when measuring his words. Yet Damian's voice bellowed out of that authoritarian throat. Damian's golden hair, the color of wheat in the summer, still hung to the prince's shoulders, fastened by *Damian's* familiar thong. And a barely noticeable scar, etched into Damian's right temple, still wrinkled when he frowned, making Mina question whom she was speaking with.

She wrung her hands in her lap and cleared her throat, setting aside her uneasiness.

This *was* Matthias, after all, and it wouldn't do either of them any good for Mina to openly display her grief and regret, to visibly demonstrate her nostalgia for the carefree, blond-haired, blue-eyed boy she had grown up with.

That man—that body—was gone.

That physical presence had died, and it was enough that Matthias had to come to grips with the change.

The least Mina could do was support him.

"So how are you feeling today?" she asked, searching for an innocuous question, one that wouldn't provoke a deep discussion.

"My prince," Matthias said.

"Pardon me?"

Matthias sighed. "How are you feeling today, *my prince.*" Mina grimaced, and Matthias intensified his reprimand. "You are still thinking of me as someone who is casually familiar, someone from your past, even if you aren't speaking that name. You have to stop."

Mina gulped.

Was he reading her mind?

That effortlessly?

"I am," he answered bluntly. "Damian was...*Damian is*...a master at such things."

"*You are,*" Mina corrected.

Matthias nodded. "Touché." And then they shared a moment of companionable silence as Mina thought about the gravity of the prince's instructive words.

Ever since that fateful day when Prince Dante had butchered his brother within the royal tent of Umbras, on the shores of Dracos Cove, he had made it abundantly clear that everything had changed. *Everything.* "From this day forward, you are not to speak the name *Matthias,* ever again. You are not to *think* the name Matthias, if you can help it. You *all* need to train your minds—as well as your mouths—to think only of Damian, to speak only of your prince. Should one of you ever slip up and make a mistake in the presence of the king, the consequences could be lethal. While my father is not as adept at mind-reading as some, he is not to be trifled with. It is a matter of habit, a matter of inner discipline, and a matter of practice through repetition. I will try to buy you as much time away from Castle Dragon as I can, but you must do the work. And you must be diligent. No exceptions. No excuses."

Mina finally broke the silence. "Apologies, *my prince.* I am not very good at this...yet."

Damian sighed. "Believe me, I understand. The one who is no more has only had seven days to come to terms with the fact that his identity is gone. He has had seven days to grieve for the loss of his family, his fiancée, and his father, knowing they will be notified of his death. He has had one week to accept the fact that he will not marry Melissa Walcott or follow in his father's footsteps as a blacksmith's apprentice...that he will live a very, *very* long time, ruling a province of shadows...ruling with an iron fist." His dark brown eyes met hers, and he softened his gaze on purpose. "That as far as the outside world is concerned, you are his mate—*his Sklavos Ahavi*—and the child that grows inside you is his offspring." He paused. "*My* offspring. At least for now. At least until my eldest brother comes of age, which is still thirty-one years away. So, yes, Mistress Mina, I understand this is a difficult transition."

She offered him a sheepish grin. "At least the vertigo and the fatigue have stopped. Yours, I mean."

He smiled and shrugged his shoulders in an awkward gesture, making his own stab at levity. "And at least my hair is still blond—*sort of*—and I can still wear it tied back in a thong. Strange, right?"

Mina tried to laugh, but it was a weak attempt at best. She was still reeling at the thought of remaining mated to Prince Damian—of pretending that Dante's child was Damian's—of remaining at the dragon's side, accompanying and serving him from Castle Umbras, until such day as Dante came of age and could shift into a full-blown dragon. Even then, the future was uncertain at best: Prince Dante believed that revealing his potential alliance with the Lycanians at just the right time, as well as outlining his authority throughout the Realm, supported by *both* his brothers and *all* their sons, would be influential enough to force the hand of the king when the day finally came, to make him step aside once and for all. And if not, then he trusted some mysterious omen—*implicitly*—although he hadn't told her what it was.

Dante believed that, in fifty-four more years, when both Damian and Drake came of age as well, the shift of power would be inevitable.

King Demitri could not oppose them all.

He could not take on three fully mature dragons.

Still, he was hesitant to overthrow his father, to usurp the traditional king by force. He was hoping that the monarch would come to see reason and bend, that the potential prosperity of the Realm, and the power of his obvious successors—his sons— would ultimately sway King Demitri's opinion and convince him to relinquish his reign. Mina had no doubt that Dante would use lethal force if he had to—*traditions, lineage, and loyalty be damned*—he would challenge his father, dragon to dragon, if King Demitri forced his hand. He had demonstrated his resolve as well as his capacity to be ruthless with Prince Damian.

She swallowed her trepidation.

And meanwhile, Prince Dante would live at Castle

Warlochia—he would rule the warlocks and his royal province—with Cassidy *at his side.*

The knowledge made her sick.

Damian's harsh, unforgiving mouth quirked up in another faintly familiar smile. "I'm sorry; I don't yet know how to turn it off, the mind reading." He brandished an apologetic hand. "But I don't think you need to worry about that, not so much."

From what Matt—what *Damian*—had told her earlier, the telepathy was really a problem: While all dragons possessed the ability to read minds, it wasn't an automatic or natural occurrence. It took a lot of deliberation and mental clarity. In other words, it didn't just happen. However, something symbiotic had taken place when the two personalities had merged. Somehow, the combination of Damian's highly developed ability and *the other one's* deep intuitive nature had led to an open telepathic channel that *the new prince* could not shut down.

Mina crooked her eyebrows in curiosity. "Well…are you going to tell me why I needn't worry?" There was no point in pretending she hadn't been thinking what she had.

The prince nodded sympathetically and chuckled.

"In the short time we spent traveling to the inn, I was able to garner a few impressions." He rotated his hand, palm facing forward, before she could jump to the wrong conclusions. "*No*, I was not able to read Prince Dante's mind. His barriers are far too strong for that—as, I assume, are my own—*but* there were several subtle impressions that lingered." He winked. "Dante is *fiercely* protective of that child—and of you—and he didn't give Cassidy a second thought on the day they were mated. He didn't care about the fertility elixir—*at all*. He was too keenly focused on the war." He leaned forward, glanced upward, and then cast his eyes to the side, as if probing for a deeper explanation. "His wheels are always turning, and he views you and that child, *not Cassidy*, as his own. She is more like a piece of furniture." He paused to take a slow, deep breath, and then he met her gaze directly. "I don't think he will follow his father's plan—*our father's plan*—going forward. I believe he will forge his own. Just as Prince Dam—*just as I*—can read minds without even trying, Prince Dante has an extremely natural command of magic. I wouldn't be surprised if he plays with Cassidy's mind or manipulates her memories. He could make her believe anything...or nothing...at will." He shrugged and inclined his head in a flippant—*almost arrogant?*—nod. "I'm just saying I wouldn't worry about it, not too much. Don't forget: I've known him for one hundred forty-nine years, and I've had... intimate dealings...with Cassidy already. A woman like that will be about as significant as a flea on a donkey's ass to Prince Dante. She isn't worth your thoughts because she won't command his."

Mina's mouth dropped open in surprise.

Trying to discern who was who when Prince Damian was speaking was like listening to twin robins sing. The notes were utterly interchangeable, yet they were distinctly different at the same time. It was truly amazing how Damian's many years of dominance and privilege, as well his formal education and training, flowed out in his cocky self-assurance, in his novel choice of words—*a flea on a donkey's ass?*—while *the other one's* careful insights and honed intuition dovetailed seamlessly throughout the examination in his cadence and his thoughts. It was mind-numbing to witness the integration, and Mina realized, perhaps for the first time, that she was truly meeting a unique and brand-new person.

Yet, when she concentrated on the meaning behind the words, she was still twisted up in knots. She didn't know how she felt about any of it. The thought of Prince Dante with Cassidy still turned her stomach, yet the thought of carrying on some secret affair with the prince of Warlochia—if, in fact, Dante was even considering the latter—made her weak at the knees with terror. The thought of living at Castle Umbras with...Damian...in light of how well she knew his predominant soul gave her a sense of peace and belonging, yet the thought of interacting with this new personality, obeying this prince and even feeding his dragon, made her want to disappear. She knew it wouldn't be easy, keeping up the ruse, but she could not have orchestrated a better twist of fate if she had tried: Compared to the future she had been facing just over one week ago, this was a thousand times more amenable.

At least *this* prince of Umbras would never beat her or rape her.

And she could definitely love "their" child.

She *would* love their child.

Her head began to hurt as she wondered how it would all play out. Would Prince Dante expect her to give him more sons? *Surely he did not expect her to couple with Prince Damian!* Her head hurt even worse, and she quickly dismissed the thoughts.

Just then, the large multi-paneled doors of the rustic castle foyer swung open, and Prince Dante strolled confidently into the room, his gorgeous onyx hair flowing like a warlock's cloak to his shoulders; his regal sapphire eyes flashing with authority and animal magnetism; his lethal, otherworldly presence permeating the entire room. She stood, out of habit, ready to bow her head and curtsey—*perhaps he would even need to feed his dragon*—and then her heart skipped several beats, her palms began to sweat, and she staggered where she stood.

Oh, dearest goddess of mercy!

She ran toward the doors.

"Raylea!"

She was utterly frantic to get to the young bright-eyed child who had just entered the foyer behind him, and when the two sisters met in the center of the hall, they embraced like the gods had commanded their union.

"Sister." Raylea wept.

"Raylea!" Mina replied, and then she started to blubber, spewing what felt like a dozen nonsensical words per second. "I got your doll! The one you made for me with the pretty button eyes and the patchwork dress. The prince told me how brave and courageous you were, going to Warlochia—*Oh my gods, I can't believe you did that!*—but I wasn't surprised at all, that you found a way to get the doll to me. Oh, and you have to know: I've kept her close to me, right next to my heart, every day since I got her. And I've kept you there, too! I love you both so much; I've missed you so dearly!" She swiped at her eyes. "But I have her—and she's so lovely!" Mina laughed at her silly, illogical speech, even as she ran her hands through Raylea's hair, cupped her cheeks in her palms, and kissed her little forehead...at least ten times.

The girl laughed amidst her tears. "I made her for you. All by myself."

Mina pulled her into another fierce hug. "I know you did. And thank you so much! I absolutely love it." She ran her hands up and down Raylea's arms and stared at her with concern. "Are you all right? Are you hurt? Do you need a physician?" She eyed her from head to toe before turning her around in order to check her back, her neck, and her shoulders. She was just about to start discreetly undressing her when Raylea slapped at her hands and smiled.

"I'm fine," she insisted, linking Mina's fingers in hers. "Well, I mean, it was awful. It was scary. The shadow who bought me was horrible, but I don't really remember. Prince Dante said I can spend the rest of the week with you, and then he's going to have his own castle guards escort me home, back to Arns, to see Mama and Papa. But I can visit whenever I want." She giggled with joy, and her dark brown eyes lit up like twin russet flames. "He saved me from the monster."

Mina's bottom lip began to tremble, and she felt like a child herself, wholly overwhelmed by her emotions and completely unable to speak. As Prince Dante stepped forward, ostensibly to explain what had happened—or to tell her what he expected her to do—she collapsed from the intensity of her grief, *her relief*, and her gratitude, and she shrouded his boots with her hair.

He bent down to place a gentle hand on her shoulder. "I told you I would bring her home," he murmured in a deep, sonorous tone.

Mina raised her head to regard him squarely beneath tearstained lashes, and he offered his hand to help her up. She took it between both of her palms and pressed it to her cheek, angling her head with affection. "My prince," she whispered softly, wetting his skin with her tears. "Thank you." Her entire body began to shake. "I have no words."

She bowed her head in the purest gesture of reverence she had ever shown, wanting to demonstrate her appreciation, and then she brought her forehead down to his feet—slowly, and with great veneration—and kissed the tips of his boots, each one in turn.

Oddly enough, she had never felt more like his equal.

"Thank you," she whispered again.

CHAPTER TWENTY-NINE

Castle Dragon ~ one month later

"COME WITH ME," Dante had said, offering no explanation, making no justification, and just like her first day at Castle Dragon, Mina had followed him into the courtyard, mounted the same white gelding, and cantered quietly beside him along the same familiar path.

In the weeks that had followed Raylea's rescue, life in the Realm had moved forward very quickly: All three dragon princes had been summoned to meet with King Demetri; they had conferred about the battle, discussed their roles going forward, and briefed him on the state of their districts.

And each one of them had managed to pull it off.

As of yet, Prince Drake did not know about the *great deception*, and Dante was waiting for the right moment to tell him, for *necessity* to warrant the admission. He wanted to bring his youngest brother into the fold, and he believed it was necessary, that he could definitely trust him; however, he was hesitant to place another innocent soul in danger, especially when they still had time.

Meanwhile, Raylea had returned to the *commonlands*, and Mina's parents had been positively elated to discover that both of their daughters were still safe and alive, that they had actually spent a week together at Castle Umbras, and that Mina would invite them *all* to visit soon, within the next couple of months.

They were, however, grieving deeply, along with Callum Gentry, over the news of Matthias's death, the fact that he had been captured at Castle Dragon and executed by the king.

Damian and Dante had given the matter a great deal of consideration—whether or not to inform the blacksmith that his son was still alive, at least his soul was—but in the end, Prince Damian had made the call. The danger was just too great. The secret was far too volatile. And there was always time to retract the decision later, once things had settled down.

Mina's heart ached at the thought of Mr. Gentry's suffering, but she understood the princes' reasoning: The fewer people who knew, the less chance there was of a leak. As it stood, Prince Dante was practically beside himself with concern over Wavani the witch. On one hand, he absolutely could not execute the king's closest advisor and hope to get away with it—King Demitri would leave no stone unturned in the search for her killer—but on the other hand, all it would take was an uneasy feeling, a haphazard toss of her runes, or a reason to consult her looking-glass, based on a passing suspicion, and the king would slay them all for their treason.

Wavani the witch and her lover were two perilous loose ends that needed to be closed.

Mina shivered, not wanting to imagine the worst…

Rather, she turned her attention to better news: They had recently learned that Tatiana was also expecting a child. She had become pregnant the first night of the war, and Prince Drake could only be described as smitten at best. For all intents and purposes, the Ahavi seemed to be happy, whereas Damian and Mina had fallen into an awkward yet familiar routine at Castle

Umbras, lending each other support, learning as they went along, and making it up when they were clueless.

Mina's pregnancy had begun to show. She was nauseated in the mornings; the smell of food made her queasy, and she required more sleep than ever before—yet she really couldn't complain. The king was satisfied with his sons and their Ahavi, he had no reason to question his choices or appointments, and the Realm was moving forward, day by day.

Life was resuming as it should.

Now, as Prince Dante reined his stallion to a halt beneath the branches of an aged sycamore tree, Mina followed his lead and dismounted. The afternoon was positively stunning: The sun was shining in a clear blue sky; the birds were singing happily in the trees; and there was a gentle summer's breeze rustling the leaves and lightly licking their skin. It was truly a beautiful afternoon.

Prince Dante tethered his horse to a fallen log, waited for Mina to do the same, and then extended his hand in her direction. "Come to me, Mina."

She couldn't help but remember that first day in the courtyard when the prince had ordered her to do the same; only this time, her arm wasn't bleeding and his dragon wasn't riding the edge—there was no hesitation or fear. Yes, she still felt intimidated by his presence, at the sheer breadth of power projected by his dragon, and her stomach still quivered with butterflies at the mere resonance of his voice; but she knew he wouldn't harm her, not indiscriminately, and she would never provoke his beast.

She curtsied. "My prince."

He smiled, *truly smiled*, and then he led her to a rise in the hill, still beneath the tree, and squatted down to remove a carefully placed bushel of branches concealing a lone gold cross behind them. The cross stood just above and beyond a flat bronzed placard, and Prince Dante burrowed his fingers into the grass. "This is my twin's final resting place."

Mina drew in a sharp intake of air. "Desmond's?"

"Yes."

The silence was palpable. She didn't know what to say.

"What does it make you feel? Seeing it, that is?"

Mina looked away. "It makes me feel sorrow…and regret. It makes me feel compassion for you and anger toward your father."

He stood up, turned around, and placed the palm of his hand over her heart in a surprisingly intimate gesture. "Don't lie to me, Mina. What does *this*"—he swept his arm around the meadow, indicating their physical surroundings as well as the two of them standing beneath the tree, and nodded—"what does *all of this* make you feel? I need to know."

Mina let out a slow, measured breath and consulted her heart.

Since the day she had first met the prince, they had been thrust into an elusive cat-and-mouse game, always testing and straining the balance of power between them. Dante had made it abundantly clear that he had to have her obedience—his dragon required the affirmation of dominance—yet she had tried to change him. And in the end, they had both fallen into their expected, prescribed roles anyway.

She bit her lip and wiped a sweaty palm against her skirt. Did she dare speak from the depths of her heart? Was that really what he wanted?

Truth be told, they were too similar to keep from clashing on occasion: They were both headstrong and proud; they were each defiant to a fault; and they were so determined to remain in control, if only of their stubborn free will, that neither one had ever truly revealed their hand, at least not entirely. And that's how Mina knew Dante's question ran much deeper than his words.

He wanted to know how she felt…*about him.*

"My prince," she murmured, her voice growing all at once subdued. "I belong to the Realm…and to Prince Damian…just as your father decreed, so it is difficult for me to speak too freely."

He placed two fingers beneath the curve of her chin and lifted it gently upward. When her gaze met his, his eyes were so intense—so dark and so full of curiosity and longing—that she couldn't hold her tongue.

Reaching into a deep well for courage, she spoke softly. "As a child, before I was taken to the Keep, I could have answered you easily: I would have said I feel like crying because a great tragedy has happened in this place. I feel like reaching out to you because you suffered." She braced her heart, refusing to allow any tears. "As a slave—as an Ahavi—the answer would be different: I feel like it is my duty to assist you, to somehow place things in order, and I wonder how I may serve you. What does he need?" She closed her eyes and steadied her breathing before she slowly ventured forward again with both eyes wide open. "But as a woman, as Mina Louvet…"

"Yes?" Dante encouraged. "As a woman?" He locked his gaze with hers, refusing to look away, and she almost staggered back, jarred by the power of the current that flowed between them: *Oh hell, what was the point in pretending?* "As a woman," she pressed on, "I can't help but wonder who Desmond was—what was he like as a boy? What were the two of you like, *together*, back then? I can't help but wonder if you laughed, or played, or dreamed anything different than you dream today. And I think, perhaps, that your bond was so tight, so unbreakable, that it survived the passage of time and the transition of death—and I'm so very jealous." He angled his head to the side, regarding her intently, and she frowned, feeling somehow ashamed. "I wonder if you loved him, and I ache inside because I know I would give all that I am to just once have you love me that deeply."

Dante absently took a step back, visibly surprised by her answer. Although he had asked her to be honest, he obviously had not expected such a confession. He wet his lips in a rare gesture of discomfort, and then he parted his mouth to speak. When nothing came out, he cleared his throat and tried again. "Why, sweet Mina? What would be different?"

At his cold, indifferent question, she wished she could just disappear.

What was the point of this banter?

As if he understood her need to pull back, he took a generous step forward, toward Desmond's grave, and glanced down at the cross. "My twin was a visionary," he said softly. "He danced to his own drum. He walked to his own mysterious beat. And he answered to a higher calling, something only known to him, something buried within his soul. He opposed my father, my mother, and his duty to the Realm because he fell in love with a commoner, and despite all the repercussions, he could not be dissuaded from that path." He knelt down to touch the placard, absently tracing the letters in Desmond's name with his forefinger. "I used to dream, Mina, a long, *long* time ago." He paused as if remembering. "I used to laugh, and feel, *and want* until my father reared it out of me...until the Realm demanded that I relinquish each and every reverie. Until I grew into a man and put away my childish longings." He looked off into the distance, and Mina approached him slowly, tentatively, pressing her thighs against his back as she reached down to place a hand on his shoulder.

She didn't utter a word.

She simply stood there, offering a sympathetic touch, and the contact brought his attention back to the present.

"I have a proposition for you, Ahavi. I would like to propose a trade. There is something I want you to consider, something I could simply require of you if I wished, but I would much rather seek your consent."

Mina stiffened, trying to find something meaningful or affectionate in his words. It was true: Dante Dragona did not have much to give—he did not have much *give* in him—so his desire to seek her *consent* in any matter, however insignificant, was no small thing. At least there was that... "Yes, my prince?"

"As you already know," he said, "I will be able to shift in thirty-one-years, and many things will change." His expression grew distant, yet resolved. "I will take over the governance of this realm, whether by diplomacy or force, and I will require the support of those who are closest to me, those I know I can trust. I do want you beside me, Mina, and I do need your help…but until such time as I am at the head of this country, you must remain at Castle Umbras with Damian. There is truly no other way." His dragon stirred, and his voice grew clipped, even as his nostrils noticeably flared. "I have made it implicitly clear that he is never, *ever* to touch you, not in *that* way, not if he desires to live." Before she could respond or react, he pressed forward, as if the statement were a mere supposition of fact. "However, I also let him know that I understand—Damian is a sovereign prince of Dragons Realm, and his dragon has many hungers. He will not be stable if he doesn't feed…all of them. There isn't a female in this kingdom who would refuse his advances, nor a maiden who would choose to deny him. He doesn't have to be alone. He may still find love or affection, albeit in the shadows, in secret, just like Desmond did. And I would look away—*I will look away*—and so will Prince Drake, once he understands."

Dante seemed to be rambling.

Yet and still, *he* had brought up the subject, and now, she had a few questions of her own: "And Cassidy, *my prince?* Where does she fit into this picture?"

Prince Dante flashed a cautionary smile, his dragon asserting his dominance. "Do you really wish to know, sweet Mina?"

"I do," she said, refusing to back off. What was good for the goose was good for the gander, assuming the gander wasn't a slave…

He sighed. "Cassidy is only too willing to fulfil her required duties, and I can't fault her for that—she was raised, trained, and *conditioned* to bear children for the Realm, and it is my solemn obligation to take care of her. *But…*" He shook his head, show-ing the first real sign of compassion. "But I do not want her to rear—or carry—my sons. She is not moral, nor is she worthy." He angled his head to look directly at Mina. "And I wouldn't do that to *you*." He glanced at her belly and then averted his eyes out of respect. "Still…at some point, if she does not become pregnant, the king will press the issue. And if I tell him I think she's barren, he will simply replace her with another Sklavos Ahavi, although we both know such females are rare. Still, I cannot make you any promises; *however*, it may not be a problem."

Mina raised her eyebrows, almost afraid to hope.

"I did not touch her before I left the castle for the battle of Dracos Cove, nor have I lain with her since, and she is growing restless, defensive, and desperate. She's been sidling up to the king, and he is starting to respond with curious glances, not-so-innocent touches, and inappropriate innuendos. If she were to be given a vial of elixir at just the right time…if I were to leave her alone with my father…I believe he would sire her offspring, albeit unwittingly. From there, it would be a simple task to manipulate her memories, to convince her that the child was ours. I have already instructed my cook to put a few drops of the elixir in her morning tea at the start of each day."

Mina gasped, stunned by the revelation. "And you would do that for me? *For us?*"

"I would," Dante answered without preamble, "and that brings me to my original proposition." He stood once more, brushed her hair out of her eyes, and bent to grasp both of her shoulders in his hands. "As for my side of the trade, I would offer you immortality, Mina Louvet. As soon as the child is born, as soon as it's safe to transform you, I would make you immortal."

Her jaw dropped open, but she didn't speak.

She couldn't.

Her head was still spinning in circles.

"If you would consent to be my lover, to come to me of your own free will, I would give you back the power of choice. You need only come to me when you choose to; you need only welcome me out of desire; and you need only surrender to my touch when you desire to share my fire." He reached down to take her hands in his, raised them to his lips, and pressed a beguiling kiss into the center of her palms, each one in turn, his passionate sapphire gaze never leaving hers. "And in return, I will give you my fealty, as both your prince and your lover. I will be yours and yours, alone."

Mina almost gasped. She nearly staggered where she stood. "W-w-why?" she murmured reflexively, stammering the word. "For what purpose? I mean, what would compel you to offer so much? Immortality, just to be your lover? Especially when you could just command it at any time?" She shook her head, knowing there had to be more to the story. After all, she had poured out her heart to him just minutes ago, and the prince had glossed right over it.

He hadn't even responded.

He didn't want her love. He didn't want her heart. But he still wanted her body.

Why?

"What else would you ask of me, my prince? What else do you want in return?"

Dante cupped her face in his hands and stared into her eyes until it seemed like he might just drown in their depths, and then he buried his face in her hair and whispered huskily in her ear. "The gods know, until this very moment, I was prepared to ask you to be the mother of *all* my sons, to agree to fulfill the Omen. Yes, Mina, you are meant to be the mother of this realm, the one who helps me fulfill the prophecy, and I was prepared to ask you to do it for your people, to do it for justice, to do it for Dragons Realm, *but...*" He drew back, turned to glance at Desmond's grave, and slowly exhaled. "But in truth, there is so much more that I want. *Teach me to love,* sweet Mina. Bring me back to life. Show me once again how to dream. Wait for me, my Ahavi, for thirty-one years. Live as you must, survive as you will, and one day, rule this realm beside me as my queen."

Mina felt the air rush out of her body, and she was certain her heart would jump out of her chest. She drew back, wresting her body away from his, and struggled to catch her breath. "Dante, I...I..." She felt like she was hyperventilating. "I hardly know what to say."

He stepped forward, brushed the pad of his thumb along her quivering bottom lip, and bent low to taste it. "Tell me you don't love me," he breathed into her mouth, "and I will never ask this of you again."

She savored the hot, wild flavor of his kiss, reveling in the smoke that tinged his breath. After several heartbeats had passed, she murmured, "I cannot."

"Cannot agree?" he asked.

"Cannot tell you I don't love you."

He nodded, and his smile illuminated his eyes. "A long time ago, I told you that I wanted you because your hair is like mine, as dark as the midnight sky." He ran his thumb along the side of her jaw, just as he had done that first day in the courtyard. "Your eyes are the color of emeralds, as rare as they are exquisite." He clasped his hands behind his back and studied her from head to toe, without apology; once again, repeating the familiar actions. "You are beautiful," he whispered, "and our sons will be strong." Only this time, he didn't stop there. "What I didn't say that day—*what I couldn't say that day*—was here is a woman who could capture my *heart*. Here is a woman who is worthy of the same." He took both of her hands in his and squeezed them, careful not to press too hard. "You understand duty and sacrifice, Mina—you are as brave as you are intelligent. You have the courage to lead, the strength to follow, and the wisdom to know the difference. You just need to live for a purpose. You have already proven that you can survive in a world full of warlocks, *shades*, and shifters; a world built by commoners, yet ruled by kings; and you have the tenacity to change it. You are a true daughter of this realm, just as I am its true son." He drew her into his arms and held her close to his heart. "I will always live for my duty and my people. I will always put the welfare of the Realm first. And I will *never* betray my royal blood, the *core* of my father's traditions, or the lineage that makes me a dragon. But I don't believe I have to…not with you." He regarded her sheepishly then, crooking his neck at an unnatural angle so he could clearly see her eyes, and the gesture was uncharacteristically boyish. "I will never be soft-hearted, sweet Mina, or gentle, or even tame. But I will be just and honest. I will be true and faithful. And I will be yours, my Ahavi, as much as I belong to the Realm." His voice dropped into a deep, languorous cadence and practically hummed with conviction. "A dragon requires fire to reanimate, and a king requires a queen, not a slave, to temper his calloused heart. You have never been the latter, so choose now to be the former, even if it's thirty years away. Teach me to love, sweet Mina. Raise my son—*our sons*—to be brave, to be strong, *to defy what isn't worthy of obeisance*. Let me be your Keep, and come to me because you wish to learn, to live…and to love."

Mina felt like she had fallen into a liquid pool of magic, of dark midnight-blue eyes, like she had been swept away by the current of a mystical fire, and she was softly, sweetly drowning beneath the swift, graceful undertow of the dragon's heartfelt words—and she wanted to just let go. She was utterly and completely lost in Dante's savage soul. Everything she had ever wanted was standing right in front of her, and she couldn't help but wonder at the sacrifice it would take to pull it off, the cunning it would require to be *this* dragon's queen, the obedience and the danger that would come with his possessive arms.

But it didn't matter.

Not at all.

If anyone could do it, she could.

She was a Sklavos Ahavi, after all, a woman born to serve the Realm.

"Yes, my prince," she whispered sweetly, her tears falling freely. "Oh, yes, Prince Dante…*yes*."

CHAPTER THIRTY

The throne room

I T WAS LATE when Prince Dante and Mina returned to
Castle Dragon, and the king, the other Ahavi, and Dante's
brothers were waiting for them in the throne room. Since
Dante had borrowed Mina under the guise of giving her several
antiquated scrolls to update and transcribe into Warlochian for
him, and since the majority of the scrolls were kept in a secure,
hidden outbuilding, a mile or two away from the main castle
library, no one seemed too concerned about where they'd been,
except...*perhaps*...for Cassidy. In truth, the king could not
have cared less if his eldest son had taken Mina Louvet out to
the pasture to feed her to the wolves, just so long as he kept her
alive long enough to birth Damian's child, and if there had been
some sort of improper dalliance between them—*so what?*—just as
long as it did not create friction between the brothers or political
unrest in the Realm.

Slaves were slaves, after all.

King Demitri scooted eagerly to the edge of his throne, the
moment they entered the hall, and bellowed, "Well, it's about

time! Are the two of you done exploring the grounds?" He narrowed his eyes in boredom and impatience.

"Forgive me, Father," Dante offered humbly, offering no further explanation.

The king turned his attention to Damian Dragona, who seemed utterly unfazed as Mina hurried to his side and curtsied apologetically. Demitri quickly harrumphed. "Very well." He gestured with his hand to indicate the other members who were present. "We were just concluding our business for the evening, discussing the importance of going forward with the Autumn Mating, if only for the kingdom's morale. I think it's important that we maintain our sense of tradition and provide a formal presentation of the matrimonial selections and district appointments, give the people something to celebrate." He sat back in his throne and shrugged. "The battle of Dracos Cove was so… anxiety-producing for some. They could use a pleasant distraction." He said it with such emotionless triviality that it gave Dante chills—*good lords,* the male had slain thousands of enemies, yet he spoke of that day like it had merely been a walk in the gardens.

"Of course, Father," he said, stepping forward to the base of the dais, just below the throne, and taking his rightful place at the head of his brothers. "As always, I will do whatever the Realm requires."

King Demitri nodded, seemingly appeased. "Good." He waved his hand to dismiss the entire subject, clearly done with it, and turned his attention to Prince Drake. "Your brother can fill you in on the details later." Prince Drake inclined his head, and the king stood up to stretch his legs, his long purple-and-gold robe brushing against the floor at his feet. "If that is all, then you are all dismissed."

All three Dragona sons bowed their heads, even as Mina and Tatiana curtsied, and then Cassidy Bondeville cleared her throat and took a brazen step toward the throne. "Excuse me, Your Majesty, but I have something I would like to announce."

There was a soft collective gasp at her unadulterated gall, and Dante placed his outstretched hand between his Ahavi and the king in a mock gesture of concern in order to usher her back. The king raised his eyebrows, and Dante waited, unable to discern whether the dragon was amused or incensed, whether he would laugh at the prima donna's antics or scorch her where she stood.

"What is it, wench?" King Demitri said with a sneer, publicly reminding her of her place.

Cassidy blanched. "Forgive me, Your Majesty: I know it is improper for a slave to speak in the presence of her king, but"—she turned to gaze at Dante, and her eyes were filled with such false worship and contrived affection that it almost made him retch—"since Prince Dante is your eldest son, I thought you would be pleased with my news." She raised her chin and drew back her shoulders, virtually beaming with pride. "I am with child," she said smugly.

Mina's eyes grew wide, and Dante bit his tongue, not knowing whether to growl or chuckle. He stared at his all-powerful father, still hovering beside his throne, and swallowed his anger. He knew it was a possibility. He knew things were heading in that direction. And he had even helped them along. *But*, it was still jarring to know that the king held him in such little regard, that after all these years, Dante had failed to earn even a modicum of his father's respect.

So King Demitri had bed his consort.

Unbelievable.

The king turned a pale shade of green, and his eyes darted nervously around the room like a guilty man's: So, he wasn't a fool, after all. The last time he had inquired about Cassidy's condition, Dante had said she wasn't pregnant, and the king had commanded him to take care of the matter as soon as they returned to Warlochia. Since a Sklavos Ahavi can recognize her pregnancy within a matter of hours—*there was some deep intuition in their makeup*—something had to have happened within the last thirty-six hours, *something named King Demitri*, and the monarch was just now realizing that if both he and Dante had bed her, then he might just be the father. Dante was at least appeased that the male looked sick.

Cassidy hurried to Dante's side, ignoring his outstretched hand, and curtsied low before him. "My prince." She offered him her cheek, ostensibly for a kiss, and he snarled.

"Are you sure?" he asked in a surly tone.

"Oh yes," she whispered, looking curiously confused by his reaction.

Dante's dragon reared its savage head, and for a moment, he felt the urge to scorch her right there, to burn her flesh from her bones, melt her cartilage to ash, and watch as she disintegrated into so much refuse...as a pile of waste on the floor. It had nothing to do with her as a person—or a woman—truly, he could not have cared less. As far as he was concerned, she would bear an incredibly powerful dragon, one he could now rear as a loyalist. However, his beast was not that cerebral or rational. It only knew that the female had disobeyed him, that she had strayed from her submissive role, and that she needed to be corrected. He restrained the impulse and gestured toward the throne-room doors. "Then I suggest you go to bed and get your rest." He narrowed his eyes in command, and she quickly scurried away, darting out of the throne room.

Drake gave Dante a questioning glance, and Damian pierced the silence with derisive laughter. "Nothing better than a wayward bitch in heat," he drawled rudely.

Dante spun around and glared at him, stunned by the unexpected outburst as well as the uncanny resemblance to the dragon he had known all his life. Prince Damian was indeed King Demitri's son—even Mina looked taken aback. Before Dante could spit out a retort, the throne-room doors swung open once more, and the temperature in the room dropped twenty degrees. For a moment, Dante thought it might be Cassidy returning to stage a scene, in which case he was going to have her head, but it wasn't Cassidy Bondeville.

Oh great lords of fire, it was not his Sklavos Ahavi, but Wavani the witch, instead. And Rafael Bishop, the high mage of Warlochia, was close on her heels.

The couple looked incensed.

*

The witch was dressed from head to toe in deep raven black. Her stiff, five-inch-high collar was turned brusquely upward; the tails of her petticoat flapped behind her like wings; and her harsh leather boots clicked noisily across the marble floor as she strode angrily toward the throne. "Your Majesty!" she called in a shrill, witchy voice, extending a long, gnarled finger to point at his guests. "This entire visitation is a travesty, and these matings are a hoax." She glared at Mina Louvet, and the Ahavi winced with fear.

The king looked absolutely stunned by her brazen entrance as well as her cryptic words, and in true Dragona fashion, his first and only reaction was anger. "What is the meaning of this!" He threw up his hand in an offensive gesture and sent Rafael Bishop spiraling through the air, slamming into a column, and dangling above the floor, pinned by invisible stakes. There was no way he was going to tolerate such a bold advance from an inferior male. Then he turned his attention back to Wavani. "Have you lost your mind, *my counselor?*" reminding her of her place.

The witch shook her head *and smiled* as she continued to approach the throne, and Dante's heart constricted in his chest. "No, Your Highness," she said with arrogant assurance, "but perhaps you have lost yours if you trust what you see."

Dante's dragon roared inside as his fight-or-flight instincts kicked in.

Son of a Jackal!

The sorceress knew, and she was going to tell the king!

In the space of a heartbeat, he surveyed the great hall and took inventory of all the players: Drake was standing beside Tatiana, about thirty paces from the throne, and they were in the king's direct line of vision, but they were far enough from the dais to escape if they had to. The prince would not understand what was happening, and he would not have time to react as an ally. Hopefully, he could save his unborn child.

Damian and Mina, on the other hand, were standing to the monarch's far right. They were at the bottom of the dais, maybe twenty paces away from the king, and he could reach them in the span of an instant. Beyond their proximity to the lethal dragon, they were three seconds too far from the doors, and two seconds too far from the nearest window, assuming that Damian could react *instantly* and use his preternatural strength and speed to get Mina out of the hall.

In all reality, the king's anger and his grief might be so great that he would strike at Damian first, *strike at Matthias Gentry*, and if he did, Mina would be caught in the crossfire.

But Dante didn't believe that was how things would play out.

From where he stood, he believed the monarch would eliminate any potential vulnerability, first. He would strike to his left instinctively, because that was his weak side, his blind spot, and Dante was his greatest threat. If Prince Dante wanted to derail the hazardous situation, he would have to strike at King Demitri first.

The moment he thought it, he dismissed it.

The idea was utterly ludicrous.

It was crazy and suicidal.

King Demitri was damn near a deity: all-powerful, nearly omniscient, and practically indestructible. Dante would never stand a chance. The king would shred his throat, disembowel his innards, and wrench out his heart in an instant, before Dante could even react. Not to mention, there would be a high mage and an angry witch at his back.

No; the only way to diffuse this situation was to go after

Wavani and Rafael, to take them out before they could expose his treason. He sought Prince Damian's eyes, knowing his brother could easily read his mind, and tried to alert him with a nod—but the witch was already speaking.

"My lord." She bowed her head deeply, and then she snarled like a fiend. "Do not attack the messenger. The child isn't his!" In her frenzy, her eyes darted around the room haphazardly, and she screeched, "Hell, *he* isn't *him*! The soul! *The soul is all wrong!*"

Somewhere in the background, Mina let out a petrified whimper, even as Dante tried to lunge in Wavani's direction, but his feet never left the ground. *So that's why she had brought the high mage with her.* The witch and the warlock were combining their powers in order to cast a spell about the room—the air had congealed into mystical quicksand, and the only being unaffected was the king, who was much too powerful to succumb.

Dante could still move, but it would require an enormous effort.

"What the hell are you saying, Wavani!" the king shouted, leaping down from the dais in one fell swoop. He glared at the hag with feverish eyes, his dragon riding perilously close to the surface.

The witch threw back her head in frustration and howled: "The boy is a bastard—"

"Shut your mouth!" the king shouted over her, and in the blink of an eye, he had the witch by her throat. Fuming, he hoisted her off the floor, and his enormous sculpted muscles bulged with unrestrained fury.

What the devil? Dante wondered, trying to make sense of the scene.

And then it suddenly dawned on him: *Blessed goddess of mercy,* the king thought Wavani was about to reveal *his* secret, the fact that he had impregnated Cassidy. After all, she was in charge of the Sklavos Ahavi, the mating, and the assurance of sacred offspring—and she took her role quite seriously. *The matings are a hoax. The child isn't his. The soul is all wrong...*

The boy is a bastard.

At this juncture, her words could still mean anything.

They still had a narrow window of time.

For a split second, Prince Dante wondered if he should let the scene play out, stand back and watch things unfold, see if his father would kill Wavani on his own, but it was far too much to hope for...

Rafael Bishop was already clearing his throat.

"My king..." the high mage drawled, using his considerable power as a warlock to descend from the post, in spite of the telepathic restraints. His eyes glowed demonic red, and his cloak fluttered behind him as he floated to the ground like a specter. *"You need to listen."* His ethereal, malevolent voice reverberated throughout the hall like a chorus of moaning ghouls. "There is an enormous deception taking place in this room."

Dante flung a sizzling bolt of lightning at the warlock's throat, catching him unaware, and rallied inside as it severed the warlock's vocal cords. "Silence!" he bellowed, pretending to support the king. Then he turned to his father and baited him. "My liege," he snarled, sounding half crazed and wholly disgusted. "Is this what the Realm has become?" He struggled to stroll toward his father, releasing his wings to propel him. "Do the *slaves* now command the *kings*? Can this hag command *you* to bow? Can a woman of lowly birth, a gifted seer or not, defile my father's throne room and order him about like a common peasant? In front of his sons? In front of his unborn grandchildren? In front of a Warlochian mage! One who just happens to be the head of the illegal slave trade and sleeping with your counselor—*enormous* deception, indeed."

Rafael Bishop shrank back in alarm, his mouth dropping open in shock, even as blood pooled from the corners of his mouth in response to his recent injury. He looked like he had just seen a ghost, and despite all of his considerable power, his legs began to tremble.

Prince Dante flashed a wicked smile. "Ah, so then it is true?" He glanced askance at the king and shook his head in disgust. "I didn't know for sure, not until now, Father. It was only a suspicion, but his reaction just confirmed it." The fool had just absolved Dante of any blame…the fact that he knew about the slave trade and kept the information from his king. He spun on his heel to glare at Wavani. Her moon-shaped pupils had just turned a vindictive shade of green, and she was trembling with rage.

"You bastard!" she choked, struggling for breath. "You clever, unholy bastard. I will see you—"

"I am your prince!" Dante thundered, drowning out her words. "How dare you." He tried to hurl a silencing spell in her direction, but she blocked it with her eyes.

"I know what you're doing, you traitorous fiend!" she hissed. "I saw it *all* in a seeking vision."

Dante's stomach clenched in fear, and for the briefest moment, he met Mina's terrified gaze. The female's eyes were as wide as saucers; she was trembling in her boots, and she looked like she might just pass out from terror, but she didn't speak a word. *She didn't dare.* She obviously understood that *all* their lives depended upon Dante Dragona and perhaps, his brother Damian.

Dante pushed through his fear and stepped forward with deliberate arrogance, taking three haughty strides toward the witch. He knew he was running out of time. Even if they managed to get out of this alive, they might not come back from the suspicions the witch was planting in King Demitri's head. Dante had to strike hard…and quick. "Traitorous fiend?" he mocked. "*Traitorous? Why?* Because I don't support your lover's unlawful enterprise? Because I don't kowtow to your visions like a superstitious little girl, like the wretch you are trying to make of my father? *Your king!* How dare you accuse me of being a traitor in the very castle I was born in, in the very hall that I revere."

"You know—"

"*I know what!*" He hurled his voice as thunder, shaking the rafters and trailing the words with flames. "What is it that you wish to tell me, witch? Please, by all means, say it! What did you *see* in your vision? What do you know about my unborn son?" He hoped to incite his father's fear of discovery—and his rage—by inciting his paranoia. "What about this mating is so wrong?"

The king roared like the Keeper of the Forgotten Realm himself had just possessed his body and clasped his hand even tighter over her throat.

And that's when Damian chimed in. "*Dear lords*, Father: I'm almost ashamed. Kill this insolent bitch before I have to do it myself."

This pushed King Demitri over the edge. He tightened his fist into an iron grasp, crushed the witch's throat, and then tossed her limp body to the ground and stomped on her head in order to annihilate her skull, before sending her body up in flames.

And then he turned to glare at Damian, took two humongous strides in the prince's direction, and backhanded him across the room. "You are ashamed, son? *Of me!?*" He sounded utterly insane.

Mina and Tatiana gasped as Damian's jawbone audibly cracked, and two bloodstained teeth ricocheted across the clean marble floors.

Dante and Drake winced and turned away.

Prince Damian stood up slowly, staggered like he was drunk, and rubbed his jaw in a lazy caress. He spit out another tooth and began to laugh in a deep, exuberant voice, his massive shoulders shaking from the mirth. "Not of you, Father," he mumbled, slurring all three of his words. "Never of you." He bowed low and groaned. "Your Majesty—*Father*— I was ashamed of my brothers, Prince Dante and Prince Drake, for forcing you to do the dirty work in your own throne room. The witch was beneath you. I meant no offense." Considering the circumstances, it was probably the best lie he could come up with, especially in light of the fact that he had just prodded the king to kill the witch himself. He stood up straight, or at least as straight as he could, turned toward Rafael, who was still trembling in the corner, unable to speak, and cocked an arrogant shoulder. "Shall I?" He inclined his head with reverence. "The bastard disobeyed your laws. He is the head of the illegal slave trade. Your will is my command."

The king took a tentative step back, visibly relaxed, and rubbed his furrowed brow. He seemed momentarily confused, like he couldn't remember Damian's original words—*thank the gods*—and then he quickly found his voice. "Did you lose a lot of teeth?"

Damian responded with more than a little swagger. "Enough." He flashed a bloody, toothless grin, and the king joined in on the banter. "You're lucky I didn't break your neck."

Damian nodded. "Indeed, Father; *my apologies.*"

The king nodded and turned to Dante. "Why *didn't* you intervene?"

Dante bit down on his bottom lip, trying not to show his irritation. "I was so…stunned…by the witch's disrespect that I couldn't think clearly. *Forgive me.*"

The king nodded his head and harrumphed. He was obviously tired. "Very well." Then he turned to glare at the quivering warlock. "The mage is your subject, Dante. Whip him until he's dead."

Dante smiled at Damian, and the two exchanged a knowing glance. *Well played, Damian.* Dante projected the thought. *Well played.*

And then he turned to wink at Mina, glanced over his shoulder at the twelve-feet-high chest, situated in the throne-room's corner, and smirked. "Damian, go pick out a lash."

EPILOGUE

Ten years later

MINA LOUVET PROPPED herself up in bed and held the sleeping infant close to her heart, glad to finally see the high priest go. The labor and delivery had taken ten long hours; she had kept the baby awake for all the necessary visitations and initiations; and now, all she wanted to do was sleep for a while, along with her newborn son.

A ruckus outside the bedchamber door jolted her back to full attention: It was her youngest two sons clamoring for another visitor's attention. "Uncle Dante! Uncle Dante!" her middle son, Azor, squealed in delight, his high-pitched voice teeming with excitement.

"Azor!" She could tell by the sudden dip in Prince Dante's voice that he had just picked the five-year-old up. "I think you must have grown a whole inch taller since I last saw you." The child chuckled with delight, and Mina sighed.

Prince Dante's relationship with his sons was priceless.

There was a deep bond of love and loyalty between the dragon and the kids; however, it still broke her heart to hear them call him *uncle*, to think of him as their father's brother, knowing how much he adored them. Yet and still, he and Damian had done everything right. Despite Damian's equal admiration for the boys, he often remained aloof. He took on a sterner, more instructive role, making sure the children had boundaries, security, and discipline, but he never completely exposed his heart; whereas, Prince Dante played the strongest paternal role. He not only offered discipline and instruction, but lots of physical contact, rough-housing, and affection. He was determined to forge an unbreakable bond with both boys—he was intent on gaining their respect as well as their deep admiration.

And he had all three.

In truth, the boys related to Dante more as a father and Damian more as an uncle. They sought Dante's approval and attention in everything they did, counted the days and the hours until his next visit, accompanied him on horseback rides and hunting trips, and wrote letters to him when he was away—at least Ari did, while Azor included his drawings. In short, they hung on Dante's every word. They loved and respected him as a dragon. And they wanted to be exactly what he was when they grew up.

It took a lot of deliberate control and discretion from both Dante and Damian to make sure these boundaries remained firm—that their separate roles were played *just so* on purpose—but the reason was clear: When the time was right, Dante would tell all three of his sons that he was their real father, and Damian would move into the role of their protective uncle. They wanted the relationships to be predictable and entrenched already, so that the young princes would have less of a transition to make when the day finally came.

Titles would change.

Roles would not.

In the meantime, Prince Dante had forged a solid bond with Cassidy's only child as well. He had taken the boy under his wing, this time as a father, and reared him as his own. He had no intention of ever telling Dario that he was actually a bastard—King Demitri was his true despicable father—but that didn't change the prophecy: *Three children; three decades; three lads with green eyes.* It simply strengthened Dante's hold on the Realm.

And he would need that added strength when the time to usurp King Demitri came, because he simply refused to father more children with his conceited Ahavi…with Cassidy. As it stood, King Demitri refused to touch the lonely female from the Warlochian district, no matter how much she flirted with the monarch. He had only wanted her body; he had never intended to sire a son; and the close call in the throne room with Wavani the witch, now ten years past, had planted the fear of the gods into the mighty dragon. There were plenty of Blood Ahavi to slake the king's every need; he was done with Cassidy Bondeville.

Mina shifted in bed, trying to find a more comfortable position, and she replaced her frown with a smile as she thought of the other Dragona children who would one day support *King Dante*: Prince Drake's wild band of five. She found herself laughing out loud at the thought of it. If Tatiana and Prince Drake had any more children, they would have to build a larger castle. As things were, Mina was thoroughly convinced they were trying to repopulate the Realm single-handedly, and her heart warmed at the thought of their pure, ever-deepening love. Tatiana had truly healed—mind, body, and soul—and she had fallen into her role as the Sklavos Ahavi of the *commonlands* with genuine alacrity and grace. The district had grown wealthier under her expert financial assistance, and Prince Drake had even made inroads with a handful of Malo Clan rebels, although a trickle of the giants was growing increasingly restless.

The door to the bedchamber opened, drawing Mina away from her thoughts, and Prince Dante entered silently, his presence filling the room. His hauntingly beautiful eyes were alight and alert; his powerful, dominating frame was regal and proud;

and his barely concealed dragon was radiating heat—the visage stole her breath. He sidled to the edge of the bed, knelt on the floor, and reached out to stroke a strong but gentle hand over her forehead. "How are you, sweet Mina?" he murmured. "Are you okay? How do you feel?"

Mina smiled wanly. "I'm well, my prince."

He nodded. "Are you sure?"

She took his hand in hers, squeezed it, and then quickly released it. "I'm sure."

He glanced absently around the room. "Then the priest and Damian were with you the entire time?"

She glanced into the distance, fixing her eyes on the fireplace mantel and the elaborate gold-and-cream tiles that rimmed its edges. "They were." She hesitated for a moment. "Prince Damian never left my side."

Dante closed his eyes in a rare, demonstrative show of emotion. "Good," he whispered absently, and then he strengthened his voice. "*Good.*"

Mina's heart constricted in her chest, but only for a moment—they all understood their respective roles. And then, the prince reached up, drew back the tip of the soft golden blanket that covered the newborn babe, and ran a finger through his fine, downy hair. "My third son," he said with awe.

Mina drew in a sharp intake of breath, both of them understanding the significance of the moment.

Dante studied the child like he was memorizing every detail of his features, and then, at last, he quirked a smile. "He is strong and handsome."

"Like his father," Mina interjected, and the prince nodded proudly.

And then he took the child from Mina's arms, stood up, and glided to the other side of the room with the grace of a panther, taking an inconspicuous place beside the fire in order to invoke the element's vitality.

Mina slowly exhaled and placed her hand over her heart, trying to calm its feverish beating, trying to garner strength. She could do this. She *would* do this. She had done it three times before.

Actually four...

Damian Dragona had already taken Asher, within an hour of his birth, and tendered the *Dragon's Kiss* in front of the high priest, as was tradition and required. Little did the priest know that the initiation had been all for show—the child was not Prince Damian's son, and so the kiss would not truly awaken Asher's dragon. Dante would have to repeat it again. And the little prince would have to endure the pain and the fear a second time.

Mina turned away, unable to watch.

Her maternal instincts simply wouldn't allow it.

Rather, she held her breath and waited as Dante proceeded to release his fangs and make a liberal exchange of saliva, blood, and heat at the sleeping child's throat.

The child came awake with a shriek, and then he began to wail for all he was worth, as Dante's dragon snarled and purred intermittently throughout the crude, possessive claiming. Little Prince Ari and little Prince Azor were at the door in an instant: knocking brusquely on the large wooden panels, yanking at the heavy knob, and peeking inside with their deep emerald-green eyes, curiosity getting the best of them.

"What's happening to my brother?" Prince Azor asked in a timid yet curious voice.

"What's Uncle Dante doing?" Prince Ari asked, sounding a bit more mature.

Mina extended a welcoming hand, ushering both children to the bed to join her, and then she cuddled the youngest of the two, rubbing calming circles along his small back. "He's just saying hello," she explained. "He wanted to take a good look at him."

"Oh," Azor replied, his eyes still wide as saucers.

"I don't see what makes Asher so special," Ari said, and Mina couldn't help but smile. The child was already jealous of the new-born babe, vying for Prince Dante's attention, and really, that was a very good thing. It meant that his bond with his *father* ran deep, and *Aurelio* was simply reacting like any natural-born son would, wanting to be his father's favorite. Little did the child know how deep his connection to Prince Dante really went. As the firstborn son of the future king, he would one day sit on the throne himself.

Another brusque knock reverberated on the outside of the door, and this time Prince Dante strolled across the room to answer it—the initiation was blessedly over. "Yes?" he growled in an impatient tone, his voice tinged with irritation. "Who is it?"

A raspy male voice echoed in answer. "My prince, it is Emory Willoughby, Prince Damian's herald. There is news from the royal province."

"What is it?" Dante snarled.

The herald cleared his throat. "A rogue band of warlocks and a handful of Malo Clan rebels tried to breach the castle's garrisons last night, demanding an audience with the king. Something about wanting immediate royal appointments and reparations. The king's guard managed to hold them off, but they have become increasingly unruly—and their numbers are growing larger. You and your brother, Prince Drake, have been summoned to Castle Dragon. As the rebels represent your respective subjects, His Majesty would like you to quell the uprising together, to make a public example of their crimes."

Prince Dante grunted, shaking his head with disgust. "Very well," he said, speaking through the door. "Send word I am on my way." He crossed the room in three long strides, placed the child back in Mina's arms, and turned his attention to the inquisitive princes. "I'll see you when I can," he said, directing the statement at the children out of propriety, but meaning it for Mina.

Her heart sank in her chest, and she suddenly felt morose. *Lords,* how she longed to spend more time with him, to simply feel his gentle touch, to speak candidly and in private. She longed to feel his powerful arms enfold her, if only for an hour, *just a frozen moment in time*, but those precious moments were few and far between.

The door opened, and Dante spun around angrily, ready to give the herald a piece of his mind, but Prince Damian entered, instead.

The children sat up straighter on the bed.

"Father," Ari said, angling his chin a little higher to show his respect and maturity.

Azor glanced back and forth between the two dragons and bit his bottom lip, looking inexplicably nervous.

"How is everyone doing?" Prince Damian asked, crossing the room to join his family at the side of the bed. "Are you all right, Azor?" he asked, speaking quietly.

The boy nodded rapidly.

"We're well," Mina replied, wanting to set Prince Damian's mind at ease.

Damian nodded, seeming to understand on a much deeper level, and then he turned to regard Prince Dante directly. "Did you have a chance—"

"Yes," Dante interrupted. "It is done."

"Good," Prince Damian said firmly. Despite his subtle, regal cast and his obvious air of confidence, Mina couldn't help but notice that the prince looked elusively out of place, even as he stood in his own suite of rooms, situated within his own sovereign castle. And she would have felt sorrow for him, perhaps even pity, except for the fact that she knew a secret...

A secret even Prince Damian hardly understood.

Over the past ten years, Mina's parents and her sister had visited Castle Umbras quite frequently, and during that time, the young, capricious Raylea had grown into a vibrant, beautiful woman, a maiden with a powerful, undeniable crush on the dangerously handsome prince.

On Damian.

Without even trying, his soul had won her over, and truth be told, she had probably recognized his spirit. Despite her believing him to be vile and wicked the first day she had met him in the Warlochian square, they had forged a strong friendship, a resilient bond, and a mutual, irrefutable attraction. It was evident in their unwitting stolen glances; in their innocent but affectionate exchanges; and in the undisguised longing that reflected in their eyes every time they locked gazes across a room.

Understanding Mina's station and loving her sister dearly, Raylea would never have acted on her feelings, and neither one of them had ever said or done anything improper. Yet and still, Mina knew the truth. The two of them were in love. And one day, albeit unknown to Raylea, they would both be free to consummate their union, to act on their powerful, unabated feelings. Mina smiled, thinking of the possibilities. She had no doubt that Matthias would make Raylea immortal, even knowing they couldn't have children, that the girl was not a Sklavos Ahavi. Mina chuckled inwardly: Somehow, she believed the future king would overlook it.

Not wanting to confuse the children, Dante bent over the bed and pressed a chaste, familial kiss on Mina's forehead. "Congratulations, Mistress Ahavi," he said in a formal register, and then he turned to shake Prince Damian's hand. "I'll return when I can."

Prince Damian nodded and stepped aside.

And as Dante turned to exit the room, the oddest thing happened: A white owl swooped down outside the bedroom chamber, perched in the windowsill, and hooted three times. Mina gasped at the blatant confirmation of the omen, and Prince Dante sucked in a harsh, knowing breath. As he passed through the threshold, through the doorway, he turned around, placed his palm over his heart, and mouthed the words *I love you*, and Mina's soul swelled with emotion.

She watched him as he made his retreat, staring at his lithe, graceful back, and then she jolted, sitting upright.

Blessed Spirit Keepers, there was a second presence walking beside him, a strong, powerful male with the bearing of a prince and the stealth of a dragon. The haunting presence placed its ghostly arm around Dante and braced his shoulders proudly, and Mina couldn't help but notice that their strides, their hair, even their proud masculine physiques were virtually identical.

It was Desmond Dragona.

The ghost turned around and smiled, and in an ethereal voice he breathed: "Behold, the greatest king to ever rule the Realm."

ABOUT THE AUTHOR

TESSA DAWN GREW up in Colorado, where she developed a deep affinity for the Rocky Mountains. After graduating with a degree in psychology, she worked for several years in criminal justice and mental health before returning to get her master's degree in nonprofit management.

Tessa began writing as a child and composed her first full-length novel at the age of eleven. By the time she graduated high school, she had a banker's box full of short stories and novels. Since then, she has published works as diverse as poetry, greeting cards, workbooks for kids with autism, and academic curricula. Her Dark Fantasy ~ Gothic Romance novels represent her long-desired return to her creative-writing roots and her passionate flair for storytelling.

Tessa currently splits her time between the Colorado suburbs and mountains with her husband, two children, and "one very crazy cat." She hopes to one day move to the country where she can own horses and what she considers "the most beautiful creature ever created"—a German shepherd.

Writing is her bliss.

OTHER BOOKS BY TESSA DAWN

To join Tessa's mailing list or view her other works, please visit:
www.TessaDawn.com

Read an Excerpt from Tessa's upcoming
Dark Fantasy Saga: *Pantheon of Dragons*

BEFORE TIME WAS a recognized construct, seven dragon lords created a parallel primordial world for their glory…and their future offspring. They harnessed seven preternatural powers from seven sacred stones and erected the *Temple of Seven* beyond the hidden passage of a mystical portal that would lead back and forth between Earth and the dragons' domain. And finally, they set about creating a race of beings—*the Dragyr*—that would exist on blood and fire, and they gifted their progeny with unimaginable powers, unearthly beauty, and immortal life.

For all of this, the dragon lords required only one thing: *absolute and unwavering obedience* to the *Four Principal Laws*…

    I.   Thou shalt pledge thy eternal fealty to the sacred Dragons Pantheon.

   II.   Thou shalt serve as a mercenary for the house of thy birth by seeking out and destroying all *pagan* enemies: whether demons, sin-eaters, shadows…or humans.

III. Thou shalt *feed* on the blood and fire of human prey in order to survive.

IV. Thou shalt propagate the species by siring *dragyri* sons and providing the realm with future warriors. In so doing, thou shalt capture, claim, and render unto thy lords whatsoever human female the gods have selected to become *dragyra*. And she shall be taken to the sacred *Temple of Seven* within seven days of discovery to die as a mortal being, to be reborn as a dragon's consort, and to forever serve the sacred pantheon.

And so it came to pass that seven sacred lairs were erected in the archaic domain of the dragons in order to house the powerful race begotten of the ancient gods, each lair in honor of its ruling dragon lord:

Lord Dragos, Keeper of the Diamond

Lord Ethyron, Keeper of the Emerald

Lord Saphyrius, Keeper of the Sapphire

Lord Amarkyus, Keeper of the Amethyst

Lord Onyhanzian, Keeper of the Onyx

Lord Cytarius, Keeper of the Citrine

& Lord Topenzi, Keeper of the Topaz

While a *dragyri* may appear to be human, *he is not.*
While a *dragyra* may appear to belong to her mate, *she does not.*
While the Dragyr may be fierce, invincible, and strong, they are *never* truly free…

COMING SOON...

Zanaikeyros: Son of Dragons
Volume One in the Pantheon of Dragons Series
by Tessa Dawn

Release date to be announced